Catch Me

BETH BOLDEN

CHAPTER ONE

Wyatt couldn't take his eyes off him. Not his face, with those dark eyes and those cheekbones. Not his hands, cradling the single glass with its inch of golden liquid. Definitely not the way his arm muscles rippled under his tan skin. Considering how many guys were packed into this bar, including the mostly naked ones dancing on the stage, that the man had caught and held Wyatt's attention was an undeniable accomplishment.

Under any other circumstance, Wyatt would have opened with that line when he approached him. But that wasn't happening tonight, or any other night.

He was definitely cute though, with smile wrinkles around his dark eyes, and close-cropped brown hair. The loose, graceful way he held himself made Wyatt believe that he had a very decent set of muscles under his t-shirt and jeans. None of that explained why Wyatt couldn't look away. Maybe it was that the man didn't smile as much as he should. Only occasionally his very white teeth would flash, a contrast to his tanned skin, but it never felt like the smile reached his eyes.

Maybe it was the way he had so easily garnered every other person's interest in the bar.

Maybe it was because he was Ryan Flores, and the first "out" professional baseball player in the history of the game. He'd come out a few years before, right before the draft, and after spending a year or so in the minors, had broken out in a huge way during a Dodgers' playoff run. So what might have become only a footnote in the history of Major League Baseball instead got a whole paragraph.

It was a Thursday night, and Wyatt had come to Temple, one of the most famous gay bars in West Hollywood, hoping for a few beers, a chill night, and some well-deserved ogling of the gorgeous dancers. One of them had always reminded him of his ex, Nate, and now that Nate's memory had faded to a pleasant afterglow rather than acute bitterness, Wyatt had thought he might appreciate the similarity a little more.

Wyatt had not expected to run into the Los Angeles Dodgers' hottest property, and it was making his previously desired chill evening not very chill at all. But everyone always said he was adaptive, and this was basically true, so Wyatt had decided that people-watching worked too, especially when the people-watching was so god damned excellent.

Person-watching, mainly.

It was unexpectedly entertaining to watch groups of interested guys approach Ryan's VIP area, be ushered inside, and then promptly ushered back out five minutes later. He'd watched close to fifty guys try to flirt with Ryan Flores, and while there had been some vaguely flirtatious behavior in return, it was clear nobody was getting anywhere with him fast. Wyatt, who also wanted Ryan to smile more, understood both their desire and their frustration.

There was too much hesitation and assessment in Ryan's eyes, and not enough pure enjoyment.

It was a problem. It wasn't Wyatt's problem though; he had enough of those. He didn't need to add yet another to the pile.

"Want another?" The cute bartender with the white fluffy angel wings sauntered up and gave Wyatt another inviting look. They'd been offhandedly chatting whenever the bartender had a free second, and on another night, when Wyatt's attention wasn't so laser-focused on another man, he might have stuck around past closing and given the angel a ride home. Maybe another kind of ride, too.

He was absolutely hot—ripped abs paired with those wet-dream angel wings and dark eyeliner emphasizing his killer baby-blue eyes. There was a glint in them that promised he'd be very good—or maybe if Wyatt was lucky, very bad.

It wasn't his fault he looked too much like Kian, one of Wyatt's roommates back in Napa. Since Wyatt felt very brotherly towards Kian, it was not a comparison the bartender would have appreciated. Not with the way he kept eyeing Wyatt.

"No, thanks," Wyatt said. It would only be his third; he was definitely sober enough to get home, but he didn't feel like drinking. He didn't know you could feel too sober to get drunk.

Definitely too sober for this crowd, anyway.

"I don't think I've seen you here before," the angel said, undeterred by Wyatt's refusal.

"I'm visiting for a few days," Wyatt said shortly. It was insanity, but he didn't want to flirt with the hot angel bartender. He didn't really want to flirt with anyone.

Lie.

The person he wanted to flirt with was acting like he was holding auditions for his next boyfriend, and Wyatt, while generally optimistic about his chances with guys, was sure he wouldn't qualify.

Broke. A line chef at a prestigious restaurant, but *only* a line chef. Painfully single. Even more painfully, still mostly in the closet.

"You know, he's never been here before either," the angel said, gesturing up to where Ryan was holding court. His voice was bitter around the edges. "You sure you're not here to see him? You've been staring at him all night."

"Pretty sure," Wyatt said.

The angel made a face, which contorted his pretty features. Wyatt had a feeling he didn't often fail to pick someone up when he made the effort. But it wasn't the bartender that Wyatt wanted to make smile more.

"You're cute and all," the angel said, a sharp glint in his blue eyes, "but I don't think you'd stand a chance with him."

Wyatt shrugged. "Not trying to," he said. It was clearly past his time to go, if he'd succeeded in pissing off the hot bartender.

It just happened that the moment he was ready to leave was also the same moment Ryan decided to venture past the velvet rope of his private section.

His security flanked him as he made his way onto the dance floor, just as Wyatt was trying to wade his way around the edges. Some idiot designer had decided that the dance floor should be between the bar and the exit, and while undeniably keeping everyone going longer, it also made leaving annoying.

Wyatt heard a wave of interested noise wash over the dance floor, and through the customers milling around the bar. Everyone turned Ryan's direction. Not because he was the cutest guy there, or the most ripped, or the most unclothed, or anything obvious like that. It must be because he was rich and famous, Wyatt assumed. A real VIP at Temple on a Thursday night.

Even though he'd spent all night looking, Wyatt deliberately turned his head away from the dance floor. He didn't want to know who had captured Ryan Flores' attention enough to risk leaving his cushy, secure prison.

He couldn't possibly be jealous over a guy he'd never even talked to. And yet.

The crowd was sweaty and close, the music thumping loudly in his ears as he skirted the edges of the mass of dancing bodies as best as he could. His ass got groped three times, and Wyatt was pretty sure at least two of those were deliberate. He kept his eyes on the big double doors of the exit, not meeting anyone's eyes. He didn't want to get drawn in; what he needed was some air.

Finally he broke through to the other side, but the crowd on this side near the door was even pushier, shoving him back and forth a lot more aggressively. Wyatt wasn't a small guy—he was almost six foot, and had the long lean build of someone who worked hard for a living and liked surfing and rock climbing in his spare time—but he was getting jostled definitely more than he was used to.

The first sign something was wrong was that the bouncer at the door looked at him weirdly. But Wyatt didn't look back behind him, even though in retrospect, he really should have.

Wyatt burst through the open door and skirting the line to get in—on a *Thursday*, no less, he thought incredulous-ly—and headed toward the next block, resting against a brick wall to catch his breath.

"I think this is when I should ask you where we're going."

Wyatt glanced up and nearly fell over.

Ryan Flores was standing in front of him, arms hanging loosely at his sides, an expectant look on his face, and the hint of a smile. Like Wyatt's shocked expression was very amusing.

"What are you doing here?" Wyatt demanded. Suddenly a lot of things made sense. Like why it had been so difficult to reach the door. Why guys had started shoving. Pushing. Trying to get to something behind him. Why he had felt like he was swimming upstream against some very determined fish. Why the bouncer had looked at him so oddly. Because it probably hadn't looked like Ryan was going with him, but *following* him.

Ryan smiled now, crooked and far more inviting up close than Wyatt had anticipated. "I thought you might know the answer to that. After all, you were staring at me for at least two hours."

"Three," Wyatt answered without thinking.

These things happened to other guys, maybe, but they didn't happen to him. Wyatt shoved his hands in the pockets of his jeans. Better to have them out of the way, better not to let himself start taking things—or *touching* things—before he figured out what the hell was going on.

"There you go," Ryan said matter-of-factly.

"I still don't understand," Wyatt said cautiously. He glanced around Ryan now, afraid they'd been followed by the crowd, but surprisingly, nobody had wandered over or was really paying any attention to them. It turned out that removed from the VIP trappings identifying him as someone important, Ryan looked like a normal guy.

Ryan smiled again, bigger this time, and it did devastating things to Wyatt's chest region. He had been right about wanting him to smile more, but it was far more treacherous than he could have ever imagined. He reminded himself that Ryan was a problem that he didn't need, but the argument wasn't exactly persuasive.

"You rescued me from the crowd. What a mob scene," Ryan said. He was a terrible actor, like he wasn't even trying. There was a conspiratorial glimmer in his dark eyes, and Wyatt wanted to just swallow the lame story and take him up on everything he was offering.

What would be the danger in that? Wyatt swallowed hard.

"At least," Ryan continued, "you could be a gentleman and offer to take me home. Especially after I followed you out here." He arched an eyebrow, and Wyatt wanted to be pinned underneath him, skin to skin, muscles clenched, the next time he did that.

"I could do that." Wyatt didn't even recognize the sound of his own voice. It wasn't like he didn't hook up occasionally. There was a decent gay community in Napa, and San Francisco was only a few hours away if he wanted something even more anonymous. But he'd never hooked up with anyone famous or anyone he'd helplessly stared at from across the bar for three hours.

"I brought my bike," Wyatt added. "I hope that's okay."

Ryan grinned. He'd smiled more in the last two minutes than Wyatt remembered from the last three hours. That couldn't have something to do with him, could it? "You wanna take me for a ride . . ." Ryan hesitated.

"Wyatt," he said, flushing, embarrassed that he hadn't introduced himself earlier. "I'm Wyatt." Flustered, he extended his hand, reminding him of the last job interview he'd gone on. Which was *stupid*, because this wasn't anything like that.

But Ryan took it anyway. His hand was big and ridged with callouses—similar to Wyatt's own knife-scarred digits, but just different enough to be exciting. Electricity flowed, making his fingers tingle, and he gripped Ryan's hand harder. Ryan's eyes crinkled with amusement.

"I'm Ryan."

"I know," Wyatt said stupidly. They weren't even shaking hands anymore, but holding them, and Wyatt wanted to hold more. He wanted to hold it *all*.

He wanted to know what those callouses felt like, deep inside him. He wanted to know if Ryan laughed in bed. He wanted to know if that tan went everywhere, or if there was paler, softer skin in places that the public didn't see.

Wyatt ignored the voice that said he couldn't have those things, and gripped Ryan's hand harder. He could be a different person, at least for tonight.

"Take me home," Ryan said quietly, earnestly, and Wyatt knew he was asking for something else completely.

He fully intended to take Ryan up on every single damn thing he was offering.

His motorcycle was around the corner, and when Wyatt tugged Ryan the right direction, to his surprise, Ryan held onto his hand. Refused to let go.

Wyatt told his ramshackle closet to fuck off, and they held hands the handful of blocks to where his bike was parked.

His hand was damp with nerves and the sharp pings of excitement flooding through his veins. His mind was swamped with a hundred fantasies, a thousand things he was dying to do with Ryan. But Wyatt knew he was only going to get a few hours. Maybe. If he was really fucking lucky. So he settled for the one that kept pushing itself to the forefront, and let out a shaky breath as Ryan settled behind him on his bike and wrapped his arms around Wyatt's waist.

His grip was tight, and Wyatt let his own hand drift down, fingertips grazing the muscular forearm resting against his t-shirt. He swore he felt goose bumps, and told himself to focus, before he killed them both.

Ryan hadn't told him where he lived, and that was fine by Wyatt, because he had no intention of taking him home just yet. He'd grown up in the LA area, before going to culinary school in New York, and the first thing he'd done when coming back to the west coast was re-acquaint himself with all the best biking roads around Mulholland and the Santa Monica mountains. He took them now, opening up the throttle, feeling the wind rush through his hair, Ryan's arms a steady, exhilarating pressure, never letting Wyatt forget what was at the end of this drive.

Well, not *quite* the end of the drive.

He took them to his favorite lookout, the one he'd come to as a teenager on his old shitty Indian, when he'd needed to get away from his brothers.

He wasn't running away from his brothers now, and he had a split second of nerves as he pulled into the dirt turnoff. Ryan's hands tensed around him, and then relaxed again. Wyatt parked his bike, and twisted in the seat, still ready to offer an apology, when calloused palms reached up, cradled his cheeks, his chin. Then Ryan's mouth was on his, and it was scorching with determination and purpose, tongue almost immediately in Wyatt's mouth, and he could only think, *I've got to feel those lips and that tongue on my dick before the night is out.*

It would be okay—he could be fine with only hooking up with Ryan for one night. He had to be. Because he couldn't imagine Ryan meant anything else. He was a broke line chef, not even a *sous*, who was still hiding from his grandmother.

There wasn't a lot that Wyatt could be proud of, but Ryan wanted him, and he intended to make good on it. Ryan climbed off the bike and Wyatt swung his legs around, leaning back against it, cradling Ryan between his legs.

His hands searched under Ryan's t-shirt, encountering tight, warm skin, only the tiniest bit chilled from their ride, and all those muscles he'd imagined he would find. Rippling abs, a pec that fit flawlessly into his hand. A tiny pebbled nipple that made Ryan groan into his mouth when Wyatt flicked it experimentally.

As far as Wyatt was concerned, Ryan went for his belt buckle too soon. Yeah, he was definitely hard, and he imagined Ryan would be too, if he followed the soft trail of hair down his chest, through the cut muscles of his abdomen. But he didn't want it to end so fast. He wanted more than just a quick, blazingly hot hand job. Even if they were on his bike and the road was just over there and anyone could drive by.

There was only a dim streetlight a few hundred yards away, but Wyatt could still see the dark intensity of Ryan's gaze as he pulled back. "You don't want to?" Ryan questioned, and there was definite disappointment in his voice.

Wyatt's voice was rough. "I've spent the whole night imagining this. Of course I want to."

"Then how do you want it?" Ryan gave Wyatt an experimental stroke through his jeans and his boxers, and he groaned. Yeah, he wanted those graceful and calloused hands all over his dick, but he also wanted his swollen lips wrapped around his cock. He wanted Ryan to bend him over the leather seat and open him wide to the cool night air, his thumbs brushing the inside of his cheeks and the furl of his hole. He wanted to fuck Ryan until they were both crying with it.

He wanted too much, and he'd experienced enough of life to know you never got everything you wanted. It was always better to temper your expectations. The problem was Wyatt couldn't do that tonight.

Not with Ryan.

He was still a stranger, but it didn't matter. Every time Ryan touched him, he went out of his mind. Every time Ryan smiled, it was the sweetest, most satisfying moment Wyatt had experienced in months. Maybe even in years.

But Wyatt knew he couldn't say any of that to Ryan. Not when he was clearly just looking for a quick hookup, so he kissed him instead. He wasn't stupid enough to believe that a kiss could make Ryan understand, but without the words, it was all he had.

He couldn't whisper it, and he couldn't scream it from the top of the tallest building in LA. His mouth, his hands, his body. That's what he had left.

Wyatt knew Ryan couldn't understand, but it was easy to imagine he had, because the kiss morphed from a solid wall of heat to something softer, something less driving and more meandering. A kiss that meant that they could take their time, even if they were on the side of the road.

Ryan followed Wyatt's lead and his fingers drifted up his abs, to his chest, touching everything under his t-shirt that he could reach.

Between kisses, Ryan murmured, "Are you sure you aren't a pro athlete?" He paused. "You're built like a fucking wall."

Wyatt took that as the compliment it was. "I'm actually a chef," he admitted.

Ryan laughed a little into the corner of Wyatt's mouth. His lips felt two sizes too big, and achingly sensitive, but he couldn't stop kissing Ryan. Couldn't get enough of the wondrous drugging feeling that took him over whenever their lips touched. Like everything, even if it all felt like it was going to shit, would be okay.

His dick was a solid, throbbing reminder that he was horny as hell, and just groping every inch of Ryan he could wasn't going to be enough. Or vice versa.

Finally, before Wyatt could say, *maybe I've finally had enough*, Ryan exhaled with a sharp, ragged breath and begged. "Can I, please?" he murmured into a particularly sensitive spot just behind Wyatt's ear. And because Wyatt didn't give a shit what Ryan wanted to do—he wanted whatever Ryan wanted—he simply nodded.

Ryan's hands went back to his jeans, unbuttoning and unzipping them, gently and carefully so that they didn't send the bike toppling over.

Not for the first time, Wyatt wondered if maybe he should have let the fantasy go, but then Ryan gestured for Wyatt to prop himself up against the bike, and lowered his mouth to the wet patch on his boxers.

His fingers dug into the leather seat, trying to steady himself, to control himself, as Ryan flicked out his tongue, tasting the wet of his pre-come on the cotton. When Ryan groaned, Wyatt had to echo him. It was so damn good already, and he'd barely touched him.

"Please," Wyatt whimpered, because even if he was dying to, there was no way he was going to last. And if all he got was some teasing, he would cry. He wanted Ryan's mouth on him, those sinfully full lips taking in his cock.

"Please what?" Ryan asked, fingers trailing up his bare thigh, tugging down his boxers finally. He knew what Wyatt wanted, he just wanted to make him crazy with need.

"Please . . . your god damn mouth," Wyatt ground out.

The moment Ryan's tongue curled around the head and then he sucked, Wyatt knew he was a dead man and the last five minutes of his life were going to be fucking brilliant.

"Knew you'd be good at this," Wyatt grunted, trying to be gentle as he reached down and cradled Ryan's head.

Then Ryan slid the rough pad on his finger to the back of his balls and pleasure exploded, whiting out his vision, making it almost impossible to avoid pressing Ryan's head down, begging him to take in more, to give him more.

There was only a split second before Wyatt knew he couldn't contain the building pressure anymore, and curled his hands possessively around Ryan's face, feeling the shape of his dick against Ryan's cheek, and it was all over.

The orgasm was like a roaring wave, overtaking him, emptying him out of everything—except this endless need to do it again, and again, and *again*.

"Sorry," Wyatt breathed out after he was able to speak again. "I'm so sorry." He'd been sort of rude, coming with almost no warning, assuming that Ryan would swallow.

But Ryan's expression as he stood was anything but pissed off. In fact, he looked smug as hell as he reached for Wyatt's hand, and placed it against his crotch. It was wet, and Wyatt stared at Ryan as he realized what had happened.

"You shouldn't be sorry," Ryan said. "Clearly I thought it was pretty damn hot."

The only problem with that was that now Wyatt wasn't going to get to take Ryan apart with his mouth, and his tongue and his fingers, or his cock. It didn't feel fair, and it left him feeling sort of hollow, now that this otherworldly encounter was drawing to an end.

"Well, uh, I just . . ." Wyatt didn't know what to say. His brain still felt sluggish after the orgasm of the millennium.

"It's okay," Ryan said, giving his thigh a reassuring squeeze. "I was staring at you too. And doing my own share of fantasizing. It was sort of inevitable."

"If you say so." Even though he'd had plenty of guys tell him how hot he was, Wyatt always had trouble accepting it. Especially now, from someone like Ryan. He could have had anyone he wanted, and he'd picked Wyatt.

"I do," Ryan said, and leaned over, kissing him again. Wyatt tasted himself on Ryan's tongue, and told himself that even if this was just a passing, quick thing to the other man, he wasn't going to forget. He would remember the rippled smoothness of skin over muscle, the strangled gasp Ryan had made when he'd pinched his nipple, the taste of his come on Ryan's tongue.

Finally, it was time for the inevitable. "I guess I'd better get you home," Wyatt said. "I promised I would."

"You strike me as the kind of guy who tries to keep his promises," Ryan said casually.

Wyatt thought he was, unless you were counting the many lies he'd told his own family about who he was. He nodded.

"Then, I guess there's nothing else for you to do," Ryan said, shooting Wyatt another one of those dimpled grins. It hurt that he seemed so casual about it, like none of this really mattered. And, Wyatt reminded himself, it probably didn't. Not to Ryan.

That was okay. Wyatt would have to be okay with it.

Ryan told Wyatt his address, and he punched it into his phone, quickly flicking through the map to make sure he knew the route. Wyatt only realized as they were near their destination, making their way up the coast, towards Santa Monica, that even though he'd had his phone out, Ryan hadn't given him his phone number.

It was hard to enjoy that last five minutes of Ryan wrapped around him, the cool night air whistling past them, because that *hurt*. It shouldn't have, because Ryan had never made him a single promise, or made a single assumption, but it still god damned ached.

But Wyatt didn't want to be *that guy*, the one who over-shared and overstayed and didn't know when to quit, so he just smiled, and then smiled more, as Ryan got off the bike in front of the big double-gated entrance to his mansion.

"Thanks for the ride," Ryan said, and leaned over, brushing a single kiss across Wyatt's cheek. Somehow, that meant more than some torrid, heated kiss, but it still hurt more than Wyatt could have guessed when Ryan turned to go.

"See you around," Wyatt said stupidly, because he didn't know what else to say. He'd had hookups before, but none of them had ever felt like this.

It had never felt like someone had carved his heart out of his chest and had taken it with them when they left.

Ryan turned, and flashed Wyatt one last smile. "Yeah," he said, clearly amused by Wyatt's choice of parting remark, "I'll see you around."

Chapter Two

It was not ideal, but Wyatt went to his interview on a handful of hours of sleep and a melancholy edge to his mood. He was generally pretty easy-going, with a sunny, optimistic disposition. Becoming the leader of the family and being forced to put his beloved Nana in a memory care facility he couldn't really afford had changed him. He knew he'd gotten quieter and more withdrawn, a heap of serious problems he couldn't solve weighing him down.

Miles, his best friend, had told him last week that he was growing up. But Wyatt didn't think so. He was the same as always, he just needed something to take the edge off. Last night, Ryan had provided a much-needed distraction, a temporary lessening of the pressure he was living with, but it hadn't been enough.

In fact, coming to terms with the fact that Ryan was so temporary was part of what caused his latest bad mood.

Even the thought that he could be making more money after today wasn't much of a consolation. "It's for a private chef position," was all Reed Ryan, the connection that had gotten Wyatt his interview, had said. Reed's description didn't exactly excite Wyatt. He didn't really want to stay at Terroir, and continue to get verbally abused by his boss, Bastian Aquino, for shitty pay, but he also didn't want to get paid to babysit and make peanut butter sandwiches with no crusts for a spoiled Beverly Hills family.

The fact that he badly needed the money was the only reason he showed up at all.

He was shown into the conference room in the trendy LA office building, and was just about to sit down at one end of the shining expanse of glass when a man entered the room, proving to Wyatt everything he'd assumed about this client.

The suit alone probably cost more than a year at Nana's facility, and Wyatt couldn't even begin to price out the watch. It was clearly expensive, real diamonds shining on the face, and the man wore it carelessly, like he had a dozen more. He probably did, Wyatt thought darkly. His face was scrunched tight and there was something untrustworthy about it, a slyness in the eyes that Wyatt couldn't miss. Wyatt didn't know if he could work for this man, even if the money was good.

"Hi, I'm Eric Talbot," the man said, extending a hand, which Wyatt shook firmly. He looked him in the eye, and tried to do everything else he remembered from that long-ago high school class in interview skills. Of course he'd had interviews after culinary school—for the jobs he'd gotten at other restaurants, and then at Terroir, but they were never like normal interviews. Nobody cared if you could communicate worth a damn in a restaurant; they only cared if you could cook.

"Wyatt Blake."

Eric settled down on one of the ultra-modern sculpted chairs, metal and clear acrylic married together in a tortured formation. Wyatt followed suit and waited a long, expectant moment for the interview to start.

"I'm sorry, we're waiting for the client," Eric said. "He's usually really punctual, but he texted me to say that traffic was brutal today."

This guy who looked like he could buy and sell Wyatt's whole family wasn't even the client? The client was even *richer*? Wyatt briefly considered telling him to just forget the whole thing, because this had been a huge mistake. He was meant to be in a restaurant kitchen. He was meant to wow patrons with his dazzling culinary skills. He wasn't meant to make peanut butter and jelly sandwiches and grilled chicken breasts with steamed vegetables on the side. Yet, he couldn't help but be relieved Eric Talbot wouldn't be his boss.

In the end, the only thing that kept Wyatt's butt in his seat were the bills that kept piling up. This job would be worth it, if Wyatt could keep them paid and at bay. The stress alone felt like it was slowly crushing him. Even making peanut butter and jelly sandwiches would be a decent exchange for a loosening of the noose around his neck.

"The client?" Wyatt asked. Reed had given him next to no information about this interview, other than date and time, and even Wyatt thought that was odd. Weren't you supposed to do research and go prepared to these sorts of things? How could he research someone he didn't know?

"My client, actually," Eric Talbot said with a friendly grin that made him look marginally less like a bloodthirsty piranha. "I manage . . ."

Eric didn't get the rest of the sentence out before the door opened and Wyatt damned everything to hell and back.

This morning Ryan Flores was dressed in jeans and a sky-blue polo shirt, looking as fucking cute as he had the night before. Wyatt would have picked him up a hundred times out of a hundred, and there was no way it was a coincidence that Ryan had picked him up first and then just happened to be interviewing him today. Ryan didn't even look surprised that Wyatt was here, asking to join his staff. Wyatt tried to let that sink in. Ryan hadn't just been out of his league, he was in a different universe. *And* he was a liar. Somehow the former felt worse than the latter.

"Hi, I'm so sorry I'm late. I'm Ryan." Ryan extended his hand towards Wyatt, clearly having decided that he was going to play this like they had never met before, like they'd never hooked up, like he'd never pursued Wyatt at all. Like Wyatt hadn't wasted three hours of his life and a hookup with the hot angel bartender, staring at Ryan like he was something important and worthwhile.

"Wyatt." He stood, held out his hand to shake. He couldn't help but think about the night before, when he'd deliberately not shared his last name. And now it felt stupid and foolish, because Ryan must have known it the whole time. "Wyatt Blake."

It was impossible to avoid touching Ryan, but Wyatt kept the handshake brief, nothing like the intimate meeting of fingers and palms that they'd experienced the night before. Still, even the echo of it rocketed through Wyatt, and as he sat down, he slipped his hand under the table, clenching it painfully around his knee. He didn't want to be affected by Ryan's touch. Or the knowledge that Ryan had known they'd meet again this morning.

His words from the night before reverberated through Wyatt's brain. *Yeah, I'll see you around.*

The joke was definitely on Wyatt.

"Your resume is certainly impressive," Eric said, kicking off the interview portion. There was nothing Wyatt wanted more than to stop him right in his tracks, and walk out. Because whatever this was, he wasn't sure he wanted a part of it. But the starting salary kept him in the chair. Maybe it would be better to work for Ryan than to work for a spoiled family. It was theoretically possible, he surmised, and he should at least listen to the pitch.

"If I'm reading this correctly," Ryan said, glancing down at the copy of the resume that Eric had slid across the table to him, "you took a position demotion and a pay cut to work at Terroir."

"I did." At the time, with Nana not yet feeling the effects of her Alzheimer's, it had been a no-brainer. He'd saved on expenses by moving in with Miles and his other roommate, Xander, and it had been worth the demotion from *sous chef* to line cook, to work at Terroir, one of the most celebrated restaurants in the United States, and the only restaurant in California to have the difficult-to-obtain Michelin stars.

Ryan leaned back in his chair, so casual, like he hadn't been on his knees less than twelve hours ago. "Can you explain your thought process behind that decision?"

"It does look like an odd choice," Wyatt admitted. He wasn't happy about defending his decisions, but he would do it. "Even with the demotion, working at Terroir transformed my resume. It's one of the best restaurants in America. Working there proved that I could cook in one of the most demanding, exacting kitchens in the world."

Ryan tapped a pen on the glass conference table. "But now, you're leaving."

"I've worked there almost two years. It's time to move on." Wyatt didn't want to bring up the pressing financial situation that was forcing this change, but he had a feeling that Ryan and Eric had already dug up that information. Eric in particular didn't seem like the kind of guy who would leave anything to chance—and he wouldn't waste his time or his client's.

So even if Ryan was choosing to grill him, Wyatt had a feeling the job was essentially his. If he wanted it.

The million-dollar question of the day.

"This job requires someone who can manage themselves successfully. You mentioned that Terroir was demanding and exacting. I've heard Bastian Aquino can be a tough boss. Do you think you can successfully transition to working without supervision?" Eric asked.

Wyatt almost laughed. "Oh, definitely. In fact, it would be pretty welcome," he admitted wryly.

"You've never been head of a kitchen before," Ryan inserted.

"Sure, I have," Wyatt said. "My own kitchen. Is yours going to be so different?"

Ryan inclined his head, a hint of a smile on his face. "No. Actually, it shouldn't be."

"Can I ask why you even need a personal chef?" Wyatt asked. He figured it was fair that he interview Ryan—especially considering he'd obscured his motives last night—even as Ryan was interviewing him.

"I'm going to be doing more entertaining. It feels like I'm always sending out for food. It would be nice to not worry about it anymore. There would be nutrition guidelines provided by my trainer that you'd have to follow."

"Not a problem. I can easily integrate those into meal plans," Wyatt said.

"Do you have any more questions, Ryan?" Eric asked.

Ryan shook his head, and that basically ended the strangest interview of Wyatt's career. He couldn't imagine that Ryan wouldn't want to taste his food if he was going to be cooking for him every day. But then, he'd never worked for someone who integrated blowjobs into his interview prep before.

Ryan's behavior should be a turnoff—and it *was*—but it also left Wyatt curious. Even if Eric left, he didn't know if he could ask Ryan what had been the goal last night. He didn't know if he could bring up last night at all. Even before running into Ryan this morning, it had felt too raw to talk about.

"Here's the compensation package." Eric slid a single sheet of paper across the conference table. The starting salary listed had an extra digit than his current salary at Terroir. It was a no-brainer, even as his brain tried to talk him out of it.

He didn't know Ryan's intentions. His motives. Would he want to keep sleeping with Wyatt? Was this some sort of combined private chef/rent-boy position? Wyatt knew he should request to speak to Ryan in private and ask those questions, but instead he kept his mouth shut and nodded.

"When can you start?" Eric asked, like he had known if he threw money at Wyatt, he'd agree. And he, Wyatt thought bitterly, had been exactly right. He could totally be bought.

"I'll give my two weeks tomorrow," Wyatt said, clearing the bitterness out of his throat, "but I fully expect Aquino to kick me out immediately. He doesn't like it when staff leaves. So I'll be able to start in a few days."

"The job includes free rent at the ADU on the back of Ryan's house," Eric said. "I don't suppose you mind us running a background check. Standard procedure for anyone granted access to the property." Another paper slid across the glass, along with a pen, and Wyatt scribbled his name without even reading the verbiage. He didn't have anything to hide—unless the tryst he'd had with Ryan counted, and maybe it didn't.

After all, Ryan was out of the closet. He could do whatever the fuck he wanted, including hook up with some random guy he met at Temple.

"Great," Eric said. "I'll also make sure to issue you a credit card for food purchases, and for any equipment purchases for the kitchen. Anything over $500 requires Ryan's approval. But it's pretty well-stocked already."

Wyatt took that with a grain of salt. Well-stocked had different meanings to a professional chef than it did a sports agent who probably hadn't been in a kitchen in years.

Ryan waved a hand, and gave Wyatt an intimate smile that made his stomach clench. "Don't worry about it. You can get whatever you need."

Eric shot his client a hard look. "We talked about this."

"Yeah, we did," Ryan retorted. "And I made my decision." If Eric wondered why Ryan would trust someone he'd only met for five minutes, he didn't question it.

Eric rolled his eyes but didn't say another word, simply got to his feet, indicating the interview was over. If it had even been an interview at all. "Nicole at the front will have the paperwork for you to fill out," he said. "I expect you'll let us know when you can officially start." He held out his hand, and Wyatt stood to shake it again, and before he realized what was about to happen, he was alone again with Ryan.

Wyatt tensed. He didn't want to have this conversation. Could he escape still? Claim he had to get back to Napa? Claim he had a desperate need to fill out paperwork?

Shoving his hands in his pockets, Ryan shot Wyatt an endearing smile. He looked more nervous now than he had picking up Wyatt last night. How was that even possible?

"I hope this is all okay," Ryan said.

Wyatt was annoyed by how endeared he was. You wanted to manipulate him? Fine, just don't pretend like you hadn't. "I wouldn't have agreed if it wasn't okay."

Ryan's smile brightened, and Wyatt was frustratingly reminded of his own expressed desire to get him to smile more. He would be in a serious position to do that, if he chose to, now. But he was feeling backed into a corner, and the thought didn't fill him with any anticipation.

"I'm glad you did."

"I'm sure you are," Wyatt said, and some of his frustration leaked into his voice. He wasn't nearly as good at fronting as Ryan was. And that just annoyed him even more.

"I want us to be friends," Ryan said.

Wyatt stared at him blankly. Seriously, *friends?* "You just hired me. I'm your employee."

Ryan shrugged, like this was hardly a barrier to friendship. "Then you're going to be around all the time. It'll be great."

"Great," Wyatt echoed. "Yeah. Definitely."

"You can always text Eric when you're going to be coming back to LA," Ryan said, "or you can always just text me. That would probably be easier. Eric is terrible at passing on messages."

It was impossible not to remember how fucking much Wyatt had wanted Ryan's number last night. How disillusioned he'd been when Ryan had not even brought it up. And now he was offering it, willingly. Wyatt, who knew just how much he and his bank account needed this job, was still struck by a petty desire to shred the contract he'd just signed.

He did not need this bullshit in his life.

Of course that didn't stop him from agreeing, and whipping out his phone to type Ryan's number in it. It didn't stop him from texting Ryan back, so that he'd have his number in his phone, and it didn't stop him from smiling despite all the irritation swirling inside him when he left Ryan to finish signing the paperwork that would tie them together.

⁂

"You're going to need to find a new roommate," Wyatt said that night to Xander and Kian when he walked in the house, to watch them vegging out on the worn couch, watching re-runs of *Iron Chef*. The dubbed English originals. Not the execrable US remake.

He loved Alton Brown, but seriously he should have stuck to *Good Eats*.

"We already found one," Kian said, barely even looking up from the TV. Someone was butchering an enormous swordfish, and he was staring intently at the process. Probably because Aquino had decided he was going to cut down all his own fish now, and Kian was desperately studying up.

"I didn't even know when I left yesterday that I'd get the job," Wyatt said, still annoyed. The six-hour drive back to Napa hadn't helped clear his head. He'd spent the whole time trying to forget the feel of his hands on the leather seat as Ryan had taken him apart with his mouth. Or the feeling of Ryan's mouth, period.

It hadn't worked.

"Of course you were going to get the job," Xander inserted with irritation. "Did you expect us to sit back and not try to find someone new when you were gonna bail?"

This was typical Xander. Usually Wyatt could brush off his abrasive comments, but he was a little tender today. "Who is it?"

"It's uh . . . I think it's going to be good. For us. I mean. Not for you. Probably." Kian stuttered awkwardly every other word and couldn't look Wyatt in the eye. It made it very obvious who he was talking about.

"There's not going to be enough room in the closet for all his shoes. Or his wine," Wyatt said.

"How did you know it was Nate?" Xander demanded. "Did he text you to ask if it was okay?"

Wyatt had blocked Nate's phone number the week after they'd broken up, so *no*, but there was a limited number of people who Xander would willingly live with, and the main thing they all had in common was that they brought something to the relationship. Nate was a sommelier who worked for one of Napa's larger wineries, and so had connections as well as access to pretty decent wine on a regular basis.

"I thought he was living with that new guy of his . . . Rabe? Rake? Rage? I can't remember." Wyatt had known he was over Nate when he had heard about him moving in with the new guy and hadn't even blinked twice.

"Rafe," Kian said. "And they broke up. I guess Nate found him in bed with someone when he came home unexpectedly."

Wyatt raised an eyebrow. "Someone?"

"His boss," Xander added. "Phillippa Winchester."

"That must have been a shock," Wyatt said. He was basically relieved that both Kian and Xander were more into the hot gossip that Nate's new boyfriend was hooking up with his female boss, and that he didn't have to discuss anything to do with his new job or *his* new boss.

Or that they had also hooked up.

"He was so angry, he stormed right out. Spent the afternoon drinking cosmos on the patio at Terroir. I had to practically pour him into the car and then drop his drunk ass off." Xander did not sound pleased about this. "But the silver lining is that we have a third roommate again."

"You're going to hate living with him. You hated him when we were dating." Wyatt was very happy he was not going to be around to witness any of the shit Nate and Xander were going to give each other.

"Probably." Xander sounded resigned to this. "Beggars can't be choosers."

"Just don't hook up with him," Wyatt warned, even when he knew his warning would be ignored.

Not that Xander would actually hook up with him. No. He would let Nate work for it, and then turn him down, because

Xander was a dick that way and also didn't like to hook up with anyone too close to home.

At least that was what Xander had always claimed whenever Wyatt and Miles went out in Napa and tried to convince him to come with them. But then maybe he just liked being celibate. Who knew.

"Like I would ever stoop that low." Xander smirked. "So what are you moving to LA for? Chasing fame and ass like Miles?"

Wyatt scoffed. "Like I care about that." He really didn't want to talk about his new job in LA—or who he was going to be working for. But Xander seemed determined to weasel it out of him.

"No," Xander said contemplatively. "But you're chasing something."

Stability, Wyatt thought, *and Ryan Flores.*

He'd gone to LA seeking the first, but never imagining he'd find the second.

"The interview was for a position as a private chef, for a high-profile athlete," Wyatt finally admitted.

"Who?" Kian asked, finally tearing his attention away from the fish butchering on *Iron Chef*.

"He doesn't want to tell us," Xander said, voice sneering just the tiniest bit.

"It's Ryan Flores, okay?" Wyatt snapped. He must really be torn up if Xander was managing to push his buttons. Usually he was able to steer clear of his friend and roommate's bad moods. But today, he'd drove right into the middle of one, and masochistically, he hadn't just walked away.

He did feel responsible for leaving them without a third roommate to split costs with, and forcing Xander to either accept a stranger or offer Wyatt's room to Nate.

"Oh, he's that cute baseball player," Kian said.

Xander said nothing, just stared moodily at the screen.

"It's a good job," Wyatt said. "He's going to be a good boss, I think."

"A lot different than Chef Aquino, that's for sure," Kian said, that worshipfulness edge appearing in his voice on cue, like it did every single damn time he talked about their illustrious boss and the owner of Terroir.

"Sometimes I think you like it when the Bastard tortures you," Xander said. And Wyatt was selfishly glad that Xander's bad mood had transferred from him to Kian. And he loved Kian. Kian was the sweetest of puppy dogs, and definitely did not deserve Xander's frustration.

Except that he totally enjoyed it when Bastian Aquino tortured him. And Wyatt knew that fact worried the hell out of both him and Xander.

"Don't call him that," Kian said automatically, and that was Wyatt's cue to check out. Go back to his room, and throw his shit in a duffel bag, donate the furniture to Nate who had picked out most of it anyway, and call it a night. He didn't have any doubts that he wouldn't make it through the dinner service tomorrow.

He probably wouldn't make it through giving his notice unscathed. Bastian Aquino's nickname was the Bastard for a reason.

"I'm going to pack," Wyatt announced to his friends, who were now glowering at each other. He didn't need any problems to add to his teetering pile, but he felt personally responsible for the fact that Kian and Xander were going to bicker all the time without him to intervene or distract, and Nate sure as hell wouldn't help out. He wasn't completely self-centered, but he was pretty damn close to it.

"Do you think Chef Aquino will let you work the two weeks?" Kian asked, even though they all knew the answer. Chef Aquino never let anyone finish their two weeks, except Miles, who had gone to professionally film his video blog series, *Pastry by Miles*. And the only reason Miles had gotten an exemption was because Aquino never cut his nose off to spite his face.

If Miles made it onto the Cooking Channel or some shit, which he and his boyfriend and producer, Evan, were always chattering about, then Aquino was going to want a piece of that action, and he was going to want to say that he'd groomed Miles and then kindly wished him on his way.

Wyatt was abandoning Terroir for a private chef job. Basically, for *money*, and Aquino, who despite having plenty of money of his own, hated that.

It should have bothered him. It should have made him even a little sad. But Wyatt found he couldn't wait to leave and head south.

To stability, and to Ryan.

Wyatt had known tying up all his loose ends in Napa would be easy. For someone who loved stability, he lived a surprisingly simple existence. His belongings—clothes, laptop, books, knives, his sous-vide—they all fit in two duffels and a handful of boxes. His furniture he donated to Xander and Kian to keep for Nate. If he knew Nate at all, he would refuse to argue with Rage or Rake or whatever the fuck he was called to get any of his own furniture back. All Nate really cared about was his clothes and his shoes and his fucking wine, anyway.

He typed out probably the shortest letter in the history of the world, giving his notice. One line, and it probably wasn't even a complete sentence. But he didn't believe Aquino would even waste time reading it, and he certainly wasn't going to reminisce fondly over the job he was leaving.

Someday, Wyatt let himself think, *someday*, I'm going to have a job where I respect people and they respect me back, and maybe I even get to call the shots. A job where I get to make the big decisions and when people love the food, it'll be because of me.

He wasn't naïve enough to think the job with Ryan was going to be like that. He was technically free of the Bastard's iron fist, but he was really only changing one controlling boss for another, slightly less controlling one. There were still going to be rules. Cook this meal, prep this week of lunches, make this protein shake every morning, follow all these dietary guidelines. Would a little bit more freedom really feel life-changing?

Wyatt didn't think so. The only life-changing part of this was the stupendous starting salary. *That* would change his life, and alleviate much of his stress.

With that thought on his mind, Wyatt drove his bike over to the memory care facility he'd moved his nana to a few months earlier.

She had gone reluctantly, and even Wyatt could acknowledge that she might not have needed the amount of care they could provide just yet, but he was terrified of getting a phone call in the middle of the night that she'd wandered away from her house or set something on fire because she'd forgotten she was using the stove.

It was a Friday afternoon, when Wyatt was usually at work, so it was great to be able to surprise her.

She was sitting by the window in her room, book upside down in her lap, eyes drifting across the gardens behind the home. The beautiful grounds had been one of the main reasons why Wyatt had picked this place for her—even if he couldn't really afford to. He'd desperately wanted to give her something beautiful, even as her life progressed further into the dark.

"Nana," he said softly, jerking her from her daydreams. She glanced up, blue eyes still bright even at her age, and the recognition in them was immediate.

Every time he came, he dreaded the first moment, the first time she might not recognize him. So far it hadn't happened, but the possibility was always there, twisting his stomach into knots.

"Wyatt," she exclaimed, getting to her feet, the book sliding to the floor with a thud. She glanced down in surprise, his gaze tracking her own, and he saw the astonishment in it.

She'd forgotten the book was on her lap. It could be the sort of momentary memory lapse everyone experienced—or it could be her disease progressing. Wyatt's stomach twisted again, but instead of letting the worry show, he smiled wide, crossing the room and wrapping her slight form in a big hug.

To him, as a boy, as a teenager, and even as a grown man, she'd always been larger than life. It was hard to feel her bony limbs under his hands as he led her to the small sofa that faced her TV.

"I didn't expect you today," Beatrice Blake said, her eyes shining like Wyatt had done something amazing, even though he still felt he wasn't doing enough.

"Had the day off," Wyatt said. He tangled his fingers in hers and held tight. Tight to anchor her to this world, and not lose her to the next. "For an interview in Los Angeles, actually."

Her smile dimmed a little, worry clouding her gaze. He'd told her a million times not to worry about the money after he'd taken over her finances, but she did anyway. "What's this new job? It can't possibly be better than Terroir."

"It's way better than Terroir," Wyatt said, and found that he wasn't even lying to her, though he had been prepared to. "It's for a really nice baseball player. He needs a private chef. It'll be a great opportunity to run my own kitchen."

Her pride in him radiated out of her sweet, barely wrinkled face. She'd never have admitted it to anyone, but she'd always been a little vain. And Wyatt liked to slip her the face cream she loved so much, and had always used religiously, even though it was expensive.

"He's a baseball player?" Bea asked.

"He plays for the Dodgers," Wyatt confirmed. "I think it's going to be a great opportunity."

"But you're moving." Her face fell a little. He already knew what she was thinking; she might not see him very much. Wyatt reminded himself to send his brothers a guilt text, trying to get them over here to see her more often, so she wouldn't be lonely.

"I'm going to be up here at least once a week, though," Wyatt insisted. "The nice thing about working for Ryan is that he's going to be on the road a lot, and I won't always be needed in LA."

"I'm just happy you're doing something for you," Nana said, a fierce edge to her voice. She might look delicate, with her spun sugar white hair in a cloud around her worn, pale face, but her blue eyes were still bright and she still wanted the very best for him. Would *fight* for the very best for him. Which was why he'd never told her about the shit that went down regularly at Terroir, or that he was taking this new job for the money, so she'd be properly taken care of.

"Tell me about what you've done this week," Wyatt said. He didn't want to lie to her. He *would*, but he didn't want to.

"It's so nice here, Wyatt," she said. "They have such nice people. And we do fun things. They take me to Mass every week. There's an art instructor once a week and we're working on a painting. I didn't think I had an artistic bone in my body, but it looks okay."

"You'll have to show it to me when it's done," he said.

She blushed. "I don't know about that. It's not exactly fine art."

"I don't care," Wyatt vowed. "I still want to see it."

"Your brothers came to see me, a few days ago," Bea said.

Something in her voice worried Wyatt. He trusted his brothers because he knew they weren't bad, trusted that they loved Nana too, but they could be careless. Selfish. "Was it good to see them?"

"Tony has a new girlfriend." Tony *always* had a new girlfriend. Wyatt barely refrained from rolling his eyes. "And Marco, I guess he got fired." That also didn't come as a surprise. Marco liked to drink more on work nights than was appropriate and probably had called in one too many days at the auto shop he worked at. "But, he tells me," Bea continued, "that he thinks he can convince the owner to rehire him."

Wyatt did roll his eyes this time, and she tapped him firmly on the shoulder. "I saw that, Wyatt."

"If they wouldn't be *so* predictable," Wyatt said.

"They're your brothers," Bea said, switching into Nana Lecture Mode, "and someday, they're going to be all the family you have left. You take care of family. Blakes always take care of family."

Something he'd been hearing his whole life. "I remember."

"When they were here, Tony and Marco didn't even say anything about you having an interview."

Wyatt hadn't told them. Hadn't much seen the point. He and his brothers were so different, and the two of them so similar, that he'd felt so many times like the outsider to their partnership. It made it hard to call or text. Especially now, that he was the only one who'd taken on the burden of Nana's care.

It *wasn't* a burden, Wyatt mentally corrected. He was grateful and privileged that he could. If only it didn't hang on his shoulders so heavily sometimes.

"I just found out about it, had to beg Chef Aquino for two days off and rush down to LA."

"And you're sure about this?" she asked, looking intently at him. "I don't want you to be unhappy."

"It's going to be good, I promise. Better for me, better for you." That was all he could say before the tears clogged his throat. He cleared it, hoping that she wasn't so aware that she'd somehow missed the flash of emotion.

"I brought you something," he said, reaching for the bag he'd brought in, hoping he could distract her. "Miles made them for you."

"Macarons?" she asked excitedly. Who would have ever thought his dear nana, Irish and traditionalist to the core, would love French pastries? Miles, that's who. And who packed her a box every time he knew Wyatt was going to see her.

"Lemon almond and raspberry chocolate," Wyatt said. "And some other strange flavors he wouldn't tell me, so I'm not taking responsibility for Miles' weird flavor combinations."

"He's a dear," Nana said, opening the box with excitement in her voice. She glanced up at him conspiratorially. "Do you think it would be wrong of me not to share these?"

"I think you should keep them if you want to," Wyatt said.

"But, Wyatt," she said earnestly. "God is always watching."

Wyatt sure hoped God hadn't been watching last night when he'd been with Ryan.

Every time she brought up God or religion, that was usually his cue to leave. It wasn't like he didn't want to tell her that he was gay. Or that he thought she'd shun him or be disgusted by him. Her beliefs were part of who she was. She'd been raised that way, and spent her whole life going to Mass. She was one of the strongest, most loyal people he'd ever met. Wyatt knew she loved him, unconditionally. But fear was irrational and he couldn't banish it and he couldn't bear to push her away from him by telling the truth.

Especially not now.

"I have to get ready to go into work, Nana," he said, rising to his feet. "Enjoy the macarons and your art class this week." He dropped a quick kiss on a papery thin cheek and felt his stomach twist again.

"Take care of yourself, darling," Bea said as he turned to leave.

If Bea had had any idea what was in store for Wyatt, she might have worried.

Which was exactly why Wyatt hadn't told her.

Bastian Aquino, AKA the Bastard, and the owner of the only Michelin-starred restaurant in California, stared down at the paper Wyatt had placed in front of him. His resignation letter.

"What is this?" Chef Aquino demanded. "What is this bullshit?" He snatched up the letter and looked ready to shred it to pieces. Wyatt wouldn't have been surprised. He'd seen it happen before and not just with paper. With homemade pasta. With fresh lettuce leaves. With a lamb chop lollipop he'd decimated, only the bone remaining. Never mind the gleaming white porcelain dishes. They routinely ended up chipped and mangled in the trash, their contents spilled across the walls of the kitchen, shards sprinkled across the floors.

It was a rare service when the Bastard didn't break *something*.

"My resignation," Wyatt said, making sure to keep his voice toneless, edgeless. Praying he wouldn't upset Aquino more than he had to.

"What, is working for the best restaurant in the world not good enough for you anymore?" Aquino sneered. "Do you fancy yourself somehow better than *my* kitchen? Feel like your shitty grillwork might be good enough to make it someplace else?"

Wyatt had a fantastic, intuitive touch with meat, especially on the grill. It was not easy, but still doable, to push that insult away and leave it behind him.

Mostly because he was going to be leaving this place and this asshole behind. Probably very shortly.

"Did someone even hire your sloppy ass?" Bastian demanded.

"Yep." Wyatt had absolutely zero intention of telling him who it was. There was a single, heart-stopping moment where they just stared at each other, Bastian's nostrils flaring with his terrible temper.

"Well fine," Bastian roared, sweeping a big hand across his desk, sending the resignation letter flying, along with cookbooks, recipe cards, a whole mug of pencils and pens, and his wireless keyboard.

The resulting clutter brought Kian to the doorway, which Wyatt had been hoping to avoid, yet also knew was inevitable.

"Get out," Bastian growled, and because Wyatt was smart, he did what he was told.

He should have spared a single sympathetic glance for Kian, who was about to head into the lion's den and be eaten alive, all because of Wyatt's defection, but he didn't. He wasn't that good of a person, apparently.

Chapter Three

"Do you think he figured it out?" Ryan's best friend in the whole world sipped her chai latte and eyed him with a keen blue stare that could sniff out a lie no matter how good it was.

Ryan was a terrible liar, and after being friends for three years, he'd learned it was always better to tell Tabitha King the truth.

"Do I think he figured out that it was weird I happened to pick him up the night before the interview? Yeah, he's not an idiot. He figured out something was up. I guess I should have told him it wasn't planned. I recognized him from the photo they'd sent with his resume, and well," Ryan shrugged, "he was so cute in person and suddenly it made sense. Two birds, one stone. A chef *and* a boyfriend."

Ryan pleated the empty sugar packet next to his coffee cup and wished that he'd texted Tabitha like he'd planned and canceled their coffee date. He was feeling weirdly guilty over his hookup with Wyatt, even though it had been unexpectedly spectacular, and he didn't want to rehash all his ugly emotions with her.

The first problem was that he'd chickened out at the last moment and went anyway, and the second problem was Tabitha was the universal expert at rehashing ugly emotions.

"You *like* him," Tabitha stated, looking very delighted at this turn of events. Ryan was not delighted at all. He was regretting the whole damn thing, even while acknowledging that it was the right thing to do under the circumstances. And all that conflict was making him feel queasy. The three sugars he'd thoughtlessly poured into his coffee weren't helping. He pushed the cup aside, wishing he could get something else to wash away the overly sweet taste lingering on his tongue. But Tabitha already knew something was up, and also that he really didn't want to talk about it.

"I thought that was the point," he pointed wryly.

"I still think you should have picked one of those randos you like hooking up with."

Ryan was glad he'd stopped drinking his coffee because he might have choked. He'd known Tabitha for three years now; he should long be used to her frank way of speaking, but she still managed to surprise the hell out of him once in awhile.

"First off, they're not *randos*, and second," Ryan paused with exaggerated faux affront, "I don't *like* hooking up with them."

"You don't like it?" Tabitha raised a flawlessly groomed blonde eyebrow. "That must be rather odd. I had this notion that sex was generally an enjoyable act."

"It is." Ryan ground his teeth together. "You know what I mean. I don't *enjoy* it because they're random guys, but a relationship just isn't for me."

Tabitha rolled her eyes. "Just because *one* relationship turned sour doesn't mean that every relationship will."

"It didn't turn sour. It became too damn boring," Ryan said.

"And yet, a relationship is exactly what you are hoping to achieve," Tabitha said, setting her latte down with a pointed click on the marble tabletop. "How do you propose to stay un-bored with Wyatt?"

"It's not going to be a real relationship," Ryan said. "You know that."

"It's real enough that you like him. It's real enough that you hired him to cook you egg white omelets every morning and grill your chicken every night. He's going to practically live in your backyard. That seems pretty damn real to me."

"I'm attracted to him. The sex was fantastic. If it's not serious and it's not real, I can't imagine why the sex wouldn't stay fantastic. And once in awhile, he'll come with me and we'll hold hands and get papped We'll host dinner parties and post sappy Instagram pics. And that'll fix all my problems."

"Sappy Instagram posts and holding hands in public once in awhile aren't going to solve everything," Tabitha said, sounding faintly exasperated. "*You* know that," she echoed him. Her eyes flitted to the coffee cup he'd bought and hadn't drank.

His stomach was still churning with all the sugar he didn't usually drink, but he still picked up his cup and took a healthy gulp, meeting Tabitha's eyes with a challenging glance of his own. "It'll fix enough," Ryan said. "The rest, I can fix on my own."

Tabitha let out an exasperated sigh. "I can't believe Eric fucking Talbot convinced you that you had to do this."

"You just don't like him," Ryan said. Which was true. Tabitha had hated his agent since day one—before Ryan and Tabitha had even met the first time, she'd hated Eric Talbot. But Ryan couldn't deny that the guy had done a very good, very aggressive job as his agent. He'd known that was what he needed, considering that even before the draft, Ryan had planned on coming out of the closet.

To his credit, Eric had not flinched once when told this, and had proceeded to make deals and eke every dollar out of Ryan's promo deals, despite that he was going to be the first professional baseball player to be out.

So when Eric said that Ryan had a problem with the new general manager of the Dodgers, and that he might choose not to sign Ryan to a new contract, Ryan couldn't help but believe him. No matter what Tabitha said.

"I hate him," Tabitha said, draining the final drops of her latte and setting the cup decisively on the table. "So when are you going to tell Mr. Blake that you've hired him as more than your personal chef?"

"I don't know," Ryan confessed. Eric had wanted to offer both jobs at the same time, and let Wyatt take his pick, but Ryan had vetoed that because after their hookup the night before, he wanted Wyatt. And Ryan knew Wyatt wouldn't agree right away.

But if Ryan could work a little charm on him? Convince him it was necessary? Seduce him with another few rounds of really good sex? Ryan's chances looked better.

"You're not going to tell him right away." Tabitha crossed her arms across her chest and looked even more pissed than when Ryan had brought up Eric Talbot.

"How can I and get him to say yes?"

Tabitha stood abruptly, and Ryan scrambled after her, as she gathered her purse and headed to the door of the café.

"Where are you going?" Ryan asked, even though he already knew.

"To go yell at your tiny-dick agent," Tabitha said between clenched teeth, turning in the direction of her car, heels clicking determinedly on the sidewalk. "If you don't think I don't see his ugly fingers all over this, then I'm a lot blinder than you were counting on. You're *better* than this, Ryan."

Despite already convincing Wyatt to take the chef job—or maybe because of it—Ryan's day was already shitty. He did not want to spend the next two hours separating his best friend and his agent in order to prevent them from kicking the shit out of each other.

Tabitha had never explicitly told him all the unsavory things she'd had to do in her career as a sports journalist, but he'd heard enough to know she'd crawled through mud and shit and blood. And not all metaphorically either. Men she hadn't liked had touched her and they'd believed they deserved that privilege.

There was an underside to professional athletics that was dark and seedy as hell. Ryan had always prided himself on avoiding it, but he knew he was sinking into the mud with this fake relationship.

But the same panic that he felt every time he thought about being traded or his contract expiring streaked through him. Shouldn't he do everything he could to prevent either possibility?

"I'm not saying don't do it," Tabitha said softer, empathy in her eyes as she reached out to squeeze his arm. "I'm saying how you go about it is the difference between sliding into the shit and rising above it. You're a riser."

Ryan raised an eyebrow and they both burst out laughing. "I'm going to text Cal and tell him you told me I was a riser," he said and Tabitha made a face, but she was still smiling.

"Like my boyfriend would actually believe I saw your dick," Tabitha retorted, rolling her eyes.

"I'm telling him anyway."

Tabitha sighed. "I'm telling you—be honest. Lay it all out on the line. Give him the option to stay your chef. I wouldn't complain if there was something edible in your fridge."

"I'll tell him in a few days. Give him time to settle in." Ryan shoved his hands into the pockets of his jeans. If he said more, if he said he was also panicking at the thought of Wyatt turning him down, Tabitha would know he *really* liked him. And she was suspicious enough as it was. He didn't need to give her any more reasons to deploy her well-meaning interference.

"Just . . . soon." Tabitha's eyes had softened, but they sharpened abruptly back into knife points. "And don't let that fucktard convince you to do anything else."

The fucktard was waiting in the driveway, having an intense conversation in his car over his Bluetooth.

It wasn't like Ryan *denied* Eric was a fucktard, but he was Ryan's fucktard, with Ryan's leash tied really tightly around his neck. Ryan reminded himself firmly of this fact as he got out of his own car, and walked over to where Eric had parked.

Eric hung up with a barked order and Ryan braced himself for an argument, because basically everything with Eric ended up an argument. Sometimes Ryan thought Eric argued because he didn't even know how to do anything else.

"I got a text from your new guy," Eric said. "As expected, Aquino threw him out when he gave his notice, so he'll be here sometime tomorrow. Probably afternoon-ish. Do you want me to be here, to go over the rest of the expectations?"

Rest of the expectations. What a nice, polite way of saying Ryan would expect him to pretend to be his boyfriend and definitely not pretend to fuck him on a regular basis. And how unlike Eric to shy away from putting it bluntly.

"Don't bother. I'll tell him myself."

"You're not changing your mind, are you?" Eric demanded.

"No. But I want to give him an out, if he's not okay with it."

"You said you two hooked up, and it was good. Why wouldn't he want to?"

"Why wouldn't he want to play my boyfriend? I don't know, maybe he just doesn't want to. Not everyone is incredibly mercenary like you," Ryan said with an eye roll as punctuation. "Anyway, if he doesn't want to, he can stay on like he planned, as my personal chef, and we'll find someone else for the boyfriend."

"Who else?" Eric said impatiently, drumming his hands on the fire engine red hood of his Maserati. "Do you even have someone in mind?"

"Not at this time."

"I have things lined up . . ." Eric started in, voice growing more intense by the second, and Ryan didn't want to hear it, because he already knew it and also because Eric really was a fucktard.

"We'll cross that bridge when we come to it," Ryan interrupted with a harsh edge to his voice. "*If* Wyatt says no."

"So when are you going to ask him?" Eric snapped.

"Soon," Ryan said. Reminded himself again that Eric worked for *him*, and whatever he wanted to do, however he wanted to proceed, everything was ultimately up to him. Eric couldn't make decisions for Ryan, he could only advise.

Eric digested this, and even though he clearly wanted to demand a specific date, probably even a specific time, if Ryan knew Eric at all, he didn't. Definitely a good thing because Eric would have gone postal if he'd discovered Ryan intended to wait a few days. At least until Wyatt got settled in, and wasn't a total stranger.

Ryan didn't expect Wyatt to trust him so quickly, but he at least needed to show Wyatt that he wasn't a manipulative jerk. Tabitha had been right about that; like she was right about so many things.

"I also have the details of the new Adidas shoot," Eric said, following Ryan as he keyed in the garage code and ducked through the opening door.

"You could have emailed it over," Ryan said, annoyed that Eric hadn't taken a hint and *left*. He walked into the kitchen, and grabbed a water bottle from the fridge. He didn't offer

Eric one and pointedly drank deeply as Eric leaned over the island counter and went over the main points of the new Adidas commercial shoot Ryan was doing soon.

"I asked them to try to downplay some of the more LGBT-friendly symbols," Eric said. "It's a contract year. I want them to emphasize that you're an athlete. A pro athlete."

Ryan made a face. "I wish you hadn't told them that. We can emphasize I'm an athlete some other way. You can get me another one of those *Men's Health* covers or something. I love that Adidas is ready and willing to embrace that I'm gay. That was why we signed with them instead of Nike."

"You can definitely do better than *Men's Health*," Eric scoffed, clearly changing the subject, which annoyed Ryan even more. "I think we can get *Sports Illustrated,* maybe even for their Opening Day special issue."

"You really think you can convince *Sports Illustrated* to pick me, instead of any of the other dozens of high-profile baseball players?" Ryan was not convinced. He had had a good year last year, and he'd made his mark in the playoffs the year before that. He'd already been a household name because he'd come out before the draft, but he was definitely beginning to be recognized for his baseball skills. As far as he was concerned, it had taken too long, though Eric kept telling him he was doing even better than the ten-year plan.

Eric was a fucktard, but he also had a ten-year plan for Ryan, which made hating him difficult. The ten-year plan also made deliberately circumventing Eric's ideas pretty stupid. Ryan usually tried to follow them, but this was a subject he was definitely willing to draw a line about.

"It's not decided yet, of course," Eric said, "but I feel good about your chances."

"I don't care. Call Adidas back," Ryan said with clipped tones.

Ryan saw Eric hold himself back for a second time in the last fifteen minutes, and that was basically a record, so it was probably better to end this conversation now, before Eric lost his temper and so did Ryan. They'd been working together for over three years now, and he'd learned that everything was just smoother if he could bring Eric around to his way of thinking without having to yell at him.

"You're sure?" Eric asked skeptically.

"Was I sure three years ago when I sat in your office for the first time and said I wanted to come out before the draft?" Ryan demanded. His temper was definitely fraying at the edges. He squished the plastic bottle in his hands and it made a satisfyingly loud crackling noise.

To his credit, Eric looked him straight in the eye. "You told me you had balls enough for both of us. I'd never had a client who questioned my balls before."

"There you go," Ryan said, tossing the bottle in the recycling bin. "Find them and call Adidas back."

Eric sighed. "Alright. I'll email you after I do."

He left without much of a goodbye, but that was fine by Ryan because he knew they were both on the edge, and the one thing he'd always sort of liked—at least *respected*—about Eric was that he knew when to quit.

Ryan flopped down on the couch in his media room and picked up the remote, even though he really didn't want to watch TV. Whenever he was this keyed up, all temper and fizzy emotions shook up with nowhere to go, he usually opened Grindr and found a hookup. Worked off his extra energy the good, old-fashioned way.

But he couldn't do that now. He was going to be in a relationship shortly—even if it was a fake one—and the only rule that Eric had laid down, with no exceptions, was that Ryan's hooking up days were over.

"Too many stories, too many rumors," was what Eric had said bluntly. "The GM doesn't like it. And if the GM doesn't like it, he doesn't like you, and then he has the ammunition not to re-sign you. And that's the last thing we want to cultivate in a contract year."

It was why they had landed on the idea of a fake relationship in the first place. The GM wanted to see Ryan steady and dedicated, on and *off* the field, because in his small, homophobic mind, being gay meant being a flighty party boy. And then Ryan had been dumb enough to give him the evidence to believe he was right.

The boyfriend was supposed to prove the opposite. But it also meant that Ryan had to walk the walk. Ryan didn't want to, but he wanted to stay in LA and play baseball more.

He couldn't help but wish Wyatt had gotten here today, instead of in a few days. Wyatt would have known what to do with all his excess energy.

Ryan flipped his phone over, the generic action movie on the TV all but forgotten. The little app icon for Grindr tempted him for half a second, but Eric had done a good job convincing him the temptation wouldn't be worth the risk. So he clicked on another icon instead.

Sorry that Aquino kicked you out, he typed out right under Wyatt's single "Hi" that he'd sent so that Ryan would have his number.

Ryan couldn't help but wonder, as he stared at the text screen, if Wyatt hadn't been annoyed at being deceived, that he might have sent something different. Something playful. Something flirtatious. Maybe even something sexy.

A ding from his phone made Ryan jump.

It wasn't exactly a surprise, Wyatt texted back. **Aquino has a temper. And he hates it when people leave.**

After the interview, Ryan had actually done a little research on Bastian Aquino, Wyatt's old boss. And after reading a handful of articles, he'd been surprised that anyone could tolerate such a dickwad for any amount of time, no matter how good the job was.

Don't worry. No plate smashing here. Unless you convince me to throw a Greek-themed party! ;) Ryan texted.

He half-expected Wyatt to brush him off because he was still pissed off that Ryan had kept the interview a secret. Ryan still didn't know why he hadn't told the truth. He'd meant to when he'd followed Wyatt outside, and then Wyatt had looked at him, awestruck that Ryan had followed *him*, and Ryan hadn't been able to confess that he'd sought him out because he looked exactly like the guy he was supposed to interview the next morning.

But, **Like it a little wild, huh** was the *very* unexpected text that Ryan got back as a response.

Wyatt had only a tiny inkling of how wild Ryan could get, but he had every intention of enlightening him.

I went off with you on your bike, didn't I? Ryan reminded him.

You did. The response came through almost instantly, like before Wyatt had put his phone away between texts, but now had kept it out, intent on talking to Ryan. And then he sent another text before Ryan could even come up with something else to say. **I really enjoyed having you behind me.**

Ryan stared at the screen. Usually it was a no-brainer that guys flirted with him. It was always overt and typically very blatant. He definitely wasn't used to trying to read between the lines. The last thing he wanted to do was guess wrong with Wyatt and scare him off.

After he typed and discarded half a dozen responses, Ryan settled on something equally as ambiguous. **I'll be happy to get behind you anytime you want.**

Wyatt clearly wasn't agonizing over Ryan's meaning the same way, because the next text came through too fast. **I got that impression. :)**

What the hell, Ryan thought. He'd done this so many times, it should have felt old and used up, but with Wyatt it was exciting again, got his blood pumping and the adrenaline fizzy in his veins like he was fourteen and it was the first time all over again. **No, you got the impression I'd get on my knees anytime I want.**

What about whenever I want? Wyatt shot back.

Ryan glanced down and wasn't surprised to see he was half-hard in his jeans. **I was pretty damn clear**, he texted.

And then . . . *nothing.* An excruciatingly long ten minutes went by without a single text. Ryan checked, then double-checked his coverage. Restarted his phone. Even wandered into the front of the house because the Wi-Fi was always stronger there.

Still nothing.

Ryan couldn't believe it, they'd had a really good, nearly sexy banter going, and the unfortunately short memories of their one encounter were already flashing through his mind in three-dimensions and full-technicolor. The sharp dig of the gravel into his knees. The clean, musky taste of Wyatt's dick, and the weight of it on his tongue. Ryan pressed the heel of his hand against his own interested dick. It didn't want to wait and entice Wyatt into repeating the past. It wanted more. It wanted everything, and it wasn't usually inclined to settle, even though Ryan was pretty sure he wouldn't need to.

Just not tonight.

Tonight, Wyatt was clearly going to leave him hanging and unsatisfied, which Ryan was man enough to admit he probably deserved. Not that he'd left Wyatt hanging the other night—he'd definitely been fully, if not completely, satisfied then.

But not entirely, Ryan thought, as he remembered the way Wyatt's face had fallen when he realized that Ryan had no intention of exchanging phone numbers with him.

No, Wyatt had definitely wanted more. He'd wanted more the next morning too, but Ryan had fucked that up by not being honest enough.

Not a mistake that Ryan or his dick were going to make again. As soon as Wyatt got here and settled in a little, he was going to find out what Ryan needed—and also what Ryan wanted—from him.

He never took a chance of being the last one interested, much preferring to cut and run and move onto something better, something more exciting, when a hookup ran its natural course. But tonight, he texted Wyatt again.

Ryan told himself it was the veneer of professionalism that he was trying to maintain because he was technically

Wyatt's boss now. Not that he'd exactly been professional the first time they'd met.

I'll be around during the day tomorrow and probably the evening too. Hope to see you.

Ryan realized as he finished typing that it wasn't only his dick that felt that way. He wanted to get to know Wyatt; he wanted to talk to him again. He wanted to convince him to take a chance on Ryan's wild plan most of all, because that meant he wouldn't have to do it with a stranger he didn't even like.

He wanted it to be Wyatt. He just needed Wyatt to want it too.

Wyatt looked at his phone and slipped it back in his pocket. Two texts unanswered now.

"You realize we threw this party for you, right?" Xander said, his voice cutting right through the grind of the guitars in the music that someone—not someone with taste, but *someone*—had put on the playlist.

Wyatt looked up at the crowded rental he was moving out of in the morning, and realized he couldn't identify more than a handful of guys he'd worked with in the Terroir kitchen.

"I don't even know half these people," Wyatt half-yelled. He knew he didn't have a voice like Xander's, that could cut through so much ambient noise, and he was usually glad about that fact.

Xander scanned over the crowd with a critical eye. "I think a lot of these are Nate's friends."

They weren't Nate's friends. If they'd been Nate's friends, Wyatt would have known them. He considered pointing this out, but Xander was in a mood—frankly had been in a mood since Miles had moved to LA—and so he didn't. Certainly Wyatt leaving and having Nate take over his part of the lease weren't helping.

If Xander wanted to throw a stupid house party, buy too much booze, and invite too many people none of them knew, then Wyatt certainly wasn't going to tell him he wasn't going to regret it in the morning.

"I haven't seen Kian yet," Wyatt said, because changing the subject was a far safer approach.

Xander's lips compressed. "I'm sure the Bastard had some sort of ridiculous project for him that kept him late again."

"While I'm in LA, I'm going to look for a different job for him," Wyatt said, even though he'd already told Xander what his plans were. Still, they both knew it was going to be in vain. There was no way Kian would leave Aquino.

Wyatt didn't want to say it was love because he'd always believed that love needed generosity and respect and admiration to grow and flourish, but maybe he was wrong.

Not about Bastian suddenly becoming generous, respectful or admiring, but about any of those being required for Kian to fall in love with him.

It was a depressing thought, and Wyatt forced his mind back to the party, because even though he was saying goodbye, this was supposed to be a somewhat happy occasion. A celebration of the potential of the future.

The truth was all Wyatt wanted to do was pull his phone back up, despite Xander's face-melting glare, and text with Ryan. He was clever and cute and just a little aggressive. Aggressive wasn't something Wyatt thought he'd want after Nate, but on Ryan it felt more natural, more an extension of a well-meaning personality than a way to go about domineering everyone and everything.

And Nate had absolutely, definitely done that.

Of course Nate also hadn't lied about his intentions either, which was something Wyatt was still confused and a little upset about. Why not tell him? Why keep it a secret?

That mystery was all caught up in his own conflicted feelings towards Ryan. He still felt everything he had the first night they'd met. He'd never stopped. He was pretty sure that stopping was totally out of the cards now that he was going to be working for Ryan and literally living in his backyard. Cooking his meals. Taking care of him. All actions that Wyatt *knew* would develop his feelings even if he tried to hold them back.

But Ryan seemed interested too, despite the mysterious intentions, and that was something Wyatt was increasingly having to come to terms with. Would he let him? Would Ryan be the guy? Wyatt had always known, in the corners of his mind, that there would be a guy that would make him *want* to come out to Nana. That there would be a guy that he'd be dying to introduce to her, and not just as a "good friend."

It seemed insane that Ryan could be the guy. It also seemed insane that Ryan was interested, but that was an undeniable fact. Wyatt felt the sharp edges of his phone through his pocket, and finally pulled it back out.

Xander had decamped to the doorway, where he was interrogating Kian. Wyatt glanced down at his screen and before he could change his mind—or chicken out—typed a response to Ryan.

I'm leaving my friends and my job and the city I've lived in for years. The only definite thing I know about the future is that I'm going to see you tomorrow.

CHAPTER FOUR

"Hɪ." Wʏᴀᴛᴛ sʜɪꜰᴛᴇᴅ ᴀᴡᴋᴡᴀʀᴅʟʏ from one foot to the other and tried not to feel like he'd fucked up already by knocking on the front door instead of doing something silly like going to the back of the house.

But mostly he tried the hardest not to stare, because he had definitely not anticipated Ryan opening the door only wearing a pair of low-slung athletic shorts and a thin sheen of sweat on his bare, muscled torso.

"Hi back," Ryan said, smiling so brightly it dismissed all of Wyatt's concerns. "Is that all you came with?" he asked, glancing at the duffel bag at Wyatt's feet.

"I have a few more boxes that are shipping down here next week," Wyatt admitted. "Other than that, yeah. I like to travel light."

"Live light too," Ryan said, and there was definitely an approving light in his dark eyes. "So do I. Come see the house."

Wyatt wasn't sure if he and Ryan had different definitions of "living light," because Ryan definitely had more than a duffel bag and a handful of boxes to his name. The house wasn't as big as it looked from the street and the gate that protected the driveway from the main road. But everything was clean and simple—lots of modern lines tempered by a worn-in homey quality that Wyatt appreciated.

"Living room," Ryan said, as Wyatt trailed behind him, trying really hard not to admire the firm roundness of his ass in those clingy shorts. "Dining room, you probably sort of care about that," he said absently. "And here's the one room you definitely care about." Ryan made some cute flourish with his hands and they stepped into the kitchen.

It wasn't a huge space but it had been well-designed, with a big island for prep, and good, professional-grade appliances. But if he was being honest, if there was one thing that could distract him from high quality appliances, it was a cute boy leaning against them. "Is there a pantry?" Wyatt asked, when he realized he'd been staring—and not even at the kitchen.

He felt the exact same magnetic pull to Ryan that he had that night. He hadn't really expected it to diminish but he also hadn't expected it to be blazing stronger than ever. Especially when they still hadn't addressed any of the growing baggage between them. Attraction didn't magically make any of that shit disappear, but it sure made it easier to ignore.

"Oh, yeah, of course," Ryan said. He walked past Wyatt, and Wyatt got one whiff of him. No cologne, but something earthy, like sunshine and dirt and grass. Wyatt wanted to know what his sweat tasted like on his tongue, what it felt like against his palms. But he kept his hands and his tongue to himself. Whatever was going to happen with them, there was no point in rushing in before they'd even talked about it.

There was a big pantry, with lots of empty shelves that Wyatt would enjoy filling. "This looks really great, actually."

Ryan shot him a lopsided, very charming smile. He probably even knew how charming it was, and it still didn't diminish the sheer wattage of it. "Are you just saying that? You can be honest with me, you know. Like I said last night, I promise no thrown dishes or hissy fits when my meat isn't precisely the right temperature."

Wyatt leaned back against the counter and shoved his hands in his pockets. Better to keep them where they needed to be, and not against Ryan's damp skin. "I wouldn't lie to you."

Ryan flushed, and looked ashamed. That had been Wyatt's original intention—to remind him that out of the two of them, Ryan had been the only one who'd lied. Despite that, Wyatt couldn't help but feel embarrassed that he'd brought it up first.

"I'm sorry, I should have told you," Ryan said. "About the interview, that is. I kept meaning to that night, and then I thought if I did, you'd really just take me home. Would you have?"

Wyatt was pretty sure Ryan already knew the answer to that question. So he deliberately skirted around it. "I don't want to be a joke or a toy to play with. Especially now that you're my boss."

"It's not like that, I promise." Ryan sounded and looked very earnest. Trustworthy, even. But Wyatt still wasn't sure that wasn't his attraction to him annoyingly surfacing and interfering again.

"Look," Ryan continued, "it'll stay separate. The professional stuff, the *you're my boss* stuff, and the personal stuff. And for the record, I don't really consider myself your boss."

"You pay my salary?" Wyatt pointed out, a little incredulously.

"Well," Ryan smiled, "technically that's Eric. And yeah, he's my agent, but it gives some separation, right?"

Wyatt wasn't sure he entirely agreed, but the attraction was still flaring up, brightly and almost painfully. He'd come here, hadn't he? He'd given up his job at Terroir, and packed his bags, and drove here, intending to work for Ryan Flores. And, if he was being really honest with himself, a good part of that was because he'd wanted more. More money *and* more time with Ryan. Was it so wrong that he might get both in the same position?

"Okay," Wyatt said, hoping that he wouldn't regret his agreement later. Hoping that even if he did regret it, that there would be some spectacular memories to make it worth it in the end.

"I guess that means I should show you the ADU," Ryan said.

"ADU?" Wyatt asked as he followed Ryan out of the kitchen, through the back door, and out to the lawn. There was a cute little cottage set a ways back from the main house, surrounded by flowering bushes and a palm tree.

"Attached dwelling unit," Ryan said, opening the door and leading Wyatt inside. "Eric said I should have it built when I remodeled the house, in case I wanted someone to stay with me but wanted to make sure we each had our privacy."

Wyatt was briefly tempted to tell Ryan that he wasn't sure he needed the privacy. He'd much rather be right in Ryan's pocket. He'd never considered his first instinct reckless before, but he knew he was acting reckless now.

"Eric seems like a good agent, that way," Wyatt said instead. Even though he'd done a very good impression of a human being encasing a blood-thirsty piranha the only time they'd ever met.

"Oh, he's an asshole," Ryan chuckled. "But he's my asshole. So it works out. Anyway, this is all yours. No kitchen, other than this little sink, mini fridge and microwave, but feel free to come use the one in the house at any time. I really mean that."

There was a tiny living room with a flat screen TV and a comfy-looking couch. A separate bedroom with a queen bed and dresser—even a miniature walk-in closet. A bathroom, with a clever closet enclosing a small washer and dryer unit, finished out the cottage.

It was everything Wyatt needed, barring the kitchen, which was just a few steps away.

What he wanted was standing in the kitchenette, examining the contents of the mini fridge.

"I told Gabriela to stock this," Ryan said, pointing out the empty shelves. "I'll have to talk to her."

"I can stock it, it's not a big deal." Wyatt was already a little embarrassed at the ridiculous salary that Ryan was paying him, never mind that he was dying to get into his pants *again*. He didn't need Ryan to pay for his groceries.

"Gabriela does the housekeeping, and runs the odd errand but she doesn't live here," Ryan said. "I don't really have a personal assistant. If I need help, Eric will usually loan me his. Nicole is intimidatingly efficient so I try to avoid it if I can."

"So it's just . . . me and you." Wyatt tried not to make that sound like an invitation, but he was acutely aware of Ryan's bare chest and the big fluffy bed in the next room. It was impossible not to think of what they could do in it. After all, it had been so good when it was just Wyatt's bike and a swath of gravel. The bed opened up endless possibilities that had Wyatt's head swimming and his cock half-erect in his jeans.

"Yep." Ryan smiled brightly. He seemed just as happy about this turn of events as Wyatt.

Wyatt wanted to reach over and pull Ryan against him, their first kiss and its incendiary intensity in sharp, perfect detail in his mind. The second, he knew, would be even better. The third might outdo every kiss he'd ever experienced before.

It was one of the reasons why he hadn't kissed Ryan yet. He didn't want this to be a casual, hookup sort of thing. He wanted to show Ryan that he wanted more. More than just a quick afternoon in bed together. Or a quick ride up in the Hills followed by a convenient blowjob.

And everything tempered by the sobering realization that Ryan was his *boss*. He'd never wanted to blow his boss before.

"We should talk about expectations," Wyatt said, dropping his duffel on the floor and digging out a worn pad from the side. He'd written a list of questions he'd needed to ask last night, after ducking out on his own farewell party.

"Expectations? You feed me when I want food. That's about it," Ryan said, and even though Wyatt didn't like the tiny crease forming Ryan's brows, he forged on.

This was stuff he needed to know to do his *job*. And for what Ryan was paying him, he couldn't shirk his responsibilities or his duties, all because he was desperate to get into his boss' pants.

"Expectations sounds more formal than I was intending," Wyatt confessed. "I just have a long list of questions, basically."

"Questions?" Ryan frowned. "We'll deal with that tomorrow. Tonight's your first night in LA. It's nice out; let's go for a drive. And this time we'll take *my* bike."

"Oh, uh, okay, sure." His first day at Terroir, Bastian Aquino definitely hadn't invited him out. Or issued the invitation with quite that fiery glint in his eye either. Ryan definitely looked like he was up to something. Wyatt might still be unsure, but he didn't think he had the willpower to turn this man down.

"I'll take a quick shower, and then we'll head out," Ryan said. "Feel free to settle in."

Settle in while Ryan was in the shower? Naked and dripping wet and only half a house away? Wyatt felt his temperature spike at the thought.

"I think I'm going to take a quick inventory in the kitchen," Wyatt said, because that felt so much safer than fantasizing about joining Ryan in the shower.

❧ ❧

Wyatt was headfirst in a cupboard, cataloging mixing bowls, when he felt a warm hand rest on his back.

"Find everything you needed?" Ryan asked when Wyatt straightened. The athletic shorts had been swapped for a pair of jeans tight enough they made his heart thump harder.

He'd done something cute and swoopy to his hair, and he smelled delectable, like spicy vanilla. Wyatt's mouth watered, and he was suddenly, painfully aware of his own faded jeans and old t-shirt.

He hadn't dressed to go out. Or to impress a cute guy, even though he'd known Ryan would probably be here. He'd dressed to drive six hours on his bike, and hadn't put anymore thought into it. Maybe he should have, instead of spending the last twenty minutes digging through Ryan's kitchen drawers and cupboards.

"You have the basics," Wyatt said, trailing after Ryan as they headed towards the garage. "I'm probably going to have to pick up some stuff."

Ryan seemed completely unconcerned by this, and Wyatt felt an awkward, embarrassed pulse at the acute financial gap between them. Ryan had enough money he didn't have to keep track, while Wyatt scraped by, even now with the increased salary.

That feeling when Ryan opened the garage door, a light shining down on a Range Rover, a Bentley, and a Tesla. And a really sweet street bike that had clearly been modified for speed, and then painted a flat, sexy matte black. In a pair of leathers, Ryan would look like fucking Batman.

It made Wyatt's serviceable bike look like garbage in comparison. And even though Ryan never seemed to compare, Wyatt couldn't help doing it.

Ryan passed by the cars without a second glance and pulled a sleek black helmet from a cubby on the wall. He extended the helmet Wyatt's direction. "You up for it?" he asked, that sly challenge back in his eyes.

It wasn't a question of what Wyatt was up for, but if the night would end without Wyatt getting everything he was up for.

He grabbed the helmet, and slid it on, watching as Ryan picked up another one, and did the same.

Ryan was maybe only an inch shorter, with slightly narrower shoulders, but it felt just as good to climb on the bike behind him as it had to feel Ryan's arms wrapped around him. It gave him hope that Ryan might echo his own versatile preferences.

Sliding his own hands around Ryan's waist, he let one drift down and feel the flexing muscle of his thigh as he pulled the bike out of the garage. Ryan's glance backwards was bright and challenging.

It shouldn't have surprised Wyatt that Ryan liked to go fast; after all, he'd seen the collection of cars, even though he only had a vague idea of what they were capable of. Wyatt knew more about motorcycles, and had definitely known this was custom and tuned for speed, but he still wasn't expecting the way Ryan floored it when they pulled onto the freeway.

The acceleration pushed Ryan's body more firmly into the cradle of Wyatt's, and he knew there was no way Ryan was going to miss how hard he was, cock aching in his jeans. He wanted everything they'd had last time they'd been on a bike like this, and so much more.

But while Ryan seemed to be in a hurry to get somewhere—weaving in and out of the traffic on the freeway, expertly maneuvering the bike even with the extra weight on it—he didn't seem to be in any hurry to go somewhere specific. They hit Highway 1, and even the early evening traffic didn't seem to phase Ryan.

The sun was setting, the sky ablaze with color as they headed further up the coast, and to his surprise, Ryan did finally pull off the road, but not towards an abandoned parking lot, but to a busy taqueria with a nearly full parking lot.

He stopped the bike with a spray of gravel, and pulled off his helmet, grinning like a loon. Wyatt reluctantly removed his hands from Ryan's waist, and took off his own helmet.

"And I thought I drove fast," Wyatt teased, pushing his hair back.

Ryan winced. "I might like speed a little too much."

"The adrenaline can be addictive," Wyatt acknowledged.

"Yeah," Ryan admitted. "You been here before?" he asked, gesturing to the building behind them.

The last thing Wyatt had expected was for Ryan to take him to a restaurant. But here they were. Wyatt shook his head, wondering if he should ask Ryan what the hell he was thinking.

"I haven't. I'm assuming I'm off the clock," Wyatt said, because he couldn't just *let* it go, not the way Ryan did. Probably because Ryan had all the advantages here, and almost certainly kept forgetting that Wyatt didn't have any.

"Of course you are." Ryan grinned recklessly. "Though maybe the apprentice has something to teach the master?"

"Master of what?" Wyatt scoffed. "You definitely know how to handle yourself on that bike."

"Master of good food, *duh*," Ryan said, slinging his helmet under his arm. "This place makes the best tacos in Southern California. Pretty good view, too."

Wyatt didn't even pretend to look out at Malibu, spread out underneath them. "Yeah, I really like it."

Ryan flushed. "You wanted to ask me some questions. I figured it might be good to grab some food."

"I'm not complaining. If you want to feed me, I'm not going to stop you," he teased back. If Ryan was going to act like this was a date, then he wasn't going to stop him from doing that either. In fact, he could definitely hold his own, if that's what this was.

Not everything had to be so black and white—either professionally or personally. Weren't the best things a gray-hued combination of both? Wyatt reminded himself of his good friend Miles and his boyfriend, Evan, who worked and loved and fought together, sometimes all at once.

If they could do it, then Wyatt could too, especially if it was Ryan he was doing it with.

There was a lengthy line at the little shack, and a lot of the picnic tables were already full of people enjoying their tacos. Wyatt half-expected someone to recognize Ryan, but everyone ignored them.

"I keep expecting everyone here to mow me down to get to you," Wyatt half-joked. "Am I going to end up being part-chef, part-bodyguard?"

Ryan shot him an incredulous look as they settled in the back of the line. "Please, I'm definitely not that famous. If Eric ever tried to saddle me with a bodyguard, I'd laugh in his face. Or something worse, like question his manhood or his net worth."

"You don't ever get people who recognize you?" Wyatt had known who Ryan was instantly, but then he'd been touched and undeniably impacted three years ago when Ryan had come out of the closet. Also he'd definitely thought he was hot back then. That feeling hadn't changed three years later, when he'd found him at Temple and had spent too many hours staring at him.

"I'm a baseball player, not a celebrity." Ryan rolled his eyes. "Every once in a while, yeah, I get someone who wants a selfie or an autograph, but it doesn't really happen all that often. Eric probably wishes it happened more. He's always wanting me to sign more deals to raise my public profile, but like I said, I'm a baseball player, not a fucking influencer, or whatever they call those assholes who take impossible

Instagram pictures. If I'm going to take pictures it's going to be of all the sick places I visit."

"You like to travel?" Wyatt asked. He kept trying to ignore how much like a first date this felt like, but it kept cropping up. But the truth was, however it felt, he wanted to get to know Ryan.

"Confession," Ryan said, leaning closer, and nudging his shoulder against Wyatt's, "it's one of my favorite parts of being a baseball player. We don't get a lot of time in cities, sometimes, but every place just *feels* different, you know? And it's an experience to be in every single one."

Wyatt wished he *did* know, but he didn't. He'd worked his ass off getting through culinary school, had spent some time in Chicago, then Portland, and then had gotten the job at Terroir, and had jumped at the chance to come back to California. But his truth was that he'd barely ever left California since he was born, and even though he felt a little wistful at the thought of exploring the world and all the culinary delights it had to offer, he'd never really felt the lack of travel.

"I haven't really traveled much," Wyatt confessed. "Not much opportunity."

Ryan's smile was bright and infectious. "Maybe we can change that."

Wyatt didn't really understand how he could do that; it wasn't like Wyatt was going to go with Ryan on road trips as his personal chef. And that was the whole issue, wasn't it? Ryan had never defined his job role, and Wyatt had a feeling that wouldn't change. Ryan wasn't really a *definer*. He liked the adrenaline rush of making it up as he went.

"We'd better figure out our order," Wyatt suggested, gesturing towards the menu. "What do you usually get?"

Ryan rattled off half a dozen types of tacos, and added, with a lopsided grin, "And definitely beer. I wasn't supposed to drink during the season so I definitely want a beer with my tacos."

"Let's get a bucket then," Wyatt suggested. "We can share. And I definitely want to try those authentic shrimp tacos. And the *al pastor*."

When they were about to get to the register, Ryan shooed him away, with directions to find a table. Wyatt decided that he didn't care if Ryan bought him some tacos and a beer. It was fine. It didn't mean this was a date. It didn't mean anything, necessarily. It was a guy welcoming his new employee. Except it hadn't felt precisely professional when they'd been pressed together on his bike earlier, and it wouldn't feel that way on the way home either. Especially with Wyatt desperate for Ryan to pull over for every dark corner.

Ryan ventured over to the table Wyatt had found with his very capable hands filled with plates and the bucket of beers dangling from one finger.

It shouldn't have reminded Wyatt of the other night, but pretty much everything reminded Wyatt of the other night. The way Ryan walked, the way he smiled—brighter now, and more spontaneously—the way he bit his lip or wet it with his tongue, and definitely his strong, calloused hands.

"Food," Ryan crowed with excitement, sliding the paper plates across the table. "And beer!"

"Do you think there's anyone on the planet who doesn't like tacos?" Wyatt asked, digging a chip into the salsa verde, heat prickling his tongue as the jalapeños hit his taste buds. "Tacos are god's food."

"Tacos are amazing," Ryan agreed.

"What else do you like to eat?" Wyatt asked, squeezing a lime over his shrimp tacos.

Ryan glanced up, attention distracted from the food in front of him. "Is this part of the interrogation? Should I find my handcuffs?"

Wyatt thought Ryan would be sufficiently pleased at how his heartbeat picked up at the mention of his handcuffs. "No," he scoffed wryly. "I promise, it'll be fine. Just a few questions. I definitely find that food is a personal thing. Besides, I want to prevent you from tossing your meal at me, and keep your broken-plate rule intact."

"It's not going to be hard," Ryan said. "I'm really laid-back about food. Most of the time, I don't really care, honestly. Just put it in front of me, and I'll eat it."

Wyatt was skeptical but maybe that was from a history of working at the most exacting restaurant in America. "Okay, tell me this. When it's just you, what do you eat? Start with breakfast."

"A banana? An orange? Sometimes a mango or a papaya if I can get my hands on it. I like to buy those pre-boiled eggs from the store for protein. Maybe a frozen turkey sausage or two, if I'm feeling like making the effort."

Wyatt had seen Ryan's kitchen and how pristine it was. He had a feeling Ryan very infrequently "made the effort."

"I'm surprised you didn't mention any protein shakes," Wyatt said, swallowing a big bite of fantastic fresh and spicy shrimp. He'd done a little research, and the shakes seemed to be the ubiquitous item that most athletes imbibed.

Ryan's grin was too cute, all lopsided and embarrassed. "Those go without saying. I like to put low-fat peanut butter in mine."

"Smooth or chunky?"

Ryan choked on his beer. "Oh, smooth." An unholy glint lit his dark eyes. "Very smooth."

Wyatt had to swallow hard, even though he wasn't even eating at that moment. "Noted."

"But you're not writing anything down?" Ryan teased.

"I have a feeling I won't have any trouble remembering any of this. So far, it's not exactly complicated. What about lunch or dinner?"

"Eric is going to be really happy that I hired someone who takes his job so seriously," Ryan said. "I don't really care, honestly. Feed me something. Whatever you feel you want to make. October and November, I don't worry too much about what I'm eating, though towards Thanksgiving, I'm going to have to watch it a little, because I have an Adidas commercial shoot. And knowing Eric, who's arranging the whole thing, they'll have me mostly naked."

Wyatt's cheeks heated at the thought of all that bare skin. Except he wasn't picturing it on an Adidas set, he was picturing it in his bed, with Ryan raising his eyebrow the same he had the night they'd met. Daring Wyatt to do everything he wanted.

Maybe a pair of those handcuffs of Ryan's thrown in for good measure.

He was all quicksilver heat, hot and swift but possibly not lasting. Considering that Wyatt already wanted more, he wasn't sure he could settle for what Ryan might give him.

Who am I kidding? Wyatt asked himself. He was going to take anything Ryan would give him, love every second, and then somehow deal with it when it ended.

Maybe if he did a really great job, Ryan might keep him on after, no matter how wretched that would feel. It wasn't something to look forward to, but Wyatt needed the money.

"Everything okay?" Ryan asked, pulling Wyatt out of his depressing thoughts. Thinking about flings ending before they even began, worrying about fallout and finances.

Wyatt grimaced. "Sorry, just got distracted."

"I must not be entertaining you enough," Ryan insisted, and suddenly, there was his foot, his boot nudging Wyatt's. And even through two layers of leather, the impact blasted through him. It wasn't the first time Ryan had touched him since he'd arrived, but this wasn't just a simple touch. It had a purpose and intent.

I'm going to touch you a lot more tonight.

"I don't have any complaints so far," Wyatt said, a little teasing edge to his voice.

"You'd tell me if you did, right?" Ryan asked.

Wyatt toyed with a chip, crumbling it onto his empty plate. "Why wouldn't I?"

The truth was Wyatt was curious why Ryan had suddenly decided he needed a private chef when he didn't even have a personal assistant, but that wasn't exactly a *complaint*. Besides, Wyatt had a feeling he'd discover the truth eventually, even if he wasn't entirely sure he wanted to hear it.

The secrecy alone should turn him off, but he was in too deep. It was that blasted attraction, rearing its head again.

"You would," Ryan confirmed. "I'm just . . . maybe *you're* not being entertaining enough."

Wyatt rolled his eyes. "That's something you're going to have to get used to, unfortunately. I'm pretty boring."

"You like to cook, but what else do you do for fun?"

"In high school, I surfed," Wyatt said. "I've been wanting to get back to it."

"I know a lot of good spots. Maybe we can go together sometime," Ryan said. "I don't get to go during the season much, so I need to get all this in before spring training starts. So, cooking, surfing. And your bike. What else makes Wyatt Blake tick?"

If Wyatt hadn't already acknowledged this felt like a first date, he definitely would have thought it now. "The first thing I try to do if I have any free time is see my nana. We're really close."

"Cooking, surfing, your motorcycle, and Nana's boy." Ryan sounded approving, and he was smiling. "Never mind that sound you make when you lose control. How is a guy like you single?"

Wyatt didn't want to talk about it. He definitely didn't want to talk about it with Ryan, who had taken the chance to come out at the most impactful moment in his career.

"You finished?" he asked, getting to his feet. His voice sounded rough, a little of his desperation leaking into it. Desperation to avoid the question. Desperation to get Ryan naked underneath him, on top of him—whichever, Wyatt didn't even care.

Ryan's dark eyes were knowing as they stared up at him. "With the food, yeah. With you, not quite."

"Then let's go," Wyatt said.

He never would have dreamed of voicing that sort of demand to his old boss, but it was becoming very clear that his old job and his new job were fundamentally different. Ryan kept saying he was nothing like Bastian Aquino, and maybe it was time to hold him to that. Ryan had also claimed they could keep their professional and personal lives separate, and had driven that point home by taking him out to dinner tonight. So, he was off the clock, right?

Wyatt scooped up the empty plates and tossed them in the trash on his way to the parking lot, hoping that Ryan was trailing after him.

He could hear footsteps behind him, and it was all the confirmation he needed to drop his helmet on the seat, and wrap one hand around Ryan's waist and pull him close. "This what you had in mind?" he demanded, right before he kissed him.

He hadn't been able to forget how intensely Ryan had kissed him the other night, and even though at the time he'd believed he'd given as good as he got, it was impossible not to catalogue every missed moment.

This time Wyatt wasn't going to miss a thing.

His mouth covered Ryan's, his arm pulling him tight against him, and he let him know explicitly, with his lips and his tongue, just how much he'd wanted him the last few days. That he hadn't stopped wanting him, that he'd wanted him even before he'd dropped him off at his front gate.

All Ryan's teasing had done was push him to a point of desperation—a point of no return. He didn't care if it was over tomorrow morning or next week or next year. He just wanted as much of Ryan as he could get, in whatever time they had.

Ryan broke away, panting, but Wyatt didn't let up. His lips only shifted to his neck, feeling the pulse point there racing. Ryan definitely wanted him just as much. His cock was a hard, burning pressure against Wyatt's thigh, and he kept shifting a little, like he was just as desperate to take the strain off. But Wyatt wasn't going to let him go that easily.

"You didn't even let me finish my beer," Ryan said, and his voice was breathless.

"I'll buy you another one," Wyatt said, between kisses against the soft skin just behind Ryan's ear. Soft and sensitive, if the way Ryan kept squirming was any indication.

"I'm going to hold you to that," Ryan laughed, and it was still breathless. "How am I supposed to drive home like this?"

"Like I've been," Wyatt said, pushing his thigh right against Ryan's cock. "Like I've been wanting and suffering."

"Suffering?" Ryan's voice went higher. "That does sound serious."

Wyatt made sure that all his desire was in his eyes as he looked straight at him. "Oh, it is."

"Maybe we should . . . uh . . . try to help you out, then?" Ryan questioned.

"I'm a pretty relaxed guy," Wyatt admitted. "Until you drive me crazy."

Ryan laughed, and it was the exact laugh that Wyatt had been dying to hear since the first moment he'd seen him sitting and bored at Temple. "I guess I *have* been entertaining you, then."

"You have no idea," Wyatt muttered.

Ryan licked his lips, and Wyatt felt a pulse of *something* at the sudden nervous hesitation in Ryan's eyes. "Why don't you show me?"

※※※※※ ※※※※※

They needed to make it back to his house in one piece though, so Ryan deliberately didn't think about it.

He didn't think about Wyatt's hands on him, clasped tightly around his waist, his thighs and stomach pressed firmly against his body.

He didn't think about how insistently and passionately Wyatt had expressed what he wanted. He definitely didn't think about the kiss they'd shared in the taqueria parking lot, or he probably would have said *fuck it*, pulled off the road, and let Wyatt demolish him in public with not a single damn ounce of shame.

But it would be worth the wait. Ryan believed that, and believed that the adrenaline spiking through his blood at the possessive curl of Wyatt's fingers into his leather jacket were going to mean fantastic things.

Wyatt had passively let him take over last time, barely issuing a single protest when Ryan had sunk to his knees in the gravel. He'd hoped that it wouldn't be like that every time, that Wyatt might appeal to the adventurous side of him that craved something different.

And Wyatt, without even having a clue, had done exactly that, yanking back the power between them in one smooth move.

Ryan pulled into the garage, and flipped off the engine. Wyatt didn't move immediately, but stayed where he was, pressing even closer into him, until Ryan didn't know where his legs ended and Wyatt's began. His fingers dug beneath his t-shirt, but instead of the rough touch he'd expected, his fingertips were featherlight on his abs, stroking all the skin they could reach, then meandering up to circle a nipple.

The visor in his helmet was fogging over, and Ryan felt lightheaded with desire, all the blood in his body rushing south. He moved restlessly against the leather seat, but Wyatt's hands were suddenly clamped around him, holding him immobile in place.

Ryan's hands clenched around his helmet, and he yanked it off. "Don't move," Wyatt said, and to Ryan's surprise, somehow he'd pulled his own off, even though it felt like his hands, those dynamite hands, had never left his body.

"Why not?" Ryan demanded, a little petulantly. If they weren't going to move off the bike, they could have taken care of this raging inferno of desire thirty minutes ago.

"Because I have too many plans for you to get off so easily," Wyatt said softly in a gravelly voice that Ryan was going to be using to get himself off for probably the next fifty years. He'd known Wyatt had a sexy voice, had experienced it on their last late-night drive, and felt the visceral impact of it during the interview. Had wanted to call him half a dozen times until Wyatt had showed up here this afternoon.

And now hearing it ordering hell and promising heaven was almost too much for Ryan.

"I'll be good," he swore, too far gone to care how shaky his voice was.

"You'd better be," Wyatt said. "Drop your helmet."

Ryan did as instructed, not even caring as the heavy plastic clattered onto the garage floor. Normally he took good care of his equipment, but right now, he didn't give a damn.

He felt the loss of Wyatt sliding off the bike, his back and ass suddenly cool without the heat of Wyatt pressed against him. "Get off the bike," Wyatt continued.

Ryan had strong knees. Non-surgically impacted knees. He still felt them shake as he dismounted.

"Good," Wyatt said from behind him. It was dim in the garage with only the emergency night light on, and he could only feel him, not see him.

"I told you I'd be good," Ryan said.

"Remains to be seen," Wyatt said. "Take me to your bedroom."

He hadn't said a word about hands, and normally Ryan wouldn't have, but he reached out and grasped Wyatt's hand. He'd asked Ryan to lead, and so Ryan was going to lead. Plus it felt good to finally be touching Wyatt back. Not nearly as much as he wanted to, but the strong clasp of his hand in Wyatt's was still a flood of sensation.

He led Wyatt through his dark house, not turning on a single light, to the master bedroom. He kicked his boots off and Wyatt followed suit. He'd deliberately omitted this part of the house in his tour earlier, imagining that they'd have sex in Wyatt's little cottage. He rarely ever invited anyone to his own bed—it always felt too personal for a hookup—but Ryan found he wanted it to be personal. He felt a little shaky with nerves, at how this whole evening had developed, even though he'd been subtly pushing Wyatt to see how far he could be pushed.

He hadn't really imagined what it would be like when Wyatt pushed back.

Wyatt hadn't issued any other instructions when they reached the bedroom, so Ryan sat on the edge of the bed, and just watched him. Wyatt flipped a bedside lamp on, barely even fumbling for the switch. "I want to see you," was all the explanation he gave. The light glinted on his blond hair, shadowing his cheekbones, and full lips.

"Then see me," Ryan said, pulling off his jacket, and then his shirt, dropping the clothes where they fell.

Wyatt took a step into the V of Ryan's legs, and kissed him again, so much like he'd kissed him in the parking lot, like he was starving and Ryan was a meal he couldn't wait to devour.

His tongue was hot and insistent in Ryan's mouth, pushing his head back, until they both fell back onto the bed together. Ryan pulled up on Wyatt's shirt, dragging it over his head. "Too many clothes," he panted into Wyatt's mouth.

He blindly rutted right onto Wyatt's crotch, feeling he was just as hard as Ryan was.

Ryan trailed his hands down Wyatt's chest, his abs, his waist. He wasn't an athlete, but like he'd said their first hookup, he was powerful. Strong. Built like a linebacker, almost. Wide shoulders, narrow waist, strong arms, thighs Ryan could have wept over.

"You want me to take your clothes off?" Wyatt asked, raising an eyebrow.

"You take them, or I'll take them," Ryan said, a little aware at how close to begging he was.

"That's an easy decision, then," Wyatt said, and he unbuttoned Ryan's jeans and lowered the zipper, making quick work of them, leaving him in his boxer briefs.

"I'm taking my time with you tonight," Wyatt announced after Ryan had reached up to kiss him again, derailing any more clothing removal.

"Whatever you want, just *get on with it*," Ryan panted. Wyatt cupped his hard bulge, Ryan's head falling back against the pillow. "Yeah, just like that."

"Don't want anything else, just my hand?" Wyatt teased, an unholy light in his light-blue eyes. "I'm a little disappointed."

"I want it all," Ryan panted as Wyatt pulled his briefs down. "I want you to fuck me."

The smug look on Wyatt's face was such a turn-on, Ryan had to bite his own lip.

"I was hoping you'd want that," Wyatt said.

Wyatt didn't know that Ryan almost never asked for it. That even for someone who liked the adrenaline rush of a risky thrill, he almost never trusted anyone to do it. Never trusted anyone to take care of it. But he trusted Wyatt, which was crazy because he was still practically a stranger.

A stranger that Ryan had lied to and persuaded to practically move into his house. He shoved that thought away. "What are you waiting for? Lube and condoms, in the drawer," he panted, eyes glued to the thick bulge in Wyatt's jeans as he perched on the bed.

Ryan was afraid Wyatt would hesitate, and his hesitation would impact Ryan's certainty, but he opened the drawer and pulled out the required items, but still didn't finish shedding his own clothes. From the flex of his abs as he positioned himself between Ryan's legs, it was clear how turned on he was, but he didn't make a move to take his pants off.

Ryan squirmed as Wyatt trailed a finger up his hard, aching cock. Like earlier, when Ryan was expecting a rougher, more intense touch, he only got a delicate, exploratory one. Like Wyatt was trying to catalog him and every single one of his reactions.

"More," he straight-up begged now. "Give me more."

Wyatt's eyes darkened. "I'll give you more," he vowed, this time his finger trailing back down, past Ryan's balls, circling his hole.

Ryan thought he might have to beg again for something more than that light, exploratory touch. But like Wyatt had presented at the interview, he was a genius with his hands. Admittedly, he'd promised he was great with his hands in the *kitchen*, but he could have also sold them as genius in bed too, because it was the most mind-blowing prep of Ryan's life.

By the time Wyatt had worked a second finger alongside the first, he had found his prostate and was wringing moans Ryan would have been embarrassed about if it didn't feel so good. He was desperate for more, desperate to come, desperate to feel something more lasting than just the ephemeral brush of Wyatt's fingertips against his spot.

He knew Wyatt could give him more, and was just holding back. "I can take it, I promise," Ryan begged, too aware of the tears forming at the corners of his eyes. "God, give it to me, *please.*"

Wyatt didn't budge, didn't go any faster than the inexorable, painfully good teasing of the past few minutes. "If you come now, can you come later?" he asked, his voice soft, but hard at the edges. The same desperation that Ryan was dying from.

He pushed harder, even though he wasn't sure he could. Wyatt's fingers felt like magic, his cock probably would feel even better. "Sure, yes, just . . . please fuck me."

"One more finger," Wyatt coaxed, and slid a third in with the other two, but still just barely grazed against the spot that kept Ryan swearing a blue streak.

"God damnit," Ryan yelled. He'd never been happier for the advice of the contractor in charge of his remodel who had suggested better soundproof insulation.

The contractor had probably been thinking about loud movies or wild parties. Except Ryan was taking advantage by having loud and very close to wild sex, if Wyatt fucking Blake would ever fucking get on with it.

"I'm good, I'm good," Ryan babbled. "I promise." He'd known Wyatt was going to be good in bed, but nothing had prepared him for the reality.

"Not quite," Wyatt said, and leaned down, and took Ryan's cock in one long suck right at the same time he suddenly pressed against the spot he'd barely been dancing around all night. Ryan barely had a second to screech before he was coming so hard he saw white spots at the edges of his vision, pleasure coursing through him like a gigantic wave.

"You promised," Wyatt reminded him, suddenly leaving him empty of fingers and, wiping his mouth on the back of his other hand. And that was all the warning Ryan got before he lined up and slid right in.

Ryan didn't even remember when he'd taken his pants off, and suddenly full of a really great cock, he realized he didn't care. Wyatt could be a fucking pants magician, and everything was still great.

Wyatt pulled back and thrust, *hard*, and everything wasn't just great, it was fucking fantastic. A little sensitive, a little raw, a little too much but still exactly what he wanted.

After the first few strokes, Wyatt pulled out and flipped him over, and Ryan went, like the limp raggedy doll Wyatt had turned him into. And then holding his head against the bed, one hand against his neck, the other at his hip, proceeded to fuck him into oblivion.

Ryan would be embarrassed at the sounds he was making, but Wyatt was grunting plenty too, spouting lots of sappy gibberish that Ryan would wish later that he could remember.

But all he remembered later was the feel of Wyatt's cock pounding into him, dismantling him from the inside out. And just when he thought it was all too much, and he was about to beg for something—not for him to stop, not for him to keep going, but some unknown action that he didn't even know—Wyatt wrapped a hand around his cock, gave him a few strokes, and Ryan managed to come all over himself for the second time that night.

He barely registered Wyatt's following bellow, or how his fingers clamped down hard on his neck. It took him a long moment to even remember his own name.

"You are a maniac," Ryan said, as Wyatt came back to bed from disposing the condom. He had found a washcloth and had wet it. The water was even warm, Ryan marveled as he took it and wiped down.

"You seemed to like it okay," Wyatt said with a blush and a self-deprecating shrug that made it even sexier. He wasn't naturally that intense; Ryan just brought it out of him. They brought it out of each other.

"It was some of the best sex I've ever had. If not *the best* sex," Ryan admitted. His brain-to-mouth filter was gone, obliterated by two fantastic, world-destroying orgasms.

Wyatt blushed again, and then shocked the hell out of Ryan for about the millionth time that night by leaning over and giving him a sweet, affectionate kiss. "You're welcome," he said when he pulled away.

"I believe," Ryan said, reaching for his boxer briefs, even though moving seemed very overrated, "that you owe me a beer. And there's some in the fridge, with our name on them."

Wyatt didn't seem to know what to do with his hands without being able to shove them in his pants pockets. Ryan wasn't surprised to see him reach for his jeans, like he needed the comfort they provided. "I could go for a beer."

Maybe a beer would give Ryan the liquid courage he'd need tell Wyatt that he wanted him to be his fake boyfriend, with all the real benefits they'd just enjoyed.

But he knew, as he slipped down the hall towards the kitchen, shirtless with jeans hanging at his hips, that he wouldn't ask tonight. Maybe he'd find his courage tomorrow. Because he suddenly wasn't sure that Wyatt was going to settle for a *fake* relationship, even with the real benefits.

CHAPTER FIVE

WYATT WOKE UP THE first day on the job in a bed that wasn't his.

Naked.

With his boss.

It was either the best first day or the worst; it was too early to say for sure.

The one thing he definitely knew was that he was hungry. His stomach was growling so loudly it was miraculous that Ryan hadn't woken up from its insistent grumbling. But, as he slipped out of the bed, Wyatt thought that it was probably better that they didn't do the whole "waking up together" thing.

It was probably going to be awkward enough, because they'd had fantastic, mind-blowing sex, had a few beers out by Ryan's fire pit in the backyard, and then had headed back inside for round number two.

Wyatt didn't exactly remember passing out in Ryan's bed, but he was pretty sure that Ryan hadn't exactly invited him. Of course, he *was* sure that Ryan was slurring with pleasure at that point, so it wasn't like Wyatt had fooled him.

Still, this would be better, Wyatt thought as he grabbed his clothes and headed towards *his* part of the house. Less awkwardness. Less questions. He'd have breakfast ready—he'd already checked, there were rudimentary supplies already in the fridge—and then he'd disappear after, and do some actual work by spending Ryan's money on groceries and more equipment.

No matter how relaxed Ryan was with him, Wyatt had no intention of shirking any of his duties. He might be doing a whole lot more than he'd been hired to do, but he was at least going to fulfill the rest of his responsibilities.

He grabbed a quick shower, appreciating the much-improved water pressure over the semi-shitty house he'd shared with Xander and Kian.

By the time he was back in the main house, letting himself in the back door, the house was still completely silent.

As far as Wyatt was concerned, that was fine by him. Ryan could sleep in if he wanted to, after all he was the boss and the professional athlete.

Wyatt raided the veggie drawer of the fridge, chopping up kale and spinach, red onion and mushrooms for a quick egg white frittata. It would have been better with a little goat cheese, but Wyatt thought, digging into his own portion, it wasn't half-bad. It was the first meal that Wyatt was preparing for Ryan, and even though he was having all sorts of un-professional feelings, he still wanted Ryan to think hiring him had been the right decision.

Breakfast finished, the dishes washed up, Wyatt went back to his cottage and grabbed his pad. Started meal plans for the week. Made an equipment list. Drank three glasses of water. Peed. And glanced at his phone, because Ryan couldn't *still* be sleeping, could he?

He'd only had two beers to Wyatt's three, and he certainly hadn't seemed drunk. A tiny bit tipsy maybe, but he'd been so adorable and then so unbearably sexy that Wyatt hadn't really worried.

He was worried now. It was past ten, and that seemed like an excessive amount of sleep even for a professional athlete during the off-season. Despite his brain screaming at him that this was a bad idea, Wyatt crept back down the hallway towards the master bedroom. He'd told himself firmly as he'd exited it this morning that he would not be taking advantage or invading Ryan's private spaces unless he was invited.

There had to be some sort of line, and Wyatt would maintain it because he was still a professional, god damnit.

Wyatt stopped short in the doorway, which was wide open. The bed, with its fluffy navy and white comforter, was empty.

"Ryan?" Wyatt called out. "I made breakfast, if you're hungry?" He was probably just in the shower or the bathroom. But the entire suite was dead quiet. Too quiet.

A growing uncertainty mounting in his stomach, Wyatt crossed the living room again and went to the garage. Flipping on the light, the bottom dropped right out of it.

The Tesla, which Ryan had told him last night he usually took in the city, was gone.

Ryan had left while Wyatt had been in the shower. And Wyatt remembered distinctly Ryan telling him last night that he hadn't had any plans for the next day. Had even hinted that he wanted to go shopping with Wyatt. But now, he wasn't even here. He'd left, without saying goodbye. Without a single god damn word.

Wyatt walked back to the kitchen in a daze, and stared at the covered plate he'd made for Ryan. His first gut reaction was to shove it all in the trash bin, but he'd seen too many documentaries and read too many articles about food waste to do so, even if he was fucking pissed. So he dug out a Tupperware container and shoved it in the fridge instead.

He couldn't explain what had happened between last night, which had been very clearly enjoyable on both their sides, and this morning. Had Ryan been pissed that he'd left the bed? Should he have left a note? Wyatt didn't know. He liked Ryan so much, but this was already messy as hell, and it had just started. How were they going to make it through with their professional and personal relationships intact?

Fuck, he didn't even know if they had either one, anymore. And it was the first god damned day.

Wyatt slammed the back door even though nobody was in the house to hear it. Grabbed the keys he'd just found and his worn leather jacket, and took off. If Ryan wanted to remind him to do his job, he'd fucking do it. If he stayed and stewed, he'd end up saying something he'd regret.

Like what a total jerk Ryan Flores had ended up being.

"I cannot believe you just *left*." Tabitha stared at him, eyes wide and disbelieving, arms crossed over a ratty UCLA sweatshirt, her mouth a thin, angry line.

Ryan really couldn't believe he'd just left either. Though, if he was getting technical about it, he hadn't left first. Of course, if he was getting technical, Wyatt hadn't really left. He couldn't leave. He lived at Ryan's house now, basically.

And Ryan had even known what Wyatt was doing. Probably some noble, professional thing—getting out of a nice warm bed to cook his bed partner, and technically his boss, breakfast. Ryan could even imagine that thought going through Wyatt's head. Wanting to stay, but feeling obligated to do what he'd been hired for.

It was why Ryan put extra time in the batting cages, why he still ran drills during the off-season. Why he'd even agreed to all of this in the first place. Because playing baseball was important, and being a professional was important. But understanding it, and facing it were apparently two different things, because Ryan had not faced it very well this morning.

Frankly, he'd not faced it at all. He'd lain awake, listening to the back door shut, and had known, deep down, that he couldn't lie to Wyatt anymore about the job. Not after last night.

Feeling raw, discombobulated, and more than a little scared, he'd run to the one place he'd never be turned away. Even when he acted like a total ass.

"Didn't I tell you that we were having breakfast this morning, darling?" he asked Tabitha, pasting on a sweet, rather saccharine smile that wasn't fooling anyone—Tabitha *or* her boyfriend.

Cal made a grumpy sound as he shoveled in toast smeared with mango jelly. He was elbow-deep in his iPad, looking at plans for his next remodel.

"Ryan," Tabitha said, her patience clearly at an end. "It is time for you to be honest with him. Completely, one hundred percent honest."

Cal said something that suspiciously might have been, "and not in our house." Which was sort of fair. It was early on a weekday and just because they both worked from home didn't mean that Ryan could just dump his problems at their doorstep.

"He is *not* going to say yes, if I ask him." Tabitha's expression softened, and Ryan had a feeling it was because of the raw fear in his eyes. He didn't know when it had become imperative that Wyatt not just be his personal chef, but that line had been crossed and there was no going back.

"I should really just call up Eric and tell him to forget the whole thing," Ryan said. Even though that sounded like both the best and the worst thing to do. Of course, not getting into a fake relationship with someone because you were scared was bad enough. How terrible was not getting into a real relationship because of good old-fashioned fear?

"And what, you're going to tell Wyatt you want to give a real relationship a shot, instead of a fake one?" Tabitha demanded.

That was exactly the problem. Ryan already knew he wasn't cut out for a "real" relationship. The fake version was probably the best he had to offer Wyatt, no matter how much he wanted to give more.

"I thought that you'd love the idea of me canning the whole fake-relationship bit," Ryan said. "You've hated it from the beginning. Of course I was never certain if you hated it because it was Eric's idea or if you just hated it."

"I hate the dishonesty of it," Tabitha said bluntly. She turned back towards the stove, babysitting the eggs in the pan. It was weird seeing Tabitha in her kitchen; it was even weirder seeing her attempt to cook.

"I'm learning," she'd said defensively when he'd nearly fallen over in shock to see her wielding a spatula and a frying pan earlier.

"You made your living being dishonest," Ryan pointed out.

Tabitha's eyes flashed, and for a single, heart-stopping moment he was sure she was going to dump the runny eggs in his lap and whack him on the head with the frying pan.

"Which is exactly why I don't want you to be dishonest. If you're going to do this—and even I can admit to the benefits—you should be honest about it. Go back to your house and tell Wyatt everything." Tabitha took a deep breath. "I lied all the time, for good reasons and for bad ones, and that's why I'm telling you that you don't want to go down that road."

"What if I'm sure he'll say no?" Ryan asked, and he hated how agonized he sounded.

"What if he says no?" Tabitha asked with an arched eyebrow. "Frankly I think more people should say no to you."

The long and short of it was that by the time Ryan slunk back to his house late morning, he was in a shitty mood. Tabitha thought he should experience people saying no to him? Well, she was going to get her wish today.

Ryan wasn't even surprised to find his house empty of Wyatt, and was even less surprised when he knocked on the addition and was met with silence and a locked door.

He knew he deserved the silence, whether Wyatt was in there or not. Ignoring him or not.

Ryan returned to the house and took a shower, taking a long time with the hot water, wishing that it could wash all his guilt away—and his feelings too, if he was being completely honest. He didn't want to like Wyatt. It had seemed so convenient at first, being so attracted to him, and genuinely wanting to know him better. But now that was backfiring because he wanted him around, he wanted *more*, and the casualty of being honest probably meant that Ryan was going to miss out on all that.

He walked back into the kitchen, half-considering another beer or maybe even something stronger, even though it was barely one in the afternoon, and nearly shrieked with surprise to see Wyatt there, unpacking a whole bunch of bags on the island.

Wyatt glanced up, eyes a stormy blue, a crease between his brows, and Ryan nearly ran back to the safety of his bedroom.

"I see you're back," Wyatt said frostily. And yeah, if Ryan thought he was going to dance around the topic, he'd been wrong. Wyatt was uncomfortably direct.

And honest.

"Yeah," Ryan admitted.

Wyatt was still staring directly at him, and Ryan shifted uncomfortably. "I see you went shopping."

"Yeah, I found the credit card and the keys on the counter." Wyatt didn't ask if it had been okay to use them; he'd just done it. "I took the Range Rover. I figured it would be better for errands."

"You can take whatever car you want, just not . . ."

Wyatt didn't even let him finish the sentence. "Just not the Tesla. Yeah, I figured that out real quick."

"You're angry," Ryan stated. Tabitha was whispering in his ear. His conscience was magnifying her whisper until it was as loud as a scream. *Be honest*, she kept repeating. "I guess it wasn't very nice of me to sneak out."

Wyatt looked away, finally breaking eye contact just when Ryan actually wanted it. "It's your house. I certainly don't have any right to be angry about what you do in it or where you go when you're not in it."

His conscience's shriek magnified to a cascading cacophony. "I don't do this very often, to be honest. And I'm not very good at it."

"Hiring a personal chef or hooking up?" Wyatt asked wryly. "Because I'm not sure which we're arguing about here." He still wasn't looking at him. He was taking those little annoying tags off the bottom of a bunch of kitchen equipment that Ryan didn't recognize. Pots and pans and some kind of whisk.

"No, I know how to hook up," Ryan said with a humorless chuckle. "The morning after. And I knew you'd be here, I definitely knew that before I started anything with you. I just didn't expect . . ."

"For it to be so awkward?" Wyatt's voice had thawed a fraction.

"Yeah, I guess you could say that."

"Well, it wasn't exactly non-awkward for me either," Wyatt said. "You're technically my boss."

"Not really," Ryan reminded him. "We talked about this. Personal and professional staying separate."

"Does it feel separate now?" Wyatt demanded. "I was handling it, I really was. And then I came to get you for breakfast and you were fucking *gone*, and you hadn't even done me the professional courtesy of telling me you didn't want me to cook for you this morning."

He glanced up now, and his eyes were blazing, a hot brilliant blue that made Ryan's chest ache. Wyatt was going to say no. He was going to say no, and Ryan couldn't do a thing to stop it. But the longer he went on without asking, the worse the ache got.

"I haven't been entirely honest with you," Ryan finally admitted.

Wyatt's expression didn't change an iota. "Imagine that," he said bitterly.

When Ryan stared at him in surprise—he'd never imagined that Wyatt would figure it out so quickly—Wyatt continued. "Yeah, I know you don't need a private chef. You don't even know what to do with me. So what am I really here for, some kind of stud escort service? You don't get enough dick on Grindr anymore? Want someone a little more dependable, with the added benefit that I can whip up some food when you get hungry for something other than cock?"

Tabitha had been right; he should have been honest from the beginning. If Wyatt said no, it was going to be because he'd lied to him from the first moment they'd met. Apparently dishonesty was a terrible foundation for a relationship, even a fake one.

"Not exactly, but you're sort of on the right track," Ryan said and watched as Wyatt's expression hardened. "Not just the sex stuff. I need . . . help with getting my contract renewed."

"How the fuck am I supposed to help you with that?" Wyatt interrupted.

"Please," Ryan asked, far too aware that he was pleading with him. "Please, let me get this out, and if you want to hate me, if you want to say no, then you can. You can keep the job being my chef. We'll figure out how to make it work. I'll be professional, we'll work out a job description and everything. I swear."

Wyatt didn't say a word, just stared defiantly at the kitchen supplies spread across the kitchen island. Ryan took a deep breath and continued. "The new general manager of the Dodgers, he's the one responsible for basically deciding whether to extend my contract or let me try the open market someplace else. I really don't want to leave LA. My family is here. I like it here. I want to keep playing for the Dodgers, but if the status quo doesn't change, the GM probably won't choose to extend me. He's not . . . precisely homophobic, but he has some fucking wrong ways of thinking. Like he thinks I'm some sort of flighty gay party boy. He wants someone who's serious, who takes baseball seriously, who isn't going to party and fuck every cute boy who crosses his path."

"How on earth am *I* going to help you reverse that impression?"

Wyatt's incredulity wasn't exactly misplaced. After all, they'd met at Temple. Ryan had undeniably picked him up, and then they'd hooked up. Twice.

"I need to have a steady, normal relationship. He needs to feel like I've settled down."

Wyatt's incredulity bubble exploded. "You *were* shopping for a boyfriend."

"A fake one, yeah. But even if the sappy feelings part isn't legit, I don't want some stranger. I want someone I would actually like. That I could like. And I like you."

A dark look passed across Wyatt's face. Ryan pressed on because he couldn't stop now. "The sex was great. Fantastic, even. We could have fun."

"So, we'd just pretend to be together, and keep having sex. Like . . . an added benefit?" Wyatt's apparent disbelief echoed Tabitha's when he'd first suggested the idea, and Ryan didn't like his deep, subterranean worry that they'd both been right. This *was* stupid.

Would it have been better to just hope that his relationship with Wyatt had turned out? That he could hold down a real boyfriend without becoming bored or boring him? But then if it didn't work out, Ryan would be right back to square one.

No, they needed parameters and guidelines and a set timeline. It was better to establish right away in cold blood that they weren't going to fall in love. It was just great sex and Wyatt helping Ryan out of a bad situation. Simple mutual benefits and nothing messy.

"This is insane," Wyatt said.

"It's all planned out," Ryan said. "You were initially just part of the setup—Eric had decided that I needed a personal chef to round out the 'settled down' vibe we were trying to portray—and then I recognized you from the photo they sent me with your resume. I met you, and I realized that I didn't want to fake date some wannabe actor. I wanted to fake date you."

The expression on Wyatt's face was terrible.

"That's all this ever was? You wanting to convince me to fake date you?"

"No, no, no, I *never* lied. I mean I omitted some stuff. But I never lied. I like you. Last night was awesome. I hope we have a hundred more nights just like it, a *thousand*." Even as he scrambled, Ryan had a sick feeling that he wasn't going to be able to convince Wyatt.

Ryan told himself the nauseous roll of his stomach at the thought was just because Wyatt was going to quit and go back to Napa, out of Ryan's life before whatever they had together ran its natural course. It always sucked when you saw the potential of something good and it ended before it ever began.

"I can't do this," Wyatt said and there was an ugly finality in his voice.

"What if it's just like last night, just a few additional and totally harmless pap shots added to the mix?" Ryan begged.

Wyatt's eyes were two hard blue stones. Opaque and closed off. From what, Ryan didn't know. He hadn't gotten to know him well enough to figure him out yet, and that shouldn't have hurt but it *did*. "I can't flounce around with you, fake holding hands for the paps." He took an unsteady breath that Ryan could hear from across the kitchen. "I'm not out. Not to my family. And I'm not going to let them find out like this."

Ryan had come up with a thousand reasons why Wyatt might tell him no. It had never occurred to him that Wyatt wasn't out, and that's why he would turn Ryan's proposal down. His sexuality felt like such a natural extension of who he was, his personality open and relaxed.

Besides, that wasn't an excuse that Ryan could ever talk his way around. He knew exactly what coming out before the draft had cost him. Not just in dollars and cents, not even with how good Eric had turned out to be.

It had taken balls of steel to come out the first time to his family and then something even greater to do the same with his friends. And then something even more momentous to do it with the world watching.

He couldn't ask Wyatt to take that step if he hadn't chosen to do it before now.

"I'm so god damned sorry," Ryan said, and he was. He was sorry he hadn't realized. He was sorry that Wyatt was in a situation where he didn't feel like he could. He was sorry for himself, that he was going to have to find some stranger to fill a void that Ryan hadn't even realized existed until he'd met Wyatt.

"It's not your fault," Wyatt said. "I'm sorry I can't help you out. It's bullshit you have to endure that sort of double fucking standard. It's not fair."

"It's not," Ryan admitted. He wasn't going to say out loud that it wasn't fair either that Wyatt couldn't be honest with his family. There was a lot of fucked-up shit in the world, and there was a lot of progress to be made with erasing homophobia. Especially the latent biases of people like the Dodgers' GM.

"It's just my nana," Wyatt said, and he sounded wrecked. "She's not intolerant. She's not mean or rude or nasty. She just . . . she's just so religious. Always going to Mass. We've never talked about it, and sometimes I swear she knows, and I never have to say it out loud. But then she asks me when I'm going to bring a girl around and give her grandchildren, and *fuck*, I'm sorry. This isn't the baggage you wanted to get into."

"I don't care. I'm here to listen." Ryan walked over to the barstool opposite Wyatt. "Anything you want to talk about."

Wyatt looked surprised, which *killed* Ryan. Did he really believe that Ryan was some sort of insensitive asshole? "Why would you even want to listen? You took the hardest road you could and you *changed the fucking world*." Wyatt flushed red, and Ryan began to realize that he was actually ashamed.

Ashamed that Ryan had come out of the closet and in such a public way, and he hadn't come out to his own family yet.

And that was the biggest bunch of bullshit yet.

"I'm not some sort of saint or god or good fucking person because I came out," Ryan said. "It doesn't make me any better than you. Any braver. Any stronger."

Wyatt's fingers clenched on the edge of the marble countertop, his knuckles going pale.

"It's different for everybody," Ryan added.

"I want to tell her," Wyatt said. "She's . . . she's . . ." And Ryan watched as his eyes glimmered with moisture suddenly. "She's not well. She's in a home. A mental care home."

"Oh god. I'm sorry." Ryan didn't think he could even express how sorry he was. At least not with words. He slid off the barstool and wrapped his body around Wyatt's tightly. "I'm so sorry," he murmured into the cotton covering his back.

"I want to tell her. I just . . . can't. What if the last thing she remembers of me is that I'm going to hell?" Wyatt choked out a sob and Ryan hung on tighter.

"I don't know her. But you love her, so I can't imagine she would think that."

Suddenly Wyatt shucked Ryan's grip and he got a single glimpse of wetness shining on Wyatt's cheek before he was across the kitchen, the back door slamming behind him.

Ryan looked at the brand-new kitchen equipment strewn across the island counter. "Fuck," he said succinctly, and pulled out his phone because he was going to have to tell Eric.

Chapter Six

ONLY THE THOUGHT THAT he was a god damn professional got Wyatt out of bed at four, where he'd spent the afternoon wallowing in self-imposed and Ryan-imposed misery.

Wyatt didn't exactly blame Ryan for the truth, and it wasn't his fault Wyatt was miserable, but so many of the reasons still originated with him.

He wanted to date Ryan *for real*, not as a front to convince his general manager that he was a reliable person. Not because Eric had decided Ryan should date someone. Not because Ryan figured they were at least sexually compatible so fake dating for the foreseeable future wouldn't be *so* terrible.

Though that reason had at least made some fucking sense.

It had brought Wyatt so high that Ryan had picked *him* and then brought him lower than he'd ever been to have to turn him down. Frankly, he didn't give a shit what his brothers thought of him; if they needed a year or two or ten to cool off, whatever. But his grandmother . . . she had always made him pause. Especially now, because the last thing he wanted was to lose whatever time he had left with her.

Wouldn't it be better to just keep his mouth shut and have her drift away from reality with her nice, innocuous, pleasant, loving memories of Wyatt?

He looked in the mirror in the bathroom and wished his eyes didn't look red still. Curse of having blue eyes; if you cried, there was no way to hide it. He wet a washcloth with cold water and tried anyway.

After a minute of dabbing and trying to take away the remaining puffiness under his eyes, he felt a little more normal. He normally couldn't give a shit, but he didn't want Ryan to know he'd spent the afternoon crying.

It would be so easy to walk back into Ryan's house and tell him that he'd changed his mind. And so hard, Wyatt reminded his reflection. If he told the truth, then his nana might have a different view of him for the last bit of her coherent life, but at least she would have the *right* view.

Tossing the washcloth into the sink, Wyatt wiped his face, gave a quick damp swipe to his hair, and hoped that nobody would be in the kitchen. He wanted to prep dinner in silence.

Before he even opened the door to the house, Wyatt knew he wouldn't get any silence. Music echoed through a few open windows and grew much louder as he stepped inside.

A beautiful blonde woman was sitting on a barstool, sipping a glass filled with clear liquid and a lime slice. Her blue eyes latched onto him instantly, and Wyatt froze.

"Hello, you must be Wyatt," she said. Her tone was brisk and straightforward. She extended a hand and he walked closer to shake it.

"I'm Tabitha. Ryan's best friend," she continued, and even though he'd known forever he was gay, he couldn't help but be struck a little dumb by how crazy gorgeous she was. Flawless features, bright hair curling around her face, and those eyes. Never mind the excessive confidence she exuded. She'd belong wherever she chose to be.

"I'm not sure where he got to," Tabitha said because Wyatt still hadn't found his voice. "We spent the last few hours figuring out where to put everything. I'm sure you'll want to re-arrange but it gave him something to do, and it kept him out of your hair, which . . . you're welcome."

Wyatt stiffened. Had Ryan told this woman all his secrets? The reason why he'd turned Ryan's proposal down?

"Don't worry," she said. "He didn't tell me why. Just that it was a really good reason, and I had to keep him occupied so he wouldn't get selfish and try to convince you anyway."

Wyatt shoved his hands in the pockets of his jeans and fervently wished he didn't feel obligated to be a professional so he could escape back to his quiet little cottage. He didn't want to be interrogated by this woman, no matter how beautiful she was. Because that's exactly what this was—a very friendly, commiserating interrogation.

"Ryan doesn't have a selfish bone in his body," he said.

Tabitha laughed. Not the Disney Princess bell laugh he'd expected, but something a little darker, a little edgier. It sounded real, and it made him like her more, even if he didn't want to.

"I've heard a lot about you," Tabitha said speculatively, and Wyatt wasn't surprised at all. This woman, as friendly as her expression was, could pry secrets out of James Bond.

"I'm sure you have," Wyatt said wryly, turning towards the fridge. If he had to give up his quiet time, at least he could do what he'd been hired for.

"Oh, are you going to cook something?" Tabitha asked when he opened the fridge and started pulling out ingredients without even looking at them. "My sister is a really fantastic chef, but that's not the only way we're different. And Ryan isn't hopeless, he just doesn't bother. I'm glad you're going to bother for him."

Wyatt was afraid too many emotions were too close to the surface, but he turned back anyway. "I'd do a lot more than bother."

Tabitha sighed and tapped a nail, blood red and dangerous, against the side of her glass. He was beginning to suspect it contained more than just water. "I figured as much. We're going to have to figure out what to do about that, that's for sure."

"I bother because I'm paid to," Wyatt tried to claim, but they both knew the truth and her eyes turned sympathetic.

He half-expected her to call his bluff, but she didn't. Merely took another drink from her glass. It made him like her more.

Of course Ryan would have a brilliant, yet terrifying friend like Tabitha.

"How did you meet?" Wyatt asked because it got her off his case, and also because he genuinely wanted to know.

"I wrote his coming out story," Tabitha said breezily. "Among other things. We met three years ago when he was just a snarky kid from Stanford."

"What about you?" Wyatt asked.

"What about me?"

Wyatt took the corn over to the sink to begin shucking and cleaning the cobs. "You said Ryan was a snarky kid from Stanford. What about you?" He glanced back, and was a little surprised to see her soft expression.

"When we met, I didn't have friends. Not like Ryan. He was my first." She hesitated. "I know you don't want me to pry, it's written all over your face, but I have to say I understand why he likes you so much. You've got this calm, zen thing that would be very appealing for him."

"Zen thing?" Wyatt asked with a low chuckle. When he'd come into this kitchen ten minutes ago, he hadn't felt less like laughing. He'd wanted nothing more than to turn around and go back to where he'd came from when he'd spotted Tabitha. But there was something about her blunt honesty coupled with the empathy in her eyes that helped.

It was very clear why the snarky kid from Stanford had wanted to be her friend. Wyatt found himself feeling the exact same way.

"All centered and shit." Tabitha waved her hand in the air. "Don't tell me you do yoga."

"I'm actually more of a surfer, to be honest," he admitted.

Tabitha groaned. "Of course you are."

"Is that a problem?" Wyatt asked over his shoulder as he continued to clean the corn from its husks with a soft brush. He was thinking a fresh corn salsa with the fresh-caught shrimp he'd picked up this morning. Maybe even add some polenta. He had the time. It was nice to be able to cook in this relaxed environment, chatting with Tabitha, and not worrying about being screamed at or pleasing a never-ending parade of particular diners paying a fortune for their dinner.

"No, you're just disgustingly perfect." He could hear the roll of her eyes in her voice.

"Hardly," Wyatt retorted. "I could give you a load of reasons why I'm not perfect."

"Oh, I'm glad I got back for this," Ryan said. Wyatt's head whipped around, and yeah, he was definitely there, standing in the doorway. Wyatt felt a little like he'd gotten caught with his hand in the cookie jar, but he was exactly where he was supposed to be.

Tabitha had just happened to be here, and he was making normal, friendly conversation with her, like anyone might.

"I got fresh supplies," Ryan said, pulling out a bottle of Grey Goose from the paper bag he was holding.

"Should have gotten tequila," Wyatt said, forcing his voice to stay even and normal. "I'm making barbecued shrimp. Great with a margarita."

"I probably have some somewhere," Ryan said. "But Tabby was determined to drink all my vodka."

"I was trying to make you feel better," Tabitha said with dignity. "And I've been telling you for years not to call me that."

"Someday," Ryan said, slinging an arm around his friend, "you're going to realize that every time you say that, it makes me more determined than ever to call you that." His affectionate gaze was completely platonic, but Wyatt couldn't help it; he burned with jealousy anyway.

Even if they couldn't be a thing—fake or real or anything else in between—he still wanted to be Ryan's friend. Not just his employee. And Wyatt was terrified that turning down his proposal had left him his job, but had demolished everything else.

He couldn't imagine how much it would burn when Ryan moved on and found someone new to pretend to date, and fuck for real.

No matter how much he needed this job or how much he didn't want to leave, Wyatt wasn't sure he could stick around and watch that.

"You are an asshole," Tabitha said. "Even though you went and bought me more vodka."

"Yeah, I'm still trying to figure out how you coming over and drinking all my booze was supposed to make me feel better." Ryan was smiling, but Wyatt thought he could see the bad mood lurking behind his dark eyes. Present, but concealed. Just like his own.

It shouldn't have made Wyatt feel any better, but it did, a little. If Ryan felt bad, at least that meant he'd cared. He'd really wanted it to be Wyatt, and Wyatt still felt incredulous that Ryan had cared so much. It shouldn't have mattered. Wyatt should have been pissed as hell that he'd concealed his motives, but there had been genuine understanding in his eyes when Wyatt had told him why he couldn't accept.

"It's a secret talent of mine," Tabitha said. She turned to Wyatt. "Don't you feel better, too?"

"I'm fine," Wyatt said stiffly, even though they all knew it was a lie. Nobody knew it more than Ryan.

"Then it's time for me to get out of your hair," Tabitha said, gracefully sliding off the barstool. Even though Wyatt was beginning to suspect she'd drank quite a bit of Ryan's vodka.

"Wyatt's making dinner, you can't leave yet," Ryan said. They all knew what he really meant was, *you can't leave me alone with Wyatt.*

Tabitha reached over and patted him on the cheek. "I'm sure I'll be back."

Wyatt threw a towel over his shoulder. "I'm holding you to that."

She batted her eyes exaggeratedly and it didn't even make her look ridiculous, only more beautiful. "It isn't every day that I get to enjoy the efforts of a Michelin-starred chef," she said.

He wasn't really Michelin-starred. That had been his boss, Bastian Aquino, but he didn't correct her, only smiled.

"I'll call you an Uber," Ryan said, "you are so damn drunk."

"Don't worry, I already texted Calvin, he'll be here in a minute."

Ryan rolled his eyes. "Next time I'm not calling you."

Tabitha's expression was dead serious. "Of course you will. That's why we're friends." She tugged Ryan into a quick, tight hug.

Wyatt turned back to his corn in the sink. He didn't want to cry again, but he felt close and he didn't even know why.

He heard Tabitha depart, her sandals clattering on the wood floor of the hallway, and scrubbed harder on the corn cob in his hand. He wanted Ryan to come back to the kitchen, but at the same time he dreaded it.

"You're making shrimp. With some sort of corn thing."

Wyatt turned and Ryan was definitely back, framed in the doorway again. This time he came in, and sat right down at the barstool Tabitha had been occupying until a few minutes ago.

"I'm making shrimp with a corn salsa," Wyatt confirmed. "I hope that's okay."

"I told you. Anything you want to do is fine by me."

"What about foods you don't like?"

Ryan shot Wyatt a teasing, chastising look. "Starting the interrogation back up, I see."

"It's not an interrogation. And yeah, we got a little . . . derailed before." Wyatt willed himself not to flush, but the reminder was all he needed to go hot and then cold all over. He didn't know how they could still work together after the sex they'd had. Maybe that was the real question he should be asking, not what Ryan's least-favorite foods were.

"It was all—okay, *mostly*—your fault. Though it wasn't like I was complaining that you decided to get a little unpro-fessional."

Wyatt stiffened. And not in the good way. "I wasn't . . . I mean . . . I'm . . ."

Ryan held up a hand, and his smile was a little sad. Too much like he'd looked that first night at Temple. "If you apol-ogize for having sex with me, *great sex*, mind you, I'm going to be offended."

"I won't, then," Wyatt said, even attempting a smile of his own. But he wasn't sure he'd been any more successful than Ryan.

Imagine being so torn up that you couldn't be in a fake relationship with someone. Wyatt figured it was pretty damn clear that he was willing to take just about anything Ryan could offer him.

"Foods I don't like . . . olives. This is an olive-free house."

"Olive oil?" Wyatt asked.

"Does it taste like olives?" Ryan asked archly.

"It'd better not," Wyatt said. He placed the cleaned cobs in a deep bowl and started slicing off corn kernels.

"I'm olive oil neutral then," Ryan said.

"What else?" Wyatt asked.

"Beets. Pickles—except maybe in a Cuban sandwich."

"Good call," Wyatt said approvingly. "There's nothing like a really good Cuban."

"Can you make one?"

Wyatt pulled tomatoes out of the wire basket he'd bought today. At least Tabitha and Ryan had known where to put these. He'd searched for the garlic for five minutes, only to find it in the produce drawer of the fridge.

He guessed Tabitha wasn't kidding that she and Ryan didn't spend much time in the kitchen.

"A Cuban? Um, yes. Definitely."

"Can I make requests? Is that allowed?"

Wyatt let his knife slice rhythmically through the tomato. It steadied him, even when he wanted to fly out of his own skin. Or fuck Ryan again. "You're the boss. What's allowed is up to you."

"What would I have been if you'd said yes this afternoon?" Ryan asked, voice soft.

Wyatt's knife hesitated. The ripe tomato, like his heart, bruised a little under the pressure of the knife. "The guy you were dating, I guess. Bonus: he cooks, too."

It was hard not to hear the hurt edge to Ryan's voice, and it was impossible to deny that he'd been eager before. Ryan had wanted this. Real or not real. And Wyatt could only assume it might have become real. Maybe.

"And now I'm your boss again," Ryan said, and he sounded frustrated.

"You made it clear this fake boyfriend was something you needed. I'm assuming you're planning on hooking up with him, whoever he is."

"That was the plan." Ryan wasn't even hiding his regret.

"So you're my boss, and hopefully, maybe we can figure out how to be friends." Wyatt already knew it wasn't going to be enough; but it was better than nothing.

"Is that what you want?" Ryan asked cautiously.

The chopped tomato got dumped unceremoniously into the bowl with the corn. Wyatt tackled a red onion next, chopping it a bit more forcefully than was entirely necessary. "It's not what I want," he said. "But it's reality."

"We can be friends," Ryan said. There was an understandable lack of enthusiasm—which Wyatt totally got. There was a decided lack of getting naked in being "just friends."

But the alternative was worse. It meant losing moments like this, and even though they'd only just met, Wyatt already knew Ryan was important. Truthfully, he'd known from the first moment, and every successive moment since convinced him he'd been right. Not for the first time, Wyatt thought that maybe even a fake relationship with Ryan might be worth jeopardizing what he'd spent so many years protecting.

Wyatt pushed the thought away, along with all the negative ones. They would make this work; they would figure something out. He hadn't missed how Ryan looked at him, too. "I asked Tabitha how you met, and she told me that you were a snotty kid from Stanford."

Ryan laughed, and like he'd hoped, the mood lightened. "I know it's tough to believe."

Wyatt finished with the onions and moved onto the bundle of cilantro by the cutting board. "Actually, not really."

In the middle of stealing a tomato chunk from the bowl between them, Ryan made an outraged noise and instead of popping it in his mouth, tossed it with deadly accuracy at Wyatt's face.

Ryan wasn't a professional baseball player—a *shortstop*, even—for nothing. The tomato landed with a plop against its target: Wyatt's cheek.

Wyatt had a vision of the walls of this kitchen spattered with red tomato juice and the floors peppered with corn kernels as Ryan pushed him up against the island, devouring him like he was all the food he needed.

"Shit. I think I promised you I wouldn't throw anything." Ryan sounded unsure, like he wasn't sure if Wyatt was pissed or not.

"It's not a plate. It's not a knife or a pot full of hot water." He looked up and shot him a quick grin. "I think I'll live from a tiny tomato." To illustrate his point, he flipped it into his open mouth.

"Imagine my relief you're going to survive," Ryan said with a laugh.

"So you were a snotty kid from Stanford and Tabitha wrote your coming out profile." Wyatt kept coming back to his friendship with Tabitha because it not only seemed fascinating from the outside, she seemed to be one of the most important people in his life.

"Did she tell you that?" Ryan asked curiously.

"Yes, but she didn't have to. I thought back to a few years ago and realized where I'd seen her before. On ESPN, giving an interview, right after the story broke."

"She's got a memorable face," Ryan said.

Wyatt rolled his eyes.

"Okay, she's generally pretty memorable," Ryan admitted.

"And nice," Wyatt added.

It was Ryan's turn to roll his eyes. "Not even close. Tabitha is a lot of things; beautiful, smart . . . unsurprisingly deadly, but she's not really *nice*."

"I think the honesty is nice." It had also been unexpected to find Ryan, a professional athlete, so close to someone who would unapologetically call him out on his own bullshit.

"She keeps me grounded. Keeps me honest. Keeps me real. Sometimes," Ryan hesitated, "sometimes it's easy to get lost. And she's always found me."

"That's what my nana has always been for me," Wyatt volunteered. He didn't want to revisit their earlier conversation; he *definitely* did not want to discuss his reluctance to come out of the closet, but Ryan still needed to understand why the reluctance was there. How vital to his life his grandmother was. "My mom died when I was a teenager, and my dad was never really around much. So she's really all I have."

"My mom is great and all," Ryan said, propping his elbows on the counter and leaning on them. His dark eyes were contemplative. "But it's my aunt I'm closest to. She could probably go toe-to-toe with you in the kitchen and might even come out on top."

"Not a professional?" Wyatt asked.

"Just a home cook, but the Puerto Rican food she makes is to die for. Better than any restaurant, here or back home."

At Wyatt's curious look, Ryan continued. "I go back. Work with some charities. I was born here, but I can't forget where I came from. I might be a good baseball player but I'd be a shitty person if I did that."

"Is she in the area?" Wyatt asked, and Ryan nodded. "Maybe she'd be willing to teach me sometime. I'd love to learn to cook some Puerto Rican specialties."

Ryan looked surprised, which Wyatt shouldn't have let get to him, but it did anyway. "Really?"

"Of course. And not just for your benefit either. For my own."

"Yeah, I'll talk to her. Maybe arrange something next week."

"Maybe she can even teach *you* something," Wyatt added slyly.

"How do you know she hasn't already?" Ryan asked with a hint of amusement in his eyes. "Maybe I'm fantastic."

Wyatt couldn't have denied it even if he wanted to; Ryan *was* fantastic. Just not in the kitchen. He held out the big chef's knife he'd been using to clean and chop the cilantro. "Come here and show me then."

The way Ryan eyed the knife was proof enough, but Wyatt was genuinely curious how much Ryan knew. He ignored the spark of electricity that pulsed through him when Ryan took the knife and their fingers brushed.

A micro-second, and he was stupidly breathless.

"What is this?" Ryan asked, frown creasing his brows. "Some sort of weed?"

Wyatt sighed. "It's official, you are *not* fantastic. It's cilantro."

"Oh, that goes in guacamole, right?"

"And about a thousand other things."

"What am I supposed to do with it?" Ryan played lost, hefting the knife up and posing like he was at the plate.

"Are you really going to pretend like you don't know how to chop so I'll conveniently come closer and show you?"

Ryan batted his eyelashes. "Would it work?"

Too well, Wyatt thought, but before he said it out loud, he remembered that they were supposed to be working on being friends.

Shoving his crotch against Ryan's incredible ass was not a proposition that would ever lead to platonic friendship.

"Sorry," Ryan said awkwardly into the silence that had descended between them. "It's sort of my natural inclination to flirt outrageously with the hottest guy in the room."

"Or the *only* guy in the room," Wyatt pointed out wryly.

Ryan didn't need to say that he'd gone after him that night at Temple, and he definitely hadn't been the only guy in the room then. He only shot Wyatt a significant look that said it for him.

"I need to check in with Eric. How long until dinner?"

As much as Wyatt wanted Ryan to stay in the kitchen and keep flirting outrageously, it was definitely better for him to put some distance between them.

It was only the first day of them attempting friendship, and Wyatt had a feeling it wasn't going to get easier—and it was already god damned hard.

"Half an hour or so?" Wyatt said, quickly calculating the remaining tasks he had to do.

"Perfect." And then he disappeared, pulling his phone out of his pocket, and leaving Wyatt to dinner and his increasing dilemma. "And you're going to eat with me. None of this upstairs, downstairs bullshit. We're friends, remember?"

Despite how terrible this day had ended up becoming, Wyatt couldn't help but smile.

⁂

"That was fucking incredible," Ryan said, leaning back on the sofa, and rubbing his flat stomach. Wyatt remembered the flex of his abs as he'd nibbled his way down them just the night before.

The night before they'd been unabashedly making out on this couch. Now they were sitting a healthy distance apart, and Ryan had put on a nature documentary without even asking Wyatt what he wanted to watch.

Wyatt had gotten the memo though; they needed to put some metaphoric and actual space between them, before they both forgot that this couldn't go anywhere.

He knew he should be relieved that Ryan had stopped trying to seduce him; he wasn't.

"Thanks," Wyatt said. "I was a little concerned that you wouldn't like my food after you hired me."

Ryan rolled his eyes. "You're one of the best chefs in the world. What is there to worry about?"

Wyatt might not have the stone-cold arrogance that some chefs had, but he'd always believed, deep down, that people should eat and enjoy what he served.

It was more complicated to address Ryan, because from the beginning he had never been just another diner to Wyatt. Not even just another boss.

It was probably a symptom of Ryan giving him a blowjob before Wyatt had ever imagined he could work for him. Or maybe it was because the first night they'd met, before they'd ever spoken, Wyatt hadn't been able to look away from his face.

"Want to make sure you're satisfied," Wyatt pointed out. And then flushed when he belatedly realized how that sounded.

Ryan chuckled humorlessly. "My stomach certainly is."

Wyatt didn't know what to say, so he said the wrong thing. It was a lifelong habit; one he regularly cursed. This was absolutely no exception. "So what happens now? You find some other guy to pretend to date?"

Ryan's face closed off instantly. "Basically, yeah," he said.

"Is that what you were calling Eric about?" Wyatt knew he was pushing; it wasn't fair to either of them, but despite all his best intentions and his resolve, he wanted to know if the offer was still open.

Could he still change his mind?

Could he still drive up to Napa and confess all to Nana?

Ryan would probably even come with him, if he asked. All he would have to do was kneel in front of her chair, feel her blue-eyed benediction on his face, and tell her the truth.

It would be wonderful, but it might also be horrible.

She might never forgive him for lying. She might not ever forgive him for who he was.

Something of his indecision must have flashed across his face because Ryan stood abruptly. "We had a lot to talk about." He barely paused as he walked out of the room, plate in hand. "That was great, thanks. I've got some . . . stuff to do."

Wyatt was barely to the kitchen when he heard the garage door open and the throaty purr of the Tesla engine as it pulled out of the driveway.

It was only when he was elbow-deep in hot soapy water, washing the dishes from dinner, that he realized that Ryan had avoided the question, and then not answered it at all.

Chapter Seven

Ryan knew he should have told Eric during their phone call that he'd asked Wyatt and Wyatt had turned down everything that didn't involve a kitchen, but Ryan was still aching over the whole conversation. Especially over the noticeable conflict and pain in Wyatt's voice when he'd turned Ryan down.

He hadn't wanted to say no, that much was obvious. But Ryan understood that sometimes coming out was difficult, and sometimes it was impossible.

That acknowledgement didn't stop him from lying in bed the next morning, staring at the ceiling, wishing that Wyatt's situation was different. Maybe it was a little selfish, because that might mean *Ryan's* situation would be different, but he reminded himself that there was no harm in wishing for things that would benefit everyone.

Just like there was no harm in a little flirting, as long as he didn't fall in too deep and hurt them both all over again.

It was also better, Ryan decided, for him to stay in his room and indulge in his melancholy mood than try to use Wyatt to improve it.

Wyatt also wanted to know when Ryan was going to start bringing around a cute boy to play his boyfriend, and probably play with other things, and he couldn't blame him for that. It was probably going to hurt like hell.

What Ryan couldn't acknowledge to him, was that it wasn't just going to hurt Wyatt. Ryan didn't want to play house with someone else. Not when who he really wanted was on the sidelines, watching.

And that was why he hadn't told Eric. Eric would have had a backup there that afternoon, probably all trendy haircut and tight pants and gym abs.

It was funny, Ryan thought as he shifted in his bed, realizing he was going to have to change his sheets because they still smelled like Wyatt and what they'd done the other night, because those things would have easily been enough to attract him only a few weeks ago.

He hadn't been picky about his hookups, but those had usually been things he wanted. And if he was lucky, he might even find them all in the same guy. But then he'd met Wyatt and suddenly he wanted something else: muscular forearms from knife work and constantly lifting heavy pans; blond hair half-messy from the wind; the intriguing hints of vulnerability that Wyatt revealed because he wasn't trying to be sexy or mysterious all the damn time.

Tabitha had been so right about what she'd whispered into his ear yesterday afternoon; he'd gotten in too deep and now he was fucked.

He could call up Eric today and tell him the whole thing was off. There had been no guarantees it would even change the GM's mind about Ryan. But Eric had unbelievable instincts when it came to contract negotiation and there was a very good chance he was right.

Telling Eric it was off was as good as acknowledging that he was willing to leave this city, his friends and his family behind. And while it was shitty that his fake boyfriend couldn't be Wyatt, this was his *life*. Even for someone who generally lived by the seat of his pants, there had to be weight to this decision.

"Fuck," Ryan told the ceiling. "Fuck all of this."

The ceiling didn't reply, which was probably better in the end.

He thought about calling Tabby and whining to her but he'd already unloaded on her *twice* yesterday, and he couldn't in good conscience do it again the next day. But he still couldn't bring himself to call Eric and tell him the truth.

Glancing out the partly open window showed a beautiful blue sky beckoned and Ryan decided that if he wanted to keep pouting, then he might as well spend time with someone who wouldn't get annoyed with him.

Or something.

He was in board shorts and a tank top, grabbing his phone and the keys to the Range Rover before he could change his mind. It was easy enough to pull his surfboard off the wall and maneuver it to the rack on top of the Range Rover.

Opening the garage door with the fob inside the Rover, Ryan realized belatedly he'd forgotten a towel and his wetsuit. Detouring back into the house, he grabbed the missing items and then stepped back into the garage with just enough time to see Wyatt coming around the corner, fresh from a run.

He was only wearing shorts, leaving his chest bare, and even though Ryan had already spent an entire evening exploring it, awareness and memory simmered in his gut, reminding him of what he couldn't have.

What he *shouldn't* have.

"Hey," Wyatt said, pulling a t-shirt from the back of his shorts and wiping his face. Ryan knew what he looked like after runs, and he never looked that god damned excellent. "Heading out?"

Ryan didn't think. That was typically his problem, and he usually knew enough about his flaws to combat them, or at least temper them with good judgement. The problem was he'd been daydreaming about Wyatt all morning, annoyed and caught in the memory of a few nights ago. And here Wyatt was, all glorious invitation.

"Yeah, I'm heading to the beach." Ryan didn't even hesitate. Just went for it. "You said you like to surf, you should come with me."

Wyatt looked regretful. "No board."

Ryan decided his brain-to-mouth filter must have died during his angsting this morning. Or maybe during the last time Wyatt had taken him apart with his mouth and those calloused fingers "I've got a spare."

Wyatt's expression moved from regret to confusion. Ryan wasn't sure he could blame him. "Are you sure?"

He was not sure at all. In fact, Ryan had no idea what the hell he thought he was doing. But he nodded anyway. "Yeah, come with me."

By the time they had gathered a second set of equipment, and were headed down the freeway towards Huntington Beach, Ryan had mentally justified that his offer fell under his agreement to be "friends." Friends totally went surfing together, right?

"I always went to Venice," Wyatt said when he saw the direction Ryan had taken the Range Rover. "It'll be fun to try somewhere new."

"How long has it been?"

"At least a few years," Wyatt admitted. "I'm sure I'll be total shit now. Last time I was in the water, I was three inches shorter and fifty pounds lighter. Before culinary school," he added as an explanation.

"I didn't realize culinary school was the same as boot camp," Ryan teased.

Yeah, they were supposed to be friends, but just Wyatt's voice was a hot lick of awareness right up his spine. When he felt that way, it was impossible not to flirt a little, and hope that Wyatt would flirt back.

"You wouldn't," Wyatt said, leaning back in his seat, the wind from the open window fluffing his blond hair.

"Professional cooking can be tough, and you need to be prepared," he continued. "There's often twelve- to four-teen-hour days. Long hours bending and lifting, all in a bru-tally hot kitchen. Not everyone can hack it. Culinary school isn't just about teaching techniques and flavors; it's about weeding out the ones without the stamina or the drive."

"So, culinary school is the educational equivalent of the Hunger Games."

Wyatt laughed. "You could say that."

Ryan glanced over and while he could imagine Wyatt a little shorter, it was hard to imagine him without his solid build or all that firm muscle.

"If it's so tough, why did you stick it out?" Ryan asked.

"It was what I wanted to do," Wyatt admitted. "I didn't care how hard it was. I sort of enjoyed how hard it was. I felt like I went in one person and came out another."

Ryan had a pretty good idea of what fifty pounds of muscle might look like on a frame the size of Wyatt's. "You *did*."

Wyatt shifted in his seat. Closer to Ryan, who didn't miss the movement. His hands clenched tighter on the steering wheel. "I don't think important things should be easy. I'm sure you worked your ass off."

"Yes, and no." Wyatt made surviving culinary school and his subsequent years in important kitchens sound like something noble. Ryan didn't want to talk about five-tool players, or how scouts evaluated them. He'd never been ashamed at how easily baseball had come to him. It was tough to imagine taking advantage of a situation when he'd had so much handed to him because of a set of natural skills, but he felt oddly shamed admitting it to Wyatt.

He drummed his fingers on the steering wheel. It wasn't shameful. It was okay to want *more*, and okay to take it. It wasn't like he'd wrested it from more-deserving hands. He'd wrested it with his own. "I've wanted to travel my entire life," Ryan admitted. "I never could see myself staying in LA."

"But you're actively trying to stay in LA," Wyatt asked with a perplexed expression on his face.

"I'm trying to stay playing for the Dodgers because my family is here," Ryan corrected. "I like baseball because the game can be great, and also because it gets me out of here on a regular basis."

Wyatt looked surprised.

"What, did you expect some paean to baseball the sport? How I love the smell of the grass and the dirt under my fingernails, and the brightness of the sun during a day game and the lights during a night game?"

"Maybe?" Wyatt said meekly.

"I do enjoy that stuff," Ryan said. "But someone said, you're a great baseball player, you could make a lot of money doing it, and travel at the same time, mostly on someone else's dime. So I said yes."

Ryan cut a quick slanted look towards Wyatt, who merely looked thoughtful and not judgmental. He hadn't really expected otherwise, but Ryan also didn't go out of his way to make this particular confession.

"You took a risk when you came out, then."

"Not really," Ryan admitted wryly. "I made sure any risk I had was mitigated. Well, technically, Eric made sure any risk I had was mitigated. He's good for that."

Bringing Eric up was the thing that hardened the look in Wyatt's eyes. Ryan told himself he shouldn't be shocked, because Eric Talbot was undoubtedly a garbage dumpster, but he also didn't think Eric had done anything to Wyatt to deserve that sort of reaction.

"And he also thinks you need to make yourself into some paragon of stability to keep your job?" Wyatt questioned. Ah, that was it. Like Tabitha, Wyatt had obviously decided that the fake-boyfriend idea was total shit. And frankly, Ryan himself had thought this same thing on and off over the last few months, so it wasn't like he blamed Wyatt.

"Sort of. And I'd get signed by someone else, probably for more money, if I wanted. So it's not exactly about keeping my job. It's about keeping LA my home base."

"For your family."

"Partly, yeah. And because I like it here. I like leaving it, but I also like coming back. If I was in Minnesota or Illinois or somewhere else, I might not feel that way."

"Minnesota would suck for sure, especially if you like surfing," Wyatt said, the corner of his lips quirking into a grin. "But you'd like Chicago."

"Not in the middle of winter," Ryan pointed out.

"Point. I was only there from March to September."

"You lived in Chicago?" Ryan asked.

"For a few months. Restaurant folded right after I got an interview at a great restaurant in Portland, so the timing was good."

"Shame you never got to experience one of those fabled Chicago winters," Ryan said.

Wyatt mock-shuddered. "I'll take California, thank you very much."

And he was the epitome of the California boy, Ryan thought as he watched Wyatt carrying his board towards the sand. Blond hair bright under the sun, the tall lanky build, all that tanned skin rippling with muscle.

Ryan hadn't thought there was a place he could look better than naked in his bed, but he was surprised to discover that he'd been wrong.

There was something in the quicksilver of Wyatt's smile as he turned to make sure Ryan was still following him. It made Ryan want more from him than just the admittedly mind-blowing sex they had had, which was something he'd thought he'd left behind years ago.

He thought about texting Tabitha and telling her she might be right, but she was already insufferable enough. Besides, if he didn't tell her, he didn't put it into words and the truth, while eye-opening, was also fucking terrifying.

"You coming?" Wyatt turned back fully this time, gracing Ryan not only with a quick glimpse of his bright smile, but his entire self. He looked worried, and Ryan wondered how long he'd been spacing out. Not something he usually did—*and* he'd already spent the morning doing it.

"Sorry," Ryan apologized. "I was distracted by such a fantastic view."

"I've always loved Huntington Beach," Wyatt replied.

Ryan snorted. "Not the view I was talking about."

Wyatt didn't say anything but the look on his face was enough for Ryan to know that comment wouldn't always go un-remarked upon. Eventually they would have to address the sexual tension simmering away between them. Eventually they would have to *do* something about it. And that day was one Ryan eagerly awaited and dreaded in equal parts.

"We gonna surf?" Wyatt asked as they set up their little camp over by one of the piers.

Ryan had tossed the wax over to Wyatt a few minutes before, and had been fidgeting with his tow strap since. He'd wanted to come out here and let the sun and the sand and the waves exorcise his bad mood, but now he wasn't sure he even wanted to go in the water.

He wanted to sit on the sand and look at the sunlight on Wyatt's hair, and ask him to tell him more about culinary school and Chicago and Terroir. Even about that nutjob Aquino.

Ryan was not used to wanting to pick social interaction over the adrenaline rush. It was weird, and he wasn't sure he liked it.

"We're here, aren't we?" Ryan asked, shooting Wyatt a disbelieving look, even though all the hesitation had been on his end. He wasn't ready to admit to anyone—never mind Wyatt—that he'd been contemplating something so out of character. "Last in the water buys burgers on the way home."

Wyatt shouldn't have been surprised but Ryan was an exceptional surfer. Great technique, perfect form, textbook pop-up, the sort of rock-steady balance that he'd always craved.

It was hard not to watch him and to focus on the upcoming waves, bobbing in the surf, waiting for the one that he might not embarrass himself on too badly. There weren't a lot of surfers here today—it was later in the day than the hardcore bunch liked—but there was a good variety of skill on display. Still, it had been a long time since Wyatt had been on a board, and it was fucking hard not to feel a little pressed when Ryan was putting on a show rare for an amateur.

Ryan finished his run, coasting into the beach with the finesse of a seal sliding through the water, and immediately glanced back, like he wanted to make sure Wyatt was okay. Or maybe check him out again, it was hard to say.

That speculative, hot look of Ryan's took the decision right out of Wyatt's hands. It was going to have to be the next wave. If he waited here for the perfect wave, he'd be waiting all day. One of his old friends from high school had once told him, "if you wait for the perfect wave to ride, you'll never ride any."

He hopped on his board, fingers gripping the fiberglass and got ready. It wasn't exactly like riding a bicycle, but his instincts, long unused, still took over. His pop-up was a little shaky but Wyatt swore under his breath, dug his toes into the board and willed himself to stay upright.

He did a quick cut against the wave, gaining speed, and managed not to wipe out as he moved towards the beach.

When he popped out of the water, Ryan was waiting for him, smirk on his face.

"Not too shabby," he said as Wyatt shook the water out of his hair.

"Yeah," Wyatt scoffed. "Compared to Mr. Amateur Pro."

He was pretty sure Ryan blushed, though it was impossible to tell under the heat of the sun. "I'm not good enough to be a pro."

Wyatt gave him a grin. "Not quite."

"I get out a lot," Ryan admitted as Wyatt adjusted his tow strap, and they prepared to go out again. "It helps clear my head. I'm technically not supposed to be out here during the season—they're always afraid I'll get hurt or be too tired or strain something—but it helps. So I keep coming."

No, he wasn't quite good enough to go pro, Wyatt thought, watching Ryan. He tried too many risky things; nearly falling off his board despite his iron balance and his great technique. He craved the challenge, Wyatt realized, as he watched him try the same trick three or four times despite no successful attempts. He craved the rush he'd get the first time he got it right.

And when he did get it right, his smile was brilliant enough that even through the spray of the salt, it was unmistakable.

When Wyatt came back in after that run, Ryan had retreated to the camp they'd set up, and was toweling his head off.

"That was pretty sick," Wyatt said and collapsed on the sand. Surfing for an hour after a lengthy jog probably hadn't been his best idea ever, and he was definitely going to be feeling it tomorrow, but this afternoon had been worth it. Both the chance to get back into the ocean, and the chance to spend more time with Ryan—even if it ended up hurting more.

"I've been trying to land that right for ages," Ryan said, smile still sparkling. On anyone else, the look might have edged towards smug, but on Ryan it just looked like pure joy at finally accomplishing something he'd been working on for a long time. "Maybe you're my lucky charm."

Wyatt doubted that. "The waves were just with you today."

"Naw," Ryan said, leaning in just enough to nudge his elbow gently into Wyatt's rib cage. If he came any closer, they'd be embracing. And Wyatt wanted it, he wanted it badly, but he also froze, because even though he typically didn't worry while out in public, Ryan was famous. People watched him. People looked at him. People *wrote* about him. And while he certainly didn't expect his nana to be reading Ryan Flores fan sites, you never knew.

Ryan must have caught the panic on his face because he eased back. He must be confused, because hadn't Wyatt made out with him in a public parking lot? And he *had*. Wyatt hadn't been thinking though. He'd only been feeling, and it had been so sweet after so long being so careful.

Look where that had gotten him.

Their burgers were sitting between them on the console, perfuming the air with grease and cheese, and Ryan was sucking away happily on his chocolate shake, when Wyatt glanced at his phone and realized the time.

"Oh crap, I didn't realize how late it was," Wyatt said. "Would you mind if I called my nana? She goes to dinner early and I don't want to miss her."

Wyatt thought he saw Ryan tense out of the corner of his eye. But that was silly, why would calling his nana upset Ryan?

He was already dialing when the answer hit him abruptly. His nana was obstinately the reason why he couldn't be with Ryan the way they both wanted; even if it wasn't her fault, he could still blame her.

"Hello?" Bea Blake's voice was tiny and faraway even though Wyatt knew the connection at the memory care facility was excellent. It was one reason why he'd chosen the carrier he had.

"Nana!" he said, trying to push away all the concern he was feeling over having the conversation in front of Ryan.

"Nana?" Her voice was questioning everything, even though she'd only said two words.

"You're Nana," Wyatt said fondly.

But instead of her bright, clear laugh, there was a puzzled, drawn-out silence.

"Who is Nana?" she repeated, clearly confused, and Wyatt's stomach tumbled to his flip-flops.

"You're Nana. I'm Wyatt," he said slowly, clearly. Maybe it was just the bad connection. Maybe she just couldn't hear him properly, and had gotten confused as a result.

"Wyatt?" she questioned. "Wyatt?"

If it was possible, his stomach sunk even lower. He tried to contain his panic, because he didn't want Ryan to hear, and he didn't want her to worry even more. It was something he'd read in the research books he'd checked out of the library when she'd first been diagnosed.

Don't panic. They'll hear the panic and panic themselves.

But it was too late, he heard it in his voice, no matter how he tried to contain it. "Wyatt is me. I'm Wyatt. I'm your grandson."

"Wyatt…" There was still that thread of uncertainty in her voice. Uncertainty that he'd been dreading hearing forever.

He remembered reading once that for patients suffering from memory lapses, just voices could sometimes be tougher than a voice and a face put together.

The rationalization didn't help extinguish his panic any.

"Yes, Wyatt. Your grandson. Wyatt."

She took a deep, shaky sigh. "Wyatt." And this time there was some semblance of normalcy in her voice as she said it. As she'd begun to place him. "You're Wyatt."

He closed his eyes, tightening his jaw, desperate not to cry. Not over this. Not in front of Ryan.

A hand reached over and lightly touched his bare knee. A reassuring touch. Even though he'd seen Ryan's uneasiness with Wyatt checking in with Nana, he was still giving Wyatt what little support he could.

It might have been small, only a light touch, but it meant everything.

"Nana," he repeated, voice breaking a little. The first time this had happened and he hadn't even been in front of her. And once it happened, it would keep happening, an inexorable tide that nothing and nobody could stop. Not even Wyatt, not even if he pushed it back with both hands and all his strength.

"I'm here, I'm here." She sounded flustered. "I'm sorry, I just got a little confused."

"It's fine," he soothed, even though it was anything but. She didn't need to know about that, or how his heart was breaking. "I just wanted to call and see how you were doing."

"I'm good. How about you, darling boy? You settle into your big fancy new job okay?"

She was back. The lapse had only lasted a minute, but it had left an indelible impression on Wyatt. He wasn't sure he would ever forget this moment. The grease in the air, the five pressure points of Ryan's hand on his knee, the sweaty grip on his phone.

He talked aimlessly for five minutes and then told Nana he had to go. He couldn't pretend like nothing had happened.

When he finally hung up, there was silence in the car.

Finally, Ryan broke it. "Was that the first time she didn't recognize your voice?"

Wyatt wasn't sure he could speak, so he just nodded.

"I'm sorry." Ryan sounded legitimately sorry, even though it was Wyatt who wanted to apologize for ruining a beautiful afternoon with this tragedy.

"Don't be. Please," Wyatt managed to say. "Please don't."

"We don't have to talk about it. But if you ever need to go see her, you just say the word," Ryan said.

"Okay. I . . . I appreciate it."

Wyatt knew he should be more grateful for Ryan's support and for his flexibility, but all he felt was a growing rage at fate and how it was trying to take yet another beloved member of his family. First his dad had left, then his mom had died, and now the one person he still felt close to was going to forget who he even was.

He clamped his hand over Ryan's, and as Wyatt gripped his hand, it struck him, suddenly and catastrophically, that the man Bea Blake would be forgetting wasn't even the *real* Wyatt.

"I texted my aunt this morning," Ryan said, clearly making good on his promise to change the subject. But Wyatt's fingers didn't let up on Ryan's for even a moment. "Would Friday afternoon work for you?"

Swallowing all the emotions back, Wyatt held on even harder. "Don't you have something important or fun to be doing besides going to your aunt's house and watching her teach me how to cook?"

Ryan laughed unexpectedly. "Obviously you've never met my *titi* Flor before, because she definitely won't let me just watch."

"I can't wait to meet her," Wyatt said, and discovered that he wasn't even lying. He wanted to meet the woman who could make Ryan laugh like that.

Ryan pulled into the driveway, the gate shutting behind them. "Do you think you could eat?" he asked, even though the bag of burgers was still sitting between them—a special detour to In-N-Out, and Ryan had whipped out his credit card despite the challenge he'd given earlier.

Wyatt still felt vaguely nauseous, but he'd only had a few eggs and some turkey sausage this morning before his run, and he'd worked up a real appetite surfing.

"Yeah, of course," Wyatt said. How had Ryan even known he'd gotten nauseous? Had it been written all over his face?

He pushed the embarrassment away. If there was ever a situation to feel sick over, it was this one.

"We could even watch some TV," Ryan suggested.

Even though Wyatt had long come to terms with the fact that Ryan was nothing like his old boss, it still felt weird that Ryan was seeking him out all the time. Either because he actually wanted to be friends, or because . . . Wyatt didn't even know how to finish that thought. Because Ryan had explicitly and clearly expressed interest in a *fake* boyfriend, someone to convince the GM that he was dependable. And if fake boyfriend had been ruled out, real boyfriend was definitely not in the cards.

"Sure, but if you turn on another of those godawful nature documentaries, I might have to pass."

But then there was the way Ryan lit up at Wyatt's teasing, defying explanation. "What about *Star Talk?*"

"With Neil deGrasse Tyson?" Wyatt opened his car door. "I thought you were a stupid athlete."

"Well, this stupid athlete went to Stanford, and attempts to combat that stereotype by arming himself with knowledge," Ryan said flippantly, but his voice was warm and comforting and certain. And Wyatt realized then that Ryan didn't want him to agonize and obsess alone.

He thought about thanking him but going back to his cottage, but then Ryan was in the house, leaving Wyatt behind in the garage, and he was babbling about Twitter and flat earth conspiracists, and instead of dwelling, Wyatt let his words wash over him, taking all the ugliness with them.

Wyatt might not know what the hell they were doing, but they were friends. And that was going to have to be enough—at least for now.

CHAPTER EIGHT

OVER THE NEXT FEW days, Wyatt worked hard to create some kind of routine for his work and his friendship with Ryan. He didn't want the other man to feel obligated to hang out with him, or eat with him, or even talk to him, but Ryan always sought him out.

"Are you trying to push me away?" Ryan asked one evening when in determination that he should get a choice, Wyatt had set a single place setting in the cavernous dining room.

Ryan had showed up in the kitchen, where Wyatt was eating at the island, with his plate and silverware and had shot him a half-hearted glare. "Do you not like eating with me?"

It had been difficult not to flush. The problem wasn't that Wyatt didn't like hanging out with him, it was that he was increasingly loving it, and he'd really liked it to begin with.

"If I want space, I'll take it," was all Ryan had said about it before setting his plate down right next to Wyatt's.

They hadn't gone surfing again, and Wyatt hadn't invited himself to use Ryan's home gym. And Ryan hadn't pushed there either, which was probably smart. The truth was getting half-naked and sweaty together was a terrible combination if they wanted to keep things platonic.

The attraction was there. The possibility for it to deepen wasn't far behind. And at least half the time, Wyatt imagined saying *fuck it*, and pinning Ryan to the nearest convenient surface.

The wall. The kitchen counter. Ryan's bed. Wyatt's bed. In his wilder daydreams, Ryan's bike again. His imagination definitely wasn't doing him any favors. He'd go to bed, and lie awake in bed, running through memories, real and otherwise, and put off jerking off as long as possible until he was burning up and there was no other way to relieve the pressure of wanting Ryan.

And every time, even as he wrapped his hand around his cock and gave himself an experimental stroke, Wyatt knew that it wouldn't help because in the end, it wasn't what he really needed.

What he needed was the god damn real thing; on top of him, under him, pressed against him. Wyatt was discovering he wasn't particularly picky except it had to be Ryan Flores.

Wyatt wasn't naïve enough to believe it might be the same for Ryan, but there was more than one morning when he swore he caught the sharpened edge of sexual frustration in Ryan's eyes. He recognized it because he saw the exact same fucking thing in his bathroom mirror each morning.

"You ready to go?" Wyatt looked up, and Ryan was standing there, board shorts and a loose tank, one nipple almost poking out the armhole.

He'd dressed in jeans and a polo shirt that he'd dug out from the back of his meager closet, because he was going to see the aunt of the guy he liked, and old habits died hard.

Now Wyatt was wondering if he was criminally overdressed.

Ryan raised an eyebrow. "You know, I have lots of money but my family rarely lets me give it to them. My *titi* won't even let me buy her an air conditioner."

Okay, so he was definitely overdressed. But changing would mean admitting why he'd pulled these clothes out in the first place, and even though Wyatt thought Ryan probably knew, admitting it was a whole different story.

"It's okay," Wyatt dismissed, "I worked in hot kitchens my whole career."

"Don't tell me the Bastard didn't give you guys even a measly fan?" Wyatt had made the mistake a few days ago of referring to Bastian Aquino by his hated nickname, and Ryan had been unexpectedly delighted and had been looking for ways to bring him up so he could use it.

Wyatt shouldn't find it adorable, but that ship had definitely sailed.

Maybe he should stop trying to fight it, and instead figure out how to embrace it—no matter how impossible the situation felt.

"I shouldn't have told you Aquino's secret nickname," Wyatt admitted.

But Ryan just kept grinning in delight as they headed down the garage steps. Ryan opened the door of the Tesla, and Wyatt followed suit, sliding into the sleek car.

"If I ever meet him, I might have to accidentally slip one or two 'Bastards' in," he said as they backed out of the driveway.

"If you ever met him, you wouldn't even dream of it."

Ryan raised a dark eyebrow and the hot, insolent look in his eyes swamped Wyatt with desire. "I don't know if you've noticed, but I like living on the edge."

He'd definitely noticed. It had been a little hard to miss, and Wyatt, who considered himself laid-back but grudgingly cautious, found it strangely appealing.

At first he'd thought it was only Ryan's looks that had attracted him, but Wyatt was beginning to realize it wasn't just his exterior that attracted him—it was the whole package.

"You drive too fast," Wyatt pointed out as they screamed onto the freeway, the Tesla handling like a dream, even as he refused to glance over and check the speedometer. "Don't tell me you're aspiring to be a professional race car driver too."

The other night, Ryan had told him that in high school, before he'd gotten the big scholarship to play baseball at

Stanford, he'd briefly considered surfing for a living. "Becoming a professional beach bum," Wyatt had teased, but it made sense. Ryan craved adventure, craved waking up and not knowing exactly where he was. Craved the liquid lighter fluid of adrenaline running through his veins.

"Maybe," Ryan said with a dimpled, slanted grin.

"All things considered, baseball must feel pretty sedate for you," Wyatt pointed out.

"Oh come on. You're not one of those idiots who think baseball is slow and boring, are you?" Ryan gave a self-conscious snort of laughter. "You totally are."

"I'm sure playing the game is a hell of a lot different than watching it," Wyatt retorted.

"This should have been my first question in the interview: do you think baseball is a boring lesser version of golf? Or curling?"

"Curling is fantastic," Wyatt argued. "Have you ever seen those Swedish guys?"

"Yes." Ryan's lip curled. "And I'm going to remember you voted baseball under curling because of the hot Swedes."

"You're very hot too," Wyatt said because he should be loyal *and* honest. Or something like that.

Ryan cut over three lanes, taking the exit ramp going at least seventy miles per hour. Wyatt didn't flinch, because he'd learned that if he flinched, Ryan would drive even faster.

"You're also a maniac," Wyatt mumbled under his breath.

"I heard that," Ryan announced cheerfully.

"Tell me about your *titi*," Wyatt suggested.

"Flor? She's been here . . . fifteen years? Twenty? We'll have to ask her. She came over with my mom."

It was on the tip of his tongue to ask about Ryan's mom, because even though he'd mentioned his aunt half a dozen times, his mother hadn't ever come up. But Wyatt didn't, because he knew how much it could hurt when someone thoughtlessly asked about his—and it had been eight years since she'd died.

Some wounds didn't heal, they just scabbed over.

"She basically raised me," Ryan continued, essentially but not completely answering the question that Wyatt hadn't asked. "She's probably my favorite person in the whole world."

The wound created by his nana not remembering him hadn't even had time to scab over yet, and it throbbed at Ryan's words.

"She and my two cousins run a cleaning business. Rich people's houses, all that bullshit. But she's good at it, and loves her clients and they love her. Someday, she wants to open a restaurant. I keep telling her I'll loan her the money, even charge interest, but she won't take a penny."

Wyatt thought of his nana, and one of the lesser lies that he'd told her recently: that the sale of her little bungalow in a Sacramento suburb would pay for her extended care in the memory care facility.

It wasn't the most painful lie he'd ever told her—that was still ongoing and likely to remain so—but it had been entirely necessary. She'd never accept Wyatt paying for her care.

"Anonymous donation?" Wyatt asked, even though they both knew it was useless because they both had tough-as-nails, independent female relatives. They were so easy to love, but almost impossible to help.

The wound ached again when Wyatt remembered that Bea Blake was no longer as independent as she'd once prided herself on being.

Ryan rolled his eyes. "If only that would work."

"You'll figure out something, eventually. You don't strike me as the kind of guy who just gives up."

"When you meet her," Ryan confessed, "you'll realize that she'll never let me. I just funnel as many nice, rich people as I can find her way, and that's how I make sure her dream comes true."

"You're a good person," Wyatt murmured.

"Not really. But at least I make an attempt," Ryan said flippantly. He pulled over next to a small house, painted bright yellow. "So, here we are."

Wyatt hadn't been nervous, but when faced with the prospect of getting out of the car, he realized he was really nervous. It wasn't so surprising that he wanted Ryan's *titi* to like him, and not because he wanted everyone to generally like him. Considering how compartmentalized Ryan typically kept his hookups, Wyatt wondered if he'd taken the job as Ryan's fake boyfriend if he would have ever met her at all.

"Just make sure you don't mention Eric," Ryan warned as they walked up the concrete path to the house. The grass on either side was neatly trimmed and there was a profusion of tropical flowers on either side of the front door.

"Eric?" Wyatt asked blankly.

"My agent. Flor hates him. She thinks he's a weasel."

The door opened and a shorter woman with dark hair pulled back in a ponytail and equally dark, intense eyes stepped out. There was a wide smile on her face, and a few laugh lines around her eyes and bracketing her lips. She looked warm and friendly and the way she immediately pulled Ryan into a big hug and then said loudly, "He *is* a weasel," made Wyatt want her to like him even more.

"No arguments from this corner," Wyatt said, extending his hand. "Thank you for inviting me into your home. I'm Wyatt Blake."

Flor let go of Ryan and gave Wyatt a quick, but very thorough look up and then down. If he'd thought Tabitha's examination had been tough, it had nothing on Flor's.

She reached out like she was going to shake his hand, but then pulled him into a hug. Wyatt got a fleeting impression of coconut and roasted pork and sunshine.

"You are ready to cook, yes?" she asked, leading them into the house. "Ryan told me you are very good."

The house was scrupulously neat, with warm wood floors and framed retro tourism posters dotting the walls. A navy-blue couch sat across from a flat screen television, with sunny orange and yellow pillows brightening its surface.

Wyatt had never felt particularly unsure about his qualifications before, but faced with Flor's fierce gaze, he wavered and Ryan ended up answering her instead.

"Yes, I told you," Ryan said. "He's a chef."

"Well, lucky you came in time. I'm making the *sofrito* first."

The kitchen was tiny, with just barely enough room for the three of them. But something incredibly delicious was already simmering on the stove, warming up the room. Ryan shot him a smug look, and Wyatt couldn't help but wish that he'd taken Ryan's advice and dressed down.

"*Sofrito?*" Wyatt asked, fully expecting that he would get incredulous looks from both Ryan and Flor.

"Oh, you didn't tell me he knew *nothing*." Flor directed this comment to Ryan.

But Ryan only laughed. "*Titi,* I told you he was a chef. He doesn't know anything about Puerto Rican food."

Flor turned to Wyatt. "*Sofrito* is . . . the most important thing in Puerto Rican food. It creates the important flavor. I usually make mine every few weeks and then freeze it."

Wyatt took in the counter full of peppers, huge bags of herbs, onions, garlic. "I can help chop," he offered.

Flor wordlessly handed him a knife. "Not perfect," she said once he began to break down the peppers. "We're going to blend it all."

But Wyatt hadn't learned knife skills in culinary school for nothing, and then honed them in one of the most exacting kitchens in the world. He knew what to do with a knife in his hand, even with Flor glancing over at him to check in every minute or so.

After he'd broken down the peppers and onions and had started mincing the garlic, Flor turned to Ryan, who despite what he'd claimed earlier, was just lounging against the kitchen counter, browsing through his phone.

"*Hijo,* he's very good with his hands." Her knowing look in his direction had him blushing and Ryan sputtering. He'd been right then, Flor had not met many—or *any*—of Ryan's boyfriends. If he'd even had one. That was still unclear and Wyatt wasn't sure it was even right to ask him.

"It's why I hired him," Ryan said.

"You didn't even give me a real interview," Wyatt pointed out. "We sat at a table and you half-heartedly asked me a few questions."

"True," Ryan admitted and Wyatt didn't miss Flor rolling her eyes.

"You're going to end up broke," she said.

"Been doing good so far," Ryan argued. "I have a huge shoot coming up for Adidas. I think I told you about that."

But Flor didn't seem to be deterred, even as she pulled out a big Vitamix blender. "You trust too many people, who want to take all of your money."

Wyatt wasn't sure he agreed. Yeah, Ryan was generous. He paid him a great salary and had insisted more than once on picking up the bill for things. Had given Wyatt a credit card to charge supplies and groceries. But more than one offhand comment he'd made had made it clear that he monitored it fairly closely. He wasn't tight-fisted by any means, but he certainly wasn't running through cash the way Flor made it sound.

"You'll have to forgive my *titi*," Ryan said. "She thinks anyone who gives a gift over a hundred bucks is careless with their finances."

Flor glared at him. "If you had told me how much this blender cost, I never would have taken it."

Ryan's eyes were guileless. "You could have given it back after you found out."

"Hardly. It saves me so much time and energy, it's cost-effective to use it," she sniffed.

Wyatt found himself chuckling into his garlic while still missing his nana so much it was hard to take a breath. He'd wanted to call her again, but frankly he was afraid to, terrified that he would dial her number and a stranger would answer again.

He knew it was something he might have to get used to—not *might*, he corrected bitterly, he *would*—but he wasn't ready. He needed more time, except that the disease wasn't exactly clued into his timetable, or anyone else's either.

"So what have you been feeding my nephew?" Flor directed this question Wyatt's direction, her bickering with Ryan over the blender concluded—at least for now.

"I've been to the farmer's market three times since I got here. So lots of fresh veggies. Salmon. Chicken. I made burgers the other night with roasted mushrooms."

Flor made a *tsking* noise as she began to load his chopped vegetables into the blender pitcher. "He takes terrible care of himself on his own. I thought this was a bad idea, but I've changed my mind."

Wyatt had a feeling that this was unusual, so he gave her a grateful nod. "It's very different from what I'm used to, but I agree. It's been good."

The toughest part had probably been being around Ryan and not being able to do what he wanted to him, with him, against him, *etcetera*, but second toughest had been all the unexpected free time he'd found himself with. He didn't know what to do with himself when he wasn't working fourteen hours a day, falling into bed, and then getting up to do it all over again.

"And you're used to what? Very long days?" Flor shot her nephew a knowing look. "I don't think you're keeping him busy enough."

"I'm only one man," Ryan complained. "I can only eat so much."

"*Sofrito* isn't cooked, then?" Wyatt asked. He'd looked up the rudiments of Puerto Rican cooking before this day, and he'd seen many recipes claiming to be authentic, but most of them cooked the pepper and herb mix down first.

Ryan groaned. "Don't get her started."

Flor shot him a glare. "Each cook does it differently. This is my way, at least for this dish."

"We're making *pasteles*," Ryan supplied. "Usually served on holidays or special occasions. Very fancy. And sort of my aunt's specialty."

"Not *sort of*," Flor corrected. "*Hijo*, come here and do something besides hold up that counter. Chop up the pork for me." She gestured to where she'd set up another plastic cutting board. A huge hunk of pork shoulder sat on it, waiting to be broken down. Wyatt's fingers itched, because he would much rather be doing that more delicate, more skilled work, than mincing another fifty cloves of garlic.

Also, despite Flor asking him to do it, Wyatt wasn't sure Ryan knew how. He'd acted very uneasy every time Wyatt had asked him to help with anything in the kitchen.

"Very fine," Flor reminded Ryan as he picked up the knife. "You know how it should be."

Ryan rolled his eyes. "*Sí*, I know."

And to Wyatt's surprise, Ryan very competently wielded the knife and began to break down the shoulder into more manageable pieces. It wasn't precisely how Wyatt would have done it, but he'd been trained in professional kitchens, and he was certain that Flor had taught Ryan.

In fact, now that Wyatt was seeing Ryan chop up the pork, he realized that Flor had been more concerned about *his* knife skills—for ingredients that were eventually going to be blended. Wyatt didn't know whether to laugh or be offended.

"Professional skills," Flor said, following Wyatt's gaze to where Ryan was working. "I only trust what I know."

Wyatt laughed. "And you taught him."

Flor broke into a huge smile. "Exactly." She turned towards Ryan. "I think I like this one. You don't let me meet many—or *any*—of your men, *hijo*, but I still like this one. Don't scare him away."

Ryan flushed red, knife pausing in the middle of a cut. "He's not *my* man, *titi*."

Throwing up her hands, Flor retreated back to the blender, and hit the power button. She didn't seem very convinced, and Wyatt was torn between embarrassment and pure satisfaction.

He'd totally dawdled through the rest of the garlic, because he'd been listening to Flor and Ryan chatter and then watching Ryan chop up the pork. So he was unexpectedly surprised when he heard a voice over his shoulder.

"You're looking awfully smug at that garlic clove," Ryan murmured near his ear. Only long practice helped Wyatt keep his rhythm and not let his knife falter.

"I don't know why I'd be staring smugly at garlic," Wyatt said.

"Okay, so you were staring at my ass at least fifty percent of the time," Ryan said, and Wyatt looked up at him to see smiling, little dimple and all.

"I think I wouldn't be staring smugly at your ass if I was getting it," Wyatt groused. Hopefully quiet enough that Flor wouldn't hear.

"True," Ryan admitted.

Wyatt wanted to ask again, *when am I going to come home to find another man in the house, the one who gets to play your boyfriend?* But Flor was right there, and Ryan had shut down the last time he'd asked. So he didn't, even though he could taste the question on his tongue.

"I'm going to smell like garlic for a month," Wyatt said, changing the subject for self-preservation reasons. "Reminds me of when I first started at Terroir, and Aquino put me on garlic duty for contradicting him once."

Ryan sighed deeply. "You're only convincing me more that I have to go up to Napa and kick the Bastard's ass. Soon."

"Language," Flor piped up from the other side of the kitchen. "I know I raised you better than that."

"That's his name," Ryan protested.

Flor raised an eyebrow. "Okay, it's his nickname, but it seems like a god damned accurate one," Ryan added.

"Bastian Aquino can be . . . well . . ." Wyatt hesitated. "He can be a bit of a jerk, sometimes. Even though Terroir was supposed to be such a great place to work, I don't miss it at all."

"When I first came here," Flor said, raising her voice to be heard over the Vitamix, "I work for company cleaning houses. They pay me a good wage. But the supervisor was awful. I quit, and started my own company. Less money, more happiness." She hesitated. "But Ryan wouldn't let you come work for him without paying you more." She sounded fond but exasperated.

"Don't worry, I'm not breaking the bank," Wyatt said. "And it's crazy how long I suffered at Terroir, just because it was *Terroir*, and a thousand chefs would have committed murder for my spot. Somehow that was supposed to make me like it more, I guess, but I didn't. Leaving was hard, I only wish I'd done it sooner."

Wyatt finished the garlic and passed it over to Flor who was still magically concocting the *sofrito*, mixing and matching ingredients and tasting each batch after she blended it. Once she determined a batch was perfect, she'd pour it into ice trays, and they went into the freezer.

"Tomorrow," she said, "I'll pop them out and stick them in freezer bags. And then they're good as long as they last, whenever I cook."

"I might do that with fresh herbs," Wyatt mused. "It's a brilliant idea."

"Not brilliant," she retorted. "Common sense."

"Amazing how the two things are often the same thing," Ryan said.

"Time for the pork," Flor announced. The skillet she produced was massive. Wyatt probably could have sat in it and paddled it out into the Pacific Ocean. "*Hijo*, will you grate the *yautia* and the bananas for the filling?"

Ryan groaned, but didn't hesitate to pull out the necessary bowl and grater, and begin what looked like an arduous job.

"I thought you said your *titi* wasn't going to make you work," Wyatt teased.

"I would never say that," Ryan loyally protested when Flor shot him a look from where she was beginning to load the pork into the hot pan.

"I hope you help Wyatt too," Flor said. "He's not your slave."

Ryan laughed. "No. Unfortunately."

"I have everything under control, usually," Wyatt inserted. He hadn't ever felt comfortable asking Ryan to help prepare meals because that was what Ryan was *technically* paying him for. Even when Ryan hung around the kitchen, which he did most days, having a beer or a bottle of water as he watched Wyatt prepare food.

"Also he's way out of my skill level," Ryan said. "He's playing dumb now, making sure not to overpromise and underdeliver, but he's got serious talent."

"Maybe he could teach you to take care of yourself better," Flor said, her voice going steely. "You eat out too much."

Teaching Ryan how to cook sounded like heaven and hell, all wrapped up in one delicious package. But Wyatt couldn't tell Ryan's aunt that he wasn't sure how much more time he could spend with him before giving in and dragging them both back to the bedroom.

Frankly, they might not even make it that far. The living room had a really nice soft carpet that had been figuring in Wyatt's imagination a lot lately.

"I do fine," Ryan argued. "You worry too much."

But Wyatt chimed in before Flor could. "That's her job," he said. "Just like yours is to hit a baseball really, really far."

"I do more than that," Ryan said. "I also run around in a circle and catch balls sometimes." The slanted, teasing look he shot Wyatt was almost more than he could bear. His fingers clenched around the edge of the counter.

Flor must have been at least partially aware of the undercurrents running through the kitchen because she waved Wyatt over and proceeded to distract him by giving him a long list of ingredients to be added to the browning pork. He was a food nerd, so it was an effective move.

"I'll send you the recipe later," Flor said when Wyatt was trying to remember everything they'd added. "We want it to be nice and cooked down. So we'll let it simmer a little, while Ryan finishes up the masa. Do you need the achiote oil yet?" She directed the question to Ryan, not even glancing his direction as she turned the pork mixture with a wooden spoon.

"Soon," Ryan said.

"When he was little he'd always beg to have *pasteles*," Flor confided in Wyatt. "But I told him he'd have to make the masa, and that usually cured his craving."

"It's a thankless job," Ryan pointed out loudly.

"But you've got a nice pair of muscles to get it done fast," Flor said.

And Wyatt couldn't exactly complain when he craned his neck to see Ryan straining against the old-fashioned box grater, biceps bulging. It was definitely a view worth turning around for.

The smug look Ryan shot him made it crystal clear he knew just how sizzling hot he was, and that he'd let Wyatt look and then keep looking any time he wanted.

He didn't know if the sudden heat in the kitchen was from the hot stove or the tiny sluggish fan pumping warm air lazily around the small room, or Ryan sweating over the grater—but Wyatt knew his polo was sticking to him in damp patches, and there was sweat beading along his hair-line.

But from the way Ryan kept gazing at him, all smolder and no stop sign, it was clear he didn't mind. Maybe he even liked it.

If they'd been alone, maybe Wyatt would've stripped his shirt off and even though his abs weren't quite the caliber of Ryan's, let him look his fill anyway.

Except there was a reason they'd stayed mostly fully clothed around each other. They were dry matches desperate to burn, and all they craved was a single flame to set them alight.

But he couldn't set them on fire, because it might burn too hot, and then they'd both be caught in the backdraft.

"Earth to Wyatt," Flor interrupted his increasingly distracted thinking.

"Sorry," Wyatt said, turning his attention back to Flor. "I got distracted."

Her smirk told him that she knew exactly why he'd been so out of it, but she didn't say anymore about it, for which he thanked all the kitchen gods.

"Are you ready to finish the filling?" Flor asked and Wyatt nodded.

Flor moved it off the heat, and they each gave it a taste. Wyatt was impressed by the complexity of the flavor, even though she'd added a fraction of the ingredients they'd used at Terroir and some of the other restaurants he'd worked at.

"Do you think it needs more oregano?" Flor asked him, and the sly light in her eyes informed him this was a test. He'd always been an achiever, and he was desperate to pass.

"He doesn't know if it needs more oregano," Ryan inserted, but Wyatt ignored him, and closed his eyes, rolling the flavor across his tongue, tasting each separate ingredient. Savoring each component, and how they became more than the sum of their parts.

"No," Wyatt finally answered. "But it does need more pepper. And a dash of red pepper, if you have it."

"Cayenne," Flor confirmed, and in her hand was the jar of bright red powder. "Agreed."

"You're pretty good," Flor said, after both peppers had been added, and the filling was off the stove, cooling. "Not many people could have figured out what was missing without knowing what it was supposed to taste like."

Wyatt shrugged. "Some people have a nose for smells. Some people are good at figuring out flavors. I happen to have a combination of both. I can usually tell what's in any particular dish by smell. Definitely by taste. Makes it pretty easy to tell what's missing."

"Seriously?" Ryan asked. "You can really do that?"

"It came in very handy, especially at Terroir. If you think your aunt is terrifying, Bastian Aquino's tests were legendary."

"And you always passed," Ryan stated, with a quick grin. "I bet you did."

"He stumped me once or twice." A lie. Bastian Aquino had never stumped him, even though he'd worked hard at it. He'd called Wyatt a freak, even in his hearing, and even implied once or twice when he was particularly nasty that all Wyatt's skill revolved around something he'd been born with, not developed.

But Ryan was glowing, he was basking in it, and Wyatt already knew what lay that direction: disaster. They couldn't go down that road again, and then end it before it ever began. If that happened, he'd end up halfway to heartbroken, and then he'd have to quit.

Wyatt needed this job. He also needed Ryan, but he was figuring out how to justify only tiny nibbles. Hanging out, being buddies, that was enough to keep his hunger at bay.

If he had another real taste . . . all bets were off.

"Finally ready for the oil," Ryan said. He was sweating too, his forehead damp. Wyatt wanted to press his lips against his skin, taste the salt and the unique taste that was Ryan.

Thank god *Titi* Flor was right there. She was an excellent dissuading tactic.

Wyatt watched as Ryan finished the *masa*, mixing in the achiote oil for color, flavor, and to bring the grated fruit together to form a thick dough.

"Finally time to stuff the leaves," Flor announced. She set up three stations and for the next half an hour, they worked like crazy, layering in *masa* and pork filling, and then bundling it together in the banana leaf, a perfect packet of tastiness.

"How do we cook these?" Wyatt asked Flor.

"Boil for an hour or so," she said. "Salted water. They also freeze beautifully, which I'll be doing with about half these."

"Really?" Ryan pouted. "I promise to take those off your hands."

"Even *you* do not need a hundred *pasteles*," Flor said sternly. "Besides, you have a very competent chef in your employ who will make them any time you ask."

"You really think so?" Ryan asked, shooting Wyatt a speculative look from under his thick, dark lashes. Wyatt felt pinned. Exposed.

"I'm not sure they would ever measure up to your *titi*'s," Wyatt said quickly.

"Maybe I want to see what you can do with them," Ryan insisted.

"They're a lot of work," Wyatt protested, even though it was weak. He'd been making complicated meals all week because he was bored and also because he wanted to give Ryan something, a little return for everything Ryan had offered so selflessly.

"Like you wouldn't do anything he asked when he bats his lashes," Flor scoffed, putting an end to the question once and for all.

Wyatt turned back to his stack of banana leaves, cheeks burning with heat and embarrassment. Was he so obvious? He thought he had his feelings at least partially under wraps.

"Well, he's not alone in that," Ryan said quietly, and Flor made an approving noise.

Wyatt and Ryan climbed back in the Tesla an hour later, fifty *pasteles* richer, with a load of unspoken, raw emotion boiling between them.

Flor had seen them off with a tight hug each. "You take care of him," she'd murmured to Wyatt under her breath during his. "He cares more than he lets on."

The problem was that Ryan already seemed to care, so if he cared even more, felt even deeper, Wyatt was afraid of what the future held for them.

He couldn't give Ryan what he wanted—what they both wanted—but they were both drowning here, and there were no good ideas left to hold onto.

"Thank you for bringing me today," Wyatt said, because trying to re-establish their friendship seemed like the safest bet.

Ryan merged onto the freeway, driving far slower than he had on the way to Flor's house. Wyatt wasn't sure if it was because he didn't want their bubble to end or if he was afraid of being alone with him.

Maybe a combination of both.

"Of course, I said I would." Ryan's voice was carefully neutral, and even though Wyatt *knew* he wasn't alone in feeling this way, it hit him hard that Ryan felt equally helpless.

A minute of silence passed between them, but it didn't seem to deflate the tension, only ratchet it higher.

Wyatt knew he had to do something to give them some space, before they made a mistake and did something they couldn't take back. "I thought tomorrow I'd head up to Napa, see my nana."

"Shouldn't be an issue," Ryan said, still so painfully neutral. Wyatt didn't know what he'd expected. Ryan to beg him to stay? To ask to go with him? Neither one was really an option, but sometimes, Wyatt realized, you wanted the impossible.

"I can make you breakfast before I leave . . ."

"No need," Ryan interrupted, finally sounding impatient. "I have a breakfast meeting with Eric tomorrow."

Wyatt knew without asking that the purpose was to discuss the faux relationship that Ryan should have already started.

Maybe when he got back from Napa, Ryan would have already found someone else. It would still be crushing, but at least it would be crushing without a single speck of hope to be found. It was the hope that was the worst; the tantalizing possibility if only Wyatt could decide the burden he'd been carrying forever suddenly weighed too much.

"I really hope you find what you need," Wyatt said quietly. He didn't say that he hoped Ryan would find what he wanted, because he was beginning to figure out that couldn't happen.

Ryan didn't respond, only gripped the steering wheel so hard his knuckles turned white, and Wyatt knew the conversation was over, and maybe even their budding friendship.

He'd have to see when he came back from Napa and surveyed the damage. He sighed; he wasn't looking forward to it.

When Ryan pulled the car into the garage, making an offhand comment about going for a jog, Wyatt did what he always did when life got too hard—he retreated to the kitchen.

It was still Ryan's kitchen, in Ryan's house, but Wyatt had a feeling that he wouldn't be disturbed.

He put the *pasteles,* carefully wrapped, into the freezer, and went to his cottage to change. Since it was still warm, he opted just for a pair of shorts, and when he got back into the main house, he opened the windows in the kitchen and turned the music up.

Moving his hips to the upbeat guitar, he pulled out ingredients for a savory goat cheese torta with roasted red peppers and a lot of garlic. He wasn't going to be kissing anyone, and if he got a perverse pleasure out of making sure that Ryan wouldn't be either, who could blame him?

He carefully lined the springform pan with plastic wrap, and then got to beating the cream cheese with the goat cheese. Frankly, he realized as he worked the whisk through the cold bricks, he should have let the ingredients get to room temperature before tackling them—his pastry chef friend Miles would be appalled at him trying to get a smooth, incorporated mixture from cold cream cheese and goat cheese, but it also gave his arm a good workout and Wyatt was in a mood where he wanted it to burn a little.

It took a few long minutes, then he added the heavy cream and started thinking about the herbs he wanted to add. The garlic was roasting in the oven still, and would be for another ten minutes. He'd add that last, to give it a little chance to cool.

Dill, he thought, pulling the leafy herb from the produce drawer in the fridge. He also had some great basil, and he added some parsley for good measure, chopping everything up finely, and mixing it into the bowl.

While he was waiting for the garlic to finish, he roasted his peppers, charring them on the gas stove, and then wrapping them in plastic so he could easily peel the skins off.

Finally he was ready to assemble everything, layering in long, thin strips of roasted red pepper in the springform pan with alternating layers of the cream cheese mixture.

Finishing wrapping it up, he stuck it in the fridge to chill, even though he already knew he wasn't ready to relax.

He whipped up a quick curry yogurt marinade and stuck it on the chicken breasts for dinner. With salad and rice, that would be a perfect dinner for him and Ryan—if he even decided to join him.

It was hard to say if the driving beat of the music was keeping him going, or all the heat in Ryan's eyes as he'd stared at him all afternoon. But the reason didn't matter, Wyatt theorized. He was still hot and worked up and frankly about to go out of his skin with desire.

He was just whipping up a batch of parmesan crackers to eat the goat cheesecake with when Ryan walked into the kitchen.

He'd also opted not to wear anything other than shorts, riding low on his narrow hips, and Wyatt's hand clenched on the handle of the cheese grater. He remembered exactly what Ryan's skin had tasted like right there, at his obliques, where the skin went from tan to something paler. He wasn't ever going to forget the salty-sweet tang of his sweat.

Here he was, driving himself up the wall with all this food they didn't need, because he couldn't forget.

Ryan hadn't forgotten either. That much was obvious.

"You're here," he said stupidly. Like Wyatt would be anywhere else.

"I'm here," Wyatt retorted testily. "I'm your private chef, remember?"

"You're hard to forget," Ryan said, a wry edge to his voice.

That was the damning part of all this. Neither of them could figure out how to get past their attraction—if that's all it was. Wyatt had his doubts at this point.

"Yeah, well it's no walk in the park for me either," Wyatt said, attacking the Parmigiano-Reggiano like it had personally insulted him.

"Really?" Ryan sounded surprised and Wyatt looked up to find that he'd come around the kitchen island and was now seriously encroaching in his personal space bubble.

It was a mistake. They both knew it. But this thing had been bubbling away all afternoon like a good Sunday meat sauce, and Wyatt was running out of ways to tell his body *no*.

Besides, he thought with resignation, they hadn't eaten the roasted garlic goat cheese yet.

Wyatt set the cheese grater down decisively. "Really," he repeated.

The earthy scent of the cheese was still floating in the air as he reached out for Ryan at the same moment Ryan reached for him. His skin was damp under Wyatt's hands, and he wanted to taste it still, to reacquaint himself with the flavor, but he was too desperate for Ryan's mouth.

Later, he told himself. Even though they both knew there wasn't going to be a later. There was just going to be this desperate, electric, sweaty kiss.

Ryan's fingers dug past the waistband of his shorts and pulled him hard, until they were crowded up together. His mouth was devouring Wyatt's, like he couldn't stop, like he wouldn't stop.

It sucked that Wyatt was going to have to be the reasonable one when the last thing he wanted was to push Ryan away.

Somehow, he did it.

"We can't do this," he gasped into the space between them. Just a moment before they'd been a moment away from taking this even further. His dick protested that it wasn't going to be happening after all.

His heart was protesting too, but Wyatt was already in trouble enough, so he ignored both of them.

"I know." Ryan sounded wrecked. Wyatt couldn't see his expression because he couldn't look at him right now. If he looked, he'd do more that he regretted.

"I'm going to Napa tomorrow," Wyatt reminded him. *Go find someone else.*

Ryan didn't say anything; he just turned and walked out of the kitchen.

Wyatt had a feeling that he wouldn't see him back for dinner.

Chapter Nine

WHEN RYAN HEARD THE engine of Wyatt's motorcycle revving to take off, and the gate closing behind him, he sighed in relief and leaned against the dresser in his room.

He was supposed to be getting ready for his meeting with Eric this morning, but he'd been fighting the compulsion to exit the house, walk across the yard, and knock on Wyatt's door. Tell him not to go. Tell him to bring Ryan with him.

Beg him to change his mind, even though that was the very last thing Ryan should ever ask him to do.

He should feel relief that he was on his own again—he'd always felt like he was the best version of himself free and unencumbered—but the house already felt empty because he knew if he walked into the kitchen, there wouldn't be a familiar pair of blue eyes or that smile.

Ryan took the bike, hoping the speed and adrenaline would dispel the frustration bubbling away inside of him. By the time he made it to the café, he felt a little better but still edgy.

"You look like someone shot your dog," Eric said when Ryan sat down at the table.

"What the hell, man," Ryan said, now even more annoyed. "Why would you even say that?" He could usually handle Eric's usual lack of tact and incredibly blunt delivery. He could even appreciate it at points.

He was not appreciating it now.

"Because you look pissed off," Eric said.

Ryan sighed and leaned back in the chair, stretching out his legs from the ride in, crossing his feet at the ankles. "You're an asshole."

"I'm an asshole because I said it looks like someone shot your dog or I'm an asshole because I'm forcing you to give up on Dream Chef and find someone else to be your fake boyfriend?"

"Both." Ryan scowled.

"But mostly the latter," Eric deduced. He wouldn't be as good of an agent if he wasn't brilliant at reading people. Or probably as much of an asshole. The realization was a cold comfort, and Ryan realized that for the first time, the possibility of being traded or waived by the Dodgers didn't fill him with the worst dread.

It was Wyatt getting on his bike and going back to Napa, never to be seen again.

Ryan pushed the thought away, rationalizing that the only reason that he felt this way was because Wyatt had left this morning. *But he's coming back*, he told himself firmly.

"Fine. Whatever. Yes."

"Dream Chef is no doubt very dreamy," Eric said dryly. "I heard you took him surfing. I also heard you took him to Flor's house."

"You heard?" Ryan raised an eyebrow, feeling dangerously on the edge of getting *very* pissed. "I thought we talked about this. I don't like being followed."

Eric usually backed down when he heard that tone of voice, but this time he didn't. "You should be happy it was me and not some random photographer."

"I'm not important enough for the paparazzi to stake out," Ryan argued.

"As soon as they scent the possibility that you've found someone, they're going to want to know who it is. And those pictures will be very valuable."

"I thought we were going to organize that so I didn't have to worry about being stalked by the paps?" Ryan said.

"We are. But you have to have a significant other to take that romantic walk on the beach at Malibu. Or however we decide to do it. You have to have *someone*."

Ryan's stomach cramped at the idea that it wasn't going to be Wyatt. He put it down to low blood sugar. Being hangry always made him crabby as hell.

"Can we order? I'm starving."

"Sure, whatever, yes." Eric raised his hand and the waitress came rushing over. She was blonde and pretty, and Ryan wondered vaguely if she was his latest affair.

They ordered. Ryan ordered too much food, everything on the menu that wasn't something Wyatt had made him already. He didn't want a direct comparison; he honestly wasn't sure he could handle it. It was already fucking difficult to push the thought of Wyatt away just so he could keep it together. He didn't need Eric watching him cry into his cereal bowl.

"I found a great guy for you," Eric said as soon as the waitress left. "You're gonna love him."

Ryan knew he was pouting. He knew it was unattractive. He didn't give a shit. "I don't wanna love him. That's not the point."

"Okay, he'll be easy to tolerate." Eric pulled a picture out of his briefcase and slid it over. The guy was very cute, just as advertised. Blond twink material; bright green eyes and an infectious smile. Ryan tried to dredge up even a fraction of interest and failed.

"What's his name?" Ryan said, because he needed to say *something*. Eric was clearly eager and they needed to get this done.

"Matt."

Ryan tried to imagine dating, fake or otherwise, Matt. He failed. "He's an actor?"

"He'll do whatever. He's very flexible."

Ryan shot Eric a dirty, dark look.

"I meant for the role," Eric clarified, but the look on his face told Ryan the whole story. He'd meant exactly what Ryan had thought he had. And maybe a few months ago, he *might* have wanted to hook up with Matt. The point of finding someone Ryan liked was to pave the way for that possibility, that eventuality.

But Ryan didn't want to hook up with Matt, no matter how flexible he was.

"I've got nudes too," Eric said, patting his briefcase. "Just in case you want to see."

"Jesus," Ryan exhaled. "You're a fucking menace."

"He offered them. He really wants the job."

Ryan was disgusted and did nothing to hide it. "He *needs* the job, you mean." He'd lived in LA almost his entire life, he knew exactly how many desperate, out-of-work actors there were, and what a lot of them would do for the money to stay, or even for a good word in the ear of the right people.

It wasn't surprising to Ryan that Eric would use that particular disadvantage to *his* advantage. Which had been one of the reasons Ryan hadn't wanted to use an actor for this.

Eric waved a hand. "They all do. It's not really a surprise."

Wyatt had needed a job, no matter what story his pride had told, and Ryan had given him one. He wanted to give Matt one for similar but very different reasons. Except even Ryan knew he couldn't employ the whole world.

"Just meet him," Eric cajoled. "One date."

Ryan didn't say a word. Just glared.

"Okay not a date. A meeting. A business meeting. Very straightforward, to the point."

"And we'll pay him for his time," Ryan said with a sharp nod. "Generously." It wasn't much, but it was what Ryan could do.

Eric frowned. "Two days. Saturday night, I'll send him to your house."

Ryan didn't really want Matt in his house. He was a stranger. Of course Wyatt had been a stranger too, though that had only felt true for a few short minutes. Maybe Ryan just needed to give Matt a chance.

"Fine."

"You know," Eric said, leaning back in his chair, looking smugly self-satisfied that he'd convinced Ryan to give Matt a chance, "you could always just fuck Wyatt on the down low if you want him so bad. Fake date Matt, and fuck Wyatt. It would work out okay."

Ryan was disgusted but even more disgusted with himself because that thought had definitely crossed his mind more than once. Except that he didn't want to *only* fuck Wyatt. They were friends. There were other undercurrents that Ryan couldn't quite explain. But while he definitely wanted to fuck him, that wasn't it.

"Thank you for the personal advice," Ryan said stiffly. "I'll take it under advisement."

The food came then, which Ryan was infinitely grateful for. He could eat and ignore Eric for the rest of the meeting.

Eric droned on as Ryan shoveled eggs and sausage into his mouth. "What about Adidas?" was the only question he inserted.

"Adidas?" Eric questioned, having the nerve to look peeved that his soliloquy was interrupted.

"Yeah, what about their direction? Did you convince them to keep the focus more LGBT-friendly?"

Eric pulled out his phone and scrolled until he found what he was looking for, and slid it across the table.

It was a mockup, with another random person standing in for Ryan. He was staring right through the screen, eyes piercing, and he was naked except for a pair of low-slung black athletic shorts and a pair of black Adidas shoes with the details picked out in a rainbow of colors. The baseball bat he was holding was the only movement in an otherwise static ad, holding it diagonally across his body, like it was just about to spring into action.

It was eye-catching and arresting and Ryan loved it.

"I don't know what you told them, but this is dynamite," Ryan enthused, something other than annoyed for the first time since he'd sat down.

"It looks good," Eric admitted. "They didn't have the bat at first, and it lacked something. Even they liked the idea of adding it."

"What about *Sports Illustrated*?" Ryan asked.

Eric chortled. "When they get a look at the preview for this ad, they're going to be falling all over themselves to do a cover shoot for Opening Day. Trust me. You're going to be the new Colin O'Connor."

It was a comparison that Ryan had experienced from the moment he'd very publicly come out of the closet right before the draft. It was one he respected and appreciated, but frankly, he was done being the next version of O'Connor. He was ready to differentiate himself and be the best version of Ryan Flores. This Adidas ad might be the first step in that direction.

"We talked about this," Ryan warned.

"I know, I know. We did. But *this*," Eric said, voice growing harsher around the edges as he pushed Matt's picture back in front of Ryan's plate, "is how we get you to the place you want to be."

"I already told you I'd meet with him," Ryan said, leaning back and crossing his arms across his chest. "You don't have to convince me."

"To *meet* with him? No. I don't. But to give up your fantasy of Dream Chef, *yes, I do*."

"Don't call him that." Ryan sighed. He ended up wanting to punch Eric in the face at some point during every meeting, but he was doing a great job of being infuriating today.

"It fits." Eric paused, and peeling a few twenties off the roll of cash he kept in his pocket, tossed them onto the table. "I have another meeting in a few. Are you done?"

Ryan was definitely done, though he was pretty sure that Eric was talking about the food still left on his plate. "Yeah," he said. He hadn't really been hungry after all. Or maybe he'd only been hungry for Wyatt's food.

If that was the case, then he was officially pathetic.

"You're wasting away," Eric said as he got up from the table. "Stop mooning after Dream Chef and get your mojo back."

"Saying shit like that is why you're getting a divorce," Ryan called out towards Eric's back, but he didn't turn around. It wasn't even true; Eric was in the middle of a horribly acrimonious divorce because he was a royal asshole.

He'd neatly maneuvered him into a corner where he couldn't help but seriously consider the possibility of fake dating Matt, no matter how much he didn't want to.

The problem, Ryan sighed, shoving his sunglasses back on his face, was that left him in a worse mood than he'd been in to begin with.

Wyatt had called his brothers and had told them to meet him at Nana's home that afternoon. Of course when he pulled into the lot, three minutes before the agreed upon time, they hadn't arrived yet.

It wasn't so much a surprise as it was a continual disappointment.

He checked his phone, cleared the handful of emails, and even though he didn't see any new texts, lingered over his conversation with Ryan anyway.

It felt stupid to text him that he'd arrived in Napa safely, because that wasn't something Ryan had asked of him. They were barely friends, clearly muddling through on that end, and anything else they could've been, Wyatt had shut down.

That didn't change the fundamental desire he felt to talk to him, even to send a short text telling him he'd arrived okay.

It was a problem, and one they were going to have to try to address when Wyatt got back to LA, because clearly it wasn't going away and it certainly wasn't getting any easier.

Wyatt checked in at the front desk, clipped the guest badge to his pocket, and went straight to his nana's room, hoping that he'd catch her in it. He hadn't told her he was coming because he hadn't known what to say to her after the incident over the phone the other day, and then the longer he'd gone without calling her had made him feel even worse.

Finally, it had just made sense to make the drive and try to find an equilibrium in person. He wasn't proud of it but he rationalized that her not recognizing his voice or his name had thrown him considerably and that she really did love surprises.

He found her in the same spot he'd left her at, only a few weeks before—sitting on her comfortable chair, a book in her lap, staring out the window at the garden.

"Nana," he said softly, and this time when she turned towards him, she didn't jerk and the book didn't fall. But her eyes were his worst nightmare come to life—completely, totally blank.

She didn't know him anymore.

Something nasty in his gut was clawing, desperate to get out, and he only held it together because he'd read that it was important not to upset the loved one when they didn't remember.

"Hello," Bea said quietly. She didn't ask his name, but she didn't have to. He saw the lack of recognition plain all over her face. He was a stranger to her, and he'd only left two weeks ago.

He should have been up here *every single damn week*, like he'd originally planned on doing. He'd not come last weekend because he'd told himself it felt wrong to leave Ryan when he'd just started the new job. But the truth cut a lot closer to the bone; he'd not wanted to leave because it was *Ryan*, and he was crazy about him, even if there was no fucking hope to be had.

"Hello," Wyatt parroted back, hands useless at his sides. He kept fucking waiting for the recognition to flash on her face, for her to realize he was her grandson, that she *loved* him. For her to throw her arms around him and proclaim how much she missed him, and how terrible her new painting was, but that she wanted him to see it anyway.

He'd even take her reciting the plot to the new romance novel she was reading this week.

"Wy, you're here," Tony's voice echoed from the doorway, but he felt growing horror as the recognition *did* begin to dawn on her, but it wasn't for him. It was for his brother.

"Tony, you came today," she exclaimed, rising to her feet and giving Tony the hug Wyatt craved.

It was even worse when she turned to him, and that little crease of uncertainty formed between her white brows when she looked at Wyatt.

"It's Wyatt, Nan, you know him. Your grandson." Tony's voice was patient, and he hadn't just had the legs cut out from under him, so he could still speak. But then it was Tony, Tony could give anyone a run for their money in the speaking department. It was probably why he went through girlfriends like candy bars.

"Wyatt," she said in a puzzled voice.

He saw the moment the fog lifted but even though he felt an incredible relief when she pulled him in for a tight hug, gripping him for far longer than she'd done with Tony, it was a bittersweet moment.

He'd known this was coming someday. He hadn't prepared for it, because he didn't think you really could prepare for the day when the woman who loved you and practically raised you didn't know who you were.

"Oh, I'm so glad you're here, Wyatt," Nana said in a soft voice. She didn't mention the lack of recognition earlier, and that was consistent too with what he'd read about her condition. "How is the new job in LA?" she asked, drawing him over to the couch, sitting down next to him.

He kept her tiny, gnarled hand curled in his. When Tony gave him a look, Wyatt glared at him. Tony could care about all that fake-machismo shit; Wyatt was going to spend time with his grandmother while he still could. Besides, Tony knew Wyatt had never given a crap about all that anyway.

And suddenly, people knowing that wasn't as terrifying as it had been only a few hours earlier. Wyatt had always heard people talk about life-changing events that drastically altered your priorities but he'd never experienced it for himself. Before today, he'd always assumed they over-dramatized the situation in the re-telling, but now Wyatt realized they hadn't. It really happened, and it was happening to him.

"It's good, it's real good," he told her. He didn't tell her that every day was an exercise in frustration. "I like my boss a lot. He's really nice. A friend, almost."

"She said you were cooking for some hotshot ball player," Tony inserted.

Wyatt looked over at his brother. His hair was cropped close, one of his tattoos poking out of his t-shirt sleeve. He looked good, better than he'd seen him in awhile. If the new girlfriend was the cause for this, then Wyatt found he might actually approve for once. "Yeah, I am." He hesitated, usually never wanting to test Tony's comfort level with anything but straight white men, but *fuck it all*. "Ryan Flores."

But there was only approval and excitement on Tony's face, and it occurred to Wyatt that even as he'd been working his ass off in Bastian Aquino's kitchen and so many others and learning a bushel of life lessons, Tony might have been growing up too. It was a strange thought, his brother acting like an adult, and it set Wyatt's world even more off-kilter.

"No shit? That's pretty cool. He's a great player. Got a bright future. Might actually get the Dodgers a ring one of these days. You're his private chef, Nan said?"

No mention of Ryan's homosexuality. No mention that he was Puerto Rican. Wyatt let out a breath. "Yeah, I'm cooking for him."

"Speaking of jobs," Nana interrupted firmly. "Where is Marco?"

"Actually working today," Tony said, turning his full-charm smile onto his grandmother. "Imagine that."

"Imagine that," Wyatt repeated back wryly.

Nana elbowed him hard in the side. "I know Marco can be difficult sometimes, but he's still your brother, and he tries."

"When it's convenient for him," Wyatt said under his breath, ribs still smarting.

"I'm cooking in the kitchen over at the Napa Tavern," Tony said. "You know the place?"

Wyatt did know the place and nodded. It was several steps above some of the shitholes Tony had worked at in the past and served good burgers. It wasn't Terroir, but then Tony had gotten kicked out of culinary school for rarely going to class, and then mouthing off when he actually went, so Terroir was way out of his league.

Stupidly, Tony had seemingly resented Wyatt's climb up the ladder of success, while never really attempting it himself. Wyatt had never understood why. Tony had lots of talent, though little taught skill, but everything he'd squandered, he'd squandered himself.

"You need to take me there sometime, Tony," Nana said kindly.

Tony and Wyatt exchanged dubious looks. The Tavern was not a place that Nana would enjoy. "We'll take you to Terroir next time they do Sunday brunch, how about that?" Wyatt asked. He could probably get Aquino to part with passes. *Probably.*

Or maybe he could convince Kian to get them on the guest list.

"Maybe Tony's new friend could join us," Nana offered.

"Yeah, I heard you had a new girlfriend," Wyatt said dutifully, because Tony was his brother and not a total waste of space. And even though she would probably be done with him in six months tops, Wyatt still felt obligated to show a vague interest.

But to Wyatt's surprise, Tony flushed. "Uh, yeah. About that . . ." He hesitated, and Wyatt didn't understand what was going on. Tony was always eager to talk about his latest hookup.

"Tony's girlfriend isn't a girlfriend, I guess," Nana said softly. "I misunderstood the last time we spoke, Wyatt."

Wyatt could not understand what was happening right now.

Tony, who had been part and parcel with Marco over the years. Not rampantly homophobic, but exuding all sorts of bullshit toxic masculinity? Who had bullied Wyatt for hitting or running like a girl? *Tony* was not straight?

"Nana," Tony hissed, but he looked pleased. Like he was happy it was finally out of the bag. "You were supposed to let me tell him."

"Oh, yes, I suppose I should have. I'm sorry, Tony."

Wyatt could only sit there in shock as his brother came out to him.

Not once in his life had he *ever* been envious of either of his brothers. Not a single fucking time. And now, he was green through and through with jealousy. Because Tony had found his nerve and his balls and his bravery before Wyatt had. He should be happy for him, proud of him, but the truth was that he was fucking envious.

"I'm just happy you're happy," Wyatt could only say woodenly.

"I am," Tony said, and for the first time, Wyatt could see that he was. And not only happy, but *free.*

The jealousy billowing in him grew exponentially.

"Let's go see my new painting, boys," Nana said, and they both stood, following her like she'd bidden them.

"I hope that everything's okay between us," Tony whispered, leaning towards Wyatt.

Wyatt could only stare back at him incredulously. He *must* know. "You know it is. You know I'm gay." He'd never explicitly told either of his brothers, but he'd always figured they must have some idea. The complete lack of girlfriends had probably tipped them off.

"Yeah, of course. I know." The sympathy in Tony's eyes was galling and it shouldn't have been. Wyatt should have been over the moon for him right now. "I just figured. She might not be around, at least as herself, for much longer." Tony shrugged. "I didn't want her memories of me to be a lie, and the more I thought about it, the righter it seemed. To tell her the truth. To tell other people the truth."

Nana brought them to the art studio at the home, and Wyatt stood in front of Nana's new painting, making all the appropriate noises, saying all the right things, but internally he was reeling.

Why hadn't he thought about this situation with Nana like Tony had? Why had he seen the situation through shades of fear, instead of trusting the woman who had raised him and loved him? Why had he doubted her inherent ability to love him unconditionally? He loved *her* unconditionally. He'd accepted everything that she was dealing with, and had done everything in his meager power to make sure she was protected and safe and taken care of.

Why had he assumed that she would feel any less towards him?

When he and Tony finally exited the home, Wyatt felt like he'd been wading through fog for the better part of the two hours he'd spend with her.

"You look thrown, man," Tony said, clapping him hard on the shoulder as they paused near Wyatt's bike. "Were you going to tell her first or?" He hesitated, like he'd been waiting for Wyatt to come out first, like Wyatt had that right in the family.

It was still too new for Wyatt to trust Tony, to confide in him. No matter what sexuality he was. "I don't know what you're talking about."

"Yes, you do," Tony said evenly. "I'm just figuring my shit out, and for awhile, I figured it was your turn first. You've been waiting a long time. New job. I figure you must be hooking up with Flores, that's why you left Terroir."

Wyatt rolled his eyes. Trust Tony to be so close, yet so far, from the truth. "I'm not hooking up with Flores." *Present tense.* "I left Terroir because the Bastard pays pennies on the dollar. I needed the money to help pay for Nana's care."

Tony had the nerve to look ashamed. "I'm sorry about that. I think in a month or two, I can start contributing too. And I'll harass Marco. He always seems to have money, though god knows I don't want to know where he gets it from."

"I don't know if I want Marco's blood money," Wyatt snarked. Was Tony even joking? Wyatt wasn't sure he wanted to know either.

"I'll just tell him to send you the legitimately earned dollars," Tony teased, sliding his sunglasses back on his face. "I've got to run, but don't be a stranger." They hugged, quick and tight, and Wyatt tried to remember the last time they'd even touched, never mind embraced. When they were kids, probably. And that made more sense now than it had ever made back then. Poor Tony, hiding for so long. It ached, that knowledge, but Wyatt still couldn't seem to assuage the jealousy.

Tony's old Mustang was parked next to Wyatt's bike. The paint looked better, and when Tony slid into it and started it, it didn't rumble like it was about to explode in fifteen seconds.

It was hard to realign his world again, but Wyatt realized as he climbed onto his bike that Tony was actually getting his shit together.

For the first time ever, maybe it was time for Wyatt to follow in his big brother's footsteps.

CHAPTER TEN

"I can't believe Tony is gay," Xander said, setting his glass down on the old picnic table they'd scrounged up and set up outside on the cracked concrete patio two summers ago.

It was a balmy fall evening in Napa, and even though it was late when Xander and Kian had gotten off work, they'd obviously sensed Wyatt was troubled, and had brought out a six-pack to join him. Or to prevent him from brooding further.

"Maybe you should hook up with him," Kian inserted slyly, and something in his tone made Wyatt sad. Melancholy and missing the old, too-innocent boy who never would have suggested that. Or teased Xander with the knowledge that he didn't hook up with anyone. Clearly Nate living here was not good for him.

"With Wyatt's older, bad-boy brother? No, thanks. I don't have that much of a masochistic streak," Xander said after taking a long gulp of beer. "What about you?" he suggested, turning the tables back on Kian. "You're about the age where making a bad romantic decision feels right."

Except they both knew that Kian was already making a bad romantic decision, and instead of it being open and then closed, it was ongoing. Never-ending, until it finally, irrevocably ended.

"Yeah, no, thanks. Gross." Kian shuddered. "No offense, Wyatt."

"None taken," Wyatt said wryly, glad he was here, and glad that his friends could distract him from brooding over this afternoon's reveal.

"Are you going to tell her then?" Xander asked. He was a huge advocate for bluntness, in just ripping the Band-Aid right off. In his mind, it might hurt, but then you knew exactly where you stood. He'd been telling Wyatt to tell his nana for years now. Wyatt was not entirely pleased that Xander had turned out to be one hundred percent right.

He also fully expected Xander to exploit that, but he hadn't so far. Maybe he was waiting until it smarted less.

"I think so, yeah." Wyatt thought about telling them about Ryan, and about Ryan's offer that he could now accept without fear.

Would Ryan still want him? Was Wyatt okay accepting his offer when he really wanted so much more?

Before, not being Ryan's fake boyfriend had seemed like the worst thing that could happen, and now that possibilities were opening up, it seemed even more devastating that he might be able to go through the motions, but could never have what he really wanted for real.

"You could have done it years ago. I told you that she wasn't going to reject you," Xander said. So much for waiting until it stung a little less.

Wyatt tipped his beer bottle at his friend. "Thank you, friend, for always being brutally honest and for never wasting an opportunity to say *I told you so.*"

"Those are Xander's four favorite words in the English language," Kian said. He sounded edgy and resentful. Wyatt could only imagine what kind of shit Xander was giving him over Bastian. Or what kind of shit Aquino was giving him.

"All I'm saying is that it's not going to end well for you," Xander said tiredly. "I don't want you to get hurt."

"You don't know that," Kian said stubbornly. Wyatt felt like he'd just been dropped into the hundredth iteration of this particular argument. Maybe the thousandth.

"He's not a good guy. He's an asshole," Xander argued. "You *know* this." And suddenly, understandably, they were talking about the Bastard.

"You're an asshole too, and I don't want you to be alone. Just because people are tough doesn't mean they don't deserve love, and doesn't mean they're incapable of returning it."

Kian, Wyatt realized, was wading in even deeper. He was going to try to "rescue" Bastian Aquino from his lonely, miserable, angry existence.

Yeah, that was going to end *really* well.

Maybe it was selfish, but Wyatt was sort of relieved that they'd at least forgotten about his own problems, and were back to focusing on their own.

"I can't talk to you about this," Xander said in mounting frustration. He got up from the table, beer bottle empty. "I worked fourteen hours today. Will probably work sixteen tomorrow. I'm going to bed. It was good to see you, Wy, don't be a stranger. And for god's sake, go tell your nana you're gay."

The door to the house slammed behind him as punctuation.

"He's gotten so grumpy," Kian said, picking at the label on his bottle.

"I think he's worried about you," Wyatt said, and it wasn't even a lie.

"Don't be ridiculous," Kian said.

"You're in love with Aquino, and he's right. If he ever returns those feelings, he's still going to eat you whole, chew you up, and then spit you out. And coming from someone who's had a fraction of that happen to them before, it's not fun. It's not something to look forward to."

Kian's voice was quiet. "What if you believed that no matter how much it hurt, it would still be worth it?"

He knew, Wyatt realized. He knew that it was going to end, and he was never going to get a happy ending with Bastian Aquino, and he didn't even care. He loved him that much. So much for this being some sort of puppy-love crush that Kian would eventually get over.

And, Wyatt realized, as Kian patted him on the shoulder on his way inside, it even made some kind of twisted sense.

It would absolutely hurt like hell whenever the professional relationship between him and Ryan ended. It would hurt if it ended and nothing ever happened between them again. It wouldn't hurt worse if he got another taste of something more personal. At least if it ended then, he would have gotten something good out of it.

He would have been able to love Ryan for the time he was able, up close and personal, instead of staring in the window, wishing for something he couldn't have.

❧❧❧❧❧ ❧❧❧❧❧

"Hi," Wyatt said, placing his drivers license on the front desk corner with a decisive click, "I'm here to visit Bea Blake. And I don't know if he's available, but I'd like to talk to the doctor in charge of her case."

"Dr. Martinez? I'm not sure if he's in today," the front desk attendant said sympathetically. "But you can speak to the nurse on call?"

"That would be fine," Wyatt said with a certainty he didn't feel. He'd spent most of the night sitting outside at the rickety old picnic table, downing beer after beer, trying to drown out the fear that kept insisting he was making a mistake.

Finding out Tony had told Nana and she hadn't thrown him out, or told him he was going to hell, or that he wasn't lovable anymore—even though he was Tony—should have swept all Wyatt's insecurities clean. But it turned out that it wasn't as easy as deciding to do it and doing it.

Fear still held him back, still whispered things in his ear. It didn't matter if his head knew they weren't true, his heart still felt the echo of them.

"I'll go get the nurse," the young lady said with a smile. "Do you want to wait in the lobby?"

Wyatt wiped his damp palms on his jeans. He'd hoped for a quick, five-minute conversation, and then he could go find Nana and finally tell her the truth. But he'd also promised himself he'd talk to someone on her case about her memory loss patches recently. He needed to know what to expect. Online research was only getting him so far.

"Sure."

"There's coffee if you'd like some," she said, gesturing to the carafe set up in the lobby. "Help yourself."

The last thing he needed was more coffee, and he'd had the coffee here before and knew it was awful. He wished he'd asked to talk to the doctor on the way out, and then he wouldn't be spending more time waiting. Waiting until visiting hours today started had been hard enough.

The dark evil sludge that came out of the coffee carafe was the same as he'd remembered it, but optimistically he thought that at least it must be strong. He stirred in a sugar packet, looked askance at the fake cups of creamer, and grimaced when he took his first sip.

Still, it had wasted at least two minutes. Two minutes was good.

Two minutes he didn't have to think about what Nana might look like when he finally told her the truth.

He'd wanted to text Ryan since last night, since he'd made up his mind, and it might have been easier to focus on the good things that would probably happen after he took this step. But he hadn't known what to say to him. After all, he'd already unequivocally told him no, with no hope that he might change his mind.

Ryan had probably already moved on to someone else. And considering how fixated he was on a fake boyfriend, how could Wyatt possibly hope to win him as a real one?

"Mr. Blake?" He turned, and a woman, mid-thirties, with blonde hair and kind eyes was standing at the entrance to the lobby. "They said you wanted to talk about your grandmother's case?"

"Yes, I did," he said, thankful that he hadn't had to wait long.

"She's in her art class now," she said. "I'll walk you down there and we can talk. I'm Gretchen, by the way."

He shook the hand she offered. Noticed it was trembling a little. Hoped that she'd put it down to the caffeine in the noxious liquid they passed for coffee.

"I've recently moved away for work," he said. "I can't get here as much as I'd like to. I know consistency and routine are really important for her mental state. But I can only get here maybe once a week. I'm still calling regularly though. And last week, she didn't recognize my voice or my name right away." His voice broke on the last few words, and he gritted his teeth, knowing that couldn't be explained by the terrible coffee and hoping that he wouldn't actually burst into tears in the middle of the lobby.

She took his elbow and steered him down one of the wide hallways. "I've consulted extensively with Dr. Martinez about your grandmother's case," she said. "I'm sorry to say, that's not a huge surprise. She's going to have lapses."

"I didn't think they'd come so quickly."

"Alzheimer's is a disease we still don't know very much about. There's going to be accelerated periods and then periods when her condition stabilizes. Moving here and uprooting her from her home probably sent her in a bit of an accelerated period, but it should stabilize. I'm assuming she does eventually recognize you."

"It's usually only a minute or so. She recognized my brother Tony right away."

"That's good," she said, even though it wasn't.

He wanted to tell her how unfair it was that Tony would be the one she'd remember. That he'd quit his prestigious job so he could earn more money to take care of her. That she was the only person in his life that he knew he couldn't lose; which meant, of course, that she was the one he was bound to lose.

"It's not good. None of this is good," he practically growled. It was instantly embarrassing, and that wasn't just because her face fell.

"Of course it's not good," she hastily corrected. "I don't mean that. I'm sorry for sounding callous or insensitive."

"You're not . . . I'm just . . . on edge," he said. Which was the best way to phrase it. He took another gulp of the devil coffee, even though there was no way it could help.

"I've spent some time with Mrs. Blake," she said, "and I promise you, she's who she was before. The disease hasn't progressed enough to erode the foundation of who she is. You have a lot of time before that happens. The best advice I can give you is to take advantage before that happens. Too many people I see wish that they'd spent more time, or called more, or made more happy times with their loved ones."

"That won't be a mistake I'll be making," Wyatt vowed. He'd figure out a regular visit schedule and call every day.

It didn't even matter if there wasn't anything to say. Just hearing her voice would be enough.

But most of all, he was going to begin this new routine by telling her the truth.

They stopped in front of a classroom with the door open. Wyatt could smell paint and thinner wafting out. "She's right in there," Gretchen said with a smile. "You want to get her?"

"Wyatt, not that I'm not glad to see you, but that was my painting class." Bea Blake didn't look very happy as he took her arm and led her out one of the big double doors to the garden. The same garden she was always looking at.

Maybe it wasn't enough to stare at the grounds out the window.

Also maybe he wouldn't cry if he told her in a semi-public place.

"I'm going back down to LA right after this," he said, leading them to a secluded corner of the garden, and sitting down on the bench there. "But I wanted to see you before I left."

Her face softened. "I can catch up later," she promised. "I'm glad you came by."

Good, because he already had enough guilt saved up to last a long while. He didn't need to add delaying her completing her painting onto his already heavy conscience.

"I wanted to tell you something, actually." He took a deep breath. For a second, he thought about bringing up Tony, but reconsidered. This needed to be just about him.

Bea reached out and took his hand in hers. "You know you could tell me anything, darling boy, and I'd love you regardless."

It wasn't as if she had ever said anything different. She'd been variations on the same theme for his entire life, but between losing both his parents, and never being close to his brothers, he'd always been too afraid to believe that she wouldn't just abandon him too. No matter what she said.

But for the very first time, he found the echo of truth ringing in her words. She meant it, and she trusted him to trust *her*.

"Nana, I'm gay." He'd thought of so many lead-ins. So many excuses. So many ways to word it over the years. He'd tasted the words on his tongue more times than he could even count. So when it came down to it, maybe it was better to keep it simple. Straightforward. The bare bones of truth.

Bea's face didn't change, her smile just softened another degree. "Oh darling, I know. It's okay. I love you no matter what."

"What? You *knew*? Who told you?" Wyatt shouldn't be panicking because he'd actually managed to tell her the truth, and nothing had changed. But he was. How had she known? And how long had she known?

He'd been torturing himself for how many years for *no good fucking reason*.

"Nobody had to tell me. I have eyes," she retorted tartly. "I know you. I love you. Also, you've never had a girlfriend. It wasn't hard to put two and two together."

"Oh." The wind out of his sails, he crumpled against her, like he was still that eight-year-old kid, whose dad had just left, abandoning his mom and his two brothers. Like he was thirteen and his mom had just passed.

"It's alright," she soothed, her hand combing his hair back from his forehead. "Everything is alright."

And for the first time in a very long time, Wyatt believed her.

⁕⁕⁕

"Thanks for coming over," Ryan said tightly, awkward as he sat across from Matt on the uncomfortable living room couch he never sat on. Why was he sitting on it now?

Because he couldn't imagine welcoming Matt into the kitchen. That was Wyatt's domain now, and Ryan wasn't going to betray him like that. He didn't want him in any part of the house he'd shared with Wyatt, and that had only left the living room.

Not that he had any intentions of hooking up with Matt. He was definitely as cute as his pictures had promised—bright, hopeful green eyes and short spiky blond hair. There had been more than one moment when Ryan had caught him checking him out.

It should have made Ryan want to lead him right back to the bedroom. Or the couch. Or any convenient horizontal surface. But instead they'd ended up in the uncomfortable, stuffy living room that he never used—for good reason.

"Are you okay?" Matt asked. "You don't seem all that happy I'm here."

"It's not you," Ryan insisted, feeling guilt swamp him. He was being an asshole, and for what? Because Matt's green eyes weren't blue, and he didn't like to surf?

It wasn't Matt's fault that he wasn't Wyatt.

"Seriously," he continued. "I'm sorry. I . . . I don't really want to do this. But I need to."

Matt's expression was sympathetic. "I get it."

Besides, if he couldn't have Wyatt, why did it matter who played his fake boyfriend?

"Let's get out of here," Ryan said with a grimace at their surroundings. Coming in here had been a bad idea. "Grab a beer and go outside to the fire pit. Try to get to know each other. We're going to be spending some time together and we can't keep acting like strangers."

Matt raised an eyebrow, getting to his feet. "Are you sure?"

He wasn't sure at all. But he had to move past this, because something kept tugging him back and Ryan didn't like anything holding him in, or holding him back. "Yeah, I am."

"Well, I'll be honest I need this job, so I'm going to stop being a selfless good guy and asking you if you're okay with it."

Ryan barked out a laugh and led him into the kitchen. "I guess being an actor in LA isn't all that easy."

Matt nodded vehemently, leaning against the island and launching into a long, over-dramatic story about some audition he'd just been on. Ryan tried to ignore the voice in the back of his head that said this was like every bad first date he'd been on, and listen to Matt's story.

Frankly, this was one of the reasons he'd stopped going on first dates.

Ryan pulled a pair of beers from the fridge and ignored the other voice that reminded him this was Wyatt's favorite brand.

Matt paused when Ryan handed him the bottle. "Are you even listening to me?" he demanded.

Ryan froze. "I'm sorry?"

Matt set the bottle on the counter with a decisive click. "You said you wanted to get to know me. You said you were doing this. And hey, I'm an actor. I can work with almost nothing. But you can't get far enough away from me and you're barely paying attention to anything I say. Honestly, usually I don't have to work this hard to make a guy interested in me."

"I'm sorry," Ryan repeated, and he *was*, but not that sorry. "It's not you, it's me." He imagined how much Eric was going to drive him crazy over this. How painful his grating, obnoxious whining would be. He imagined Wyatt coming back and Ryan dropping to his knees and *begging* him to reconsider. He imagined leaving Flor and LA and everything he loved. He imagined terrible winters in Ohio or Wisconsin or the death trap of the Trop.

But nothing seemed quite as terrible as doing this.

"Seriously?" Matt demanded, and the worst thing was that Ryan even sympathized with him. "What is with you? It's not like we're going to declare our eternal love or register at Macy's or adopt a kid. We're going to hold hands and I'm going to go to your games and wear your jersey and be cute in the wives' section. We don't even have to hook up if you don't want to, though I wouldn't exactly mind."

Alarm bells were clanging in his head. It wasn't like he *wanted* to do any of those things. Not even with Wyatt—though it was scary as fuck that doing them with him didn't sound all that bad—but he didn't want to hook up with this cute guy.

He couldn't have gotten it up right now if he was being paid or he was being jacked full of Viagra.

Of course that was the moment the back door to the kitchen opened and a pair of blue eyes narrowed, taking in the scene in front of him.

Ryan. And a young, cute guy. Beers in front of them. *Wyatt's* favorite brand, even.

"You're back," Ryan said, fifty percent excited, fifty percent panicked.

Matt's sympathetic look at Ryan was galling, and definitely deserved. He was totally fucked over this guy, and if even Matt could tell with about ten seconds of evidence, then it was probably extremely obvious.

"I'm back," Wyatt said slowly. His hand was still on the doorknob, and he hadn't taken a single step into the kitchen.

"This is Matt," Ryan said, because Flor had drilled good manners into him. "This is my private chef. And friend. Wyatt."

"I'm going to be Ryan's fake boyfriend," Matt said, piping up, and fucking him over big-time. Even though Ryan had literally been about to tell him that *no*, he wasn't about to be his fake boyfriend. Ryan had been about to say that if he couldn't have Wyatt, he didn't want anyone, no matter how insane that sounded.

It *was* insane; Wyatt would never believe it. And from the doubting, incredulous expression on his face now, Ryan wondered if he could even keep him in his life after this clusterfuck.

"No, you're not," Ryan insisted desperately.

Matt crossed his arms and raised his eyebrows.

Wyatt wasn't reacting at all, though. He still had that deadened expression on his face, completely shut down, like this was his worst nightmare and he couldn't quite process it.

Ryan totally understood that mind frame; he was smack in the middle of it right now.

"I need to talk to you," Ryan said, directing his desperation in the right direction this time.

Wyatt crossed his arms over his chest, mimicking Matt. He didn't really have a right to be upset. Jealous, maybe, but Ryan found he didn't give a shit right now what was deserved and what wasn't.

Ryan wasn't going to beg in front of that little snot Matt, so he did the next best thing. He walked towards the doorway, stopped right in front of Wyatt, and waited for him to give in.

"Fine," Wyatt said, breaking after half a minute of tense silence. He backed up and Ryan followed him out to his little cottage. Wyatt had left the door open behind him, but Ryan shut it decisively. He didn't even care if Matt decided to help himself to whatever in the house. If Matt robbed him blind, it still wouldn't matter.

"I'm sorry about that," Ryan said.

But Wyatt only shrugged. "You said you were going to do it. You had to find someone else. I didn't really expect to come home and find him in the kitchen, but it's your house."

Ryan opened his mouth to say that it *was* his house, but that it didn't matter because in the end, Matt wasn't going to be his fake boyfriend. Not now, not in a day or a week or in a hundred years. Except Wyatt kept talking.

"The thing is," he continued, beginning to pace back in forth in the tiny living room, "I realized something in Napa this weekend. And I came home because I wanted to tell you that I'd changed my mind. So seeing him in there threw me. I didn't like it."

Ryan gaped. "You didn't like it?"

"I fucking hated it, okay?" Wyatt turned and there was something fierce and hot in his blue eyes. They latched right onto Ryan's face and he felt like he was burning under the heat of that gaze. "If you need a fake boyfriend, I want it to be me."

He stalked right up to where Ryan was standing mute and disbelieving. "Tell me it can be me."

Ryan did the only thing that made any sense in this fucked-up situation: he placed his hands on Wyatt's chest, and kissed him.

He didn't react, just stayed frozen in place. Ryan pulled back a fraction. "Please," Wyatt begged, voice cracking, "please tell me that this means yes."

Ryan laughed, and it felt like the weight of the decision lifted with each exhale. "Yes. Yes. Yes."

"Oh thank god," Wyatt breathed out, and his hands reached out, grasping Ryan's waist. "Because I missed this too much."

I missed you too. The thought was instant, but Ryan was prevented from saying it because Wyatt pulled him even closer, until they were flush against each other, and kissed him.

It was everything like their first kiss—the sudden burst of heat and electricity that had flared between them from the first moment—but even though the intensity was just as fierce, it felt calmer, mellower. Much more certain. As if Wyatt had finally realized that this wouldn't be their last kiss, but the first in a long chain of them.

"Fuck it," Ryan breathed into Wyatt's mouth, every nerve ending in his body lighting the way they never could for Matt. He dropped his hand to the growing bulge in Wyatt's jeans, because now that he was allowed, that he was allowing himself, he didn't want to waste another second doing something other than touching Wyatt every way he'd dreamt about.

"Right now?" Wyatt murmured wryly. "But there's that guy in your kitchen." It wasn't like Matt was stopping Wyatt either, because his hands were already at the waist of Ryan's shorts, hooking into the elastic and pulling them down.

"You want to wait any longer?" Ryan asked, breathless because Wyatt's big capable hands were already curling around his dick, and he hadn't been completely hard before, but he definitely was now.

It was like Wyatt knew he needed it a little rough, because his callouses were sliding along his length and his thumb was curling around the head of his cock and it felt so good, he could only pant into Wyatt's neck.

"I'm done waiting," Wyatt said, sounding so final that Ryan quivered at the implications. This was supposed to be them agreeing to be *fake* boyfriends. But it felt real, like it was so much more than just playacting in front of a camera.

But then, there wasn't a camera here now, was there? And they were both so into each other that nothing, including Matt stealing all his worldly possessions, would have torn him away from Wyatt.

Wyatt twisted especially hard, and Ryan groaned. "I said," Wyatt repeated with a grin, "that I was done waiting."

"Oh. Right." Ryan scrambled for the button and the fly on Wyatt's jeans, and tugged them down, along with his boxer briefs. Wyatt's cock was just as perfect as Ryan had remembered (and fantasized about). He'd been wanting this for weeks now, and now that he was finally going to get it again, he wasn't going to half-ass it.

Ryan matched Wyatt's pumping rhythm, slow and a little rough, because he'd figured out that was how Wyatt must like it. And sure enough, his head lolled back, eyes glazing over, as Ryan worked his hand over his dick.

"Tonight," Wyatt panted, "we're going to do this again. Slower. Better."

Ryan definitely remembered how it had been last time. Not exactly slow, but a steady, inexorable burn of pleasure that had left him hazy for hours after. And if that happened again, Ryan definitely wasn't going to complain. But that wasn't what he was in the mood for.

"Oh, yeah, it's gonna be better," Ryan promised. "Slow. Definitely." Gasped as Wyatt's hand tugged him just right. He was going to lose it, because it had been too long without those hands on him. "But it's gonna be you at my mercy."

Wyatt's sly expression, agreeing to all that and more was what did it for Ryan, and he came with a low cry, orgasming over Wyatt's hand.

"Shit," Wyatt groaned, and followed right after Ryan.

Laughing, Ryan steered them over to the kitchenette and with a free hand grabbed some paper towels. They cleaned up, but he couldn't quite meet Wyatt's eyes. This was just supposed to be about them hooking up, but because of how much they'd wanted each other it had somehow felt like more.

Ryan wasn't sure how he felt about that.

He did know he had to go see what Matt was doing in his kitchen, though.

"Are you just going to kick that guy out?" Wyatt asked as he zipped his jeans up.

Ryan raised an eyebrow. "Well he's definitely not staying."

"He doesn't seem like a bad guy."

Only Wyatt would find his rival nice.

"You talked to him for about thirty seconds and said less than ten words," Ryan pointed out.

"But you talked to him longer. He couldn't be all that bad," Wyatt said.

"Except," Ryan said, opening the door to head back to the house, "I only have one opening for a fake boyfriend, and that is currently filled."

To Ryan's surprise, Matt was still sitting in the kitchen, sipping on a beer, scrolling through his phone.

When they walked in, he looked up. "Ah, must have been a pretty good conversation," Matt said.

"It was okay," Ryan said nonchalantly.

Next to him, Wyatt tried—and failed—to stifle his laughter.

"I guess this means I didn't get the job," Matt observed, and Ryan felt a pulse of guilt at how bummed he sounded.

But before Ryan could tell him that he was sorry and that Eric would be in touch for the payment for this evening's "work," Wyatt was leaning over on the counter by him. "I know, it probably sounded really cushy," he said sympathetically. He glanced back at Ryan, but now he was smirking, and Ryan knew that expression promised bad things. "Hanging out with a cute guy, holding hands, going to free dinners and events and sitting in the wives' section at the Dodgers' stadium. But trust me, you dodged a bullet here."

"What?" Ryan squeaked out in surprise.

Matt's eyes had gone sly and calculating. "How so?"

Wyatt gestured to where Ryan was standing, but didn't take his eyes off Matt. "He's a spoiled brat of epic proportions. Expects you to wait on him, hand and foot. Expects you to tell him all the time how gorgeous he is, like the mirror isn't telling him the truth. And in bed? All taking and no giving. Trust me. You really ended up with the better part of this bargain."

Matt's eyes narrowed. "How do you know all this?"

"Duh. I'm his real boyfriend," Wyatt said. "Or maybe his sex slave. We haven't really put a label on it yet."

"I'm not really big on labels, *honey*," Ryan said, coming over, and slinging an arm roughly around Wyatt's shoulders. "Isn't that true?"

Wyatt barely lost a beat. "*And* he won't actually define your role, which means that he can decide it's whatever the fuck he needs *right now*."

Matt took another gulp of his beer. "If you're trying to make me feel better, it's not working."

Wyatt looked very surprised, and Ryan was very amused. He clearly had no idea what a terrible liar he was. "Why?"

"Because you're a really shitty liar, so I'd guess that whatever you're telling me is exactly the opposite of how he really is." Matt paused. "*Plus*, he hasn't exactly kicked you out of the house for saying all that, *and* he looks like he wants to drag you back to wherever you just went for round two. So I call bullshit."

Wyatt shrugged. "It was worth a try."

"I can do better than that," Ryan offered. "I'll find you another job. It won't be free dinners or holding hands or wearing my jersey in the wives' section, but I can see what I can do."

"Really?"

Ryan sighed at Matt's disbelieving tone. "Like I said, this was all me. Nothing to do with you. I'm sure you would have been a fantastic fake boyfriend, but there's someone a little more my style."

Matt raised an eyebrow. "I'm really not stupid, guys."

"What do you mean?" Wyatt asked.

"I mean, there *is* no fake-boyfriend position. You're clearly Ryan's *real* boyfriend," Matt said, slipping off the barstool. "Thanks for the entertainment and the spank bank material for later, but my Uber is here."

Ryan and Wyatt stood there, more than a little shocked, as Matt went out the back door with a single jaunty hand wave that just as easily could have been a middle finger.

"I don't think he likes us very much," was what Wyatt said after a silent moment.

Ryan was relieved that Wyatt was pointedly ignoring Matt's final comment about how they looked like they were really together. Wyatt had *just* agreed to play Ryan's boyfriend. He didn't need to have issues already with either of them believing it was more real than it actually was.

"He wasn't so bad," Ryan teased, turning in Wyatt's embrace. "Now maybe I should drag you back where we came from and do what Matt suggested and have round two."

Ryan swore he saw something flicker in Wyatt's eyes. Was it unease? Fear? Something else? But then Wyatt leaned down and kissed him, quick and fierce, and Ryan decided it was nothing. Nothing worth worrying over, anyway. Not when Wyatt's mouth was on his and his hands were all over his body. Everything that had been so close but so far these last few weeks.

He wasn't the type to deprive himself when he found something he really wanted, and he wasn't about to start now.

CHAPTER ELEVEN

Before he even opened his eyes, Wyatt knew the bed he'd been sleeping in wasn't his.

He knew this bed, though. Knew the mattress, the sheets, the particular natural scent of its regular occupant. Knew the occupant, intimately.

It was hard to forget the last time he'd woken up in this bed. He'd gone to make breakfast and had only figured out too late that Ryan had bailed. Escaped. Disappeared.

Wyatt reached out hesitantly, brushing the skin of Ryan's arm. His rhythmic breathing didn't change. Lying there, close enough to touch Ryan, he figured he had two choices.

One, get up and go start breakfast, like he'd done the last time. Hope that things would go differently and that Ryan wouldn't leave.

Two, wake Ryan up himself, and guarantee that he wouldn't leave because he didn't *want* to.

It wasn't even a choice. Door number one never had a chance. And maybe, Wyatt thought, pushing the sheet down his naked body, that wasn't fair, but he'd been trying to play fair up until now, and that hadn't gotten him anywhere.

Maybe it was time to play unfair.

Ryan's breathing barely changed as Wyatt rolled over, and then nestled himself in the blankets kicked to Ryan's feet.

His dick was still soft, but as Wyatt ran a tentative finger up the underside of his balls, he had a feeling that wouldn't last long.

Wyatt had just wrapped his tongue around the head, and started sucking when he felt Ryan tense.

"I thought you were a dream," Ryan said, voice soft and rough, as he reached down to cradle Wyatt's head with his palm, running his fingers through his hair.

Wyatt traced a pattern on Ryan's hardening cock with his tongue. "A good dream, I hope."

He shouldn't have worried, but some things were hard to shake, and Ryan literally running away after their first—or second, but who was counting?—night together was one of those. Maybe it would have been easier if they were something more than employee and employer, or convenience with added benefits.

But Ryan had made his feelings very clear, and Wyatt, having just gotten at least part of what he wanted, wasn't about to look a gift horse in the mouth.

Speaking of gift horses and mouths, he lapped at the head of his, sucking off a little bit of pre-come.

"It had real potential," Ryan observed sleepily.

Wyatt took that as a request to continue, so he did, trying to lose himself in Ryan's taste and scent and the feel of his hardness against his tongue, in his mouth. And he did, swallowing his come with the glow of satisfaction on a job well done.

Almost.

Even when Ryan wrapped his big calloused hand around Wyatt's dick, pumping him until he felt woozy from pleasure, he couldn't quite forget that this was all supposed to mean nothing.

He'd never been good with hookups, he reasoned as he wandered back to his place for a quick shower before making breakfast. He just had to adjust to this new normal. Having Ryan was definitely better than not having him at all. That much was true.

"You're quiet this morning," Ryan said, pushing his toast around his plate, trying to sop up the rest of his over easy eggs. He looked up, grinning. "I figured earlier it was because you had my dick in your mouth but now you don't have any excuses."

"Maybe I'm tired," Wyatt said, trying to match Ryan's sly, teasing tone. "Someone kept me up most of the night."

It had been so good it was hardly anything to complain about. But last night Wyatt had felt lost to the pleasure of finally getting what he'd craved so badly, and this morning he felt like he couldn't drown out the voice in the back of his head that kept whispering, *what's next?*

"And maybe," he added, Ryan looking up, surprised at his serious tone, "I'm curious what happens next."

"What happens next? Now that we're faux-happily-ever-after poster children?"

Wyatt nodded and told himself firmly that the word shouldn't sting. It was just a word. It didn't *mean* anything, and Ryan didn't mean anything cruel by it. It was the truth, plain and simple. He had agreed to be Ryan's fake boyfriend, not his real one. Ryan couldn't be held responsible for the feelings Wyatt couldn't seem to help.

"Oh, I guess I should call Eric. I'm sure he's been blowing my phone up with a bazillion messages after Matt left here last night."

"Is there some sort of plan?" Wyatt didn't even care what it was. But maybe if he knew, if he prepared himself in advance, it would be easier to deal with.

"Lots of plans, to be honest," Ryan said. "Dozens, probably. Eric likes contingency plans. I think the last one he had involving you, and not someone else, was hosting a dinner party here. Something super couple-y, with lots of social media posts from the people invited. Way to generate some news buzz before we confirmed it."

Wyatt cleared his throat. "We should do a barbecue instead of a dinner party. Something a little more casual."

Ryan brightened at the idea. "That's a good idea, actually. I knew you'd be great at this."

Great at being a fake boyfriend. Wyatt internally raised his hand in a mini, half-hearted fist pump of triumph.

"Let me call Eric, and I'll run the idea by him. Maybe in a day or two? How long do you need to plan something like that?"

"Plan it?"

Ryan laughed. "Like the food, silly. I'll take care of the rest. Or Eric will. Or actually Eric's assistant."

"The food's the easiest part," Wyatt said with an eye roll as punctuation. "Promise, I can handle it. How many people?"

"Maybe ten? Fifteen? Tabitha and her boyfriend. Flor. Her kids. A few teammates if they're in town. Eric, of course."

"You're going to invite Eric?" Wyatt was still on the fence about Ryan's agent. He wasn't sure which side he was on, or if he even acknowledged there were sides. Or if he just played everyone, maneuvering everyone exactly where he wanted them, like pieces on a chess board.

"Of course. He's got to orchestrate this whole thing, right?" Ryan laughed, and the carefree edge to it hurt. Unintentionally of course.

You need to get yourself together.

This was what he had agreed to. This was the new normal. It was time to get his head and his heart on the same page, onto the same plan.

"Right, *duh*," Wyatt said.

"But you liked Tabitha, right? And Flor?" Ryan sounded a little concerned, as if Wyatt might not like his friends or his family, which was ridiculous. Because what fake boyfriend required their approval?

"Of course I did," Wyatt teased. "They're hella intimidating, but strangely, unexpectedly, nice."

Ryan beamed. "I think they'd take that as a high form of praise."

"Well, I meant it." Wyatt shoved his hands in his pockets. "So barbecue for fifteen. I can do that in my sleep."

"That's because you're brilliant." Ryan hopped off the barstool, slid his empty plate into the sink, and kissed Wyatt's cheek. "I'm gonna go call Eric."

"How about . . ." Wyatt hesitated, and then decided to just go for it. "Would it be okay if I invited some friends too?"

"I didn't even know you knew anyone in LA. I'd love to meet your friends," Ryan said, and sounded so god damned sincere, Wyatt wasn't even sure he was acting. And maybe he wasn't. Maybe that was the attitude Wyatt should take. It was all real, until it wasn't.

"They've been super busy filming, but I bet I could drag them away for an evening," Wyatt said. "You probably don't watch any of the *Five Points* culinary shows, but they star in *Pastry by Miles*."

Ryan rolled his eyes. "Tabitha works for *Five Points*. Not in the culinary department, because that would be an epic fucking disaster, but yeah, I do. Once in awhile. I heard about that new show. Heard it's good."

"Yeah, I worked at Terroir with Miles Costa. He and his boyfriend, Evan, produce the show and star in it."

"Well, I'm dying to meet them," Ryan declared. "Invite them!"

It was easy to suggest inviting Miles and Evan to the barbecue. It was another to actually do it.

"Did you drown in the Pacific?" Miles asked when he picked up the phone.

Like Miles hadn't been so overwhelmed with filming the second season of *Pastry by Miles*, practically on top of finishing the first season, that he hadn't bothered to keep in touch either.

"No," Wyatt said testily, flicking through recipes on the iPad he'd set up on a cookbook stand. "I've been busy." That was actually a lie, but Miles didn't need to know that.

"Actually, Xander told me that you're barely working at this private chef gig. Lots of time to experiment in the kitchen, time off to go surfing, all those extended naps in the afternoons." Miles made the fairly innocent word *nap* sound as dirty as it could.

"That is . . . almost completely a lie," Wyatt protested. He hadn't been whiling away the afternoons by having wild sex with Ryan every day, though if the opportunity had come up, he wouldn't have said no.

"Xander doesn't lie," Miles retorted. "That's his whole problem."

It was definitely *one* of Xander's problems; he was painfully, bitterly honest. Wyatt wouldn't say he was lacking in tact, more like it was completely absent from his vocabulary.

But Wyatt didn't want to talk about Xander. Of course he didn't really want to talk about himself either, so changed the subject. "How's season two going?"

"Going to be a wild success, of course. Even better than season one. Cooking Channel has been making overtures about season three but I need to get Evan away from the studio before he forgets where we live."

"You should get away like . . . tomorrow night, for example," Wyatt offered.

"Tomorrow night? I was thinking more like a three-week trip to Fiji. One of those huts overlooking the water. No Wi-Fi, no laptop, no cellphones. Definitely no clothes."

"That too," Wyatt said, leaning against the kitchen counter. "But circling back to tomorrow night, Ryan and I are hosting a barbecue at his place, and you and Evan should definitely come."

"You and Ryan?" Miles sounded suspicious, like he had a feeling where this was going, and really, honestly, he didn't have a fucking clue.

"Ryan needs to give the impression that he's settled and responsible to his team, so I've agreed to act as his . . . partner socially," Wyatt improvised. It didn't sound much better than saying the phrase, *fake boyfriend*, and Miles was going to figure it out in ten seconds flat, but it made *him* feel better.

"You're going to be his fake boyfriend," Miles said flatly. "And this barbecue is what, your coming out party?"

Miles had always been too smart for his own good.

"Yes," was all Wyatt could say.

"We'll be there," Miles said with absolute finality, shocking the hell out of him. Wyatt had at least expected him to have to consult Evan and their mutual schedule together.

"Really?"

"You like the guy, right?" Miles asked.

"Uh, yeah, I guess. I mean, I don't guess. I do. I do like him."

"And you're sleeping together." Miles didn't even phrase this as a question.

"How did you know?"

"Because," Miles said impatiently, "that's what always happens in these scenarios."

"It's not what you think," Wyatt protested.

"I don't think anything," Miles said gently. "Only that you'll probably put yourself out there and then get crushed to shit by the hot football player."

"Baseball. He plays baseball."

Miles' silence in response was telling. So he'd nailed it on the head. It wasn't necessarily going to end that way, there were lots of ways it *could* end. That was definitely the way Wyatt kept imagining though, and dreading.

"We'll be there," Miles finally repeated. "What time? Text me the address. Actually," he paused. "Text Evan the address. He can add it to the schedule."

"Sure."

"Xander said he seemed nice."

Wyatt nearly dropped the phone. "Xander hasn't even met him yet!"

"I'm sure he did some sort of creepy digging. YouTube binge-watching all his interviews or whatever."

"He means well," Wyatt said. "He's really worried about Kian. I'm surprised he made the time from his schedule of worrying about Kian to worry about me."

Miles sighed. "When we first met him, I didn't expect that he would end up so fiercely protective."

Wyatt couldn't help but be reminded of something Kian had said the other night. That just because he was an asshole didn't mean he wasn't deserving of love.

"Someday," Wyatt promised, "we need to figure his shit out."

Miles laughed. "Maybe when we don't have enough shit of our own."

"There," Wyatt said, "I just texted Evan the address, and now he's going to find you in approximately five point three seconds and demand to know what's going on."

"Probably." Miles sounded happy about it. "Hey, you don't need me to bring anything? Some sort of dessert?"

Miles was an incredibly talented pastry chef, and Wyatt probably should have taken him up on the offer. It wouldn't be any trouble for him, even as busy as he was, and trouble and the effort for Wyatt would be far more substantial. But there was some stubborn part of him that wanted to make this dinner all himself. Also, it would definitely keep him involved and busy enough that he wouldn't have the time to worry about what might happen at it.

"Nah, I'm good," Wyatt said.

"Your loss," Miles retorted. "We'll see you tomorrow."

Ryan walked back into the kitchen five minutes after he'd hung up with Miles.

"Everyone on my side is confirmed. Eric is *thrilled,*" Ryan said, making an expressive face of distaste.

"I bet he is," Wyatt said. "Miles said he and Evan could come too."

"Eric practically fell over himself at how excited he was that you knew the stars of *Pastry by Miles*. He likes the connection and they're popular on social media. He thinks it'll be a great fit."

Wyatt had thought it would be a great fit because Miles and Evan were his friends. But apparently genuine friendship wasn't all that was required these days.

"I'm sure he's disappointed that you ended up with the slightly less famous chef from Terroir," Wyatt said wryly.

Ryan surprised him by coming up next to him, and wrapping an arm around his waist, leaning in to brush a quick kiss across his lips. "But I'm not disappointed, and that's all that matters," he said seriously.

"Say that after I've attempted to make a dessert," Wyatt joked weakly. He felt even less comfortable with how demonstrative and affectionate Ryan was now. Like the last barrier had been lifted and he could act however he wanted—and what he wanted was to act like Wyatt was his boyfriend.

Just go with it, don't fight it, he reminded himself.

And in this scenario it meant acting like he'd just gotten what he wanted too: Ryan as *his* boyfriend.

"I'm sure it's going to be great," Ryan said loyally. "And I'm happy to help with whatever you need."

Wyatt turned slightly, pulling Ryan fully into his arms. "What if what I need is a very dirty nap?"

Tugging on his hand, Ryan smiled slyly. "Then let's go take a nap."

The next day it was tough not to regret spending hours "napping" in Ryan's bed. He'd had a big list of stuff to do, including shopping and prep, and instead he'd let himself be talked into a few hours of sex alternated by actual sleeping, followed by ordering pizza in and making out on the couch.

Frankly, it hadn't even required much convincing on Ryan's part, but Wyatt was slowly, but surely, getting to a better place with that.

Acting like they were just together with no weird *faux* bullshit had been the answer to all of Wyatt's questions about what he should do. The strangest—and the best—thing was that Ryan didn't ever hesitate, or pull back, or question anything Wyatt was doing.

It was all good. Great, really. Except that how great it had been yesterday meant that he was now at the grocery store at six in the morning, shopping for the barbecue.

"You really made me come grocery shopping," Ryan whined, slouching against the cart, a hoody pulled over his head, eyes sleepy. "At *six* a.m."

"Didn't you tell me once that Colin O'Connor does his own grocery shopping?" Wyatt asked.

Ryan sighed. "I did tell you that, didn't I?"

"He probably doesn't go this early," Wyatt suggested.

"I was going to say that if you'd ever met O'Connor, you'd know he probably does. But why would you have met Colin O'Connor?"

Wyatt elbowed him in the ribs. "Unfair. True, but unfair."

"I mean, he's okay. Everyone always wants us to be great friends, I guess because we're both gay and athletes and out of the closet. But that's not really much basis for a friendship, is it?"

Wyatt piled a handful of watermelons into the cart that Ryan was half-heartedly pushing. "You have a point."

"He's nice and all. But we're not friends."

"Yeah," Wyatt teased, "you seem really happy about that."

This time Wyatt caught an elbow to the ribs. "If he wanted to be friends, it's not like I'd turn him down, but he's so serious and settled down. I heard he and his husband were adopting. Or doing in vitro or something. That's not really my scene."

Wyatt could see that. "I think people who believe you're friends are probably assuming that you two have experienced situations that nobody else has."

"You're saying he's punched out a homophobic asshole on his team?" Ryan sounded so hopeful, it was hard not to be endeared even further. And Wyatt was already *very* endeared. He kept expecting to reach the ceiling on endeared, only to discover that it kept going up and up and *up*.

"He might have. That seems like the sort of thing he'd do," Wyatt said. "And if you want me to be impressed at your prowess and convictions, I sure am."

Ryan scoffed. "If I was trying to impress you, I'd do this." And he pressed Wyatt against the cart in the middle of the produce section, hands pulling up Wyatt's t-shirt and settling, cold and certain against his stomach. Wyatt was just about to protest, but Ryan kissed him instead, swallowing all his words.

There wasn't anyone to see; nobody to photograph them. But Ryan did it anyway, so Wyatt decided when they finally broke apart that spontaneous kissing was definitely allowed. He was going to be taking a lot of advantage of that ability.

"Where are we on the list?" Ryan asked breathlessly, digging for it in his pocket. "You got watermelons. Did you get strawberries or mangos?"

"I think there's also pineapple and avocado," Wyatt said, pulling the cart towards the fruit displays because Ryan had given up on pushing it. He was whipped because that fact didn't even annoy him.

"Double strawberries," Ryan pointed out as Wyatt began to sort through the plastic containers. "Whatever that means."

"It means that I need strawberries for the salsa and for dessert."

"You know, you didn't have to do this. We could have just gotten the dinner catered."

Wyatt was still absorbed in picking strawberries. "I'm going to pretend you didn't say that. I'm a *professional*, I can handle a little dinner party. Also, isn't this why you hired me? Because I don't think you hired me to make your smoothie or grill your chicken at night. Or give you a morning blowjob."

"You're very handy," Ryan said in lieu of an apology. "I'm spoiled rotten, I know."

Wyatt began loading pineapples in the cart, then moved onto mangos. "You absolutely are."

"You love it," Ryan teased, and Wyatt had to hold the answer back, because damnit, he did. He kept creeping closer to that revelation, and every minute they spent together like this, he sped up. Soon enough it was going to be inevitable that he didn't just love that Ryan was spoiled rotten, but every damn thing about him.

"Where to next?" Ryan asked, shoving the pen behind his ear. "I think you got all the produce and the fruit."

"You're a good grocery shopping partner," Wyatt pointed out as they headed towards the butcher. "I'm impressed."

Ryan preened. "You're never going to regret agreeing to be with me."

He wasn't wrong; even if it all went wrong, and Wyatt ended up with a broken, demolished heart, he didn't think he'd regret it.

❧❦

"Hiding out?"

Wyatt glanced up and saw Tabitha lingering in the kitchen doorway. He was putting the final touches on the main course of the barbecue—tri-tip steaks that he was planning on grilling and slicing thin.

All the cold salads were prepped and in the fridge. He'd set up the appetizer buffet in the backyard, and put Ryan in charge of drinks. Everything was coming together, and he was feeling calm and collected, until Ryan's best friend decided to drop by the kitchen to check in.

He knew he wasn't intimidated by Tabitha because of her beauty. It was probably because it felt like she saw right through him, past his skin and his rib cage, to the frantically beating heart underneath. The traitorous heart who was just about ready to topple head over heels in love with Ryan.

"I'm finishing up prep," he said. "I'm not just here as the eye candy hanging off Ryan's arm."

Tabitha walked in, setting her glass on the counter with a click. "You're not even here as eye candy."

"Tell Eric, who's already been through here, telling me to change my shirt, fix my hair, get ready for a hundred pictures that I'm apparently going to have to take tonight. All demonstrating just how hot Ryan's new boyfriend is."

Wyatt had told himself not to let Eric get to him, but it seemed to be a losing battle.

"Eric's an asshole," Tabitha said.

"That's what everyone keeps saying," Wyatt said crossly, "and yet we all still have to deal with him."

"Someday, Ryan will get fed up, and he'll dump him. For someone with an actual shred of empathy. But Eric makes him lots of money so that probably won't happen for awhile."

Tabitha didn't need to point out that Wyatt would likely be long gone by that point.

"Are you here to take a selfie with me?" Wyatt finished rubbing the dry seasoning mix onto the meat, and then transferred it to the tray.

"Actually," she said, "I'm here to ask if you need any help. Which seems a little ridiculous, I'll admit, but my mother always tried to drill manners into me. Even if it was mostly unsuccessful."

"Actually, you can help me," Wyatt said. "Grab that salt, I need to season the meat and I don't want to wash my hands again."

"You're going to let me do something this important?" Tabitha asked skeptically, while still coming around the corner of the island and picking up the salt shaker.

"It's just salt. You seem very intelligent. I'm sure you can manage," he teased.

"How much?" she asked, shooting him a grateful look. He didn't imagine that many people upon meeting her for the first time noticed her intelligence first.

"Just shake it liberally all over," he said. "And then the pepper grinder next."

She did as directed, as he rubbed in the seasonings further. "Would it be patronizing to tell you that you did a good job?"

Tabitha shook her head. "I like praise, and you're good at it."

"Praise?" Wyatt questioned, as he walked over to the sink, scrubbing his hands under the spray.

"Yes, and putting people at ease," she said. "That's one of the reasons Ryan likes you."

He turned, grabbing a paper towel to dry his hands off. "You mean that's why Ryan picked me."

"No," she insisted with a sharp shake of her head, "that's not what I said. That's why he *likes* you."

Before she could elaborate, Ryan burst in. "The grill's ready, I think."

"Good," Wyatt said, hefting the tray.

"Miles and Evan just got here," Ryan said, trailing after him, Tabitha bringing up the rear. "I love them already, though I was surprised at how uptight Evan is."

"Everyone is, after they meet Miles," Wyatt said.

"Miles and Evan?" Tabitha questioned. "From *Pastry by Miles*?"

"Yeah, they're friends of mine. Miles and I worked together. Lived together too, for awhile."

She let out a heavy sigh and shot a glare at her best friend. "And you didn't tell me they were here? I've been *dying* to meet them!" She elbowed her way between Wyatt and Ryan, escaping out the back door first.

"Are you ready for this?" Ryan asked quietly as they paused on the threshold. To Wyatt's surprise, he didn't sound ready; he sounded apprehensive.

Wyatt looked out over at the crowd milling around the backyard. It had definitely looked more intimidating in his mind. But he wanted to reassure Ryan, so he leaned over, brushing a quick kiss over Ryan's mouth. "Never readier."

Wyatt headed straight to the grill; he needed to get the meat on so all these guests could get fed. He was glad, as he used the tongs to position it just so on the metal grid, that he'd planned for far more people, because there were definitely more than that in the backyard.

Probably more like twenty-five or thirty, if he was being honest.

"So this is the LA life, huh?" Miles asked from behind him.

Wyatt turned, and pulled him into a quick hug. "I'd like to remind you that you moved to LA before I ever thought about it."

Evan was next to him, and got hugged too, because Wyatt was happy and feeling generous. "I'm so glad you guys are here," he said.

"I can't believe you're dating Ryan Flores," Evan said.

"I told you, babe," Miles said, voice dropping in volume, "he's not *really* dating Ryan Flores."

Evan waved a dismissive hand. "Isn't that all a matter of semantics?"

Technically, Wyatt didn't think that Eric would think of it that way—and probably not Ryan either, no matter how affectionate he liked to be in bed. And outside of it. And in grocery stores.

"It's a good move for you," Miles said, clearly trying to sound positive. Except that while he'd never been a Debbie Downer like Xander, he'd never exactly been the cheerleader type either.

"The private chef job was a good move," Wyatt corrected. "This is probably stupid, but I'm doing it anyway."

Miles shrugged, and it was clear from his expression that he agreed with Wyatt. "As long as you're happy."

"I'd be happier with a drink," Wyatt admitted. "Make sure the tri-tip doesn't spontaneously combust while I grab one."

Miles nodded, but eyed the grill with trepidation. He was a pastry chef, and happiest—and most comfortable—around desserts. He could deal with some savory preparations, but barbecue was definitely beyond his skill level.

Meanwhile Wyatt headed towards the makeshift bar that Ryan had set up in the shade. There were metal bins full of ice and bottles of beer, as well as a few bottles of various white wines.

He grabbed a beer from the bin and was just looking around for a bottle opener, when Tabitha showed up, a handsome blond man in tow.

"Wyatt, I'd like you to meet my boyfriend, Calvin."

Wyatt reached out and shook his hand. He had frankly appraising blue eyes and a firm grip. The fact that Tabitha's expression and voice softened as she talked about him made him like Calvin already.

"Cal," he said in a friendly voice. "Call me Cal. If you do, I'll keep pretending that I don't already know all about you."

Wyatt raised an eyebrow. He finally located the bottle opener and popped the top off. Taking a long drink, he realized mid-sip that meant Ryan had been talking about him.

"What do I have to do to get the details?" he asked with a grin.

Cal laughed and Tabitha snickered. "You're going to feed me homemade tri-tip with the fixings," he said. "And I'm sure Tabitha told you she can't cook. I'm grateful enough that I'll tell you anything you want to know."

"Calvin," Tabitha admonished in a low voice.

"What?" he asked innocently. "Should I not tell him how crazy we know Ryan is for him?"

"We could," she said primly, "but *that* is none of our business."

It wasn't, but Wyatt couldn't help but wonder if it was true. And then, if it *was* true, why Ryan kept insisting that their relationship had to be pretend.

"How about you tell me why Ryan is so scared of relationships that he has to hire a boyfriend who'd be perfectly happy to date him for real?" Wyatt asked, wondering if he was giving too much away, then deciding he didn't give a crap.

Tabitha definitely had seen through him, and he wouldn't be shocked if Calvin weren't right there behind her.

"That," Cal said, "is unfortunately beyond my pay grade. You're going to have to ask Ryan about that."

Tabitha muttered something that suspiciously sounded like, *"but he won't tell you."*

It wasn't like Wyatt had necessarily expected Ryan's friends to sell him out, even to a guy who was crazy about him. But he did learn one thing; that there was definitely some reason why Ryan would opt for something pretend instead of something real.

"I've got to go check on the meat," he said, "but it was great to meet you." They shook hands again, and Wyatt was off to the grill again, but Eric waylaid him in the middle of the yard.

"There you are," he said, putting his arm around him, like Wyatt had seen him do with Ryan more than once. Ryan hadn't seemed to have much compunction in just shrugging him off, like a pesky fly, but Wyatt knew he should tread a little more carefully. After all, while Ryan signed the checks for both Wyatt's jobs, Eric cut them.

He didn't know if he should feel more or less bothered thinking of Eric as his boss, instead of Ryan.

"I need to check on the food," Wyatt protested, even as Eric steered him towards a pocket of people underneath one of the big trees. The group included Ryan, and Wyatt shouldn't have felt a twinge of nerves, but he did. This was it, then, the very first time he met strangers and got introduced as Ryan's new boyfriend.

"What you need is to mingle, and meet your boyfriend's friends," Eric said pointedly, hitting Wyatt's suspicions right on the head.

Wyatt felt his palm dampen against the beer bottle in his hand, but he lifted his chin. "Hey, babe," he said, directing his comment at Ryan.

"Look who I found, hiding out," Eric said, laughing obnoxiously. "I told him he needed to join the party."

Wyatt's dislike of the man grew exponentially. He hadn't been *hiding*; he was in charge of the food for this party so if he disappeared to take care of something, he shouldn't need an excuse. And now he was being forced to present one.

"This your new guy?" a gorgeous African-American guy with dreads and kind eyes asked.

On cue, Ryan walked over to Wyatt, and finally Eric let him go—probably only because it was Ryan's turn to take over. Except that Ryan didn't eagerly walk over, excited to introduce his new boyfriend to his friends. He practically dragged his feet and his whole persona exuded reluctance.

"Yeah, this is Wyatt."

Wyatt couldn't explain it. Ryan had kissed him in the middle of the grocery store. He'd hardly been private about it. Never mind that this was all his idea. Wyatt was only playing the part that he'd been asked to play.

Ryan leaned and gave him a quick, perfunctory kiss that didn't resemble anything like one he'd given Wyatt before the party. Wyatt told himself that he was thinking too much; if Ryan was a little apprehensive over this whole charade, that was fine. It wasn't like Wyatt himself hadn't had a few anxious moments. This was a big deal, and the very first time. It would get better, and Ryan would seem less stiff and less like he wanted to be somewhere else—or with someone else.

"Picture," Eric demanded, and while Wyatt wanted to refuse, he didn't.

It was easy enough for him to wrap his arms around Ryan and press a loud kiss to his cheek as the camera clicked, because he wasn't playing a role. Ryan let him, even leaning in a little, and the soft look in his eyes as Wyatt pulled away made him think that maybe he'd imagined the whole thing.

"Hi, I'm Andrew," the handsome man said, reaching out to shake his hand, acting like this was all normal. "I'm happy that Ryan's finally met someone. Where *did* you meet, if you don't mind me asking?"

"Temple, actually," Ryan said quickly. "Can you believe it?"

If Andrew looked a little more disbelieving now, it wasn't like Wyatt could blame him. Nobody ever met a boyfriend at Temple. Found hookups, yeah, but long-term happy relationships, rarely.

"You should go with me sometime," Ryan added.

This time Andrew looked at him weirdly. "You're still going to Temple? By yourself?"

Of course he wouldn't be. You went to Temple alone or with a group of friends to find a hookup. And Ryan didn't need a hookup if he had a boyfriend at home.

"We like to dance," Wyatt covered for Ryan, who was just standing there, silent.

"Then maybe I will," Andrew said. He seemed nice and very friendly, and Wyatt thought they might be friends, except that he had a feeling Ryan wouldn't be on board with that plan.

He couldn't say why, exactly, though the reason probably lay with the guarded look in Ryan's eyes.

"I've got to go check on the food," Wyatt said, excusing himself. "But it was great to meet you."

Wyatt rarely checked his social media accounts and rarely posted on them. That hadn't stopped Eric's "communications manager" from vetting all of them, even though he had nothing to hide. He'd been reminded by Eric three times tonight that he would be expected to start posting, beginning with tonight and for the foreseeable future.

So when he checked the tri-tip, he took a pic of the grill, and posted to Instagram. He was still a chef, and food had always figured so prominently in his posts before. He figured it would be good to keep things normal.

He did notice that several people had taken pics of him, and tagged him in them. One of the posters was Andrew, who was apparently a third baseman for the Dodgers. Andrew, who Wyatt was about sixty-five percent sure was gay and still in the closet, had tagged him in the picture of him and Ryan, and called them the "cutest couple I know #relationshipgoals."

They weren't relationship goals. They could barely speak to each other out here in the yard, though everything had felt perfectly fine before they'd walked out here. Wyatt fought back the inclination to announce that the party was over, and drag Ryan back in the house, where everything made sense.

"Hey."

Wyatt glanced up and Ryan was standing there, an apology in his eyes.

"Everything okay?" Wyatt asked, keeping his voice light and casual. They were still figuring this fake relationship out, and balancing it with their private lives. That was hard. They wouldn't get it right instantly.

"That was weird back there," Ryan confessed. "I knew we were going to do it, I just didn't think it through."

"It's okay, I think everyone assumed it was normal," Wyatt said.

"Yeah," Ryan grinned, "because you're a stealth ninja and you slipped that line in about liking to dance. I thought I'd blown it big-time."

So Ryan wasn't really apologizing—or *not* apologizing—for his general standoffish behavior, but for accidentally inviting Andrew to Temple without Wyatt.

Still, he was here and he was sorry. Even if he hadn't said it explicitly.

"A ninja, huh?" Wyatt grinned. "I love the sound of that."

Ryan leaned in and kissed him, this time nothing perfunctory or quick. He even slipped in a little tongue, wrapping his arm firmly around Wyatt's waist. It was easy to forgive him when he kissed like that—like Wyatt was his whole world and this wasn't a charade at all.

"Food's almost done?" Ryan asked, stroking a hand up and down his back. "Smells awesome."

"Yeah, could you go grab the cold salads? You might need an extra pair of hands. Then we can get ready to slice this in a few minutes."

Ryan nodded, and took off, collecting Cal to help.

It was so easy to forget the early uncomfortableness in the low-key excitement of the party as the food was served, everyone gathering family style around a big table Ryan had set up outside in the yard.

He took about twenty selfies, and from his constantly vibrating phone in his back pocket, assumed most of them had been posted and he'd been tagged.

The party started slowing down a few hours later, even though Ryan had lit the fire pit.

Wyatt had gravitated towards it, lounging against a bench seat, with a beer dangling in his hand. He felt so mellow, like nothing could disturb his much-won peace. A few people had stopped by to chat, including Tabitha and Andrew. When Ryan slid in next to him, his arm going around his shoulders, Wyatt assumed the party was mostly over.

"It went well, don't you think?" Ryan asked. He sounded just about as relaxed as Wyatt felt, and he couldn't help but be relieved at that. He'd worried that Ryan would stay uptight, but that hadn't happened. He'd relaxed into the role, and even though he didn't act exactly as he did when they were alone, it was close enough that Wyatt wasn't going to angst about it.

"I think it went great," Wyatt said honestly.

"Eric said a few outlets have already picked it up. They all think you're very cute and that we're very cute together."

"Well, that doesn't feel too far from the truth," Wyatt said smugly.

"Even TMZ posted," Ryan said.

"Who's TMZ?"

Ryan laughed. "I think we did forget one thing tonight, though." He held up his phone. "We didn't take a selfie together to cement our very cute couple-ship."

"I took about a thousand selfies," Wyatt protested.

"So, what's one more?" Ryan pointed out.

Which is how they ended up with a very cute picture on Ryan's Instagram—the palms and twinkly lights of the backyard in the background, with the glow of the fire pit reflected in their faces, pressed closely together.

"I'm going to caption this #bestnightever," Ryan announced.

"You don't think that's a bit of an exaggeration?" Wyatt asked lazily. He was dreaming about bed. Ryan's or his—he wasn't sure he cared at the moment. It had been a long day.

"I don't, actually." Ryan's voice sounded serious, devoid of any teasing edge, and Wyatt thought that he might actually be telling the truth.

CHAPTER TWELVE

"HOW DO YOU FEEL about going up to Napa this weekend?"

Ryan looked up from where he was checking his email. Wyatt's head was still mostly in the fridge, as he put together a quick lunch for them.

"I feel good about it," Ryan said. "No plans here. Did you have something in mind?"

"This weekend is one of Bastian Aquino's famous invite-only brunches at Terroir. I promised my nana I'd take her, and Tony, my brother, is going too. I could add you to the list, if you wanted."

"Does this mean I can finally meet the Bastard?"

Wyatt laughed as he began to spread pesto on one side of the bread. "I'm not sure I want you meeting him if you're going to call him by his infamous nickname. He's killed people for less. But yes, he does generally make a pass through the dining room to take his allotment of praise."

"Excellent, I'd love to come and meet your nana. Plus, I have an idea for something else we can do in Napa." Ryan had a feeling Wyatt wasn't going to like it as much as he was; Wyatt didn't have the same craving for adrenaline that Ryan had.

But Wyatt kept piling sliced turkey and cheese on the sandwiches like he wasn't concerned. Of course Ryan had discovered that when Wyatt was cooking, even if it was as simple as building some paninis, he was usually absorbed in his task.

"Napa Skydive is up there," Ryan threw out casually, leaning back, and taking a long drink of his iced tea. "I thought we could give it a try."

The shocked, apprehensive look in Wyatt's eyes was priceless as he looked up at him.

"Oh, it'll be fun," Ryan teased. "You're gonna love it."

"I'm not an adrenaline junkie like you," Wyatt protested.

"Yeah, you play it downright safe when we surf," Ryan teased. Like just this morning Wyatt hadn't been attempting tricks that Ryan wouldn't even try. "I'll tell that to the gigantic bruise you're probably going to be sporting tomorrow."

"I already told you," Wyatt said as he slid the sandwiches into the pan, and weighed them down with another big heavy skillet, "I did that on purpose. So you'd kiss every inch of it."

Ryan couldn't help but laugh. Hanging out with Wyatt was fun and always so unexpected. If he'd known that hanging out with your hookups was like this, he would've been tempted to do it before. But then, he had a feeling there weren't many Wyatt Blakes out there in the world.

If he'd ever run across someone like him before, Ryan wanted to believe that he'd have realized it right away, the exact same way he had this time, and done whatever he could not to lose him.

The adjustment to being together, even if it was fake, had seemed pretty smooth, despite his sudden anxiousness the night of the party, and so much of that had been because of Wyatt. He was calm and collected, and endlessly supportive. He made doing this easy, and every hour they spent together further convinced him of the truth he'd known from the first moment they'd met: he could only have this fake relationship if it was with Wyatt. He couldn't have done it with anybody else.

"I guess if you come to brunch with my nana and my brother and endure not calling Aquino the Bastard to his face, I could skydive. Besides, isn't that super safe now? And don't they hook you up to the instructor?"

"Luckily for you," Ryan said, "I've got enough hours to be considered an instructor. We can get hooked together."

Wyatt's response was a smoky, hot look shot from his cool, blue eyes. "How did you guess that's my favorite position?"

Ryan snorted. "It wasn't very difficult, considering how often it occurs."

"Are you complaining?" Wyatt slid the sandwich onto a plate and pushed it in front of Ryan. "Because I sure as hell am not."

Ryan definitely wasn't. He'd unapologetically had a lot of sex and lots of it had been good, some of it had been great, and a little had even been extraordinary, which is why he'd expected some of his sexual obsession with Wyatt to wane as the novelty faded. But there was something addictive about him, and whenever Wyatt offhandedly mentioned how much he enjoyed them together, Ryan couldn't help but be a tiny bit embarrassed at how much he agreed.

With how much experience he had, Ryan wasn't the one who was supposed to be so into it, but he'd definitely passed casual bystander by a while ago. It wasn't that it hadn't *ever* happened, but it was definitely unusual.

He took a bite of the sandwich, and nearly moaned. It was perfect—the bread, the meat, the cheese, with the herb notes in the pesto. "I'd ask how you keep doing this," Ryan said, "but you'd just tell me you're a professional. Even when you're only making a sandwich."

Wyatt smiled, looking very pleased with himself. "It's never *just* a sandwich," he said. And Ryan was pretty sure that the end of the sentence was *when it's for you*, and he didn't know how he felt about that.

Except that wasn't even true. He knew. He liked it. He loved it. That was probably selfish but Ryan couldn't help himself.

"Should we take the Tesla or maybe the Maserati? Or the Ducati?"

Wyatt shrugged, in the middle of his own sandwich.

"I have an even better idea," Ryan said. Wyatt didn't like it when he, in his words, "threw his money around," but he decided he'd be okay taking that risk. "You take care of getting Bastian Aquino to let us into this fancy brunch, and I'll take care of the transportation and the hotel. Okay?"

Wyatt looked suspicious but nodded in agreement.

It was still worth it four days later when, instead of staying on I-5 to drive up to Napa, Ryan pulled off the freeway, and pulled up to the private terminal at LAX.

"I thought I told you I didn't like you throwing your money around," Wyatt said, frustrated edge to his voice, as they embarked onto the small private plane. "We could've driven."

"And wasted six hours on the road, when this way, we can check in to the hotel early, get a massage, spend some time in the sauna, and have sex before we have to meet your brother Tony for dinner."

"You are incorrigible," Wyatt said, finally cracking a smile as they settled into their plush leather seats. "I'm not sure whether to encourage or discourage you."

"I think you should wait until we get to the hotel before deciding," Ryan teased.

Wyatt rolled his eyes and settled back in for takeoff. "I told you we could stay with the guys. They have some extra room, since both Miles and I moved out."

"I am not staying with your ex," Ryan stated. He'd known that from the first moment Wyatt had confessed that his ex-boyfriend had ended up moving in with his old roommates. He kept telling himself it wasn't a jealousy thing, but when he couldn't come up with an alternative explanation, he'd been forced to conclude it turned out he *was* the jealous type, at least when it came to Wyatt.

Of course he hadn't been able to admit that to Wyatt, so he'd used some bullshit privacy excuse that he was pretty sure was horribly transparent. But Wyatt was such a good guy, he'd let it go gracefully and not made it an issue.

But it also meant that Ryan could check them into his favorite hotel and Wyatt couldn't complain about the price.

"I'm not arguing about staying with Kian, Xander, and Nate, but I recognize that expression," Wyatt grumbled. "It usually means you're up to something."

"I'm totally up to something," Ryan agreed cheerfully. "But you're gonna like it."

"Does this have something to do with the massage, sauna, and sex you mentioned earlier?" Wyatt couldn't quite hide the eagerness in his voice.

"You're just gonna have to wait and see." Ryan mimed zipping his lips shut, and tossing the key over his shoulder.

"Gentlemen," the stewardess said, entering the main cabin, "we're just about ready to take off. Would you like something to drink before we do?"

"Mimosas?" Ryan asked. Wyatt rolled his eyes but nodded in agreement.

"Are we celebrating something?" she asked when she returned to the cabin with two crystal flutes.

"Us," Ryan said, shooting her his most charming smile. "I think that's something worth celebrating."

She laughed. "I'd agree. Now please keep your seatbelts fastened. It's a quick, short flight and the pilot probably won't turn off the seatbelt sign. But you can press this little button," she indicated a discreet call button by Ryan's seat, "if you need anything during the flight."

"Cheers," Ryan said, tipping his glass Wyatt's direction. He rolled his eyes again, but toasted back.

"I'll admit," Wyatt said a few minutes after takeoff, "this is better than driving."

"I'm glad you approve," Ryan teased.

"I worked at Terroir, which is pretty much synonymous with wealth and excess, but we didn't get to experience any of it."

"That doesn't seem fair," Ryan said, but he wasn't very surprised. Wyatt had let slip a few days ago how much money he'd been making before working for him, and it had been appallingly low, considering how many hours Wyatt had worked, and how tough his job had been.

"Bring it up with the Bastard," Wyatt said with a resigned sigh. "Actually, I shouldn't say that, because you might."

"Wyatt," Ryan asked seriously. "Your nana is coming with us to brunch, right?"

"I told you she was."

"I'd never do anything to embarrass you in front of her. I promise."

Wyatt downed the rest of his mimosa. "But we should tell her about our relationship."

"You don't want to lie to her," Ryan guessed.

"I don't."

"Then we don't." It didn't matter that Eric had asked him to post some photos of their trip and the brunch. To show their "deepening" relationship, he'd said, because Wyatt wouldn't introduce him to his grandmother unless Ryan was important.

But then, Ryan had a feeling that Wyatt hadn't asked him to come with him this weekend to perpetrate their fake-relationship agenda. He'd wanted Ryan to meet his nana because it was important to him.

"Are you sure?"

"Don't tell me you asked me to come because you imagined a whole bunch of cute staged Instagram photos," Ryan said.

"I thought you should meet her while she still might remember you," Wyatt said and Ryan could hear the pain in his voice.

"Then that's what we'll do."

Ryan closed his eyes and leaned back in the chair and wondered if Wyatt realized he'd just revealed how much he cared. If he knew Wyatt at all, he probably didn't care. He'd volunteer it if Ryan asked.

The problem was Ryan wasn't sure if he wanted to ask.

A little over an hour later, they landed in Napa, and Ryan led Wyatt to the car he'd rented and asked to be left near the private terminal.

He was happy to see they'd even gotten exactly what he'd requested—a Tesla Model X, which he'd been dying to test drive for awhile now.

"You're awfully spoiled, I hope you realize this," Wyatt said, as he loaded their bags into the back.

"I was thinking about trading in the Range Rover. Combining a trip with a test drive was efficient." Ryan checked his phone for the time, typing in the address of the hotel in the mapping app. "We made great time. Even with the traffic on a Saturday, we should have just enough time until we meet your brother."

Twenty minutes later, they pulled up to the hotel. As soon as Ryan was out of the car, the valet was at the door, taking his keys. He didn't always expect to be recognized, but it was a nice perk when he was and he got great service as a result.

"I'm internally rolling my eyes," Wyatt hissed in his ear as they walked up to the front desk.

"Why just internally?" Ryan teased.

Wyatt flushed. "I don't want to embarrass you by looking uncomfortable with all this."

Ryan assumed by "all this," Wyatt meant the expansive lobby with its shining wood floors and soaring vaulted ceiling, the metal and glass modern chandeliers echoing the design of a wine bottle.

Maybe he meant the way the manager recognized him and pulled him aside, checking him in ahead of the rest of the line waiting for service. Or that he showed them to the suite personally.

"I didn't realize you came here so often," Wyatt said as he dropped his bag on the sofa.

"Flor likes to go wine tasting," Ryan said with a shrug. "And I like to give her trips because she can't argue with those."

Wyatt raised an eyebrow.

"Okay," Ryan corrected, "she argues about them *less*."

"I don't blame her," Wyatt admitted. "I don't want you to think you *have* to do any of this. It's nice, and I appreciate it, but I don't need it."

Ryan wondered if Matt would have expected all this, part and parcel with his position as Ryan's public boyfriend. He wouldn't have blamed him for expecting the private jet, the luxury suite, the couples' massage booked in fifteen minutes.

In some ways, Wyatt was the perfect fake boyfriend, but in others, the role didn't sit right at all. Ryan was just now beginning to figure out the reasons why that was—or else he would have, if he'd allowed himself to think about it. Instead, he shoved the logic aside, and settled his hip on the edge of the couch.

"Noted," he said, feigning a pout. "Now come over here and kiss me. We've got a few minutes until our massage and I'm feeling neglected."

Wyatt laughed, but Wyatt came, and his lips on Ryan's were the last piece of the puzzle he needed to shove the rest of those annoying thoughts aside.

***

Introducing his boyfriend to Tony was blowing Wyatt's mind for several distinct reasons.

One, Tony was accepting of aforementioned boyfriend.

Two, Tony had mentioned his own boyfriend several times since they'd arrived an hour earlier.

Three, Tony was definitely flirting with Ryan.

Wyatt didn't feel comfortable bringing Nana to Tony's new gig at the Napa Tavern, but it was exactly the sort of place he wanted to bring Ryan. Laid-back and chill, with great food and an extensive draft beer list. He might be recognized, but none of the people in the bar would give two shits.

Tomorrow was going to be enough of a clusterfuck, Wyatt didn't want to make a public production of the night before.

"Wyatt, you didn't tell me your brother was this cute," Ryan said, eyeing Tony up and down. It was still weird enough watching Tony flush and look undeniably pleased. It was even weirder that Ryan was the one causing the reaction.

"When we talked about my family, I didn't really think it mattered how cute my brother was," Wyatt retorted fondly.

Ryan was two and a half beers in, and for someone who didn't drink much, it was enough to make him a little tipsy and a lot more daring than usual.

Anyone else might feel threatened, but Wyatt was feeling especially chill from the massage/sauna/sex combination that Ryan had arranged for the afternoon. It turned out it was difficult to feel threatened when the sex they'd had was so spectacular.

Ryan made a face. "I sort of expected you to get all hot. Jealous and protective and all that."

"Wyatt's never been like that," Tony answered for him. "He's always gone with the flow."

Maybe that was true. Maybe it was also true that Wyatt had never felt like he'd had something to lose before.

"Are we really going to talk about going with the flow?" Wyatt teased. "You've flowed around plenty."

Tony's grin was wolfish. He set his elbows on the table, his tattooed forearms on full display and leaned forward, dark eyes sly. "Guilty as charged."

"I also did not expect for you to have a bad boy as a brother," Ryan said.

"He's not bad," Wyatt said, rolling his eyes, before Tony could even tee off on that particularly juicy bit of bait. "He just wants everyone to think so. He's always just been a mouthy, snotty asshole."

"Also guilty," Tony said with a laugh.

"I've definitely had a thing for bad boys," Ryan mused, pausing to drink his beer. "Sorry, but my current tastes are running more towards Cali beach boys." He reached out and touched Wyatt's neck, his hand warm against his hairline. "I've got to piss, be right back."

Tony barely waited until Ryan had cleared the table.

"I thought you said you weren't really together," Tony demanded, his expression going from playful to serious. "You said it was just an image thing." And Wyatt *had* told Tony that, when he'd called to make the plans for this weekend, but the fake-boyfriend thing had still been so new that Wyatt hadn't expected Ryan to be so touchy-feely even when they weren't trying to pretend anything.

"We're not," Wyatt said.

"Could've fooled me, and just about everyone else in this place," Tony muttered.

"It's . . . complicated," Wyatt said, which was an expression he normally hated. The fact that he didn't even hate it now spoke volumes.

"You like him," Tony stated, like he fully expected Wyatt to argue with him. Wyatt wasn't sure what he'd have to gain from that. His like was pretty fucking obvious, there wasn't much point in denying it.

"Yeah, I do."

"You need to figure your shit out. You've always had your shit together. A lot better than me, that's for sure. It doesn't feel right to watch you playing free and easy with this guy, not when you obviously like him."

"It's still developing," Wyatt defended. "We're figuring it out." Technically a lie, but Wyatt was scrambling still, trying to acclimate himself to this bizarre new world where Tony felt able and obligated to give him advice on his love life.

"You and Nate, that was doomed to fail because he loved you more than you loved him."

Wyatt rolled his eyes. "Why am I not surprised you knew about that and pretended not to?"

"Because we live in the same town and you weren't exactly subtle?" Tony shrugged. "I've got to get back to the kitchen, but I just wanted to say, don't let the opposite happen here. He's obviously having fun, but it's more than that for you."

"Thank you, Captain Obvious," Wyatt hissed through gritted teeth as Ryan emerged from the bathroom and made his way back to the table.

"Hey, it was great to meet you," Tony said, standing as Ryan approached the table. "I've got to get back to the kitchen. I'll send some food out for you guys."

Ryan grinned, and Wyatt realized that somehow in the last hour, between all the flirting and the beers, Ryan had become friends with his brother. "You too, and thanks for that. We'll see you tomorrow."

They didn't hug as Tony departed, but it was a near thing. Wyatt set his forehead against the table and considered banging it against the wood.

"What is your deal? I thought you'd like that I liked him," Ryan questioned, downing the rest of his beer.

"I did. I do. I'm just . . . acclimating," Wyatt protested.

"Is it weird?"

"I'm almost thirty years old, and my brother just met my first boyfriend. And I've found out that not only has he known basically this whole time that I was gay, but that he's bisexual. And very curious. So to answer your question: yes, it's weird."

Ryan rubbed a reassuring hand across Wyatt's shoulders. "Should I tell you about the time Flor walked in on me giving our next-door neighbor a blowjob?"

Wyatt let his head fall back against the table. "God, no. Definitely not."

Ryan was Ryan and didn't listen to Wyatt's half-hearted denial. "He was so hot, and liked to wash his car. Like, *every* weekend. And since it was LA, and usually at least eighty, he never wore a shirt. I spent three summers on the front porch, tongue on the ground, desperate for a chance to show him that I wasn't a little punk teenager anymore."

Wyatt wanted to stick his fingers in his ears and yell *la la la la la* until the story stopped, but the only person possibly more stubborn than himself was Ryan. There was no way he wasn't going to hear this story, eventually. It might as well be now, when he was already two beers in.

"Anyway, the summer I turned eighteen, he finally invited me over to help him wax."

"Him?" Wyatt nearly yelped.

"No, no," Ryan laughed, "but that would have been a great pickup line. He invited me over to wax his *car*."

"You went, obviously," Wyatt said.

"Obviously," Ryan teased. "How else was I supposed to get my mouth on his cock?"

"I can't think of any other way." And somehow, Wyatt was smiling again, and the world didn't feel quite so weird anymore.

"Right, it was brilliant. So we ended up in my house."

"Wait," Wyatt interrupted. "I thought you were waxing *his* car?"

"We were, I had to invite him for a soda. I didn't want him to get heatstroke, right?"

"You're such a good Samaritan," Wyatt said sarcastically. "Was the blowjob to make sure his pipes didn't get clogged?"

"Actually," Ryan said thoughtfully, "we were in the kitchen, and suddenly he dropped his jeans. Said that he knew I'd been waiting for it."

"You had," Wyatt pointed out. "You said you'd been flirting with him for years."

"It was everything I'd been fantasizing about, but then Flor walked in, and yeah . . . not the ending I'd anticipated. She dragged him out by his ear, and he moved six months later."

Wyatt chuckled. "Am I supposed to feel sorry for him or for you in this story?"

"Him, obviously. You know how good my blowjobs are and his got interrupted mid-suck."

Wyatt snorted his beer as he laughed helplessly. "Just don't tell my nana that story."

Ryan's expression was angelic as he said, "Oh, I've got lots of others." He turned, so he was straddling the bench, and put his hands on Wyatt's shoulder. "Do we have to let your brother feed us?"

"Did you telling me about giving the hot guy next door head *then* being caught by Flor turn you on?"

Ryan shrugged, eyes so bright, the curve of his lip giving away that he was trying hard not to grin. "Maybe? No shame." His hands slid down Wyatt's chest, and found their target—the waist of Wyatt's jeans, tucking his fingers under, and tugging him closer. "Let's go," he murmured. "We can always order room service later. I've got a pressing . . . issue that we need to discuss."

Wyatt leaned in, his lips almost brushing Ryan's. His eyes had darkened so much it was tough to see the pupils in the dim room. "Is there a fire?"

Ryan lost the fight, and grinned wide, lighting up like a neon sign. "In my pants? Yes. Absolutely." Wyatt felt his heart thump arrhythmically in his chest, and wondered if this was what really falling for someone felt like. Uneven and uncertain and all-consuming. He didn't know what he'd been doing before meeting Ryan. Maybe just marking time until this moment?

This moment right here, right now, his brain and his heart and his dick screamed at him, and it was the easiest decision in the world to grin right back and say, as serious as he could, "That sounds serious, we should go take care of that situation."

"I don't think you've ever driven faster," Ryan said, sounding breathless and approving as Wyatt pushed him back up against the door.

"Like that, huh?" Wyatt asked, nudging his neck to the side so he could kiss his way down to it, and then back up to the sensitive spot on his ear.

He'd been spending the last week cataloging every especially sensitive spot on Ryan's body and felt he had a bit more to explore tonight.

"You driving fast or you exploiting my ears?" Ryan teased.

"Yes," Wyatt said.

"Watching you drive fast was one of the sexiest things I've ever seen," Ryan confessed, and the truth in his tone made Wyatt's traitorous heart beat even faster. Did Ryan know statements like that affected him? Did he care? Was that why he made them?

The questions distracted Wyatt for a split second, and that was all it took for his back to be the one flat against the door.

"This is much, much better. More my style," Ryan purred as he lifted Wyatt's t-shirt off and slid a hand down the center of his chest, pausing right over the button of his jeans. "I love it when you're at my mercy."

"Am I?" Wyatt questioned. "Or are you at mine?"

Ryan's fingers hesitated on the button he was working open, and he glanced up from his crouched position. "Because I want this so badly?" He ghosted his palm against Wyatt's erection and he hissed through his teeth at the sudden pleasure.

"Yeah, I want it too," Wyatt admitted. "Did you think I didn't?"

"Doing this to you," Ryan said, his voice low and gravelly, as he popped the button and pulled Wyatt's jeans and boxer briefs down, "reminds me of the night we met."

For Wyatt, it was a reminder that he'd been falling from the first time he'd glanced up from the bar and seen Ryan across the dance floor, in the VIP section. Roped off. Exclusive. Unobtainable. Until suddenly, they were on Wyatt's bike, flying across the Hollywood Hills and none of those things were true.

"Doing this to you," Ryan continued, tongue slicking across Wyatt's abs between hissed words, "reminds me that I wanted to the first second I ever saw you."

It was the echo of Wyatt's thoughts, and that was too much. Wyatt's fists flexed against the wood of the door, and he wanted to drag Ryan up by his hair, and crush his mouth to his. Tell him everything he felt, that it was so much more than sexual desire. That it had always been more than just a hookup. That he'd been a fucking light in the midst of the darkness that Wyatt had been trudging through for too damn long.

But that was edging far too close to the other feelings spilling over and they weren't really together. Not the way Wyatt was desperate for them to be.

Ryan's tongue teased against the head of his leaking cock, and Wyatt pushed away everything else but the way it felt. Hot and silky, wrapping around him as perfect as it had the very first time they'd done this. When Wyatt hadn't realized that it could feel like this.

"God damnit," he gritted out as Ryan sucked him down. "You're too god damn good."

Ryan's glance up was half-angelic, half-devilish tease. Wyatt loved it all; the way he loved all of him.

"You want it like this?" Ryan asked, cock slipping out of his mouth, his lips red and swollen and perfect.

Wyatt was undone and could only nod, watching as Ryan began to expertly work him over, everything blending together in a red-hot wave of bliss, so much more intense than it had ever been before.

When he finally let go, shooting down Ryan's throat, they both hesitated for a long moment after, and Wyatt could hear himself panting in the quiet of the room.

Or maybe that was Ryan.

"Give me a sec," Wyatt said, every nerve ending feeling raw and over-exposed.

"You can fuck me later," Ryan said, and he sounded equally breathless, even though Wyatt knew he hadn't lasted long enough for Ryan to have made a real effort.

Wyatt slid down the door, and landed in an awkward heap next to Ryan. "Whatever you want," he said, and knew it was true no matter how you sliced it. Whatever Ryan wanted; that was what Wyatt was going to do.

It probably had something to do with falling in love with him.

Chapter Thirteen

"Oh, Wyatt, you didn't tell me how cute he was," Bea said as Tony helped her out of the car. "He's adorable."

"And now he also has a much bigger head. I'm not sure how we're going to fit through the front door," Wyatt teased as he and Ryan walked up to meet her.

"I'm Ryan, Mrs. Blake," Ryan said, reaching out to clasp her hand in his. He leaned down and brushed a quick kiss across her cheek. "It's so nice to finally meet you."

"You as well, dear boy." Nana beamed up at him. "You're much cuter than you are on TV."

Wyatt didn't know his grandmother even watched baseball. Tony, who was just finishing with the valet, gave him a distracted shrug that meant he didn't know either.

"I didn't know you followed the Dodgers," Ryan said, sounding surprised and pleased, before Wyatt could even ask her what she was talking about.

"I didn't, not before now," she said, tucking her arm into Ryan's proffered one. "But they replay games all the time on MLB Network. Who knew?"

Wyatt fell back, next to Tony and watched them walk up the steps into the big patio that surrounded Terroir on all sides. There were a number of people milling around, holding glasses of champagne and coffee cups, all chattering away, looking superior because they'd managed to score an invite to the most exclusive brunch in Napa.

He, Tony, and Ryan barely looked like they belonged—Tony least of all with his close-shaved head and tattoos peeking out of his short-sleeve button-down. His nana, with her sweet smile, and brightly printed floral day dress, looked like she never belonged anywhere else, and it filled his heart with a bittersweet joy that he was able to give her this, even as her memory began to fail. She might not remember today's details exactly, but hopefully she'd remember that she had grandsons that loved her very much.

"I'll go grab us some drinks," Wyatt said as Ryan made sure to get them close to the trellis, where the front gave some shade from the sun.

"I'll help," Tony said.

As they approached the outdoor bar to order, Tony leaned in and asked, "You okay leaving your boyfriend with Nana? She might grill him."

"And find out what?" Wyatt asked with exasperation. "That he's an awesome guy? I hope so. I've never gotten to introduce her to someone I really cared about before, and you know what? I'm glad I could with Ryan."

But Tony just shook his head, a look on his face that made Wyatt's stomach wrench. "I heard some stuff," he said. "After you left, I heard from a guy in the kitchen that knows someone else who used to hook up with him all the time."

"*Used to,*" Wyatt emphasized. Did he like thinking about Ryan's history of various hookups? Not particularly, but he hardly expected him to be a saint before they'd even met. Sex was amazing; it was a perfectly natural reaction to want to have it if you could.

"I'm just saying," Tony hissed as the person in front of them picked up their drink and departed from the bar. "You need to think about this."

"I'm done thinking," Wyatt said, and turned to the bartender. "Nico, it's so good to see you."

"You too, Wy," he said, "what can I get you?"

"Two mimosas, a coffee with cream, no sugar, and a Bloody Mary."

"You catch sight of the big boss yet?" Nico asked as he began to prepare the drinks. "Or should I ask, has the big boss seen you yet?"

"Thankfully, no." Wyatt wasn't under any impression that Aquino felt any less betrayed now than he had before. Just because Kian had worked his magic and gotten his hands on the brunch tickets didn't mean Wyatt was forgiven for the ultimate betrayal: leaving Terroir behind.

"Better keep it that way," Nico said, placing the drinks on the bar. "He's on the warpath today."

This was nothing new, but the extra heads-up was nice, and Wyatt was reminded of how much he'd always liked Nico.

"Thanks," he said, throwing some bills on the bar, tipping generously and happy that now he could, after leaving Terroir and going to work for Ryan.

"I think it was Nico," Tony said under his breath as they picked up the drinks and made their way to where Ryan and Nana were sitting in the shade. "Conner said it was some bartender at Terroir that he'd been hooking up with."

"Nico isn't even gay," Wyatt protested. "I don't know why we're even talking about this still."

"Because, baby bro, I don't want to see you hurt. And you really like this guy."

"And this guy really likes me," Wyatt said defensively. After all, Ryan had made it clear that if he couldn't have Wyatt, he hadn't wanted to have anyone. As his *fake* boyfriend, sure, but that must mean something?

Wyatt wanted it to mean something so badly.

"Here's your mimosa," Wyatt said, and he knew he sounded short as he handed Ryan his glass, but Tony was reminding him that only a short while ago, they hadn't gotten along.

"Thanks," Ryan said, beaming up at him, making Wyatt feel guilty. "We've just been chatting about my new ad campaign for Adidas."

"He says he might even be on the cover of some magazine," Nana said, smile bright as she looked up at Wyatt. "He's definitely cute enough."

"And now his head is definitely not going to fit through the front door," Wyatt teased. He hadn't explicitly told Nana what he and Ryan were—he hadn't wanted to lie to her, and Ryan had been surprisingly okay with that—but she'd clearly connected the dots anyway.

A man approached their group, and Wyatt tensed. Had Aquino found out he was here and sent security to boot them out? But no, the man was dressed in a pair of preppy khakis and a blue chambray button-down and had a combination of nerves and eagerness in his dark eyes.

"Ryan Flores?" the man asked, gesturing with the phone in his hand. "I was wondering if I could take a pic with you."

This had happened to them before when they were out. Once when they were surfing, once when they were grabbing food. It wasn't a big deal, and Ryan dealt with it like it wasn't, giving the fan a selfie and a smile both times.

But this time, Wyatt caught a flicker of annoyance on his face before he quickly covered it.

"Sure," he said, rising to his feet and going over to where the guy was standing, anticipating the selfie request.

"Actually," the man hedged, "a selfie would be great, but what about a pic with your boyfriend? You guys are so cute. I follow your Insta, and my husband laughs, but I swear I can never decide if I want to *be* you or hire you to come cook for us."

The hesitation on Ryan's face was distinct this time, and he didn't cover it up. Wyatt told himself it didn't matter, but it was hard to convince himself. After all, what was so different about taking a picture here, when they took pictures together on a regular basis and posted them—just so everyone, like the man in front of them, would think exactly what he thought?

"Uh, I think he'd probably prefer his privacy today," Ryan said awkwardly. "Selfie instead?"

They took the selfie and though the man thanked him and wished him luck in the upcoming season, Wyatt got the distinct impression that nobody had come out of that encounter happy. Not Ryan, whose smile had dimmed considerably, not the fan, who seemed pretty disappointed, and definitely not Wyatt, who now couldn't help but wonder why Ryan had turned him down.

Thankfully, Tony had kept Nana distracted, so Wyatt didn't have to answer any questions right now about why that man had believed he and Ryan were together. He'd had an answer ready, but he felt a little too raw to explain anything right now.

"I'm going to go check on the seating time," Wyatt said, and wasn't even embarrassed it looked like he was escaping because he *was.*

Callie, the hostess, had a permanent smile etched on her face, but the smile deepened a little as Wyatt approached her. "Oh, Wyatt, it's so good to see you," she said. "We've missed you around here."

"You're a gem. Do you have any idea when the seating is going to begin? I've got my nana here, and she's not great in the sun."

"And your boyfriend too, if I hear the rumors right," Callie said with a sly wink. "Ryan Flores, what a great catch."

It was exactly the impression they were explicitly and implicitly trying to give, but Wyatt still felt himself shy away from the implication. "Yeah," he said, neither confirming nor denying anything. "Any idea on the time?"

"Five minutes," she said. "And I don't know if anyone told you but the Bastard is on fire today. Steer clear."

Wyatt hadn't been too worried before because Kian *had* managed to get the tickets, and they were unequivocally in his name. He knew Aquino often reviewed the guest list himself, so if there'd been an issue, Wyatt had always expected Kian to call him and cancel the tickets.

But now, he wasn't sure. Not when the Bastard was in apparently a very bad mood.

When he returned to the waiting trio, there was unexpectedly two others that had joined their party.

"I'm sorry," Ryan said, not sounding very sorry at all, "but I'm not taking pictures today."

Wyatt's heart clenched. How many times had they been out and Ryan had agreed to pictures? At least half a dozen times. He'd never denied fans before, not when Wyatt was present, and suddenly Wyatt couldn't help but wonder if this had something to do with him?

Was Ryan avoiding a situation like the request he'd denied earlier? Wyatt wasn't sure he could feel worse, and yet his stomach kept falling. But he plastered a smile on his face and sank to the bench next to Nana.

"Only a few minutes to go," Wyatt promised, reaching over and holding her hand. "You're going to love it."

"It's a beautiful place," she said, her eyes sparkling. "But then I'd never expect anything else from you. You've only ever kept your eye on the biggest prize, determined to win it." Her gaze strayed over to Ryan, and Wyatt had a feeling he knew what she was really referring to.

"Being the best, working for the best, that's always been important to me," Wyatt agreed. "But some things are just as important. Like being able to spend time with you." He didn't add that making more money was important, so that she could stay in the home she was at and be well cared for. But it meant something to him, that he was able to give that to her. More than the worthless prestige of Terroir had ever brought him, anyway.

"You're a good grandson," Nana said, her tender expression putting to rest forever his worries that she wouldn't care about him because he was gay. He'd made a mistake by not telling her before, but maybe she'd been a convenient excuse because *he* wasn't ready to finish telling the world yet.

The truth was, he'd never appreciated how much Nate had pushed him, but he was beginning to wonder if that was because he'd never really loved Nate. Because now he wished Ryan would push a little harder.

"Let's go have a fabulous brunch," Wyatt said, helping her to her feet. "I see people starting to go in."

Tony and Ryan trailed behind them as they headed towards the front door. Wyatt had a single moment of unease when he handed the tickets to a woman he didn't recognize manning the entrance. But she checked his party off the list, and then Callie led them to their table. It wasn't the best table, off in the corner, away from the main dining room, but Wyatt could care less. The food would taste just as good here, and this way he might avoid seeing Aquino.

"Tell me about the menu," Nana asked as they sat down.

"Chef Aquino doesn't typically like menus," Wyatt explained, "but he knows he couldn't get away without a menu during regular dining hours. People like to know what they're eating and have some input into what it is. But during Chef's bi-annual brunches, he serves whatever he feels like. Usually three or four courses, with pastries."

"It's a stupid affectation," Tony said.

"Yet it's packed," Wyatt said wryly. "I guess when you're as famous as Chef Aquino, you don't care how egotistical it looks."

"Or you do it *because* it looks egotistical," Tony said under his breath as the waiter approached their table. He was new, because Wyatt didn't recognize him either. One month out of this place, and already he didn't recognize all the staff. Of course turnover was to be expected when the boss was often referred to as the Bastard.

"I don't think he cares much about what people think," Wyatt said.

"Actually," Ryan inserted. "I'd disagree. He probably cares too much."

Wyatt had never thought of it that way before, and maybe it didn't make him like his ex-boss any more, but it did help shed some light on his personality.

"I had a coach like that once," Ryan said with a shrug. "It's so important what people think of them, they're willing to bulldoze everyone and everything to look good. Sound familiar?"

Wyatt had to nod.

"Is there any way we could see Kian and Xander while we're here?" Nana asked. "I know they're working, but maybe they have a break and could come say hi?"

"Never going to happen. I'm sorry, Nana. Chef Aquino is the only kitchen employee allowed on the dining room floor. But maybe we can steal them away after brunch is over. I'll see." Wyatt didn't think it was likely, and also didn't want to attempt it because doing so would mean getting into the kitchen. Putting himself straight in the crosshairs of the Bastard was definitely a bad idea, but he didn't want to tell Nana no. He also didn't want to have to explain that despite being back in the Terroir dining room, he was definitely not allowed back in the kitchens.

The waiter returned with their drink refills, and as he was distributing glasses, looked over at Ryan in a way that was not very casual. Wyatt resisted the urge to nudge his chair closer, because jealousy was stupid, and also they weren't really together anyway.

"I'm sorry, but you're Ryan Flores, aren't you?" the waiter asked as he set Ryan's mimosa in front of him.

If Wyatt had needed other proof that the waiter was new, here it was. Being fired for this was the very least thing Aquino would do. Waitstaff were given very strict instructions not to call attention to celebrity visitors to Terroir. Asking if he was Ryan Flores was breaking every one of those rules.

"I am," he confirmed.

"I'm such a big Dodgers fan," the waiter gushed, and Wyatt told himself that this was cute, it was adorable, it was anything but annoying, but he couldn't quite pull it off. "I lived here as a kid, and just came back a few months ago."

Which explained why he was breaking the cardinal rule of the Terroir dining room and also why he wasn't acting chill like most LA fans did.

"Great," Ryan said, and sounded just as annoyed as Wyatt felt.

"I'll have your first course up shortly. It's a lavender chamomile honey yogurt with fresh berry compote," he said.

"Chamomile," Tony said in disgust as the waiter departed. Wyatt found what he hoped was his brother's foot under the table and kicked.

"What?" Tony demanded. "Is Aquino trying to put us to sleep?"

"It's so interesting to me that chefs these days find inspiration everywhere," Nana said loyally. "Imagine using lavender in food. I used to grow lavender in my garden."

"You're not a fan of these unique inspirations?" Ryan asked Tony.

"I prefer simple food, prepared really well," Tony said. "Farm to table is well and good. But it needs to be something the diner recognizes. I like the way the Tavern does it."

Wyatt bit his tongue and did not remind Tony that the reason he'd ended up on this "simple is better" path was because he'd been booted out of culinary school and had never had an opportunity to cook at a restaurant with a reputation for complexity like Terroir.

"What do you think, Wyatt?" Nana asked him.

"I think there's room for both points of view, and both types of food preparation. Some people aren't going to want lavender in their food, and that's fine, and then there are some diners who want to try something that nobody else has made before."

"I've always wanted to try a more mobile approach to dining," Tony said. "I love the food cart concept, where you can change the menu up at will, and always try something different. I think people are a lot more apt to try something if it comes from a food truck with a cute name, and in something recognizable, like a taco shell or a burger bun."

"That's . . . actually really interesting," Wyatt said. "I'd love to work in that sort of framework."

He knew he wouldn't be Ryan's personal chef forever. After all, despite taking the job and keeping it, they both knew Ryan didn't really need one. Eventually he'd have to move on, and maybe the idea was one to tuck away for a rainy day. He couldn't really imagine working with his brother, but Tony had clearly matured and changed. Maybe it was time to put all that past history aside and give something a try.

"Your first course," the waiter said with a flourish, setting down bowls of yogurt, beautifully arranged with a floral pattern of bright-red berry sauce traced across the surface.

Nana's face said it all; that coming here to this had been worth the risk of Aquino's wrath and worth Ryan's uncomfortable fan encounters.

"Oh, Wyatt, this is so beautiful," she exclaimed. "I'm not sure I can even eat it, it's so pretty."

The brunch passed with Bea raving over each and every dish, her smile growing brighter with every moment that passed. Even Wyatt managed to relax—though he wasn't sure if that was because Aquino didn't make his way into the dining room or because Ryan had relaxed, too. In any case, no other fans approached them, and even their waiter toned down his interest which Wyatt sensed Ryan was grateful for.

As the meal drew to a close, and he pulled out his wallet to pay the bill, Wyatt checked his phone. To his shock there were three texts from Xander. Xander wasn't much of a texter, even on his best day, and he, like the rest of the kitchen staff, always put his phone into the storage lockers during a shift. Three texts during Terroir's famous brunch service was the equivalent of a 911 call, complete with SWAT team and Life Flight.

Just as Wyatt expected, when he opened the texts, they were supremely unhelpful—cryptic one-word messages like "emergency," and "help," and the last one, "this is bad."

Wyatt felt himself tense. If Xander thought something was bad, then it was very bad. But how bad could it be, he reasoned. The food coming out of the kitchens was as flawless as ever, and none of the waiters looked worried or harassed. If something bad had gone down in the kitchens, then it was at least somewhat contained.

The thought didn't really set Wyatt's mind at ease. He texted back, "I'll be at the back door in five," and hoped that Xander still had his phone on him so he'd see the message.

"I need to check on something," he told Nana, Tony, and Ryan. "I'll be right back."

"Are you going to see Xander and Kian, dear?" Nana asked, oblivious to the undercurrents of Wyatt's worry.

"Something like that," he told her, rising to his feet.

"Make sure to pass on how wonderful the meal was," she insisted. Ryan's eyes were questioning across the table, but Wyatt gave a quick shake of his head to indicate that he didn't need to accompany him.

Exiting the front door, Wyatt made his way around the side of the building, down to the employee parking and entrance.

Xander was leaning against the wall next to the door, eyes closed. He was still in his whites, with one of his trademark chili pepper head-wraps on.

"What's going on?" Wyatt demanded.

Xander's eyes opened and Wyatt realized how weary he looked. There was no shift you took at Terroir where you didn't feel exhausted by the end, but this was an emotional weariness and a clear concern that got Wyatt's stomach churning.

"Kian," Xander said simply.

"Callie and Nico both warned me he was in a mood today," Wyatt said. "I hoped that it didn't have anything to do with Kian."

"Do you remember when someone sent overcooked branzino to the governor?"

Wyatt remembered. They'd all walked on eggshells for at least a week, everyone terrified to provoke Aquino into another angry explosion. His ears had rung for at least a day from the blistering lecture they'd all been given, even though at best they'd all been tangentially involved in the branzino incident. The culprit, of course, had been summarily fired, after a rant that promised he'd never again work in food service in California.

As far as Wyatt knew, that had held, and the guy wasn't even able to get a job at McDonald's, working the fryer.

"It would be hard to forget."

"This was . . . minor in comparison. Except," Xander said, taking a shuddering breath, "it was all on Kian. The Bastard found out he'd gotten you tickets. I guess he felt it was a betrayal."

Wyatt was speechless. He'd expected Kian to get a minor lecture for the infraction, if it could even be termed that. He'd never imagined that Kian would bear the brunt of Aquino's temper.

"It wouldn't have been so bad," Xander continued, "except that Kian didn't just stand there and take it. He dished it right back. I guess that's maybe why it didn't touch the rest of us.

Chef was too busy trying to contain Kian, and then too busy weeping in his arms about how Kian doesn't care about him after all."

"*What?*" That seemed both improbable and impossible. Chef didn't have personal feelings. Everything was directed to and from the professional side. It was never a personal betrayal—only a professional one, and according to Aquino, that was always worse.

Wyatt didn't personally agree, but then he'd never had the balls to tell him that before. Kian apparently had.

"Kian started to let him have it, telling him he was being unreasonable and mean, and it was all so true and so pointed, and I couldn't help but think he'd been listening to both of us too long. Mostly me, because it was all there in the delivery, which probably could have given industrial-grade acid a run for its money. But Aquino didn't take that lying down, so he started screaming back. Then suddenly . . . Kian said one sentence, and he stopped yelling, so we couldn't hear it. But Aquino shut right up, and we all heard him beg Kian not to leave."

"I don't understand," Wyatt said. "He begged him not to leave? *Bastian Aquino* begged him not to leave?"

"Exactly," Xander said. "Worst day ever."

"I'm failing to see how this is bad for Kian. It clearly means he's got a hold on Aquino, and frankly it's terrifying, but maybe Kian can handle it."

"Kian can't handle it," Xander growled. He started pacing back and forth. "All this means is that they've got a terrible hold on each other. If Aquino had yelled at him and then fired him, then he would've been hurt, devastated probably, but he would've gotten over it eventually. Found a new job, fallen in love with someone more appropriate. But all this proves is that Aquino feels the same, and if Kian figures this out, he's never going to get out while he still can."

Wyatt hadn't thought of it that way before. But then he remembered what Kian had said the other night, about it being worth it, no matter the cost.

"I don't think he's going to get out. No matter what, he's not going to," Wyatt said slowly. "I think it's time to let it go, Xander."

Xander threw up his hands in frustration. "Would you have stopped that chef from overcooking his branzino and saved his career if you'd been able to?"

"Of course I would have," Wyatt said, crossing his arms over his chest. "You know I would have. But this is different. This is personal, not professional, and they're already halfway in it. You can't stop it now. All you can do is support him, now, and if it goes bad."

"Not if, *when*," Xander predicted darkly.

Wyatt knew better than to ask why Xander was so convinced it was going to end badly. He wouldn't get an answer. Not a real one, anyway. Xander kept all those feelings locked up tight—except for the little that escaped when he worried about someone he cared about.

"That's all we can do," Wyatt repeated.

The door next to them opened, and Xander jumped, which proved how worked up he was. But it was just one of the bartenders from upstairs. Nico, in fact.

Wyatt was the one who froze when he saw who it was. "Oh, Wyatt," he said. "I think they're about finished upstairs."

"I know, I was just checking in with Xander," Wyatt said.

"I've got to go back in," Xander muttered, and shouldered his way through the door without even saying goodbye. Which was to be expected in Xander World, even when he wasn't in a bad mood. And he was in a terrible mood.

"So," Nico said slyly, not leaving, and filling Wyatt with foreboding. He remembered what Tony had said about him, and wished that he could forget. "I heard you're here with Ryan Flores."

"Yeah," Wyatt said, hoping that a short answer would keep Nico from continuing the conversation. But Nico wanted to talk, and nothing was going to stop him.

"And that you're living with him."

"I'm his personal chef," Wyatt inserted.

"Yeah." Nico sounded like he hadn't bought that for a second. "I know all about his arrangements."

"I'm not stupid enough to think I'm the first guy he's been with," Wyatt defended.

"Possibly," Nico said. "But he's never gonna stay with one guy. He's not built that way. He likes it all kinds of ways, with all kinds of guys. Likes to keep it exciting."

That sounded like Ryan, the adrenaline junkie, and even though Wyatt had always loved that part of his personality, suddenly he wasn't entirely sure.

"There's no crime in enjoying sex," Wyatt said shortly.

But Nico was determined to torpedo everything—or do *something,* Wyatt still wasn't sure. Was he jealous? Was he hoping that if he got Wyatt to leave, his hookups with Ryan might continue? Wyatt didn't know. All he knew was that Nico kept fucking talking and wouldn't stop.

"Just . . . lower your expectations," Nico counseled. "Actually, scratch that. Obliterate your expectations. Because he's never going to let you have any."

That *didn't* sound like the Ryan that Wyatt had come to know. At least most of the time. He couldn't help but think of the few awkward instances that Wyatt had desperately tried to write off as growing pains with a new very public relationship.

But maybe it was more. Wyatt cursed Nico for getting into his head, when that was the very thing that he'd clearly set out to do.

"I'll take that under consideration," Wyatt said. "And I've got to go. Thanks for the advice, I guess."

"You've been quiet," Ryan said.

"Yeah, I can't imagine why," Wyatt grumbled. "I'm only preparing to throw myself out of an airplane."

"But you're going to be with me," Ryan said, as the plane taxied towards the runway. "It's all gonna be good."

"I guess I should be happy you settle for skydiving and aren't into BASE jumping," Wyatt said. The truth was Nico's confessions had him worked up far more than the possibility of launching himself out of an airplane with only a parachute to stand between him and death.

"Oh, I've tried that too," Ryan said. "But I like myself in one solid piece, thank you very much, and management didn't like it when they found out. I guess it made them think I was a bad investment. They aren't exactly wild about the skydiving either, to be honest. Or my collection of fast cars. They called Eric in and yelled at him for half an hour over the Maserati I bought at the end of the season."

"Gee, I can't imagine why."

"I know it's stupid, but it's an addiction," Ryan said, with a helpless little shrug that Wyatt found adorable, even when he didn't want to.

It wasn't Ryan's fault that Nico existed. It wasn't Ryan's fault that Nico had decided to give him unsolicited advice. It definitely wasn't Ryan's fault that Wyatt had listened despite all his intentions not to. But despite all those things that Wyatt knew to be true, it was impossible not to feel a little frustrated. Maybe even a little angry.

If Ryan hadn't been so awkward about their relationship today, Wyatt knew he wouldn't have listened to Nico. How was it that Ryan could be perfectly normal and perfect boyfriend material except when he was trying to prove he was Wyatt's boyfriend?

It made no sense, and Wyatt liked things to make sense. The culinary arts were full of irrefutable facts, and there was a comforting certainty in the kitchen. At first, when Ryan had been so determined that his boyfriend had to be Wyatt, it had been easy to believe that he'd meant more than just a random guy he'd picked to play a lover.

Now, Wyatt couldn't be sure. And yet, he was allowing himself to be strapped to him anyway, doubt be damned.

"What other crazy things have you done?" Wyatt asked, because hearing how many ways Ryan had conspired to kill himself was somehow easier than wallowing in his own confusion.

"Besides BASE jumping? Last year I was trying to get my wingsuit certification, but I got busy and had to let it go. I actually like it better than BASE jumping, because it's a longer flight, more like flying."

"Is it just shit in the air?" Wyatt asked.

The airplane engine revved up and they started down the runway. "I love this part, so maybe it *is* just shit in the air?" Ryan said.

"Taking off?"

"It's the anticipation in the air," Ryan said with relish. "Knowing I'm going to choose to jump out of this plane."

Wyatt shook his head. "I think I'll stick with surfing."

"Have you gone deep-sea diving? That's pretty wild, too. Totally different vibe, but still gets the blood pumping."

"Do you swim with sharks too?" Wyatt asked sarcastically.

"Once," Ryan said with a grin. Wyatt regretted asking.

"Don't worry, I'll try to contain your life-threatening ac-tivities to waking me up in the morning and this skydive," Ryan said, and Wyatt wanted to find him as endearing as he had only this morning. It wasn't that he loved him any less, it was that he doubted him more. Right about now he wished he could push Nico out of the plane.

"I appreciate that," Wyatt retorted dryly. "Now go over the steps again, please."

"Again?"

"I'm a chef, I like to be prepared," Wyatt said.

"Okay, it's gonna be great, I promise. When we get close to altitude, I'll hook us together. You'll be attached to my front." Ryan paused, and Wyatt realized that he was waiting for him to make a sexual joke. "Okay, maybe not your favorite place to be after all," he teased. "Anyway, when we reach altitude, we'll inch our way to the door, and then I'll push us off."

"I can't believe I let you talk me into this," Wyatt said. The plane was flying higher and higher, and it was impossible not to look out the window and see the fields of Napa getting smaller and smaller beneath them.

"It'll be about a minute of free fall," Ryan continued, "and then I'll pull the parachute."

"And there's a backup, right?"

"Of course there is," Ryan retorted. "I told you not to worry. This is safe. I mean, not *safe*, because we are jumping out of a plane, but as safe as that gets. You remember the landing I told you about?"

"Yeah," Wyatt said. They'd practiced it a few times on land. Speaking of land, he was really wishing he was back on it. He eyed the toy-sized trees with trepidation.

"We're about to altitude," the pilot said over the intercom. "We'll open the door shortly."

"Just take a breath," Ryan counseled as he began to hook them together. "Maybe a few breaths. It's gonna be great."

"If you say that one more time," Wyatt hissed.

The door opened, and Ryan didn't have another chance to say it again, because suddenly they were at the edge of the plane, and then they weren't in the plane at all.

The wind rushed past Wyatt's ears as they free-fell in the deep-blue sky. He could feel Ryan's excitement even though he couldn't see his face. As for himself? It wasn't . . . terrible he decided as they continued to fall, the ground rushing closer and closer.

It was even sort of a pleasant rush. Kind of like when Ryan had climbed on the back of his bike. When he climbed on the back of Ryan's. A feeling of putting yourself in someone else's hands with the hope that you'd be safe.

After today, Wyatt didn't know for sure if he was still safe in Ryan's hands. But he loved him enough that he couldn't just pull away. His whole body jolted suddenly, and he realized that Ryan had pulled the parachute.

After a few minutes of coasting to the ground, they landed, legs getting a bit tangled, and they fell to a heap on the ground before Ryan could unclip them. Wyatt pulled his helmet off and took one deep breath, and then another. He didn't think he'd get his breath back so quickly.

Ryan finally unclipped them, and Wyatt did the only thing he'd wanted since they'd jumped out of an airplane—he leaned down, yanked his helmet off, and kissed him. Ryan tasted like air and sky and fresh air, and his breath was coming in short, breathless pants as he pulled back.

"You loved it, didn't you?" Ryan grinned, eyes glittering from the adrenaline rush. "I knew you would."

I love you.

Wyatt shrugged, faking nonchalance, and Ryan stared at him for a moment, then tackled him to the ground, hovering above him for a split second before covering Wyatt's mouth with his own.

Chapter Fourteen

"This is a really big deal," Eric said, reaching out to smooth down the collar of Wyatt's shirt.

Ryan had to stop himself from pushing Eric's hands away, and doing it himself. He wasn't sure if Wyatt's eye roll was more to do with Eric stating the obvious or Eric invading his personal space.

"Believe me, I'm aware," Wyatt retorted dryly, at the same time, shucking the hand off his collar with a shrug of his shoulder.

So, maybe both.

Ryan wished that Eric hadn't decided that he needed to show up to give them a last-minute pep talk on their first public outing, because he had a few much more fun ideas to give everyone the indelible impression he and Wyatt were definitely together.

But apparently showing up with their hair and clothes messed up, looking like they'd just fucked on the car didn't give the impression Eric was looking for.

Ryan maintained it still would've been a lot more fun than the lecture they were currently receiving.

"I don't want you to spend the whole evening together," Eric continued, even though Ryan knew he was barely paying any attention and Wyatt had clearly tuned him out altogether. "Constantly hanging on each other gives the idea that you're insecure in your relationship.

"The car will be here any minute. I just spoke to the event concierge at Temple, she's going to make sure you guys have a great time, and will let you know when there's something you need to participate in." He paused, and Ryan thought for one miraculous second that Eric was done talking, but then he kept going. "It goes without saying that you need to both be on your best behavior tonight. Have a few drinks, but don't get drunk. No crazy antics. No semi-public sexual exploits."

"Awwww, there goes everything I wanted to do," Ryan teased and to his disappointment, Wyatt's expression didn't change. Instead of the melting smile that he'd grown to expect, Wyatt looked stiff and nervous. Withdrawn, almost, which had been the norm since they got back from Napa a week ago. There'd been a few times when Ryan had really been able to get him to relax, and laugh with him like he had at the beginning—usually after a few beers or a really intense workout—and he still approached sex with a fierce intensity that Ryan definitely enjoyed.

More than once, he'd considered asking Wyatt what was wrong, but in his head, that conversation fell exclusively into the "relationship" category, and since he couldn't go there, he avoided it.

Eric shook his head, amused despite his own lecture, and went to go see if the car had arrived yet, finally leaving them alone. Maybe Ryan couldn't ask Wyatt what was wrong, but he could make sure this was still something he wanted to do. It was hard to doubt that Ryan was still something he wanted, because the sex was so raw and consuming, but maybe it wouldn't hurt to ask.

"Is this still okay?" Ryan asked, turning towards the other man. Wyatt looked up, surprise in his expression.

"Why wouldn't it be?"

Ryan might be a baseball player, but he wasn't dumb. Even he knew that answering a question with a question was a great way to deflect.

"You just seem quiet, that's all," Ryan observed. It occurred to him suddenly that he'd made this exact same comment before they'd gone skydiving.

Ryan didn't think he was getting bored; the very nature of their relationship was designed so he *wouldn't,* so he *couldn't* get bored, but maybe Ryan had miscalculated?

Maybe even though they weren't technically in a relationship, they were doing too many relationship-like things—like going to Napa, spending time with Flor and Wyatt's nana and his brother, going to brunch, now this couples outing to Temple.

Boredom was something that wasn't allowed to happen. Ryan couldn't let him pull away, and not only because of the fake relationship that Wyatt had committed to, but because the more Wyatt retreated, the more attached Ryan realized he'd become.

He needed to fix this, because whatever this was, because it definitely had morphed into something more than Ryan had ever anticipated or expected.

"It's gonna be great," Ryan said, feeling stupid because he kept saying that and he wasn't sure that Wyatt believed him anymore.

But Wyatt smiled this time, and pulled him close, and brushed a brief kiss across his lips. "It will," Wyatt agreed, "I'm just disappointed we couldn't take the bike. Re-enact the night we met."

"Maybe tomorrow," Ryan said, hating the hope that bloomed through his system. All he wanted was to get back to how good they were together. The fantastic sex they were having should have been enough—it had always been enough before—but now he wasn't sure. They were missing something else; Wyatt was holding it back, and even though Ryan didn't know what it was, he craved it anyway.

"The car's here," Eric announced in the foyer.

Ryan slipped his hand into Wyatt's, and gave him a bright smile. "Let's do this," he said.

The concierge, Anne-Marie, met them at the private back entrance of the club. Eric had decided, in his fake-relationship wisdom, that it would be better for the photographers to get them on the way out of the club, instead of heading in.

Ryan didn't know why this was, but he'd learned to save his energy to argue with Eric on the major points, not the minor ones.

"Around midnight, we'll bring you up to the stage, as you're our VIP hosts for the evening," Anne-Marie said, as they walked into the back of the dim club.

"What are we supposed to do?" Wyatt asked.

"On stage?" Anne-Marie questioned as she tucked a strand of bright-red hair behind her ear. "Whatever you like. Dance. Kiss. Each other? The dancers?" She waved a hand. "You two are so cute, I'm sure you'll come up with something."

Wyatt raised an eyebrow, like this wasn't something they heard all the damn time. Like it wasn't something they had *planned*.

"I mean, your Insta pictures are so gorgeous, like some sort of fairy tale," Anne-Marie said. "And obviously, yeah, you set them up to look that way, but there's a truth in them that you don't see very often. I can tell you're both very fond of each other."

She turned to them. "I'll escort you to the VIP booth now, if that's okay?"

Ryan was officially pathetic. He wanted to beg her to tell him more about how they cared about each other, even while he argued with himself that caring about each other had never been the point of this. They were only supposed to *seem* authentic, while having great sex, but something had gotten crossed along the way.

"Sure, yeah, that'll be great," Ryan said when Wyatt stayed quiet.

The VIP area was the exact same one that Ryan had occupied the night he'd gone looking for a fake boyfriend and had found his personal chef instead.

He wanted to ask Anne-Marie if that was something Eric had arranged, but decided against it because it exposed too much of his nostalgia and stupid feelings in front of Wyatt.

"I'll see that the waiter brings over your bottle service," Anne-Marie said, as they settled on the plush velvet couch. Wyatt looked way more comfortable than Ryan felt, but he tried to copy the other man's relaxed posture. The reason, Ryan realized as Anne-Marie left, was because he'd never been here with another man before. Definitely not with one that he was pretending he was in a relationship with.

Definitely not one that he apparently had stronger feelings for.

When you fell in love with someone, Ryan reasoned as the waiter approached, you were supposed to feel excited and happy, not greet the discovery with dread. Except that was all he could feel, as he envisioned Wyatt growing bored, just as his ex had described, and then having zero choice but to seek excitement somewhere else. In someone else's bed.

"Welcome to Temple," the waiter said, and for the first time Ryan looked up at the man. He was dressed in a pair of tight black leather pants, riding low on his hips, his rippling obliques exposed, and a pair of black feathery wings. His light-blue eyes were rimmed with black, making them pop even more. He looked like a just-debauched fallen angel, which was just the sort of fantasy theater that Temple liked to indulge in.

There was no excuse except that the guy was objectively hot, there was undeniably interest in his baby blue eyes, and Ryan was both miserable and desperate.

"I feel like I must have died and gone to heaven," he teased the waiter.

The waiter perched a hip on the edge of the couch, leaning in closer, and Ryan didn't have to be looking at Wyatt to imagine his expression. "I'll tell you a secret," the angel murmured low, so Ryan had to scoot even closer to hear, "I got kicked out of heaven."

Ryan heard Wyatt's incredulous scoffing noise behind him, and yes, it was silly and ridiculous and over-the-top dramatic, but the guy was gorgeous and no doubt this was a very common fantasy.

"Were you very, very bad?" Wyatt asked from over Ryan's shoulder, in a faux-serious voice. "I bet you were super naughty."

The angel rolled his eyes, but his voice kept that faux-conspiratorial tone that had pulled Ryan into the fantasy from the first moment. "I discovered being bad is a lot more fun than being good."

Ryan sympathized; he'd discovered this same thing himself, at sixteen. And at eighteen. And at twenty-one. And again, at twenty-five, when he'd been unable to stay away from Wyatt Blake.

It was a lesson he kept re-learning. Maybe it was a lesson he could re-learn tonight.

"That's definitely a lesson we don't need to be taught." Wyatt sounded amused and vaguely interested and Ryan leaned back, tucking himself against Wyatt's side. It wasn't a shock when Wyatt's arm curled around him. Protectively, Ryan told himself. Wyatt was jealous. Normally, Ryan hated dealing with jealous guys, but he'd take jealousy over boredom, especially if it was Wyatt.

"I'll stay close," the waiter said. "Just in case you need anything. Or need a refresher course."

"We'll take a few beers, too," Ryan said, because he remembered Eric's warning, and he might as well try to keep to one of his admonitions.

To Ryan's surprise though, Wyatt bypassed the beers, and went to the bottles of liquor, pouring a few fingers of vodka into a glass, splashing in a little juice and nothing else.

"I thought he was flirting with you, at first," Wyatt said, mouth drifting towards Ryan's ear so he could hear him over the music, which was increasing in volume by the minute, "but actually I think he was flirting with both of us."

Wyatt again proved how observant he was.

"I think so too," Ryan said, sneaking in a little ear nibble as he turned to talk in Wyatt's ear.

Wyatt shrugged. "He's cute but the whole act is too much for me."

Wyatt was always so damn straight forward, it wasn't a surprise that the act was too theatrical for him. Ryan didn't even like it all that much, but he intended to use it.

"I don't know, cute goes a long way," Ryan said, smiling up at him. "Let's go dance."

Wyatt threw the rest of his vodka back, and Ryan set his beer down. Wyatt caught up Ryan's hand and they walked down the set of stairs to where the rest of the club was partying. Ryan intended to keep to the edges—after all, they needed to be seen, and not just because they were the VIP guests for the evening—but Wyatt took them deeper into the crowd. Ryan should have protested but he just followed.

"You didn't dance last time you were here," Wyatt observed, lips right against his as his hips ground into Ryan's.

"You weren't dancing," Ryan retorted, hands gripping his shoulders firmly, and Wyatt just smirked back.

Wyatt had a natural rhythm that Ryan had already observed from their surfing sessions, and he was a decent dancer, though frankly most of what they were doing was pseudo-dry humping anyway. The crowd and the feeling of Wyatt's hips grinding into his, hands a possessive brand on his back, creeping down towards his ass, raised his temperature quick, and after only a few songs, he felt damp all over. There was sweat slicked at Wyatt's temple, and Ryan wanted to lick it up.

As one song changed to another, Ryan tugged Wyatt towards their VIP area, and he followed easily.

It was a little easier to talk when they were away from the pounding bass emanating from the speakers. Wyatt leaned down. "I think we should tell the angel that you've been very bad indeed." Ryan could tell from their close proximity that Wyatt was hard in his jeans. He wanted to tell him, screw this, and let's go home and screw me, but the voice in the back of his head whispered that he couldn't let this go. He couldn't let Wyatt become complacent and bored and end up in someone like the angel's bed, only without Ryan.

Wyatt threw back another shot of vodka, this time with no juice, and Ryan opened the bottle of tequila with a quick wrench of his fingers. He'd just taken a shot and was sucking on a slice of lime when the angel waiter approached again.

"Need anything?" he asked. "Maybe some help with your shots?"

Wyatt's eyes were blank as Ryan looked at the waiter.

"Sure, sounds like fun," Ryan said carelessly. He couldn't look at Wyatt as the guy reclined on the table, like a tempting buffet, and poured a shot of vodka right into his abs.

There was no backing out now, he could hear the whoops from the crowd, which meant they'd been spotted, and he couldn't push him away.

Besides, he told himself as he leaned down, slurping the tequila off the guy's skin, it was the least boring thing he'd done in ages.

The slice of lime was waiting for him in the angel's mouth and he took it with his own, lingering for a long second. Ryan knew it was all part of the act and the fantasy the club provided, but there was undeniable interest flashing in his light-blue eyes. He wanted Ryan, and he'd probably even take Wyatt too, if that's what it took.

"Can I get you anything else?" the angel asked huskily, partially sitting up. The tequila left his bare chest shiny and Ryan could see exactly where his tongue had been in the flashing lights.

And that was the real question. How far was Ryan willing to take this? How far was *Wyatt* willing to take this?

Anne-Marie chose this particular moment to return. Ryan was pretty sure it wasn't even midnight on the nose, but certainly she'd been observing the activities with everyone else, and had decided the best time to drag them to the main stage was when the entire club was already watching.

"Time to go," she said.

Ryan decided that she must have seen a lot of shit in her tenure because she barely batted an eyelash at what they'd been up to.

Before they went, Ryan turned back to the waiter. "Your name," he asked. "And a dance when we get back."

He could feel Wyatt tense next to him. "With both of us," Ryan clarified, making sure that his intentions were clear.

"Alex," he said, as he began to pile empty glasses on the tray. "And I'll be around when you're done."

That was exactly what Wyatt was afraid of—that Alex would be there when they got back to the VIP area, and Wyatt would have to decide where he stood on the subject that Ryan had spent the whole evening hinting at.

It could have been worse, Wyatt thought as he climbed the stairs, trying to look calm and not nervous because he was about to get in front of about a thousand people, not because Ryan kept trying to set them up a threesome. Ryan could have dragged Alex up there to the stage with them and forced the decision in front of the entire club.

They got to the stage, and the DJ announced them. Wyatt kept a firm grip around Ryan's hips, feeling zero compunction about pulling him a little rough towards him. Ryan leaned over and played it up, kissing him noisily on the cheek and then moving to his lips.

If this was happening, it was happening on *his* terms. Wyatt yanked Ryan even closer and made it even showier, playing to the crowd by dipping him low, and pouring all his frustration into the kiss. The noisy crowd faded away, giving way to a low roaring in his ears. He opened his eyes as the kiss finally ended, and Ryan was staring at him, an inscrutable expression on his face.

The DJ said more nonsense that Wyatt didn't understand even though they were practically on top of one of the speakers, and then finally Anne-Marie led them down the stairs and off the stage.

But it wasn't a solution, because they were still under the crowd's microscope and Alex was waiting, an impatient look of excitement plain on his features, for them to collect him and give him the dance he'd been promised.

Maybe under different circumstances, Wyatt might have enjoyed dancing with him. Would have definitely entertained the threesome idea, but right now, it didn't feel right. Not now. Not under these tenuous circumstances. Not when Wyatt felt five seconds away from grabbing Ryan back and keeping him all to himself.

The uncertainty was breeding jealousy and envy in him, and Wyatt didn't like it, but he didn't know how to exorcise it either.

Wyatt grabbed Ryan's hand just before they were about to head up to the VIP area. "Wait," he said loud enough that he could be heard even over the pounding bass of the music. "Wait. We need to talk."

Ryan turned back to him, pulled his hand back and crossed his arms over his chest. "Are you okay with this?"

The question was a challenge and it was stark black and white, with none of the shades of gray Wyatt knew were important. At least to him.

"We need to talk," he repeated. Even though there was no possible way to talk in here. Not with the music and the strobe lights, and Alex practically hovering over Ryan's shoulder.

He wasn't stupid enough to think they'd get away with it again, but Wyatt decided he was going to try anyway. He pulled Ryan's hand back, and led him the same way he'd gone the first night they met, winding through the crowd and right out the front door, leading him past the bouncers and the eager partiers waiting to get in, down the street, and into the mouth of the alley they'd first spoken in a month ago.

Every second, Wyatt expected Ryan to pull away, to go back to the club, to go back to Alex. And that, Wyatt realized as quiet finally surrounded them, was a microcosm of the whole problem.

He didn't trust Ryan not to break his heart. He didn't trust Ryan to pull the parachute if things got hairy.

"What are we doing here?" Wyatt asked, the question spilling out before he could stop it. If Ryan's earlier question had been a challenge, this was a demand.

"Drinking, partying? Eventually getting photographed and introducing all the housewives in the grocery store checkout line to our relationship?"

"I don't want a cute answer," Wyatt said. "I want the truth."

"Keeping it fun. Keeping it exciting." Ryan's voice sounded brittle. Wyatt's first instinct was to claim bullshit on that too, but he was beginning to think Ryan was actually telling the truth.

"Why can't we have a drink and dance some and make out in the car on the way home, and have undeniably spectacular sex when we do? Isn't that exciting enough for you?"

Ryan hugged himself and Wyatt wasn't sure it was because of the temperature, which seemed mild enough, even for November.

"It's *always* going to get boring. That's what *always* happens."

"Bullshit," Wyatt retorted. "I jumped out of a fucking plane for you. If you want exciting, I'm going to give it to you, because I care about you. But I'm done playing games."

"I don't . . . I don't understand." Another lie. Wyatt found his normally moderate temper beginning to spike. The one thing he hated was being lied to, and Ryan was doing it a lot, and not just tonight.

"Sure, that guy in there is hot, I'm not going to deny it, but we don't need him. Do you need him?"

"I . . . you don't want to go home with him?" Ryan sounded incredulous. When Ryan had been the one flirting with him all night, not Wyatt.

"I want to go home with *you*," Wyatt bit out.

"I'm not dumb," Ryan sneered. "I don't believe that you'll want that forever. You'll get bored, you'll start looking, and someday you're going to wish we took him home. And instead of the three of us, it'll just be the two of you."

"Tell me *you* don't need that guy," Wyatt said again. "Tell me you just want that guy, and we'll figure this out. Because it's not about what I want. It's about what you want."

The look in Ryan's eyes was pure stubbornness. "I want to have fun. I never want to be bored. Never again."

It shouldn't have hurt so much because he'd anticipated it, but it burned like hell anyway. "And I'd bore you, eventually," Wyatt said quietly. "I get it. Thank you for being so clear."

He turned to go, because he couldn't stand there any longer and try to figure out which stupidity coming out of Ryan's mouth were lies and which was the truth. But Ryan caught his arm. For a split second, Wyatt's heart rose, because maybe now he would finally get the answers he wanted. Maybe he could finally break through this barrier that Ryan had insisted on erecting.

"Where are you going?" Ryan demanded. "We're supposed to get photographed together."

The hope hit the barrier straight on and crashed and burned. Because to Ryan, the games were all that mattered. He hadn't even listened when Wyatt had tried to lay his heart on the line for him.

All he could do was shrug. "Go get the fucking angel to do it with you. I'm done." And he walked out of the alley alone.

⚜

Ryan was still unsteady when he walked back into the club. The moment Wyatt had walked away, he'd wanted to run after him, and beg him not to give up on him.

But he'd been really fucking clear, hadn't he? He'd laid out the details of the arrangement and had never given Wyatt any expectation that he would change the rules. And now that Wyatt wasn't getting what he thought he wanted out of the deal, he was done?

Fuck that. Fuck him.

His temper had boiled over after that, leaving him raw and shaky, and clenching his hands over and over again, wishing for a bat to hold onto. To ground him. To beat against the most convenient stationary object.

It wasn't supposed to go this way, and it definitely wasn't supposed to end like this.

He went back to Temple because he didn't know what else to do. Marching back up to his VIP section, he unscrewed the lid off the tequila and took a shot from the bottle. He was buying it after all, he could do whatever the fuck he wanted to with it.

"You okay?"

Ryan looked up and the angelic waiter was standing there, looking confused. Well, that made two of them. "Not really," he admitted. He took another long swig of tequila and wiped his mouth with the back of his hand.

There was part of him that really wanted to take the angel home anyway. Keep Wyatt up all night with the sounds of their fucking. Make it crystal clear that whatever Wyatt thought Ryan felt, he was wrong.

The truth was, he didn't know if Wyatt was wrong. Maybe Ryan was wrong. Maybe whatever they'd been doing was bound to crash and burn at some point. Nothing simple ever stayed simple, and even Ryan could acknowledge they'd crossed over into complicated awhile ago.

"You want a drink?" he asked Alex, extending the bottle towards him. "I probably shouldn't be drinking alone."

"Can't, sorry, I'm working, and I'll get fired if they catch it on the cameras," Alex said apologetically.

Ryan took another long drink from the bottle, large enough for both of them. It suddenly occurred to him that while the interest in Alex's eyes might have been genuine, he'd probably been paid to flirt outrageously with them.

It wasn't so much different than Wyatt, who he was paying to be his boyfriend and to cook cute, couple-y meals that he could post to his Instagram. But even then he knew it was a lie, because even though he'd been paying Wyatt since day one, money had never been part of what existed between them.

"Was that your boyfriend who left?" Alex asked, perching just on the end of the couch.

"Yes. No. I don't know," Ryan admitted. His total ignorance of the realities of the situation made him want to drink more. But he didn't, because he'd learned a long time ago that getting drunk never really helped. Tomorrow morning he would wake up hungover and miserable and still fucking clueless.

Alex shrugged. It was clear he thought Ryan should go figure that situation out before trying to make threesomes with hot Temple waiters happen. And the galling part was that he was absolutely fucking right.

"I don't suppose I can give you a ride back to my place," Ryan said, even though he didn't even want to. He wasn't even sure anymore if *Alex* wanted to, but this situation was already so monumentally messed up, surely fucking it up more couldn't make it worse.

"You're cute. You're rich. You're famous. Normally, sure. But not tonight. Not when it's not even me you're thinking about."

"We can just not think at all," Ryan said, sounding a little desperate. The last thing he wanted to do was go home alone, and sit in his empty house, imagining the conversation if he went and knocked on Wyatt's door.

Nothing good, that was for fucking sure. But the thought would tempt him all night.

The look Alex shot him was pitying. "You can't turn that off," he said, and got up to leave.

Ryan ended up alone on the couch in his VIP section, sipping his tequila, and trying to figure out how to text Eric that the photos tonight were off.

He'd composed version fifty-three of the message when instead, Eric texted him.

Why am I not hearing rapturous reports of your cute coupledom? Eric said.

Slight snag, Ryan texted back before he could lose his nerve. The tequila also helped with that. **Photos tonight off.**

He sent another text to call the car, and then turned his phone off, gripping the neck of the bottle of tequila.

Maybe waking up hungover would at least fuzzy up some of the extraneous feelings he was never supposed to have in the first place.

CHAPTER FIFTEEN

"Are you going to tell me what the fuck happened last night?"

Ryan came awake slowly and painfully, aware at first only of a bright, hideous light shining in his eyes and an annoyed voice looming over him.

"What are you doing here?" he groaned, turning over, trying to take his sheets with him. The empty tequila bottle thumped to the floor from the bed.

Not his greatest plan, taking the bottle to bed. But Alex wouldn't come, even if Ryan had wanted him anyway, and Wyatt . . . Ryan pushed the thought of him from his head, because that pain was even worse than the ache in his head.

"You are certifiably insane," Eric retorted. "What the fuck happened? All I'm hearing last night is rumors you're cheating on Wyatt, there are reports of you flirting with some waiter with angel wings on, and then you cancel the pictures?"

Ryan groaned again.

"Do you need me to go remind him that he signed a contract? That he is *legally obligated* to be your boyfriend until we tell him otherwise? Because I can do that."

It was funny how everything seemed bad, until Eric waded into the middle of it and things suddenly became catastrophically terrible.

"Please do not do that," Ryan said, all too aware he was begging. "And for the love of god, turn the fucking light off."

"Did you have a fight?" Eric demanded. "Where is he?"

"In the cottage, I don't know. I didn't have a GPS tracker put on him."

"He didn't answer the door, and I realized I don't have a key," Eric said impatiently.

"A situation I'm incredibly jealous of right now," Ryan moaned into the pillow. "Just leave me alone."

"No," Eric said. "We need to fix this problem you created last night. And fix it quick. The rumors are flying fast and loose, and I need something concrete to combat them. Do I need to remind you why we came up with this plan in the first place? This is not making you look great."

"It's not my fault," Ryan said. He didn't know if he was lying or not. Only that he wanted to make Eric stop.

"You're the one with the high profile," Eric countered. "So automatically, everything is your fault."

"You're fired."

Eric ignored that which was probably better for everyone. "Tonight you're going to go out to dinner, and there are going to be photographers and you're going to sit in the most public table in the whole fucking restaurant, and you are going to be the cutest couple LA has ever fucking seen. I don't care if you hate each other right now, you're going to put all that aside and *fix this*."

It sounded hideous. The Temple thing had been so much more their speed, with the added bonus of a cute twist that it was the place they'd met. A twist that Eric had made sure all the gossip columnists knew about. And now that was all ruined because Wyatt had decided that Ryan's determination to never give him a reason to cheat was stupid.

If anything, Ryan reasoned despite his pounding headache, that proved just how much he cared. Ryan had been about to propose that threesome for *Wyatt*. A completely selfless act if there ever was one.

The problem was, he wasn't sure if it was the tacky taste of tequila poisoning his mouth or the bright light shining in through the window, it no longer made quite as much sense as it had the night before.

"Fine, we'll go to the dinner," Ryan said. He could admit he'd been at least partially wrong. He could go knock on Wyatt's door and grovel, apologize for the stupid threesome idea, hope they could go back to where they'd been, and beg him to go to dinner.

He could do that.

He groaned into the pillow again.

Maybe.

"I think you need more of an intervention than I have the patience to give," Eric said. And the worst part of that was Ryan knew exactly who he meant instead, and that was even worse than Eric.

And when something was even worse than Eric, it was a very serious problem.

⟡ ⟡

"You look incredibly shitty," Tabitha said when he opened the door.

It wasn't entirely fair. He'd at least managed to drag himself out of bed, and into the shower, knowing she'd be coming and would expect brushed teeth and no tequila body odor at a bare minimum.

"I feel incredibly shitty," Ryan retorted, shutting the door behind her.

"I should have known you'd fuck it up with him," Tabitha muttered to herself as she made her way through the foyer and down the hall towards the kitchen.

Ryan stopped in the doorway when he realized where she was headed.

"Oh, don't be ridiculous," she chided him. "He's not even here. He's hiding too, I'm sure. Probably angry at you, and I'm sure it's mostly, if not completely, deserved."

"You're my best friend, you're supposed to take my side," Ryan said petulantly, sliding onto one of the barstools and setting his aching head gently against the marble countertop.

"That's not what best friends do," Tabitha said briskly, opening the fridge. "They give you the unvarnished, ugly truth and help you deal with it. Thus, why I am here."

"You're here because Eric bribed you with the newest Gucci bag," Ryan said. "I heard him on the phone."

"I would have come anyway, darling. I didn't want to waste a chance to get something out of that asshole." She placed an ice pack against his forehead. "Wyatt's not here so you might as well tell me everything that happened."

"I don't want to talk about it," Ryan said, his voice muffled by the countertop.

"But you should, and you're going to. Otherwise how are you going to tell Wyatt that you have to go to dinner tonight?"

"Eric told you about that too, I assume," Ryan groaned.

"If you are going to enact this charade," Tabitha said, far more kindly than he probably deserved, "you need to actually put the effort in. It's not all cute Instagram photos and rumors of you surfing together. You dropped the fly ball last night, and threw an interception, to mix metaphors. Time to fix it and show all those fans of yours that you're actually very happy together."

"I'm not sure it can be fixed," he admitted. The look on Wyatt's face had been blank and devoid of anything, like he'd shut down and then shut it all away. Maybe Ryan couldn't get it back. Maybe Wyatt didn't want him to.

"I'm certain there will be some groveling involved," Tabitha pointed out sternly, pulling out the barstool next to him and settling in. "Now, from the top please. I need to know how bad it is before we pick the appropriate groveling method."

"He's been . . . quiet since Napa," Ryan said. "I thought maybe he'd changed his mind about us. The sex was still so good, though, so maybe it was nothing. Maybe I misjudged."

"Did you ask him if he'd changed his mind?"

Ryan shook his head and almost instantly regretted it. "No," he murmured.

"And did you ask him what was wrong?"

"No." Ryan hesitated. "I was afraid it would feel too . . . boyfriend-y. That it would open up what we had to even more complexities. And I wanted to keep it simple."

Ryan didn't even have to look at Tabitha to know the look she was giving him was galling.

"It was stupid, okay? I should have asked. I wanted to ask."

"That isn't why I'm annoyed with you, and definitely not why he's annoyed with you," Tabitha said. "So, he was quiet, and you didn't ask, and then you went to Temple, and decided to pick up a waiter dressed like an angel? I'm not following that logic."

"I thought he was bored, okay? I thought he was bored of . . ." Ryan paused, because he didn't want to say *me* and he definitely didn't want to say *our relationship*. That was the whole problem. He'd gone into this very deliberately trying to avoid a relationship, but they'd ended up there anyway.

"Bored? Let me tell you, Wyatt Blake does not strike me as the kind of guy who sticks around when he's bored."

"Exactly," Ryan said miserably.

"You thought he'd get bored and leave you? Really?" Tabitha's incredulous voice didn't help. "Wyatt is crazy about you."

"It sounds stupid but I had an ex, well, you knew him actually. David. He cheated on me, at the end. And he told me that he'd been driven to do it because he was bored. You know how much that relationship ending hurt me, and since that point I've made sure to never let things get that far. Ever."

"David cheated on you? That miserable small-dicked bastard," Tabitha muttered. "You never told me."

"It was fucking embarrassing," Ryan admitted.

"I just can't believe he had the balls to use that excuse and then you actually *believed* it," Tabitha said.

"How was I supposed to know? I was bored too! I didn't get why everyone was so hot to be in a relationship, because I was just as bored as he was."

"Darling," Tabitha said carefully, "I think that was because *he* was boring and you were not right for each other. Not everyone with a little hiccup in their relationship adds excitement via cheating."

"I know that, of course I know that," Ryan retorted.

"So that was what you were trying to do last night? Add in excitement so that Wyatt wouldn't cheat on you and leave you because he was bored?"

"It sounds so stupid when you say it."

"Well," Tabitha hedged.

"He didn't understand," Ryan said. "He just said he wanted to stop playing games and kept demanding to know if I was enough for him."

"Oh dear," Tabitha said. "What did you tell him?"

"That I didn't want him to get bored! I wasn't thinking about me, I could go on like this for . . . I don't know, a long time probably. I'm not bored."

Ryan realized what he'd said just as he said it.

"Oh fuck," he groaned. "I'm in love with him, aren't I?"

Tabitha put a reassuring arm around his shoulders. "It's not that bad, I promise."

"I was so worried he'd leave me that I actually drove him away." Ryan slammed a fist on the counter. "I'm a fucking idiot."

"I'm pretty sure he's in love with you too, so maybe tone down the *woe is me* inevitability that he's gone for good," Tabitha said. "You can still fix this."

"If I agree to make it official, probably," Ryan admitted.

"You just admitted that you're in love with him. Isn't that something you want?"

"What if it happens again?" Ryan asked seriously. "What if he cheats on me? What if he leaves? David, I didn't love him at all, I don't think, and that was so humiliating. I don't think I could survive it, if it happened with Wyatt."

"Darling," Tabitha said softly, "you can't go into a relationship expecting it to end. You have to believe in each other and trust each other. Trust that Wyatt isn't going to use some bullshit excuse to cheat on you. And that if you get worried he will, or that he's not happy with you, communication is key. You'd be surprised what people can figure out when they actually talk to each other."

"You think I should do this," Ryan stated. He couldn't even believe that after being *so* clear upfront, he'd gone and done the exact thing he'd warned Wyatt not to do.

"I think it's worth a shot. You two clearly care about each other. I want you to be happy, and I think you were really happy with him."

"I was." Ryan hesitated. "I am."

"Then you should go for it," Tabitha said, giving him an extra encouraging squeeze.

"What if he turns me down?" Ryan asked, because the fear of that eventuality was terrifying, squeezing the breath out of his lungs.

"Do I think you're going to say, *let's get together for real*, and he falls all over you? No. It's not that simple. Love isn't that simple."

"Groveling, then," Ryan said.

"There will probably be some groveling involved," Tabitha hedged.

"Do I get on my knees or . . ."

Tabitha held up a hand. "And that's where I step out. Whatever you two do in the bedroom or any other room of the house is between you."

"No, I meant, how should I grovel? Begging? Promises? Gifts?"

"I think," Tabitha said slowly, "that's going to depend on two factors. One, who Wyatt is as a person. And two, how pissed off he is at you."

"And you think he's really pissed off." It was unreal that while facing that particular fact, which was something he'd suspected since Wyatt had walked out of the alley, something in his chest started to ache even worse than his head.

"I think that Wyatt is an honorable guy, who keeps his promises, and that he's in love with you. He wouldn't ditch you last night if he wasn't really pissed off." Tabitha stared at him frankly, and Ryan realized there was actually something that she was insinuating but not actually saying. Which was the scariest thing of all, because Tabitha was renowned for telling the unapologetic truth. If she was trying to cushion this, then it must be really bad.

"Oh god," Ryan said, a spike of panic rising through him. He'd thought the worst it could be was groveling, maybe even begging Wyatt to forgive him. And then in the twenty or so minutes since he'd come to terms with his own feelings, he'd seen them in a sort of nebulous, happy-ever-after future.

But what if Wyatt didn't come back? What if Wyatt came back and didn't forgive him?

It could be so much worse.

"You might as well just lay it on me," Ryan said bluntly. "I know you're holding back, and it doesn't suit you. I'm already down; I'm not sure it's going to get much worse."

"He's pissed, he's embarrassed, his pride is in shambles because during your first night out as an official couple, you were all over some waiter dressed in a trashy Halloween costume. But the worst of it is that you definitely hurt him a lot."

The ache in Ryan's chest intensified. "I don't suppose me explaining I was incredibly stupid and never meant to will fix that?"

Tabitha's look was soft and sympathetic. "We can sure hope it will. Or else I'll be back here in a few hours with ice cream and more tequila."

"I have a great idea. We should hire an assassin," Evan said excitedly.

Wyatt looked up from his hot fudge brownie sundae in surprise.

"He really doesn't mean that, I swear," Miles said.

"Doesn't he?" Wyatt said dully. He shoved the hot fudge around in his bowl and didn't put the spoon in his mouth. He'd been sitting here for half an hour, watching Miles' famous caramel crunch ice cream melt in a puddle of hot fudge, barely able to stick a spoonful in his mouth.

He must really look awful because Miles usually took exception to his friends not eating the desserts he made for them, but he hadn't said a word.

"I'm not sure I do," Evan revised. "It sounded really badass, though. At one point I thought about hiring an assassin to kill you, Miles, when we first started working together."

Wyatt was not as surprised by this as he should have been. Evan and Miles, while rapturously in love now, had not always gotten along. And Evan was all for finding unusual solutions to problems, thus the assassin.

"True love," Miles announced proudly. "That's really true love right there. You were willing to pay someone a lot more money to get rid of me."

Evan rolled his eyes but they were still so fond that Wyatt's heart ached. Just yesterday it felt like he and Ryan had been on the same path as Miles and Evan. Instead they'd been heading in the opposite trajectory. Instead of hating each other at first like his friends, they'd immediately connected. That first night had been magical, and Wyatt had been so sure that *this* was the guy. He was still pretty sure he still felt the same way, under all the anger and the humiliation and the hurt, but he couldn't believe anymore that Ryan was the right guy.

The right guy wouldn't want to keep pretending when the reality was better than any fantasy.

Still, he'd come here to Evan and Miles' place early this morning and after plying him with a gourmet breakfast he had barely been able to choke down, they'd sat him down in front of bad reality television for two hours. Then Miles had made him the sundae, proclaiming that brownies and caramel crunch ice cream topped with hot fudge could cure any problem. At the very least distract from one.

Wyatt was marginally distracted, but he didn't really feel any better. Miles would try to keep him here, and away from Ryan, but Wyatt was beginning to think he should go home, and try to figure out how they were going to proceed. Would Wyatt stay his personal chef? Would the fake relationship be on? Could he even get out of that contract he'd stupidly signed, all hopeful and optimistic only a few weeks ago?

Knowing Ryan's shark of an agent, getting out of it was probably going to be a nightmare. But on the upside, Ryan could probably hire the waiter to take his place pretty easily.

"You don't have to go back there, you know. We can go get your stuff. And you can stay with us for awhile." Like Wyatt didn't know Miles and Evan had marathon sex sessions complete with noises he'd really prefer never to hear. "I can even put out feelers for a new job. There's so many more opportunities in LA. With your resume, you'll get something fast."

He probably would, Wyatt reasoned. Miles wasn't even lying. But despite everything, he wasn't really sure he was ready to quit his current job just yet.

Wyatt didn't think he was nearly as stubborn as some people—like say, *Xander*—but once on a path, it was hard to shove him off of it. And he'd fallen in love with Ryan pretty irrevocably. It was probably going to take more than an angel to change his mind.

"I'm tired," Wyatt finally said. "I'm going home to try to get some sleep."

He'd gone home from Temple the night before, and had lain awake in bed all night, fully expecting that he would hear Ryan come home from the club with company. He'd tortured himself for hours, preparing his heart for what he might hear or see the next day. But he wasn't sure that Ryan had come home at all, or else he'd come home and been too quiet for Wyatt to hear.

Removing himself from the house and going to Miles' had seemed like such a good plan, but now he wasn't sure that being around Miles and Evan was helping him at all, no matter how sympathetic they were.

Or how many assassins Evan was willing to hire.

Miles opened his mouth and Wyatt held up a hand. "I know, I don't have to. I need to."

"Well, make sure to text me, tell me how it goes," Miles said quietly. Evan had faded into the living room, leaving the two friends alone in the kitchen. "I know how rotten you must feel if you can't even work up an appetite for my caramel crunch ice cream and homemade hot fudge."

"You even made brownies without walnuts," Wyatt said ruefully. "I'm sorry I couldn't enjoy them."

"I'll wrap them up," Miles said, beginning to do just that. "You can snack yourself into a chocolate coma later."

"Thank you," Wyatt said. And to his embarrassment, he was near tears. Again.

Miles walked over, handing him the container full of brownies, and wrapped him in a big hug. "You're a great guy," he said. "Either Ryan realizes he needs to do better by you, or you'll find a guy who will. You deserve that."

Wyatt left, saying a quick goodbye and drove his bike home to Ryan's house.

Wyatt was not ashamed that when he reached the gate, he kicked off the power on his bike and walked it in. Ryan wouldn't even know he'd come back. Of course that was assuming he'd noticed he was gone in the first place or that he even gave a shit.

He collapsed in his bed, and as he snuggled into the pillow, couldn't help but be grateful that they'd been sharing Ryan's bed. His sheets were thankfully completely Ryan-free.

He fell asleep hoping that Ryan was suffering a little because, unlike his own, his bed wasn't a Wyatt-free zone.

⚘ ⚘

Ryan took a deep, steadying breath and braced himself for the difficult conversation to come. He knocked twice, trying for soft but determined. If you could even interpret that from a knock.

Nothing.

Wyatt was either ignoring him or he wasn't home. Normally, Ryan would have been fine giving him the space he wanted, but after last night's relationship debut had not gone as planned, Eric was chomping at the bit to get things back on track.

He'd given Ryan stern orders that they would go to dinner tonight and they would at least pretend to be the most loved-up couple in LA.

That meant that knocking again wasn't an option, it was a requirement.

He did it, a little louder this time. More authoritarian.

Still nothing.

The third set of knocks were more door *thumps*, and they must have done the trick because the door swung open, revealing a sleepy-looking Wyatt, shoving a hand through his hair.

His expression went from confused to angry to hurt. And it was the last that made Ryan's heart ache. It hadn't been very hard to figure out that was what was hurting so much in the vicinity of his chest. Even Tabitha hadn't had to tell him.

"What are you doing here?" Wyatt demanded.

Ryan discarded the immediate and obvious explanation that this was his property and attached to his house. "I wanted to apologize," he said.

"Not interested," Wyatt said, and tried to slam the door shut, but Ryan got his foot and calf in before he could. Usually Wyatt had incredible reflexes, even more deft than Ryan's, but he'd clearly just woken up.

"I was an asshole last night. Rude and thoughtless and cruel. I genuinely am very sorry," Ryan said.

Wyatt had taken a step back away from Ryan's entry into the house and took another. And then another. Ryan shut the door behind him. His neighbors didn't need to hear this and send the scoop to TMZ.

Wyatt didn't look convinced, so Ryan tried again.

"You're right, I was playing games. And I'm done."

"Done how?" Wyatt asked.

"You were right about so much," Ryan said, desperately latching onto the tiny opening that Wyatt had just given him. "About how the boredom thing was about me, and not about you. I should have told you I wasn't going to get bored, and should have listened when you said you wouldn't either."

Wyatt sighed. "Listen, I don't really give a shit that you're not going to get bored in a fake relationship. Or by hooking up with me, or whatever. I don't care."

"What if it wasn't just a fake relationship? What if we weren't just hooking up?" The Ryan of six months ago would have been aghast at the direction this conversation had taken, but frankly the Ryan of six months ago had been a tool.

Wyatt hadn't just made him a better person; Wyatt made him *want* to be a better person.

"You want to be together? For real?" Wyatt sounded very skeptical, and Ryan honestly could not blame him. He sat down on the couch, leaving Wyatt hovering around the TV. He'd read once that if you wanted someone to believe you, you needed to be absolutely sure of your own actions. Sitting down on the couch like he belonged there seemed the most affirmative action that Ryan could take at the moment.

"I do," Ryan said.

There was a flash of hope in Wyatt's eyes as he sat down on the chair opposite and leaned over, his elbows resting on his knees. "I want to believe that," Wyatt said. But then his face hardened. "I'm just not sure I can."

Ryan figured this was the best time to lay all his cards on the table. Tabitha had warned him as she was leaving that going to dinner tonight in an attempt to fulfill the original agreement was going to fuck with Wyatt's ability to forgive. Ryan's apology would just look like he was manipulating Wyatt to get what he needed from him.

"You need to nip that right in the bud," Tabitha had cautioned. "Tell him right away and be as honest as you can. Tell him your hands are tied with this. Otherwise he'll have every reason to believe you're lying."

"There's something else," Ryan added. "Last night . . . I don't even need to tell you that last night I monumentally fucked up. Not just with you, though that's the part that possibly has the worst and most lasting consequences. I also fucked up our agreement. I fucked up the impression I was trying to give people. I was trying to look like someone responsible and trustworthy, someone who cared about you, and instead I made it look like the opposite."

"Believe me, I was there. We don't have to rehash it," Wyatt said dryly.

"What I'm trying to say is that Eric has set up a redo. For tonight."

Wyatt stared at him incredulously, then jumped up and started pacing between the living room and the kitchen. "Are you fucking kidding me? That's why you're here? That's why you're apologizing? Because you need me to go play nice with you in front of some fucking photographer?"

"No. I'm here because I'm sorry. But yes, we do need to do that."

Wyatt looked straight at him, a challenging look in his eyes. "How can I ever believe you if you make me go do this tonight?"

"I don't know," Ryan said and it was the most wretched truth he'd ever told. "I really wish I could figure it out, because this is killing me."

"It didn't seem to be killing you last night," Wyatt said, and there was a cruel edge to his tone that Ryan told himself that he absolutely deserved.

"I know. I was . . . I guess I should tell you why I acted that way. I probably should have started with that. When I first got drafted by the Dodgers, I had a boyfriend. And he was a little older, and exciting, and I loved that. I thought I loved him. And then one day, I came home early, and he was fucking some guy in our bed. I kicked him out, of course, but not before he told me that he'd had to do it because we'd gotten too boring. We'd stayed in and ordered pizza and watched Netflix and he'd gotten *bored*. I realized then that I'd been bored too. After that, I swore that I'd only do hookups. Because that would never happen in a hookup."

"Because you'd never stay long enough for anyone to get bored," Wyatt said slowly. "I want to say that's really stupid of you, to believe something a cheating asshole tells you, but you thought you loved him. And he echoed something you were feeling too."

Ryan nodded miserably. "Tabitha said we were both wrong for each other, and that if it's right, it doesn't matter if you're boring together, because you never get bored."

"I don't know, I could go for boring sometimes," Wyatt said ruefully.

"I just want you to know why I would do something like last night," Ryan said. "I was confused, things between us had gotten so complicated and you'd gone sort of quiet, and I thought, completely stupidly, that you were bored."

"I wasn't bored," Wyatt admitted. His eyes looked so blue from across the room, boring into Ryan. "I was falling in love with you and afraid that you didn't feel that way about me."

"Oh." Ryan had said plenty of times how stupid he'd been, but this really drove the point home. If he'd only *asked*, instead of assuming that Wyatt pulling away was a bad thing. "You said, *was*."

Wyatt shrugged. "That's not something that changes. I'm just not sure I trust you. Those are two separate things."

"Because of the dinner tonight."

"Because of the dinner tonight," Wyatt repeated. "Because of a hundred other things that I shouldn't question but I am anyway." He sounded upset and conflicted, and Ryan probably should have felt more sympathy for him, but he was also doing a little happy dance internally that he sounded conflicted at all. Wyatt could have just kicked him out, but he'd listened, and they were trying to figure things out. Of all the ways this could have gone, it certainly hadn't gone the worst.

"I really am sorry, but I can't get us out of the dinner. Believe me, if I could, I would. I would do it, if it helped you trust me again," Ryan said. He knew he was begging; he'd always assumed it would feel worse. More demeaning, maybe. But it felt right. Like putting everything on the line for someone he loved.

"That's okay," Wyatt said, and for the first time, there was a hint of a smile on the corner of his mouth. "I could think of worse ways to spend an evening than being wined and dined by a cute guy."

"You'll go?"

"I didn't think I had much of a choice," Wyatt said wryly. "Not if I don't want to get sued by Eric."

"Threats and blackmail are really more his style," Ryan said. "But yes."

"You need to get a new agent," Wyatt said.

"Sadly, you are not the first person to tell me that." Ryan took a deep breath, and asked the question that really worried him. "What are we going to do about going forward? After tonight?"

Wyatt sighed. "I care about you. I care about what I started building here. I don't want to leave, even if I'm mad at you, even if you've embarrassed me. So I won't. But I don't think we can go back to where we were right away. I need time. I need to figure out if I can trust you again."

"Okay." Ryan was feeling cautiously optimistic. Wyatt had agreed to go to dinner. Wyatt wasn't leaving. Wyatt was willing to wait and see if he could give Ryan another chance.

Best-case scenario, considering how catastrophically he'd torpedoed things the night before.

He'd considered more than once if he should tell Wyatt he loved him too—because now the other man had told him twice he felt the same. Once in anger and now again, while they were trying to resolve things. But Ryan hadn't wanted to tell him as an apology. He wanted it to be a moment of celebration and happiness. Something bigger and brighter. Special. Just like Wyatt was to him.

So the three little words would have to wait but he had another ace up his sleeve. Tabitha had suggested presents, and though people usually gave apology roses or apology chocolates, Ryan was betting on his apology gift being a hell of a lot more successful than that. He'd wanted something concrete that could say so much better than he could two important things: *one*, that he knew he'd messed up and *two*, that he was willing to put the work in to fix it. But the present wasn't going to be delivered until late tonight, or early to-morrow, no matter how much he'd pleaded, so Ryan would have to wait.

And waiting was really not his strong suit.

Chapter Sixteen

Ryan didn't know what to do with himself. In his own house.

This was why he'd avoided dating for so long; it always turned him into an unsure neurotic who was always afraid every decision was the wrong one and would doom the relationship before it even got off the ground.

The one good thing, he thought as he loitered in the hallway between the living room and the kitchen, waiting for Wyatt to appear for their dinner date, was that he'd already done the fucking up and probably couldn't mess the relationship up any worse.

He heard the back door open and close and Ryan sauntered a few casual steps to the right so he could see Wyatt walk in and through the kitchen. He was wearing dark jeans and a light-blue button-up nearly the shade of his eyes. His face was still shadowed, faint circles under his eyes, but he'd lost that pinched, angry, hurt look from earlier, and Ryan was relieved. He didn't think he could sit through a whole dinner, seeing that look while knowing it was all his fault.

"You look great," Ryan said enthusiastically. Tabitha had told him how important it was he take every opportunity to show Wyatt how much he meant to him. But that had probably been too much enthusiasm, deployed too quickly.

Wyatt looked taken aback. "Okay. Thanks, I guess?"

Definitely too enthusiastically.

Honesty and the communication were the key, Ryan reminded himself. "That . . . came out wrong. I don't know how to do this—not the right way anyway. I've only had one boyfriend, and it didn't end well. So I'm almost definitely going to mess up again." Admitting to failure in advance was not easy, but he did it anyway because it was *true*.

"I don't want a perfect boyfriend, I want a real one," Wyatt told him, voice soft and pleading. "I want *you*."

"I want you too," Ryan said, and he couldn't help the ache that spiraled through him at just how much. "Exactly as you are. And you do look good. That wasn't . . . I wasn't lying. I just haven't always said what was on my mind, how much I care about you, and I'm trying to fix that. Trying to be better, for you."

"I want the Ryan I've spent the last month with," Wyatt said, walking over and pulling Ryan into an unexpected hug. "Not some other version of you. Not someone who's trying to be someone they're not. When I said I want you, that's exactly what I meant."

Ryan ordered himself not to get too comfortable, and not to turn Wyatt's innocent embrace into something else. To just enjoy it, and not grab hold too tight, afraid that this would be his last chance. Wyatt wasn't going anywhere. He was sticking around and letting Ryan prove that he was telling the truth.

He let him go reluctantly. "We should go, our reservations are soon." And because he hadn't asked last time, he asked this time. "Are you okay doing this?"

Wyatt shrugged. "Do I wish we didn't have to do this tonight? Yeah. But I understand the reasons why we need to."

"I'm sorry," Ryan automatically apologized as they moved towards the garage. "That's my fault."

"You can stop apologizing," Wyatt pointed out wryly.

"Sorry," Ryan said and grimaced. "I told you I'd be bad at this."

"Just relax," he coaxed, reaching out to give Ryan's shoulder a quick squeeze.

Ryan moved through the garage and opened the passenger door of the Maserati. He'd had it washed and detailed this afternoon until the midnight-blue paint gleamed in the dusk light.

"What's this?" Wyatt asked, stopping short. "We're taking the Maserati?"

"You want a real boyfriend, and this real boyfriend intends to give you the best he can," Ryan admitted.

"Also, because it looks pretty damn cool in the pictures," Wyatt said, sliding in. Ryan snorted as he closed the door.

"You're not wrong," Ryan admitted as he got in the driver's side. "I'll admit about ten percent of the decision was how killer we're going to look pulling up in it."

Wyatt rolled his eyes as Ryan pulled out of the driveway.

"Where are we going?"

"Some place in Malibu that's apparently *the* new restaurant," Ryan said. "I thought you'd enjoy it. I made sure Eric got us a good table."

"A public table, you mean," Wyatt retorted, and there was the faintest edge of bitterness to his voice. And Ryan couldn't help but think that he also wished they hadn't had to do this so soon after their fight. They both would have benefited from some time. Even if it was hard. Even if it hurt. Throwing them in together so fast had left a lot of issues unresolved.

Fear bubbled up inside him, but he didn't have an outlet for it, so he pushed his foot down on the accelerator, feeling the engine roar to life.

"Yes, a public table," Ryan said. "You know why we have to sit at a public table. And I'd apologize, but you just told me I've apologized enough already."

Wyatt didn't say anything, just looked out the passenger window as Calabasas passed by. Ryan turned onto a windier road, but didn't slow down. Pressed down harder on the accelerator, actually. When he'd bought this car, the salesman had promised second-to-none acceleration and handling, and he'd never had a chance to take it out like he should have after it had been delivered.

What was the point of owning a car like this if you didn't test its limits a little?

"I wish you wouldn't drive so fast," Wyatt said to the window, and yeah, he was definitely still annoyed.

Instead of slowing down, Ryan took the next turn at seventy. It was a stupid thing to do. Stupid and reckless, and a remnant of a time when he hadn't cared what sort of attention he got, even if it was negative. He'd thought he'd left that attention-seeking behind in high school, but the fear kept creeping up.

He didn't like Wyatt ignoring him. Even if it was Wyatt trying to avoid an argument.

"God damnit, Ryan," Wyatt ground out as the car flew around another curve in the road, tires squealing.

"What? Is this too fast for you?" Ryan teased darkly as he stepped on the accelerator in the flat, jumping up to triple digits as easily as breathing. Reveling in the attention he was getting again.

"I don't care if you're hooked on adrenaline, but this is stupid and reckless," Wyatt ground out.

Ryan glanced over at Wyatt, and registered how pissed off he looked. But it was a split second too long, especially when he was going over a hundred miles per hour. Especially when the next turn was a lot tighter than he remembered.

He jerked the wheel reflexively, and knew a moment too late that he'd miscalculated. He'd forgotten about the damp road. It had rained early this morning, just enough to bring out the oil on the road, but not enough to wash it away. The tires tried to grip but failed, and before Ryan could even yell out a warning, or brace himself against the roof, the car was flipping, his stomach heaving as they rolled down the road in a cacophony of metal scraping against asphalt.

They finally slid to a halt, and the first thing Ryan did was frantically look over at Wyatt, who was slumped against the leather seat, eyes closed. He unbuckled, and immediately started checking him for injuries, heart beating a thousand miles per hour. Faster than he'd ever driven. Faster than he'd ever drive again.

"Oh god, oh god, oh god," he chanted under his breath as he realized Wyatt's arm was crooked at an awkward angle. And when his hands reached up to set his head at a better angle, they came away wet and red.

He smeared blood everywhere as he dug his phone out of his pocket and dialed 911. All over his phone and his shirt and the leather interior of the car. Streaks of rusty red everywhere.

The operator answered immediately, asking him the emergency and taking down the information as Ryan spit it out, voice shaky.

"Are you hurt?" the operator asked.

"No, I'm fine, I'm fine. But my boyfriend, he's not fine. I think his arm is broken, and he's knocked out. I think he hit his head against the window. Oh god, what if he's dead?" It had never occurred to Ryan to check his breathing, but now he did, pressing his fingers against the artery in his neck to feel the blood beating there.

The pulse was faint but it was there, sluggishly beating against his fingertips. "We need an ambulance *now*," Ryan demanded. Fear was making him nauseous. Wyatt still hadn't moved. His face was pale and unresponsive.

"Don't move him out of the car," the operator ordered. "The ambulance will be there shortly. Maybe keep talking to him, see if you can wake him up. And if he does, keep him calm."

Ryan set the phone down and did his best to cradle Wyatt's head so it wouldn't flop. "I'm so fucking sorry," he whispered to him. "And I'm going to damn well apologize for this because it's my fault again. Showing off, trying to get your attention. I just . . . I'm so afraid you won't see me otherwise. That you won't stay. That you'll find someone else, someone who doesn't have any problems. Someone who doesn't do stupid shit like drive too fast and end up hurting you."

Wyatt's fingers quivered against Ryan's, and he took that as the right sign and kept going.

"I love you," he said. And it felt like such a waste to say it now, when he could have said it fifteen minutes ago, when they were both fine. Angry, but fine. When Wyatt might have been more receptive to hearing it. When they weren't lying in a heap of mangled metal and plastic, and Wyatt's blood wasn't all over Ryan's hands.

"I love you," he repeated again, heart in his throat, "please don't fucking leave me. Not like this."

"Let me get this straight," Eric said, his voice a hardened mask, no doubt hiding apoplectic anger. He hadn't been still since arriving at the hospital five minutes earlier, pacing in the hallway with Ryan outside of Wyatt's room. "Instead of going out tonight and fixing *last night,* you took Wyatt out to dinner. But you never made it to the restaurant because you crashed your Maserati and now Wyatt has a broken arm and a concussion."

Ryan hadn't thought it was possible for the events of the evening to sound any worse, but somehow they did, recited through Eric's clenched teeth.

"That sounds about right," he said morosely.

"You told me you want this," Eric said. "You begged me to find a way to fix your management's opinion that you're reckless and careless with your personal safety. I told you I'd help you, and I've been fucking *trying.*"

Nobody liked Eric much, Ryan included, but it was hard to deny that he'd been trying, despite all the ways Ryan fucked up.

Eric threw his hands up in frustration. "I can't help you if you won't help yourself," he continued.

"It was a mistake. A mistake that won't happen again. I was . . . messed up over Wyatt."

"And just like that, you're *not* messed up over Wyatt?" Eric asked in disbelief. "To be honest, he's messed you up since the first night you met him. I don't think crashing your Maserati is going to help with that."

"It's not, it's not. I've been messed up because I was fighting how much I cared about him, but I'm not fighting it anymore. This is where I'm meant to be."

"In a hospital," Eric muttered under his breath. "Standing vigil over your injured boyfriend."

Ryan couldn't help but admit he wasn't always the world's quickest learner, but he'd learned now. He'd felt how easily it all could end. How silly it felt to keep fighting something when it felt so natural. He didn't know how he could have let it go on so long. He'd been a fucking moron, and maybe he could get out of this without paying the heaviest price. He leaned against the wall and wished Wyatt would wake up so he would know if he'd ever forgive him for almost killing both of them.

"I called you because you always told me to call if you things got . . . rough."

"It got rough alright. I'll clean this up because that's my job," Eric said. "But no more bullshit. It doesn't suit you."

"Agreed," Ryan said miserably.

Eric turned to go, but held back for a split second. He reached out, and for a grade A asshole, he had a pretty convincing sympathy face. "You're a good kid, Flores. Don't let the system change you."

Then he was gone, walking down the corridor with purpose, no doubt to start handing out non-disclosure agreements like party favors.

Ryan heard a very familiar shriek and looked up to see Flor walking fast and determined towards him, fury in her eyes.

He closed his own in supplication. This night had already been so long, and was growing longer.

❧ ❧

Wyatt's arm really hurt. His head too. He didn't want to open his eyes because he was pretty sure that would hurt just as badly, but he needed to know who was saying those words. It was a voice he recognized. He was sure of it. He just couldn't place it right now because his brain was so fuzzy. He didn't even know why he was hurting.

"We could charge you for reckless driving," he heard someone say. Not a voice he recognized. It was harsh at the edges, and clearly pissed off. "And even though there weren't any other vehicles involved in the accident, your passenger could file charges since he ended up in the hospital."

Accident. He had vague flashes of screaming metal and a surge of fear and then nothing. A voice in the darkness, reaching out to him. Begging for him to wake up.

Wyatt strained, anxious to hear the other voice in the conversation, hoping that it was the man who had been so desperate for him to be alright.

The man who loved him.

But the voice who responded wasn't his at all. "Officer," the accented voice said insistently, "it was just an accident. The road was slick. You said so. And Ryan, he's sorry. He's learned his lesson."

"To the tune of a wrecked Maserati?" the same official voice retorted dryly. "I'm sure he has. But I will need to check in with Mr. Blake and make sure that he doesn't want to file charges."

"When he's awake, you can speak to him if you like," the accented voice continued. "Right, Ryan?"

Ryan. That sounded familiar. Was Ryan the man who'd professed his love in the car?

Wyatt, struggling through the fog in his brain, thought that might be the same man.

"I . . . Ryan . . ." he forced in a harsh whisper. His mouth was so dry and tasted smoky and metallic. The echo of blood and pain.

He hadn't managed to open his eyes yet, but the moment he spoke, there was a person at the bed next to him, cradling his hand in his two hands. They were big palms, creased with callouses. Capable hands, hands he could be safe with, despite his presence in a hospital bed that seemed to prove otherwise.

"Wyatt, are you awake?"

That was the voice. This was the man.

He finally opened his eyes and a thousand memories came rushing back at the sight of his face. Dark eyes, pleading and terrified, stared back at him. Blood spatter on his white button-down shirt.

They were supposed to be on a date. At a restaurant. At a public place. Getting their pictures taken. He'd been angry; *so* angry, but that felt so far away now.

"I'm sorry," Wyatt said, and Ryan laughed wetly, wiping his face with a blood-splattered hand.

"If I'm not allowed to apologize again, neither are you," he said, leaning down so Wyatt could catch the words.

"My arm hurts," Wyatt said matter-of-factly. He didn't want to look over and see why it was immobilized. Did he even still have it? Was the pain just a phantom reminder of the limb he'd used to have?

"It's broken, but it was a clean break. The doctor thinks it'll heal quick and you'll be back in the ocean with me soon," Ryan promised. "And you have a mild concussion, from a contusion on the back of your head."

"The blood?" Wyatt asked, lifting his good hand, and gesturing to the bright red all of Ryan's shirt.

"It's yours," Ryan said wryly. "I only have a few minor scratches. A bruise or two. I'll be fine."

And then it hit Wyatt head-on. Ryan had been the driver of the car. The rest came rushing back: Ryan driving way too fast. Wyatt demanding he slow down and Ryan not listening. Hitting the slick spot.

"Eric is gonna kill you," Wyatt said. "If I don't first."

"You're upset," Ryan suggested hesitantly.

"What the fuck were you thinking?" Wyatt demanded, even though the tone of his own voice made his heart hurt worse.

Ryan shoved his hands into his pockets. "I'm not sure we should be talking about this now," he said hesitantly, voice wavering. Wyatt had seen Ryan Flores in a lot of moods, but never like this. Never diminished, scared, *guilty*.

Wyatt looked around, taking in Flor hovering in the doorway, blocking the police officer he'd heard earlier. "Can we have the room, please?" he asked, and Flor nodded immediately, shutting the door behind her a moment later.

Leaving him and Ryan alone.

"If you want to call it off, you can," Ryan said nervously.

"I don't want to call it off." Wyatt's head kept aching and Ryan's behavior was somehow making it ache worse. "I want to figure this shit out, once and for all." He paused, collecting his thoughts, the shards of memory that kept fitting back in place, one at a time. "You told me you loved me."

"I do, I do love you. I was . . . so scared you'd leave. Scared you were only sticking around because you said you would. Maybe because you didn't want to get sued." Ryan laughed, self-consciously and without much humor. "You told me you'd stick around because you wanted to learn to trust me again. But you were angry in the car, and I was afraid it was all ending again, and I . . . got desperate."

Wyatt took a deep breath, trying to keep his temper because the closer he got to the edge, the more he hurt. And he didn't want to have any more to blame Ryan for. "I love you, you fucking idiot. I'm not going anywhere."

Hope flared in Ryan's eyes. "How can you even say that after . . ."

"After you wrecked your Maserati and almost killed us?" It was Wyatt's turn to chuckle at the irony. "God only knows. Maybe because I know how much fear can control you. It controlled me for so long, how can I blame you for falling victim to it?"

"I didn't think about it that way," Ryan said and the stiffness in his back was softening a little, bringing him closer to Wyatt's side.

It was all instinct to reach out and take Ryan's hand, curl it in his own, despite the ache in his bones. Ryan gripped it fiercely, like a lifeline.

"We don't have to know everything right now. We don't have to figure everything out right now," Wyatt said. "That's all I meant earlier. Honestly . . . I couldn't leave. Not now. Not before. I . . ." Maybe he should have felt ashamed as the tears clogged this throat and made it difficult to speak, but it had been an emotionally trying forty-eight hours, and he was reaching the end of his rope.

"I love you," Ryan said, finishing his own sentence. "I meant it earlier. I'm not . . . going to do this right. I promise. But I promise you that I will be there to figure it out afterwards. Every single time."

There wasn't complete peace and acceptance in Ryan's dark eyes as he gazed down at Wyatt, but there was more. The fear was receding, and Wyatt felt it leaking out his own mind, along with the anger.

On cue, there was a brisk knock at the door. Ryan raised his head and reluctantly let go of Wyatt's hand to answer it.

It was the police officer. Of course.

"I need to take his statement," he said gruffly. "Now that he's awake."

Ryan looked over at Wyatt, who inclined his head in agreement.

The police officer walked in, and took up a spot at the end of Wyatt's hospital bed. Ryan resumed his previous spot, and grasped Wyatt's hand like he'd never let it go again.

"Mr. Blake," the officer said, "could you please tell me what you remember about the accident?"

"Do we have to do this right now?" Wyatt asked, even though he already knew the answer.

"Yes," the officer said, unrelenting.

So Wyatt quickly and efficiently rehashed what he remembered from the accident. They'd been driving fast, maybe, he relented, but not outrageously fast. The road had definitely been slick. They'd flipped a couple of times. He didn't remember much else.

"And what about charges, Mr. Blake?" the officer asked expectantly.

"Charges?" he asked blankly. "Why would I want to file charges?"

"Mr. Flores' reckless driving endangered your life," he reminded Wyatt.

"Mr. Flores," Wyatt pointed out, voice as clear and strong as he could make it, "despite some lapses in judgment, is *mine.*" Ryan's fingers spasmed against his. Flor reached out a reassuring hand towards Ryan, but he brushed it away. "I'm not pressing charges against him."

"Are you sure?" Ryan asked, but his voice was so hopeful. So full of love that Wyatt could almost block out the pain in his head.

"I'm definitely sure," Wyatt retorted dryly, tugging his hand and bringing Ryan closer. Close enough to kiss. Maybe he shouldn't have been, but he was.

The nurse outside must have heard the commotion, because she bustled in then, giving him some ice chips for his dry mouth, and talking about discharge papers after he saw the doctor again.

"I called Miles," Ryan admitted. "I left a voicemail. I think he was filming or something."

"Why did you call Miles?" Wyatt questioned.

"I wasn't sure . . . wasn't sure you wanted to be in the same car as me again. Not so soon, anyway," Ryan said, voice halting.

"Do you think I didn't mean it?" Wyatt asked.

"I know you do," Ryan said, his voice growing stronger again. "But I didn't know that then, and I wasn't ever going to presume your feelings for you again. But," he added, a wry grin blooming on his face, "I should probably call Miles and let him know his services are no longer required. And that you're not dead."

"Does this mean we can finally go home?" Wyatt said, in relief.

"I think the doctor needs to discharge you still," Ryan said.

Wyatt knew the look he shot his boyfriend was unfair. He did it anyway. He hated these hospital sheets—they were scratchy, and he had a feeling they'd frown at Ryan climbing into bed with him. And he definitely needed to feel Ryan against him very soon.

Ryan reached out and carefully pulled him against his side, hugging him close. "You want me to go get the doctor and get it over with," he stated, amusement bright in his voice.

"I do," Wyatt admitted. "Let's go home."

Ryan reached out and intertwined their hands together, and helped him sit upright in the bed. "Let's go home," he agreed easily, giving his hand a final squeeze before he turned away to go take care of the rest of the paperwork.

Ryan drove like Wyatt's nana the whole way home. Wyatt, a little tired and loopy from the pain pills, didn't tease him about it. He figured there was lots of time for that later. And just that thought was miraculous. Instead of an enforced ending, and a time limit, there was endless time extending before them, the possibilities never-ending and boundless.

The gate opened and Ryan carefully drove the rental Prius into the driveway. Right next to a looming black mass that hadn't been there when they'd left in the Maserati earlier in the evening.

"What's this?" Wyatt asked as Ryan came around to help him out of the car. He was a little unsteady on his feet, and the doctor hadn't wanted his arm jostled the first few days. Of course, that was the excuse Ryan had latched onto to practically never let go of him. Wyatt was definitely not going to tease him about that, because he was enjoying it too much.

It all felt like a dream come true, a hope and a wish coalesced into reality.

A fake boyfriend evolving into a real one.

Ryan helped him out of the car and they walked a few feet to the left of the big mass, just enough so that with the lights of the house, Wyatt could make out the faded writing on the stainless steel side.

"Tacos," Wyatt recited, realization dawning. "It's an old food truck."

"It's yours," Ryan said. "I love you being my personal chef. I hope you never stop. But I'm not selfish enough to want to keep you all to myself. You need to spread your wings. Experiment somewhere other than our kitchen."

Wyatt was speechless, staring at the stainless steel shell.

"It needs a lot of work," Ryan rambled on, "but I'm going to help you. It can be our project. Maybe even Tony will want to help. I got the impression he might, and you and your brother could use something to bring you together."

"You bought this for me," Wyatt said incredulously.

"I was trying to grovel. Might have gone over better if I hadn't wrecked the Maserati first. Oh, well. Anyway, in the morning, you can look in it. It's basically a wreck. I wanted to buy you a brand-new one, but Tabitha said that was overdoing it."

"She would be right," Wyatt said. "This is still too much."

"Trust me, you haven't seen the interior. It needs a *lot* of work. You might think it's not enough in the light of day."

"I don't think so," Wyatt said, and turned towards Ryan. "I thought you were afraid of me leaving. But you just gave me the ability to leave."

"I was, I *am*. But someone told me once that letting love in means you need to accept what you're afraid of." Ryan's voice was wry. "I told you before I'm not going to be good at this. But I'm going to try, every single day. Today, this is me trying."

Wyatt raised his good hand to Ryan's face, cradling his jaw. "I love you. I'm not going anywhere. Even if you try and fail. Even when I fail. We're in this together."

"Together," Ryan echoed, and leaned in and kissed him.

EPILOGUE

THE FOOD TRUCK SHONE bright silver under the merciless LA sun. "What A Catch" was painted in a handwritten green script along the side of the truck, the letters nearly reaching the top of Wyatt's head as he stood in front and critically eyed the setup.

"I still don't think the menu is big enough. The letters are still hard to read from a medium distance," Wyatt said, raising his voice so Tony could hear him from inside.

"We sell enough tacos to buy a new chalkboard today, you can have it," Tony shouted back at him, the rhythmic chopping sound of his knife against the butcher block countertops they'd installed last week nearly drowning out his voice, and the Foo Fighters playing on the Bluetooth speaker.

The Foos were more Tony's scene than Wyatt's—he liked his food prep music a little chiller—but in this brand-new joint venture between the brothers, compromise had quickly become one of the most vital ingredients.

Wyatt rolled his eyes even though Tony couldn't see him. "We're not selling any tacos today, dipshit."

Tony popped his head out the back door. His hair had grown out a little in the six months since they'd started rehabbing this truck, but it was still cut close to his skull, and a few more tattoos decorated his forearms. The two most important were also the smallest: a bright pink, yellow, and blue pansexual flag and a tiny, red, split heart. Tony had opened up much more about the former than the latter. He still wouldn't talk about the first guy to break his heart—the first *person* to break his heart, if Wyatt was being specific, because Tony had always been the one to do the heart-breaking—but Wyatt hoped he would soon. Tony was clearly hurting, no matter what sort of jovial front he put on.

"That's right," Tony snarked right back. "We're *giving* them away to your boyfriend."

"My boyfriend's team," Wyatt corrected. "And I think catering a charity event of the Los Angeles Dodgers our first time out is a really great achievement."

"I'll say this," Tony said casually, and Wyatt almost missed the hint of pride in his voice, "you don't like to start small."

Wyatt didn't have to ask who Tony was proud of. It was definitely both of them. Probably because they'd managed to do it together, without killing each other. A real achievement that had never been a sure thing, and had been touch-and-go more than once.

The truth was, Wyatt didn't like taking charity from Ryan. They'd begun their relationship—the fake one at least—with inequality, and Wyatt had spent the last eight months trying to figure out the right balance between them.

"He offered to pay for them," Wyatt pointed out. He had, and Wyatt had turned him down flat. Ryan had already done enough getting them the gig and an opportunity to iron out the kinks that went with opening a restaurant, even if it was on wheels.

Especially if it was on wheels.

"Where is he, anyway? I thought he was getting here early to help us set up?"

"I think he had a last-minute meeting come up," Wyatt said. "I'll come in and help you finish prep. It's not like he could've helped with that anyway."

Wyatt followed Tony into the small cabin of the food truck. It was a tight fit with the two of them, but at least he didn't have to stoop. He'd paid a lot more than he should have to get the roof raised just enough that neither of them had to stoop.

They fell into their regular rhythm which until eight months ago, Wyatt never would have guessed even existed. He'd believed he and Tony were so different for so long that figuring they were more alike than he'd ever imagined had turned his world topsy-turvy.

As soon as he'd regained his equilibrium, he'd realized just how much he *liked* his brother.

Ryan had looked very smug when Wyatt had admitted this one night.

"I knew you would. Or that you did? I'm not sure which is right," Ryan admitted. "Sometimes it takes a shakeup to see what's right in front of you."

"A shakeup in the form of a wrecked Maserati?" Wyatt had teased.

Ryan hit him hard in the shoulder. It stung, offsetting the pleasurable afterglow from the sex they'd just had.

"I told you that wasn't going to get old," Wyatt teased again.

"I thought real dating would mean more sappy, cheesy fluff, and less tormenting me," Ryan said mournfully.

"But the tormenting is so fun," Wyatt said with a chuckle.

Wyatt could still feel the warmth of Ryan's smile as he'd gazed lovingly at him, even months later.

"Hey, you sappy idiot," Tony called over, "did you get the pulled pork on to heat?"

Wyatt awkwardly pointed an elbow at where the big hotel pans were warming in a water bath. "I might be sappy but I'm not an idiot," he retorted.

"You and Ryan disgust me," Tony said, shaking his head. "You were just thinking about him, I could tell you were. You get this incredibly fond look on your face, like you're staring at him and he's not even fucking there."

"I spend a lot of time imagining his face instead of actually seeing it," Wyatt argued.

"Even the long distance hasn't dimmed your honeymoon period." Tony lifted up a big cardboard box of butter lettuce and with a few efficient movements began breaking each head into individual leaves.

"And it's not going to," Wyatt said. "Not even now that Ryan's signed his new contract and he's going to be playing for the Dodgers for years to come."

Wyatt wanted to tell his brother he was just jealous, but he didn't because he *was* and that was the whole problem. Not of Ryan, specifically, but of the forever happiness that Wyatt had found with him.

Frankly they were so blissfully in love, it was a miracle the world wasn't jealous. Instead, the world ate it up with a spoon. Without even trying, Wyatt had somehow become *the* chef in LA to follow on Instagram, and when he'd worn Ryan's jersey to Opening Day, the picture had gone viral.

It would have been so easy to lose their way with all the publicity and the attention, and with the shaky beginning of their relationship, Wyatt should have been more worried. But Ryan had never once given him cause to worry.

For someone who'd claimed he didn't want a relationship because all relationships became boring eventually, Ryan had fully and completely embraced their coupledom.

And when, late one night while binge-watching a show on Netflix, Ryan had leaned over and said, "I think I'm bored now," Wyatt had never been happier.

It was the only time since the accident that he'd ever brought it up, and the last time too.

"Hey, you guys in there?"

Wyatt turned around, and Ryan had just pulled up next to the food truck, driving a white Range Rover. He'd stuck his head out the open window, and Wyatt put down the knife and emerged just as he climbed out.

"You're late," Tony grumped, though his tone didn't have any heat in it.

"I know, but I was running an important errand. Picking someone up from the airport, actually," Ryan said, going to the passenger door and opening it. To Wyatt's shock, the snowy-white hair of his nana emerged, shining in the sun.

"You brought Nana," Wyatt said, dumbfounded.

Ryan's smile was warm as he carefully helped Bea out of the back of the SUV. "I did. She deserved to be here, to watch her boys open their brand-new food truck."

"Wyatt," Bea exclaimed, walking towards the truck and intercepting Tony, giving him a hug, "it looks even better than the pictures. And, Tony, I'm so proud of you."

Wyatt climbed down, and wrapped her in a long hug after his brother released her. "I'm so glad you came," he whispered into her shoulder, glancing up to see Ryan staring at them, a soft look in his dark eyes. "Ryan always has the best surprises."

"That's because he's lovely, darling," Nana whispered to him. "You marry that boy, you hear me?"

Wyatt surreptitiously wiped the moisture out of his eyes before Tony could see and make fun of him. "I'm sure going to try."

"It's beautiful, *hijo*. You didn't tell me how shiny it is." Wyatt finally let go of Bea, and met *Titi* Flor's loving stare.

"Wyatt, you have much to be proud of," she said, reaching him and wrapping him in a big, warm hug.

Wyatt's gaze locked with Ryan's. He looked only a little embarrassed. "I figured it would be good for Nana to have someone to look after her," he said, "and Flor wasn't going to be left at home today."

"You should all be here today," Wyatt said, throat suddenly tight with emotion. "Tony and I couldn't have done it without you."

"You could have," Ryan said, his voice a vow, "but we're happy we could be here to share it with you."

Flor led Bea off to one of the decorated picnic tables, chattering the whole way, the older lady smiling and offering her own opinion right back.

"Those two could run the world if they set their mind to it," Ryan said fondly, as Wyatt wrapped an arm around his waist.

"It was a great surprise," Wyatt said seriously, "thank you for making sure she was here."

"You want to make the most of the time you have left with her, and whatever you want is what I want," Ryan said, reaching over to cup Wyatt's cheek in his palm. "I love you."

It wasn't the right time, or the right place, or like anything that Wyatt had started vaguely planning in his head. But suddenly the thought was there, stark and bright and so right it overpowered everything else.

"Marry me," Wyatt choked out. Ryan's eyes grew wide. "Not today, not now. Just someday. Promise me, we'll do it before she can't remember."

Wyatt remembered all too well those dark times before he'd met Ryan when he'd been determined that the last memory his nana had of him would be a lie. Now he wanted to shine as much light and beauty and truth onto her last days as he could.

And what was lighter or more beautiful or more full of honesty than a wedding?

"Damn you," Ryan laughed, the love in his eyes swamping Wyatt, "just had to steal my thunder."

"You were going to propose?" They hadn't even talked about it, but Wyatt couldn't say he was surprised. Ryan, once he had figured out that Wyatt was what he wanted, had been the best boyfriend. Not a perfect one, but he'd kept his promise and was a real one.

"Someday," Ryan said with a bright grin.

"I think that's a yes," Wyatt said, pulling him in even tighter.

His only answer was to put his hand in Wyatt's, and kiss him hot and fierce—for forever.

Check out ***Savor Me***, the next Kitchen Gods book, about notorious grump Xander, and the man who melts his heart, ex-winemaker and new restaurant owner, Damon Hess.

Interested in reading more about Tony and his search for love? Check out ***Drive Me Crazy***, the first book in the spinoff Food Truck Warriors series.

INTERESTED IN READING MORE OF
BETH'S BOOKS?

CHECK OUT A FULL LIST OF TILES
BY SCANNING THE QR CODE
OR VISITING HER WEBSITE

WWW.BETHBOLDEN.COM/BOOKLIST

WANT TO FOLLOW BETH?

MAKE SURE YOU NEVER
MISS A RELEASE?

SCAN THE QR CODE BELOW
OR VISIT HER WEBSITE
FOR A SOCIAL MEDIA LIST,
NEWSLETTER SIGNUP,
AND SO MUCH MORE!

WWW.BETHBOLDEN.COM/ABOUT